AF MC OHIO
THE COMPLETE SERIES

By
Esther E. Schmidt

Copyright © 2019 by Esther E. Schmidt All rights reserved.

No part of this book may be reproduced in any form, without permission in writing from the author.

This book is a work of fiction. Incidents, names, places, characters and other stuff mentioned in this book is the results of the author's imagination. AF MC OHIO is a work of fiction. If there is any resemblance, it is entirely coincidental.

This content is for mature audiences only. Please do not read if sexual situations, paranormal, violence and explicit language offends you.

Cover design by:
Esther E. Schmidt

Editor #1:
Christi Durbin

Editor #2:
Virginia Tesi Carey

AF MC · OHIO
—— BOOK ONE ——

One incident after another has shaken Ransom's life to its foundations. Yet when he returns home and faces his neighbor—with whom he had a soul scorching one-night stand—everything suddenly slides into place.

Hedwig wasn't expecting the news she received after an intense one-night stand with the rough, tattooed biker from next door. Months later she finally gets the chance to share her news and once again, she didn't expect what she gets in return.

Will this couple face their future together and grow stronger as each day passes? Or will danger spark in their direction, risking their future and every life involved.

When you've been riding a dark road, it's hard to see the light at the end of the tunnel. But when you do? You ride full throttle until you've claimed what's rightfully yours. Jump into the lives of Ransom and Hedwig, book one in the AF MC Ohio duet.

PROLOGUE

HEDWIG

"I don't have any sugar," I sigh in frustration into my phone.

Wendy, my bestie, is at her parents' house in Vermont for the holidays. Yet she's the one I call when I'm in need, of anything for that matter. She's my rock, even more so since I broke up with my cheating boyfriend. Well, ex-boyfriend now.

I kicked him out of my life four months ago when I stumbled onto him screwing my assistant on her desk. Kicked that bitch out of my office too. Okay...that makes me sound kickass but to be honest...she quit. They walked out of my business holding hands. About an hour later I got a call from the cops with the news that my house was on fire. They later said it was the electrical wiring, a short circuit, overheating causing the fire...but maybe it was a sign that I needed to burn my past.

Long story short...I'm just barely getting back on my feet. I bought this amazing house in a friendly neighborhood seven weeks ago. I've been living here for twelve days now. Before I was living with Wendy, but I finally finished painting and decorating, and it was time to get my life back on the road.

"Then go ask your sexy, biker neighbor for a little sugar." Wendy giggles and draws me back into our discussion.

"You did not just say that. I should never have told you about that guy," I squeak.

Good thing she was already on her way to her parents' house when I found out who lived next door to me. Because she would drag me over to introduce myself. Then I would be standing there mimicking a goldfish. I'm good like that when it comes to social interactions. Or maybe it was my ex-boyfriend sneering 'sex with you is like screwing a cold fish'.

"Go. Just ring that doorbell and shake those hips. I'm serious. It's the time to be jolly and surprise your V-jay with a big present." Wendy's voice carries no hint of laughter.

"You're kidding." Walking toward the kitchen window, I pull down the blinds with two fingers. "Tell me you're kidding."

"I'm not," Wendy sighs. "You have to put yourself out there. It's Christmas, Hedwig. You need to do something out of the box. I hate that you're alone in a new house all by yourself without having something nice to look forward to. It must be a sign that you're all out of sugar. Go and…"

"He's coming home," I whisper into the phone and I rip my fingers out of the blinds. I don't know why I'm whispering, maybe because I feel caught or something. "God he's hot."

"Don't gimme 'God he's hot'. You said that the first time you laid eyes on him. More details, woman!" Wendy pants like a dog whose owner just got back from a day's work. All excited and bouncing around.

"You know I don't have details," I sigh, again frustrated because I wish I had those details to share. "He's wearing a helmet, sitting on that amazing vintage bike and he's wearing a…oh, my…"

"What's an oh, my? Spill!" Wendy demands.

"He's only wearing that leather thing with Areion Fury written on it and a horse with wings." I have to swallow away some drool because…

"And he's not wearing pants?" Wendy gasps. "Yikes, that doesn't seem right."

"Wendy! Of course he's wearing pants. He's not wearing a shirt. The porch light is on and I just noticed he's covered in tattoos. And why isn't he cold? It's like mid-winter…shit, he's looking right at me.

I gotta..."

"I'm hanging up. You're going out there and asking for sugar, or better yet...jump his bones. Now, damn you, or I'll come over and kick your ass." Wendy hangs up and all this time my neighbor keeps staring at me.

While still sitting on his bike I might add. Gosh he looks completely edible. Shit. I'm really hungry. I was going to make...Okay, still staring. Screw it.

I dash into the hallway, swing the door open and step outside. My door swings back and closes.

"Finally, I get to meet Miss Sunshine. Gonna tell me your name there, little one?" Gravelly. His voice sounds low and rough in a way I've never heard before.

Good thing too because it's doing crazy things to my body. Well, not so good right now because it causes the goldfish reaction I mentioned before.

– RANSOM –

Fuck. Why do I torture myself like this? I'm a damn nomad who spends more time on a bike than in the comfort of a home. I've inherited this house and I can't bear to sell it. Every once in a while, I check on it and spend a few nights here when I'm in town. Except every night for the last week or so, I've come here solely to check if I can catch an image of my neighbor standing in the kitchen.

The first time I saw her, she was hanging up the blinds. Great set of tits in a yellow tank top. Her dark hair was pinned at the top of her head, and her face? She might have been painting something before she started working on the blinds because there were white smudges all over it. She was clearly having a hard time hanging up the blinds. Her face was all red and I could hear her curses flowing through the open window. Being the asshole that I am, I didn't even offer to help, or say hi for that matter. I just stalked off and rubbed one out in the shower with the visual of her tits dancing in my head.

Like I plan to do right now...get my fill so I can picture her clearly while I go fuck my hand...shit. She's gone from the window but a few heartbeats later the door swings open so hard it falls shut behind her. Not that she notices because her eyes are locked on mine.

"Finally, I get to meet Miss Sunshine. Gonna tell me your name there, little one?" I ask.

Seems like she wants to say something. I mean her mouth moves but no sound tumbles from those fuckable lips. The corner of my mouth twitches, just like my dick. Both want to silence her even more than she already is. The kickstand takes the weight of my bike and I swing my leg over and take my backpack from my saddlebag.

My sexy neighbor is still standing there when I face her again. "Did you need something? Or did you just come out to say hi?" To my cock.

Shit. Maybe she heard my unspoken remark I mentally added about my cock because she flushes so damn adorably.

"Sugar," she blurts out. "Hedwig. Me." She stomps her foot and releases a tiny growl of frustration before she takes a step toward me. "Sorry. You're a bit huge and…"

I should interrupt and tell her that my cock appreciates the compliment. But in fact, it's annoying because the chicks I've fucked over the years throw themselves at me. Most do it because they want the bad boy thrill. Not that I'm complaining about any fuckable pussy, but I just left the Areion Fury clubhouse that was filled with cheerful Christmas shit. Family stuff in the way of babies, ol'ladies, happily ever after relationships.

I'm not cut out for that stuff. As I told my brother, Pokey, a while ago… I don't ride into sunsets …I ride in darkness, trees flashing by like memories haunting the tainted parts of my soul. Yet my chest burns with longing to have something I'm never capable of giving back or opening up to.

"Never mind, I'm sure you get that a lot." Hedwig gives me a stunning smile before she adds, "I need sugar. Do you have any?" She keeps her gaze locked with mine.

I'm about to dismiss her, being rude is always better than hurting something so enthralling, when my dick is acting like a damn compass...pointing right at her with a slight curve.

"Come on in." Fuck. Why did I say that?

"Okay, lemme get my key." She turns to face her house but notices the door that locked behind her. "Shit," Hedwig mutters before she looks over her shoulder. "Do you happen to know how to get inside a house without using a key? I've seemed to have locked myself out."

"Quite a list of demands there, sunshine. Something sweet and criminal." Snow starts to fall. Sure...rub the Christmas shit in some more. "Come on, let's get inside my house first, then we'll work on that list of yours."

– HEDWIG –

I need to add more to my list. Like a V-jay massage. Shit. I manage to make myself flush with that thought.

"Why aren't you with family and friends?" his rough voice rumbles when we're standing in his living room.

I glance around the somewhat empty space. There's a large wooden statue of an Indian in the corner, and it's the size of a real life one. On the wall next to it hangs the skull of a buffalo. Add a large black leather couch and a TV and that's all there is.

"I could ask you the same thing," I shoot back without thinking.

The man snorts. "I just came from one cheerful get-together with my brothers from Areion Fury." He taps his pecs where it says just that. "Motorcycle club. Even though they're my family, I've never liked the crowds, or the babies the ol'ladies are popping out one after the other nowadays. I'm the loner type. That's why I'm a nomad and never stay in one place long. Never have, never will."

"That's your choice. Mine is different and yet the same. My parents went on a cruise. They asked me to go with them in case you're wondering, but I declined. My best friend is in Vermont with her parents, she invited me too. I also declined. Four months ago my boyfriend cheated on me with my assistant...I'm just getting back on my feet with this new house and wanted to spend some time by myself, baking. For me." Why in the hell did I blurt out that last stuff? Probably because he shared something about him. Ugh. Of all the things...

"You're not taking that douchebag back, are ya?" the huge man in front of me growls in my face.

Wow. I should be scared with the growling and towering over me...and yet my body fills with tingles and my breath catches. "No way."

"Good." He keeps crowding me in my personal space. With his gaze locked on mine it's like we're having an intense discussion and yet there are no words between us. That is until he says, "Wanna fuck?"

Wanna fuck? "Right now?" I squeak.

"No. About fifteen minutes from now because I wanna explore your mouth first with my tongue. That will give your body enough time to make your cunt drool and beg for my cock to fill you up. Or do you need more time, sunshine? How tight is your cunt?" The corner of his mouth twitches.

I'm sure this guy in front of me thinks he's scaring me, or not… either way I'm taking Wendy's advice; jump his bones. Hell, I can't bake without sugar to put inside my body, so I'm grabbing the next best thing. Scratch that…by the looks of him it might be the only shot in my life I get to do something this impulsive.

"It's not like I have a lot to compare with…so you be the judge. I reckon you've seen, or felt?" Shit. Focus, stay cool. "More…cunts than mine."

Dammit, why can't I ever keep my cool? What I just said came out like a little mouse who had a mouth full of cheese. Fingers crossed I can still pull this one-night stand thing off.

For a moment I think I've insulted him until he leans even closer, his mouth hovering over mine. "Well then, I guess there's only one way to find out."

I swallow in an effort to gather some nerve before I ask, "Wait…I know this is a one-night stand thing…but do you mind telling me your name first?"

"Ransom. And that's exactly what I'm planning with your body; keeping it ransom for the rest of the day." With a promise in his voice, he buries his fingers into my hair and tightens them into a fist.

I can only gasp at the bite of pain that flows into desire when he pulls my head back and slams his mouth over mine.

– RANSOM –

Holy hell, I need to make this last. The way her curves mold against my hard body is enticing. The chicks I allow to kiss me seem to all have a finish line they run for; hard, fast, hurry up and fuck me. But this one? Hedwig? Lazily she licks around as if she's branding every microsecond into her brain. And fuck if I'm not doing the same thing.

I guide her to the wall behind her, taking that soft, round ass into my hands and allowing her to wrap her legs around me. I must be imagining the heat that hits my cock when I grind myself against her.

Sure feels like fucking Christmas right now where I wanna unwrap and own the best gift ever.

My tongue traces her teeth one more time as I regretfully pull away and put her back on her feet. "Let's go upstairs."

My heart is racing and this woman has me out of breath with a mere kiss. I need some distance to make this last and the only thing I can think of is moving this into the bedroom where I can spread her out on my bed.

She takes my hand and follows me up the stairs. First door on the left is the master bedroom where I have a king-size bed waiting to be used. It's new and I've never brought a woman home with me. All of this is a first and somehow that's a settling thought. Hedwig deserves it.

Shrugging off my cut, I let it drop to the floor. My boots are next and so are my pants. Yeah, I'm taking shit slow but I'm not going to keep my cock, which has become the size of a tree, strangled inside a matchbox. Or so it feels; the pants need to go. But not before I grab a condom out of my wallet and put it on.

Just making sure I'm wrapped up because this woman might be the only one who can drive me nuts and make me forget such a crucial thing. Can't have any of my swimmers getting friendly inside her cunt. I'm too dark to be tied down, let alone bring kids into this cold world.

Fuck. Or maybe that wouldn't be such a bad thing. The way the light from the hallway falls inside the bedroom with her standing there in all her naked glory? Hedwig looks like a Goddess who's been sent to bring heavenly joy to my cock. And the look of appreciation radiating from her eyes while she's caressing my length almost make my knees buckle.

"On the bed, hands and knees," I growl to regain some control.

She darts toward the bed like a little deer and jumps on, presenting that fine cunt without any further question. Pink, bare, and glistening. I slide one finger through her lips while I palm my cock in my other hand. We both groan in contentment but when I enter her with one digit a sultry moan rings out while her cunt clamps down. That's when I lose it and the choice of prolonging it just went out the fucking window.

The head of my cock replaces my digit and with a tender ease I just obtained in this moment in life, I begin to surround myself with the hottest, cock-hugging euphoria I've ever had the pleasure of taking.

And I am taking because when I'm finally balls deep, I drag out and slam right back in, making her stumble and catch herself on her elbows. No. Fucking. Remorse. It's like my normal restraints have fallen off, a beast that's burst out of his cage. I grip her hips and start to fuck her like my life depends on it. Maybe it does because my heart feels like it's ready to burst out of my chest.

I feel so damn selfish when I suddenly experience her starting to grip my cock into a turmoil of spasms. Where I usually have to fumble for a clit to rub to get the chick off, this special one only needs my cock pounding inside her. Can it be any more perfect? Yeah. Because she needs to do it again. But this time, I'll taste her when I make her come with my mouth.

– HEDWIG –

I feel empty when he suddenly pulls out and has me on my back the next instant.

"Spread your cunt open for me," Ransom's gravel voice tells me and I'm completely stunned.

"What?" I manage.

"Hands on your cunt and spread those lips open for me." He goes down and his face is now hovering above my pussy, waiting.

Oh. His words finally make sense and my hands obey. I understand his reasoning when he tweaks my nipple with one set of fingers while entertaining my pussy with his other set. "Oooohhhh," I groan.

His mouth sucks the next orgasm right out of me. My whole body shakes as his name tumbles over my lips. I'm struggling to keep my sanity and I'm sure my sex life will be nonexistent after having this man. Because no other will compare to this.

I'm still recovering, my body limp, when he enters me again. "Fuck, you feel good. Cunt rippling in anticipation. No worries, sunshine. You won't be able to get out of bed when I'm finished with you tomorrow morning. Because although I'll be taking you hard and rough in a few breaths…we're going to take a moment waiting for my cock to harden before we fuck this night away. Understood?"

My pussy just clapped in reply but in case he needs a verbal agreement, I add, "Yesss" and moan because clearly my body's answer was enough for him to grab my neck, holding me down as he starts to pound inside me.

There's nothing else for me to do than surrender to the pleasure this guy gives me. Falling right into the next wave of pleasure when he grinds himself deep and grunts as I feel him pulse inside me.

There are hot breaths from both of us and sweat running down his muscled, inked body while I manage to drift back into reality. Damn… is it too soon to ask if we could do this again?

His sexy chuckle fills the room. "I like that look on your face. Makes me want to fuck you again."

Ransom pulls out slowly but the confident, lust filled gaze slips from his face when he looks down. I want to ask if something's wrong but he turns and stalks to the bathroom. I'm about to sit up, but his voice makes me freeze.

"Lie back down so I can clean you up." He's holding a cloth and with wide eyes I feel him cleaning my pussy.

"There. All pretty, puffy, and pink. Ready for round two." He throws the cloth over his shoulder and crawls up my body. "You're so damn beautiful," he says tenderly before he gives me a hard kiss that makes me dig my nails into his back to pull him even closer.

One thing is certain…if this is the only night I'm going to have with this man…I'll be spending it with my legs and eyes open, enjoying every micro-second. So, I can remember this moment for a lifetime.

AF MC OHIO

CHAPTER 01

RANSOM *Four Months Later*

"Just fucking go," I grumble, and turn to brace myself on the kitchen counter.

I need to be left alone. Not that my asshole brother will do what I ask. The fucker knows me too well to back off. Casey isn't my brother by blood, but I consider him my sibling nonetheless. Ever since we were placed in the same foster home over twenty years ago, it's been the two of us and we consider our bond closer than blood.

"Seeing you don't want me staying here…I've rented a room at the hotel down the block." What did I just say? The asshole never does as I ask.

He's FBI, I'm an Areion Fury MC nomad, and even if Casey craves a leather cut to complete his bike like I have, he wouldn't give up his day job to wear one. Mainly because he doesn't want to risk leaving the FBI for anything. He enjoys catching bad guys and finding out what makes them tick. Even if I balance the fine line of outlaw life…we've never let that shit come between us.

But I can't bear having anyone around me. Not now, not even the man I consider my brother in all ways. All of this because of a confrontation with a gang. Lemme explain a bit. A few months ago, a damn gang came after the Old Lady of one of the brothers of an Areion Fury MC charter. The one where Zack's the president. I've been there loads of times, off and on, and have known all these brothers for years. When shit went down, me and Casey were both there. Zack asked me if I could stick around and help. The both of us did seeing my brother is FBI and dove into the matter in his own way. Long story short, we had a confrontation with the gang where I took a bullet to the leg and had some muscle damage.

That's not the worst of it though; my leg I can manage since it only bothers me if I overuse it, like I did now with the last fucking PT session with those assholes. But, I also took a bullet in my arm and some knife wounds to add to it.

They said there's a big chance I won't regain full function of my arm—and with it the strength in my hand—ever again. Meaning I could lock up my fucking bike and never feel the rumble of it underneath me because I can't fucking trust my own goddamn hand to keep a tight grip. You might as well put me in the fucking ground if I can't feel alive anymore.

And don't call me a fucking drama queen, I know I'm sulking but when you can't even trust yourself to hold a good grip on a damn cup of coffee…Yeah, no need to talk about my bike, right? I feel less than a fucking man. Hence the reason I want to be alone; Casey needs to leave.

"I'll swing by tomorrow," Casey starts, but I cut him right off.

"No. I won't let you in," I snap. "I'm blocking the fucking door. Call me next week or I'll send you a fucking text every damn day if it gets you to back off. I need time alone and you butting the fuck in ain't gonna do shit to heal me, all it does is piss me the fuck off."

"Fucking hell, Ransom, you need someone to,"

"Wipe my fucking ass?" I growl and grab an apple off the fruit bowl to throw at his head. At least my other arm still works.

The idiot dodges it effortlessly and my head swings back to the fruit bowl. What the hell? I don't own a fucking fruit bowl. I haven't been back to this house since Christmas. Best fucking night of my life…but it was over four months ago. That's right before that gang shit started. I didn't want to taint this place and risk them showing up here. Then I got fucking injured, so I couldn't get back until now.

"Who the fuck has been here and put this fruit shit in my fucking kitchen?" I growl, knowing it wasn't Casey because he was with me when I was at PT. Fucking PT. Also, something I don't need. Fucking positive, cheer you on, 'we'll fix you' shit that won't ever work. Like I said; they all need to leave me the fuck alone. "Never mind, just leave, man. I'll check in later," I sigh and hope he will take the hint.

"If you don't text me later tonight, I'm coming over in the morning. Understood?" The fucker narrows his eyes at me.

"Yeah, mom." The corner of my mouth twitches when I see him wince at my words.

Between me and him…he has always been the one with the 'do the right thing' mentality, making me call him mom whenever he tried to steer us on the right path. You know those shirts with pointing out the one who causes trouble and the one who gets them out, best buds and shit? Yeah, I would be wearing the troublemaker one while Casey is the 'fix this shit' one.

Casey glances over my shoulder and his eyes light up. What the hell is he looking at? I turn and instantly regret the move. Fuck. It's my neighbor, Hedwig. My sexy as fuck neighbor I met for the first time at Christmas time. Do I dare say we fucked our brains out all night long before I had to leave and then I had to stay away due to the fucking gang issues. Yeah, best damn night of my life followed by a turmoil of bad shit.

She's the whole reason I kept away from this place, to keep her safe. But does she know that? Nope, she thinks I bailed. Shit. Gotta admit, I've been watching her like a creepy stalker through the security system I have in place around my house. Not to keep an eye on her, but the house since it is special to me, though it definitely came in handy.

It's actually the house that belonged to the woman who raised Casey and me. Casey and I both inherited the house when she died. Though Casey gave his half to me…something about me needing to fix the place up so I had something to do and a place to go.

Sneaky fucker, but he was right. I fixed it up and it somehow gave me gratification by doing it. Hence the reason this place is fully registered to my name, and I'm never ever gonna sell it. This place is a piece of our history with meaning to the both of us.

Also the reason why I come and stay in it a few times a year. And why I went there to be by myself at Christmas, and now when I feel like shit. It's my safe haven, there when I need it.

I even gave Hedwig a key to keep an eye on my place, being all neighborly and all. But also to give her the option to go out and have the key to crawl back into my bed if I wasn't back yet.

I left her in my house with the full assumption I was gonna return later that day, but that gang...fucking hell, that gang caused me to turn into a lesser man with my injuries and robbed me from returning to a woman who filled my every fucking need.

Oh, shit. She's the one who put the fruit in my kitchen, I'm sure of it. The kindhearted, shy, bright as fuck beam of light I had underneath me...what a fucking night...I ripped two condoms straight in half. Never happened before, but with her? Twice. Cum leaking out and everything, that's how rough and consumed we were with one another.

"Please tell me the curly redhead isn't the one you nailed and pined over for months. Because I'm leaving right now to ask for her number if she's free play," Casey says and backs away from me as I see another girl standing next to Hedwig.

I hear the front door slam shut and see Casey walking over to the two women. Talk about more frustration. Hedwig turns her face toward me and smiles. I can't even lift my arm correctly to fucking wave. Angry at myself, I spin around and move away from the window, ignoring the outside world and everyone in it.

I plunk my ass down on the couch and wince at the pain that shoots through my leg. "Massage the muscle" the annoying voice of the fucker from PT goes through my head. The one who caused the pain to begin with by wearing me out today. I'm glad I won't be going back to fucking PT anymore. Screw it. Screw every-fucking-thing.

I grab the remote and flip through some channels. A shark documentary spikes my interest when I hear the front door open and close. What the hell?

"I told you to fucking leave, asshole," I bark, hoping Casey will turn on his heels and get the hell out of my damn house.

"Oh, the asshole did leave. It's only me dropping by to give you the lasagna I made. You know how to handle a microwave, right? Just heat it up a few minutes. Hey, is your leg giving you trouble?"

The first fucking time I met this woman, she was mimicking a damn goldfish; completely speechless. Opening and closing her mouth...stunned without a working brain cell to kick in and save her. I guess the tables are turned now because I can't seem to find a working brain cell myself to understand what the hell she's doing here. On. Her. Knees. In fucking front of me massaging my leg. Shit. That feels so good. Not only does she drive away the muscle cramp but my cock is trying to escape my damn pants to give her the warm welcome she deserves.

Fucking hell, the reality courses through me; I can't even reach out and fist her hair to guide her head toward my cock to suck me off. See? Lesser. Man. All because of my fucked-up arm.

"That's enough," I growl, more frustrated at myself than at the kind beauty who's on her knees in front of me. "Get out and don't come back. I don't need you to come here and bring food either. Leave the key I gave you on the kitchen counter and focus on your own damn life instead of butting into mine."

"Yeah...about that. It's not going to happen." She shoots me a cute as fuck smile. "I'm going to be here a few times a day, and,"

"No fucking way," I seethe.

"Sit. Down," she snaps and I let myself drop back on the couch.

Again, I'm stunned by this tiny as shit woman lashing out at me. Me. Inked all over every inch of my body. Even my face and damn ears carry ink. I have men crossing the road when they see me walking toward them but this woman—who's still massaging my damn leg—thinks she can order me a-fucking-round?

My arm goes up and my fingers find her throat. I order them to squeeze with my brain but I only manage to have her in a soft grip. Dammit.

"Okay, that's perfect." Little Miss Sunshine is giving me another fucking smile. "This will give me a good idea how your arm is progressing. Try and give it a squeeze for me."

"I'm focusing to snap your annoying neck, be fucking glad I'm failing," I growl.

She grabs my forearm with her delicate fingers and slides up.

Did she have those magical fingers the last time? When I fucked her all night at Christmas? I do remember her nails in my back, and those tiny fingers wrapped tightly around my cock, but this? I manage to catch myself before I let a moan of contentment slip past my lips.

I clear my throat and dash up to stumble away from her. "Okay, that's enough."

"No, that wasn't nearly enough," she snaps, again, and transforms those magical fingers into tiny fists and places them on her hips. "Your muscles are too tight and if I read your file correctly, you still need PT but bailed."

My file? "My. Fucking. File? How the fuck...that motherfucker. Casey gave it to you, didn't he? Are you fucking him now?"

"Oh, shush it, Moby, there are more people who seem to like and care about you other than Casey. I can't see a reason right now with you acting like this, but you know what? I'm used to outbursts and difficult clients. You're stuck with me and we'll have daily sessions to get you back on your bike."

Moby? This is getting more fucked up by the damn minute. "Who the hell are you calling Moby?"

"You, sir, are a dick. There, I've said it. I didn't want to call you out on being one, so I morphed it into something nice, but you forced me to say it anyway. Now heat up your lasagna and I'll be back later when you're hopefully in a better mood." She spins on her heels and is out the door before I can insult her.

I regain my bodily functions and rush after her. My door slams shut behind me, fuck...no keys. Just fucking great, add that to the pile of shit that just keeps getting higher. My fist meets her door and I don't stop pounding until it swings open.

"You can't just sashay your ass out of a discussion like that," I growl in her face.

"I can when you're being unreasonable." She crosses her arms in front of her chest and pushes her fine tits up.

Have they gotten bigger? Shit. They were perfect in my memory but seeing them—even hidden by layers of fabric—is making my mouth water. In the back of my mind I hear her rambling but her tits are mesmerizing. I feel a hand on my chest, giving me a hard shove.

"Oh, wow. I can't walk out of a discussion but you can have silent discussions with my tits while ignoring me, huh? Well, how about this?" She steps back and slams the door in my face.

What the? This woman, fucking hell. My fist meets the door again. "Open the fuck up, Hedwig."

"No," she yells through the door.

"Open up because I've locked myself out," I grumble, embarrassed I have to admit it to her like this.

Full. Blown. Laughter. And she's still not opening the damn door.

"Come on, Hedwig, I helped you out when you locked yourself out of your damn house last Christmas," I sigh, hating the fact I just reminded her of how we left things between us. How I left and never returned till now.

The door swings open. 'Yeah, let's not ever repeat what happened then." She trots over to my door and instead of opening it, she points at me. "I will be coming over two times a day to give your leg, but mainly your arm, the attention it needs to get you back on your bike. Understood?"

"You're negotiating demands for opening my own fucking door to my own fucking house? I'm twice your size and could snatch away those damn keys before you have time to fuckin' blink. Know how to pick your fights, sunshine." The corner of my mouth twitches, and I have to fight to keep my laughter inside.

Fucking hell, this is what she does to me; spiking damn emotions no one ever brings out inside me. All at a time I only want to ignore everyone, and this fucked up world along with it.

Again, she pushes up her tits. It's as if she knows it's my weakness when it comes to her. "It's not about fighting me, Ransom. But you're right…and it raises the question; do you know how to pick your fights? Even as we're standing here, we're wasting time. Fight for what you want. Fight for something that's worth freaking risking your life and dying for. We might have had one night together, you and I, and I know damn well I don't have a clue who you really are, but even I know that a bike—and everything connected to it—is worth everything to you. Time to man up, Moby…what's your answer? What do you want to fight for?"

Now this? This makes me fucking angry. Her words are slicing through my bare soul. "Are you a fucking miracle worker? You said you read my fucking file. The damn doctors at the hospital told me there's only a tiny as shit chance I'll ever regain full use of my arm again. So, don't you fucking dare stand in front of me blabbering about imaginary shit."

"That's their job to give you the cold hard truth. Reality is hard but so is your body. If you give up or stay mediocre at your actions, you'll never obtain dreams. Truth strips you bare but also gives you the foundation of knowledge, to move forward from that point on. Hence the reason I asked what you wanted to fight for, because your whole demeanor? It's telling me there's enough anger to get where you want to be. Now use that fuel to get somewhere instead of lashing out at me—at the whole freaking world." Her voice lowers to a minimum when she adds, "I'm here to help, so manage a fragment of politeness for me, Ransom. It's all I ask in return." Her words are still echoing through my head when she opens my door. "There, go inside and hide from the rest of the world. It's what you want to do, right?" She dismisses me and mutters mainly to herself, "Go and lick your wounds, asshole," right before she walks inside her own home and shuts the door behind her.

CHAPTER 02

HEDWIG

"Asshole!" I seethe as I stride to the kitchen and grab the chewy candy I hid yesterday.

Shit. No green ones. Weird statement, huh? I know. But I only crave green chewy candy. I sort them out and give the rest of them to Wendy, my best friend. She's been staying with me and eats the rest of my chewy candy but told me to hide it because she keeps eating them when they're in plain sight.

She's got a sweet tooth, and to put it in her words 'my ass don't need the extra calories, now hide those fuckers from me before I hunt and devour every last one of them.' Wendy will be here later, she just went out to get some files from work for me.

Ugh, the bumping heads with my neighbor doesn't brighten my mood. I need a distraction. A new series to binge on, some chips, and most definitely my apple juice. I grab all those things and rush up the stairs and into my bedroom.

I don't need the frustration and anger my neighbor brings out in me. He's had enough of an impact on my life. So much in fact my whole future changed because of it. All thanks to one freaking night.

Worst thing? He doesn't even know how much of an impact. One freaking night where we used a condom, more than one I might add. Clearly it didn't stop his seed from hitting home. That's right, I'm pregnant. It's his and no one else's. Hell, my ex cheated on me and we broke up way before I bought the house next to Ransom. So no, I didn't have sex months before I had sex with Ransom or the months after it. So yes, one hundred percent it's Ransom's, even if we used condoms.

Insane, I know, and I still can't wrap my mind around the fact I got pregnant while using condoms. But does he know? Nope. Is it my fault? Nope. Is it his? Nope. He gave me a key the morning he had to leave and said he'd come back later. He didn't leave his phone number and didn't return until today.

So how was I to contact him to let him know our one-night stand on Christmas left us with a little present? Right, there wasn't. But I do have to tell him. And maybe I should have the second I laid eyes on him but he's in such a bad place right now…wrong of me, believe me, I know.

And it's safe to say he doesn't even want me around him, let alone have a kid in a few months to add to it. What a freaking mess. Shit. I should have grabbed the ice cream too since I clearly need it. I'll tell him in the morning, for sure. It's not like his mood will improve any time soon.

And who could blame him? I certainly don't. Before the night we had sex I only saw him a handful of times through my kitchen window while I was settling in next door to him. Back then I just bought this house—to have a fresh start—and was cleaning and hanging up the blinds. He would ride up with that amazing custom made bike of his. Just a few glances had me drooling.

Then Christmas Eve came along. I was baking and didn't have any sugar and Ransom rode up to his house…I thought, what the hell… and rushed outside to ask for sugar. It didn't go as smooth as I thought it would. I locked myself out and all I could do was gape at him without getting any words out.

Good thing he was as straightforward as my V-jay would have liked me to be. One moment we were discussing why and how the both of us were home alone on Christmas Eve and the next…I sigh and let my mind wander to the memories of that blissful night.

My body still tingles with the reminder of how we enjoyed and explored each other's bodies. His hands, his mouth, his...nope, not going to think about how good it felt when he filled me up with his dick because I've never had such an intense connection or such soul-crushing sex. Incomparable and insatiable, that's how we were. Both of us couldn't get enough and every thrust of his hips was better than the next.

Yup, waaaaayyyy over my head this man, but that night? Worth it. Even if it left me with a surprise I wasn't prepared for. I still can't believe I'm pregnant. Seriously, I wake up every day and then seconds tick by as the thought flashes through my head. A few breaths of panic before it settles and I know I will make it work.

I'm financially stable, I don't do any hard labor, I have my own practice to run, and I can afford to take time off if needed. The house I live in is all done and has a spare room I'm turning into a nursery. See? No concerns, I will make things work.

If Ransom welcomes becoming a father, I'd be thrilled. If not... I'm not going to force his hand or keep my hand up to demand his money. Like I said, he's got enough issues to deal with and I will tell him tomorrow; he has a right to know.

Great, he hates me already by butting in, trying to help with his recovery. Now he will have another good reason to push me away and lock himself in his own home to distance himself from the outside world. Because I've heard from his friends, Sico, Everleigh, and Casey too, how he wants nothing more but to shut everyone out.

I won't let him, though. Like I mentioned, it's his choice if he wants to be a part of this baby's life or not. But I won't be standing around to watch a strong man wither away with no reason at all. The human body is strong. The mental state is even stronger—and can have a huge impact if you have the right mindset—you can carry on. Do things you never thought would be possible. You just have to be strong, take that step and face your fears.

Awesome. I should really take some of my mental boosts and step up to face my fears myself. Shit. I should have told him the second I laid eyes on him again, huh? Dammit. Ice cream. I really need ice cream.

Good thing I bought large sweaters and hoodies to keep my stomach covered. Rephrase; keep my ass covered. It's growing even faster than my darn breasts or stomach for that matter. I am already showing though—a cute little baby bump—and I have an appointment set to find out if I'm having a boy or a girl. Dammit, I haven't even told my parents yet.

I make my way downstairs and a scream rips from my throat when I see a man standing in front of my kitchen window. Holy shit, I almost peed myself. Now that I've calmed myself down, I see who it is and anger overtakes me. The asshole called me out of the blue about an hour ago and I didn't pick up, and now he thinks he can just show up here instead?

Rushing to the door, I swing it open and start to bark out my words. "Get lost, Theodore."

"Come on, cupcake, hear me out," my ex says, sending chills up my spine by calling me cupcake. Stupid freaking term of endearment if you ask me, and I now realize I didn't even like him when we were together.

And for real, hear him out? Seven months ago, I stumbled into him screwing my assistant on her desk, they walked out of my office holding hands for Pete's sake. Not to mention I haven't heard one peep from him since. What the hell is he doing here? If he thinks he can give me another go after screwing someone else for all those months, and easily switch back to me, he's dead wrong.

"Who are you?" I hear Ransom growl from my right. He steps closer to me and glances down. "You okay? I heard you scream."

"I'll be okay if Theodore here leaves." I direct my attention to my ex. "And if my not answering your call an hour ago wasn't a clear indication I don't ever want to talk to you, I will spell it out; we were done the day you put your dick in my assistant. Do I need to remind you it all happened seven months ago? Seven. Months. Why are you even here?"

"This is the fucking ex you mentioned?" Ransom growls.

"The one and only," I reply.

Theodore steps closer. "It was one mistake, cupcake. Sandy and I aren't even together anymore, and you need to give her her old job back. She needs it. Come on, cupcake, we were good together, let's get past this like adults."

Give the bitch—who was employed by me at the time—who screwed my boyfriend on her freaking desk, her job back? Is he kidding me? And for real…'we were good together'? This guy can't hold a freaking candle against the mere hours I spent with Ransom that one night.

For starters, Theodore never even once gave me an orgasm. Yikes, even the reminder of him being my ex is making me gag, no matter how short it was; both his dick and our time together.

"Get lost, fucker. You and her ain't ever gonna happen again," Ransom states. "And for sure as shit she ain't hiring back a cunt who fucked her ex."

A little crass, but Ransom hits the nail on the head. He actually voices it the way it should be said because this asshole doesn't seem to listen to a word I've said when he starts to ramble again.

"This is none of your business. This is something between me and Hedwig, we have a history," Theodore dismisses Ransom and steps closer to me. "Please, cupcake."

Ransom steps in front of me. "For fuck's sake, stop with the fucking cupcake. She ain't, nor will she ever be, a fucking cupcake. Now fuck off and never come back or I'll kick you off our fucking property."

Theodore narrows his eyes. "You might scare people with your leather cut and your tattoos on your face but truth is, you're scum. Why don't you go away so I can talk to my,"

"Not. Yours," I snarl and dash around Ransom to give Theodore a push against his chest.

I want to give him another push but Ransom catches me around my waist and pulls me against his body. Shit. My belly. I gasp and grab his forearm but it's too late. Ransom's hand slides from my side over to my belly and he spreads his fingers. His whole body locks tight and he steps away from me.

Ransom doesn't even look at me but mutters, "You guys need to talk shit out. You owe it to him."

Wait...what? "I don't owe him shit," I seethe.

Ransom points at my belly. "You're pregnant, right? You owe the father of the child you're carrying."

"I do." I swallow at the sound of his words.

"You're pregnant?" Theodore squeaks.

Ransom stalks toward his house.

Dammit. This is so not the way I wanted things to go. "It's not yours, Theodore...it's his."

CHAPTER 03

RANSOM

I'm about to lose my shit when this Theodore fucker almost says Hedwig is his. Jealousy is coursing through me, something new and utterly vicious. Thank fuck Hedwig dashes forward and pushes him away.

She's about to push him again so I grab her just in time and drag her against my body. My hand slides from her side over her belly. She feels different. Not the flat belly she had when…fuck. She's pregnant?

Pregnant…does this mean that fucker is the father? Must be the reason why he's here. I release her, step away and mutter, "You guys need to talk shit out. You owe it to him."

"I don't owe him shit," she seethes.

I point at her belly. "You're pregnant, right? You owe the father of the child your carrying."

If there's something I hate in this world it's failed parenthood, even worse…a person who would prevent a parent from obtaining a connection with their kid. Fuck this. I turn my back on the whole situation.

I hear Theodore ask if she's pregnant. I'm about to enter my house when Hedwig's words make me stop dead in my tracks. "It's not yours, Theodore...it's his."

Mine? Mine? She's pregnant with my kid? It could be. Shit. It fucking well is. We ripped the condom when we fucked on Christmas. I even had to clean my cum from her cunt. She didn't know, though. I didn't fucking tell her we snapped the condom. Fucking twice we ripped a condom, so hell to the fuck yes, her swollen belly shows my kid's inside with the months I've been gone after.

"How can it be? He hasn't even been here for months!" Theodore snaps. "Or did you give a happy ending at work? Is that how you do business nowadays?"

His words rip me straight out of my train of thoughts, what did the fucker just say? How the hell did he know I wasn't around for the last few months? "How the fuck do you know this, you little shit? Are you stalking her?"

Theodore's eyes widen then narrow. "None of your business."

"I beg to fucking-differ, you heard the woman, she's carrying my kid. Now fuck off like I told you to, and never look back, because if you do...I'm gonna be standing there, ready to poke your fucking eyes out before I slice your fucking throat, get me?"

I have to give it to the guy, he doesn't so much as blink. He does however glare at Hedwig before he steps back and walks over to a high-class car, gets in and speeds away.

"I'm sorry," Hedwig mutters. "I should have told you when I walked into your house."

I sigh and rub my hand over my face. "And I'm fucking sorry I didn't tell you the fucking condom ripped...twice."

When I meet her eyes, they are wide and she's got her fists perched on her hips. "That would have given me some kind of heads-up, asshole." She groans and presses her fingertips against her forehead and starts to rub before her hands fall away. "Sorry, this isn't helping. We both screwed up and you didn't leave a phone number and I had no way of contacting you. I really didn't think an abortion was an option and, I couldn't discuss it with you or anyone else, so now I'm having a baby."

A fucking baby. One I probably can't even hold with my fucked-up arm. "How long?"

Her forehead scrunches up. "How long, what?"

"How long until the baby comes?" I sigh. "And did you mean what you said? About my arm?"

"Do the math, between us having sex on Christmas, just add nine months." She rolls her eyes. "And yes, I did mean…oh, wait…you're telling me, what? You want me to help you but you don't want anything to do with the baby? Is that it?"

"What the hell, woman? I'm counting how many months I have to strengthen my fucking arm or I won't trust myself to be able to hold my own fucking kid," I growl in her face.

"Oh," she gasps.

"Yeah, oh," I snap. "Now let's go inside to talk some more instead of standing out here in the cold."

"Right. Yes. Of course." She stalks over to her house.

"Let's go to mine," I say.

"No." She doesn't even stop but stalks to her house and throws over her shoulder, "I need ice cream if we're having this discussion."

"I gotta go lock my door, be right there." I rush over to my house and lock up.

Hedwig already went inside hers and when I stalk into her kitchen, she's leaning against the counter, holding a tub of salted caramel ice cream. She scoops a large chunk into her mouth and closes her eyes to savor the taste.

It's getting dark so I hit the lights, allowing me to watch her closely. I have to admit, she's more gorgeous than I remember. Even if I watched her through the security feed for all those months I couldn't be here, it holds no reality to the vision before me.

Maybe it's because I now know she's carrying my child. And I have no fucking doubts it's mine since there hasn't been any other men coming over to see her. Add the fact she doesn't strike me as a chick who'd jump from cock to cock, even though she jumped right onto mine minutes after we met.

Fuck. Call it a gut instinct or my damn stalker issues, I just know she's got my kid inside her. I've seen with my own eyes how the condom was snapped in half, and I've cleaned my cum leaking out of her cunt. Twice. Like I said…I've been watching her closely—fucking stalker level—and she's been in no contact with men. Not to mention the condoms ripping, yeah…it's mine all right. No. Fucking. Doubt.

I don't even know why I thought this Theodore fucker could be the father, I just assumed with him being her ex and standing on her front lawn. I should have known better. The way she reacted to him, all fierce and with pure anger…and shit, the way that fucker reacted? I doubt we've seen the last of him. But let him fucking come. Hedwig is carrying my kid, therefore she's mine. I protect what's mine at all cost, and I'll fucking fight for my kid till my last damn breath.

Limp arm, fucked-up leg, or not…my kid will have a fucking father he can count on. I never had a chance growing up and with what I had to live through I won't ever wish upon my own fucking enemy. I fucking swear my kid will have a better future and I'll make sure to be there every step of the way.

I have issues. I have a lot of fucking issues and not just my past, my fucked-up body or the reasons why I'm a nomad and never stay in one place longer than a few months. All of it seems less important than the woman standing before me, eating fucking ice cream with the cute as fuck tiny baby bump I now clearly see with her hoodie unzipped and hanging open.

There are so many thoughts flowing through my head it should scare the fuck out of me but instead there's an eerie calm of righteousness overtaking me. There's a reason I came here Christmas Eve. There's a reason she moved into the house right next to mine—the only safe haven I return to every now and then. There's a reason why the condom ripped. There's a fucked-up reason I got injured and crawled my way back here. All of it involves the burst of sunshine currently eating her way through a tub of ice cream.

"Any chance you're gonna share that?" I question, though I'm pretty sure she'd kick my ass if I come any closer.

Her eyes flash open and narrow, and fuck…are her fingers tightening around the tub?

"You said yourself we needed ice cream for this discussion," I offer.

Not that I want the sweet and cold shit, but the way she's clutching it? I feel the need to ruffle her feathers. Hell, it's the first time in months I feel lighter—fucking playful—instead of everything comin' at me and pressing on my fucking shoulders, trying to drag me down.

Even the huge change coming up with the baby and all…I remember all too vividly when I rolled the condom up and the thought came to mind how I couldn't have any of my swimmers getting friendly inside her cunt. I'm too dark to be tied down, let alone bring kids into this cold world. Back then I doubted, that maybe it wouldn't be such a bad thing.

Now? With the certainty of becoming a father? Every single inch of doubt falls away. And let's not forget the monstrosity of motivation for becoming my old self. I have to. For my kid. Or at least gain enough function in my arm to hold the tiny fucker. Her question comes back to mind… 'what do you want to fight for.'

"That," I state and point at her belly. "You asked me what I want to fight for…now I know."

Her eyebrows scrunch up. "You want to fight for my ice cream? What the hell? You're not getting it."

My head falls back and laughter rips free. Fuck. It's been months since I've been so carefree to laugh. "No, sunshine. I need to fight for myself because of the kid growing inside your belly. I owe it to him, or her."

She places the ice cream on the counter behind her. "I have an appointment set where we could find out if it's a him or a her."

"Do we want to know?" Fuck. First thing in this discussion and I'm not even sure I want to decide on this.

"I don't know. I'm just saying we could." She shrugs. "It's more important to hear the baby has all their toes and fingers, right?"

"It is," I murmur and think things through.

"Nothing weird in my family, I'm not implying anything," she hastily adds.

It makes me shrug. "I wouldn't know if anything runs in my family, it's just me."

But I'm pretty sure my bloodline is tainted with crazy, though I don't have the fucking nerve to say anything. She bites her lip and I know she wants to ask to get to know some more but I ain't in the mood to share. Not now, and probably not fucking-ever.

"It's in the past. I've moved forward and will always keep my eyes on the future. The only one I consider family is Casey. My brothers of Areion Fury MC too, except with me being a nomad I never stay in one place long. I tend to go where I'm needed."

"I won't hold you back." The fierce look she's giving me makes my stomach clench. Her voice is determined as she goes on, "I've got my own practice, money saved, I won't ever force you into anything or make you stay because,"

"Stop talking," I growl, unable to hear her finish her rambling. "Let me make something very fucking clear. I'm going to be there for the kid and for you. I won't tell you everything about my fucking past, but I will tell you this, so listen close and don't ask any damn questions afterwards, understood?" I wait for her nod and take a deep breath to throw out details I've buried a long time ago. "My father murdered my mother before my very eyes. I ended up at my uncle's house for three months before social services took me away when I was admitted for the second time in three weeks for a broken arm because of the abuse I endured. All before the age of twelve. Believe me when I say I won't ever walk out on a kid that's mine. I know what it's like to have no fucking parents and no safe arms to hold you. And I will fucking protect the mother of my child at any cost along with it."

I'm expecting pity and compassion, but instead there's anger and understanding radiating.

"That makes me very happy," she states and turns fiery red right after. "I didn't mean...shit, that came out weird. What I meant to say was...I'd love for you to be involved in any way possible. I just didn't want you to think you didn't have a choice or that I would suffocate you."

"Good. Then it's settled," I tell her and I watch her whole face light up, making my cock stand to attention. It's been way too fucking long since I've gotten my cock wet. Come to think of it...the last time I seemed to have made a fucking baby. Common sense evaporates when I state, "Wanna fuck?"

"What? No! We both know what happened the last time you said that," she sputters and it makes my cock even harder.

I shrug. "It's not like you can get pregnant again."

"You were gone for months, doing who knows what...or who for that matter. I can't just...we can't just...it's not...no," she huffs, and grabs the ice cream from the counter and shoves a huge chunk inside her mouth as if she needs to shut herself up.

Fuck. With me gone for months without a single explanation she must think the worst of me. Time to make shit very clear. "I didn't stay away because of you. Nor am I the kind of guy who'd fuck and leave the woman who gave me the best fucking night in years of my fucked-up life," I growl, unable to keep the anger and frustration out of my words. "Shit happened, club business I can't talk about. I didn't want any danger coming your way and to do so, I had to stay away. Then I got injured. I know it's fucked-up but one thing is for fucking sure...my cock hasn't seen any action this year and the last cunt it's been inside was yours."

She starts to sputter and cough, the spoon and ice cream both end up in the sink. I rush forward and rub her back. But she jumps away from my touch. What the hell?

CHAPTER 04

HEDWIG

Things were so much better this morning. I had come to terms with my neighbor—father of my unborn child, whatever—being nonexistent. Then his two friends, Everleigh and Sico, show up today and told me how Ransom was injured a while ago and needs help. I was determined to be there for him, and grab the chance to finally tell him about the baby.

What I didn't expect was the turmoil of emotions swirling inside me with his return. How could I even think I would be able to handle this? Shit. It's the hormones. Making my feelings jump all over the place and pull on my damn emotions with what this man's youth must have been like.

No wonder he wants to be there for his own child with his own experience tainting his very soul. Add the reasons why he didn't return... because he did want to come back to me. If I only knew back then. Why the hell didn't we exchange phone numbers? Breathe. I need to breathe and not choke. Not have his hands on me. Space. I need space between us, and oxygen.

"You need to leave," I croak.

"Like fuck I will," he replies in all fierceness before grabbing me around my waist and pulling me close.

I want to push him away. My fist digs into his leather cut but instead of pushing, I pull him closer and bury my face against his chest. My next breath fills my lungs with his scent. His strong arms wrapped around me, sweet words while he's stroking my back, it's everything that makes an impact. Shit. Here come the waterworks.

Tears stream down my face and all I can do is sigh and bury myself tighter against his chest. I have no shame when I wipe my face on his shirt and start to ramble how sorry I am for breaking down like this. Though deep down? With every tear I shed, I feel lighter. As if he lifted the anvil off my chest with just being here, arms wrapped tight, keeping me grounded.

Ransom curses underneath his breath, something about not being able to scoop me off my feet and carry me. Instead, he gently guides me over to the couch. He sits down while he places me on his lap. I finally manage to stop crying and release a deep breath while snuggling into his warm embrace.

"And this is the whole fucking reason I ain't leaving," he mutters into my hair. "All those months...anyone been there for you?"

"I haven't told anyone except for Wendy. She's my best friend, and she's always been there for me. She's been staying here with me on and off a few days at a time. And I can't believe you just spilled it to Theodore," I grumble, not liking it one bit the asshole knows.

And why the heck does he pop up after all these months? Right after Ransom got home? Weird.

Ransom tightens his fingers into my hair and gently pulls my head back to connect our gaze. "That's it? You've only told one person?"

Shit. "Two of your friends came around earlier today...Everleigh and Sico. I didn't mean to tell them anything but Everleigh guessed when she saw me put my hand on the bump where my flat belly once was."

"Should have known those fuckers would interfere," Ransom grumbles as he guides my head back against his chest. "I got injured at their place, Everleigh is Sico's Old Lady. She caught me watching you on my phone a few times. Fuck. That doesn't sound...well, it sounds like it is, but..."

"You've been watching me?" I gasp and push myself up with both hands.

How's that for creepy stalker level? Watching me but not making any attempts to contact me at all. Yet it does give me the realization he didn't just leave, I meant something to him if he's stooped to that level, and how his attention was directed fully at me...even if it's freakishly weird.

He diverts his gaze and sighs. "I've got a security system set up and it covers the front of your house too. You do a lot of gardening during the winter, which I think is strange, though. But...I just wanted to make sure you were okay. Watching you was all I could do."

"Oh, that doesn't sound creepy at all," I mutter. "And for your information, I like outdoors. Even if it's to sweep my porch during the rain or whatever. It's my porch, it makes me feel better," I grumble.

"I really wanted to come back but with each day passing it became harder and harder. The risk of drawing attention to you, my injuries. Hell, when I woke up in the hospital all I wanted to do was return to this house with you living right next door. And I never want to come home, I'm a fucking nomad without a fucking home that ties me to one place but I felt the need to return here. The house where the best memories of my life were made, and it's only fuckin' walls keeping a roof up, but now...with you living next door...it's become so much more." His confession and the way he's pinning me with a fierce look makes me swallow at the emotion tightening my throat.

"I guess we can't change the why and how there was so many months in between us meeting again, huh? Maybe we could start fresh?" I take a deep breath and rush out the rest before I lose my nerves. "As friends, neighbors or at least friendly enough to make it work for the baby?"

"No," he rumbles. "My cock, tongue, and fingers were buried deep inside your cunt and it's what kept me going all those fucking months. I ain't settling for some friends shit now that I know you're carrying my kid inside you. Things drastically changed for the both of us; you're mine now."

"You do know we live in a society where we don't need to have a relationship of any kind to be parents, right? I'm not a person to tie a man down just because..."

He leans forward, taking up all my personal space. "Do I fucking look like a person who would let anyone tie me down?"

"But we don't even know each other," I squeak. "It was a one-night stand! We don't even know if we're compatible."

Ransom snorts. "My seed took root in your womb at first strike, I'd say we're very compatible."

I'm not sure how to respond to that so I can only stare while mimicking a goldfish. Shit. All this time I was only dealing with the issue of telling him about the baby, not with how we would be moving forward once we're both aware of the fact we're going to be parents.

"Relax, sunshine. We have months. Months we both need to figure out how shit will go but don't make any assumptions, you're mine and I'm yours. But I do need your help with my fucked-up arm."

"Your arm is nothing compared to the little thing growing inside me," I mutter. "Your arm I can handle, it's muscle and willpower, you need to build it up. I've had a few cases similar to yours. If you want to, you can regain enough strength back."

"What's your profession, miracle worker?" The man chuckles, but it sounds forced.

"Doctor of Physical Therapy, so you might say I know damn well what I'm talking about. And I'm not as easily shoved away by your attitude as I can imagine you did with those others who tried to help you. I've seen your file, you quit." His eyes narrow but even with the fierce look he's giving me, I know deep down he wouldn't hurt me in any way. Even more with the tiny fragment of his background he shared with me. This gives me the strength to continue. "My parents own a wellness center chain. I'm managing the one located here. I've shown my parents I'm very capable of handling everything myself, and in return they don't interfere. Well, unless my mom steps foot here, then she always takes over as if I can't do anything right." I confess to that last line with a deep sigh because my mom likes to interfere with a double dose of mom issues. I clear my throat and raise my chin. "Basically, it's my business, but we also work together to accommodate a number of VIPs who travel. Like I said, it's a wellness center, but the one I run is always top of the list when you look at all the numbers. Though it's not just about profit; it's also about quality and service. So, now you know; I have the skills and everything else I need to help you. But like I've mentioned before…you need to want to fight for it. It's a team effort, the whole shebang. I've had a few clients of mine, even some VIPs who've come to my wellness center expecting a miracle worker. With everything in life, you have to take steps yourself, even if someone is there to back you up and pull you through it, it all comes down to yourself and how bad you want it."

"I wanted to fucking sulk," he grumbles, and I can't help but laugh, earning me a glare.

"Sorry." I bite my bottom lip in an effort to stop the laughter. "You're absolutely entitled to sulk. And I do have to tell you that there are no guarantees in life. You could work hard and not see any progress for weeks. It's a process, and a huge impact on your body. It's going to hurt and drain you. Frustrate you…but in the end, it might be worth it if you can ride that bike of yours again, right?"

Ransom shakes his head, a small smile tugging his lips. "Baby steps, huh?"

"Baby steps and diapers filled with shit you're gonna hate to handle," I agree, secretly relishing about the metaphor I used to freak him out.

He looks horrified. "Woman, that's no fucking way to motivate me. Not with the prospect of having a baby in our near future. Fuck. My cock was hard at the thought of your belly swelling because you're carrying our child…not about the cock-block you'll squeeze out of your tight cunt in a few months, I didn't even think about the diaper filling part."

"Breathe, Ransom. It's the exact reason people don't just pop out kids, you have to slowly grow into it. We have months. Months. Just… breathe."

"I am, and it's causing me to hyperventilate. Fuck," Ransom gasps and I can't help but laugh. "I'm not kidding, Hedwig."

"I know," I wheeze, hearing him growl while my laughter intensifies.

I'm being lifted off his lap and placed on the couch. Ransom stands and grabs his phone. "I need to call Casey, he doesn't know yet, right?"

I tuck my feet underneath my butt and shake my head. "I don't think Sico and Everleigh told anyone else. Sico said he'd let Casey know I would keep an eye on you since I live next door, but nothing more."

He holds the phone to his ear and locks eyes with me. "Yeah, it's me, hey…you ready to be an uncle? Well, tough shit, I'm gonna be a father in a few months so I guess we both need to man up, huh?" Ransom gives me a wink and a goofy grin and starts to chuckle. "No, I ain't kidding…yes, I did. Yes, I'm very much aware you're right and I'll have the fifty bucks when you get here tomorrow. I know I said that shit but things are different now. No, I ain't putting her on the phone. Fuck no...well, yeah, I'm spending the night at her place. Fine. See you then."

Weird phone call, and it makes me wonder, "What's with the fifty bucks?"

He rubs a hand over his head and it makes my eyes slide over his whole appearance. There isn't an inch of skin not touched by ink. Even his face is covered with statements he deems worthy of turning into an eternal memory to carry with him. His hands, his head...the place where normal people would have a thick head of hair, this man has inked it all.

The sneer Theodore threw out? About scaring people, and labeling him scum by his appearance? It says more about Theodore's own insecurities. I hate it when people place a label on others with just one glance.

Judging people is wrong. One can only define another when you've walked in their shoes—know their motivations and actions—why they live their life the way they deem worthy. And then still you can't say shit because it's their life, not yours.

"I told Casey about you the day I left here," Ransom sighs and sits down next to me. "He basically said it didn't matter if I took time to return to you, because if it was meant to be, you'd have me by the balls someday soon anyway...fifty bucks said my balls would be chained within six months."

"Don't give him the fifty bucks," I snap, annoyed by the fact Casey thinks I'd be the kind of woman who will tie a man down. "Or at least shove the fifty bucks in one dollar bills down his freaking throat."

"Now that," Ransom chuckles and throws his arm around me to pull me close, "is exactly why I know we'd fit very well together."

CHAPTER 05

RANSOM

"I'm serious, Ransom. I'm not the type of person who would tie you down all because,"

I don't let her finish her sentence but slam my mouth over hers. It's been too fucking long since I've tasted her. I'm about to deepen the kiss when the room goes completely dark. Fuck. First time I've felt serenity overtake me and we get inter-fucking-rupted.

"Stay here," I grunt and start to check why the power blew.

I can't find anything wrong inside so I open the door and see my own porch light still on, it's most definitely not the whole block, just Hedwig's house. Stalking around the house, I come to an abrupt stop when I notice someone cut the fucking power intentionally.

I snatch my phone from my jeans and call Casey. "Get over here right fucking now, someone cut the power from Hedwig's house. Run a full check on her ex-boyfriend, Theodore something. Fuck, I don't know his last name."

"Butler, his last name is Butler," Hedwig quips from behind me.

"What the fuck? I told you to wait inside," I growl.

"I don't care what you said. I didn't want to wait inside in the freaking dark." She puts her fists on her hips and it's a damn adorable sight.

I hear Casey stating he heard the name and is comin' right over. I put my phone in my jeans and hold out my hand. "Come on, we're going over to my house and waiting till Casey gets here."

"I can't, Wendy is supposed to come over and...oh, there she is," Hedwig says and stalks to a car that's parking in her driveway.

The curly redhead steps out of the car and holds out a bag for Hedwig to take. "Here are the files you asked me to pick up. Did you want me to help out with the VIPs coming? It's going to be hectic with the two of them. I've also added the list with the guys from the security company, be sure to pick a few and I'll let them know. Timing sucks with two VIPs at the same time, but we can manage if we put one in the...oh, hi. Ransom, right?" Wendy steps forward and I take her hand in mine to give it a firm grip in return.

"Right. Hedwig's neighbor, and the father of our unborn child." The corner of my mouth twitches as I watch her eyes widen and lock on my woman. Fuck, that sounds so damn right; my woman.

Casey parks his black SUV behind Wendy's car and jumps out. "The fucker is an electrician." He notices Wendy and his voice drops to a seductive tone. "Oh, hey there, back here again too, huh?"

She graces him with a beaming smile while we're out here in the fucking cold, power cut, and I'm damn sure Hedwig's ex cut the power to her house. "For fuck's sake, everyone get inside my fucking house. I don't want my Old Lady standing in the damn cold and out in the open."

"Old Lady? I've got both Calix and Zack on speed dial. Shall I repeat that little slip of the tongue to any of those Prezs? Calix would be a better fit since we're in Ohio and he's the closest." Casey raises his eyebrow in a challenge, but for real, I don't give a flyin' fuck.

"I'll do you one better, brother," I growl and grab my phone, keeping my eyes locked with him as I wait for Calix to pick up. "Calix, Ransom here. I'd like to request a meeting since I'm done being a nomad. Zack would be an equally good choice, but I'd rather stay closer to home, hence my reason for calling you and offering you my request. Can you bring it to the table? If you guys want me that is...great, see you in the morning. Oh, and Calix? Hedwig is my Old Lady." I don't wait for Calix's reaction, I don't need to, my waterfall of information says it all.

Calix is the President of AF MC, Ohio. I've been an AF MC nomad for as long as I can remember, but with a kid coming in a few months—and let's not forget I can't even ride a fucking bike as it is—it's time to stay in one place. Ohio being the nearest AF MC, and with me knowing Calix, C.Rash, and a few of the other guys for years…it's the most logical choice.

Casey keeps staring at me and it's annoying, so I give him the truth. "I don't expect you to understand. It's a moment in time where everything lines up and seem to fall into place. I need to do this, it feels fucking right. You of all people should know how righteous it is to settle down in this house, this fucking town, and to be able to be here for my kid."

He curses underneath his breath and gives me a chin lift. "You guys go inside, I want to check things first. I'll be there in a few minutes."

"Well, I would if I was going to spend the night like every other night I've been here. But I just came by to drop something off, I'm on call and I can't stay." Wendy flips her keys in the palm of her hand and addresses Casey. "Could you move your car? I'd like to grab a bite to eat before…"

Wendy can't finish her sentence because Casey is crowding her. "I'm not moving my car. You need to listen to me and go inside so I can make sure all is clear."

Wendy jabs a finger against his chest. "And I just told you I need to go."

"I'm sure work can wait a few minutes," Casey says, totally ignoring the furious look Wendy is giving him. "What do you do for a living anyway, sweetheart? What on earth could have a pretty face like yours on call this late in the evening?"

Wendy locks her lips and dismisses Casey as she steps toward Hedwig. I swear I hear her mutter something that sounds like "Fucking cavemen bikers."

Casey's clearly pissed and grabs his phone. The way he's eying her car…I bet he's putting in a request to run her license plate to gain information about her. It doesn't take long for his eyes to bulge.

Striding over, he steps into her personal space again and growls, "You're a fucking coroner?"

Wendy narrows her eyes. "What's the matter, asshole? Don't think a pretty face can handle a scalpel and some dead people?" she sneers, totally missing the fact Casey found out her info with a few thumb strokes.

"Okay, that's enough, you two. Like I've said a few times before… it's late, it's cold, my pregnant woman is standing here and I need to get her inside. You two can continue your fighting for all I care but Hedwig and I are going inside." I don't wait but guide Hedwig inside my house and start to relay my concerns. "Is what Casey said true? Theodore is an electrician? You do know one and one is two, right? With this fucker showing up on your doorstep and when he supposedly leaves the power gets cut."

My gut clenches as I see Hedwig rub her own arms. I turn up the heat, though I know the cold doesn't have anything to do with it. This fucked up situation with her ex is screwing shit up.

"And I said you can shove your lame excuse where the sun doesn't shine," Wendy's fierce voice sings through the air but changes to warm laced with concern when her eyes find Hedwig. "Hey, what's wrong, sweetie?"

Hedwig replies to Wendy but her eyes find mine. "I don't like any of this, it's all a bit too much, I guess. Ransom coming back, Theodore popping up. The power being cut…remember what happened when Theodore and I ended things? I just…like I said, a bit too much."

"What happened when y'alls shit ended?" I question. Casey crosses his arms in front of his chest, also waiting for Hedwig to elaborate.

"An hour after she found Theodore screwing Sandy, she got a call from the police that her house was on fire." Wendy curses. "They later found out it was the electrical wiring. Dammit, Heddy, you're coming with me tonight. I'll make a few calls and I'll bring you somewhere safe since we can't stay at my place either. Shit, talk about weird coincidences with the electrical wiring. Dammit, I'm on call…doesn't matter, you're coming with me anyway. And why the hell does your ex pop up after all these months? Talk about shit being dang creepy."

My gaze finds Casey's and a silent agreement settles as he gives me a tight nod. "On it, brother."

Wendy bounces her gaze between us. "What does he mean with 'on it, brother'? Care to share or do I get the standard 'club business' reply you bikers use to shut chicks up?"

Casey steps into Wendy's personal space. "No, sweetheart. It means I'm going to look into it, you know…do my job. Wanna know what I do for a living?"

"No thanks," Wendy quips. "Pretty sure you're an asshole by day and an even greater one at night."

Hedwig and I share a look before we both burst out in laughter. Fuck. What a way to break the tension. Casey just shakes his head, steps back, and thumbs off a message through his phone, probably requesting the info about Hedwig's house. If anyone can dig for information, it's Casey.

Wendy's phone rings. When she answers it's clear she's needed somewhere for her job. She glances at Hedwig. "Are you sure you're okay? I can try to see if someone can take over my shift if you need me. Just say the words, Heddy."

"I got this, Wendy. I won't leave her sight," I vow.

"I suggest you call Calix and see if he's got a room you guys can bunk at. Might give everyone here some peace of mind for the evening," Casey says, and even though I know it's a smart thing to do, I won't let anyone drive me out of my own fucking house.

I'm about to state those very words but it's then I notice Hedwig rubbing her belly. Fuck. He's right. It's not just me, it's not just my woman, it's everything I've never had and wanted in my life.

Now I realize the most treasured thing in life isn't anything money can buy; it's the life you have at your fingertips. And I won't fucking jeopardize the most precious of gifts I just got handed.

"You're right." I grab my phone and shoot a text to Calix.

"Call me later, or text if I'm not answering…I don't know if they want me to dig in straight away," Wendy says to Hedwig.

"I will," Hedwig replies.

"Want me to come with?" Casey asks Wendy whose eyes go wide.

"Something wrong with your head? You can't come along with me, you're a civilian," she says and shakes her head, muttering, "cocky bikers," as she tries to step around him.

"I very well can," Casey snaps. "And I'm not a damn biker, but I could also easily enough throw you off the case you're headed to. If it even is a case." He now smirks as he flashes her his badge. "FBI, sweetheart."

Wendy manages to keep her gasp to a minimum. Recovering fast, she narrows her eyes. "Asshole with a badge, got it."

Casey growls but the lights in the living room flash, making their banter fall flat.

"I'm gonna get her out of here and ask Calix to have their tech guy tap into my security feed. I want eyes on my place, and hers, at all fucking times. I don't care about coincidences or lack of power, I'm not taking any fucking risks," I growl and put my phone to my ear, I don't want to wait for an answer to my text, I need to handle this now. "Calix, it's me. Something's happening at my Old Lady's place which happens to be right next to my house. You got a room available for me and my Old Lady to crash in? Thanks. Coming right over." I lace my fingers with Hedwig. "Come on, let's pack an overnight bag real quick and get you warm and comfy."

She nods warily and I fucking hate the way her life has shaken up today while mine suddenly feels as if shit is finally falling into place.

CHAPTER 06

HEDWIG

"Are you sure you're okay? Need anything else? Don't be afraid to speak up or feel like you're imposing, 'cause you're not," Tenley says and keeps her blue hawk eyes centered on me as she brushes a stray blonde hair behind her ear.

Ransom introduced me to her when we got to the clubhouse, before he rushed into a room they called church along with Calix, the president of this MC.

I give her a warm smile. "I'm fine, thanks."

"I can tell you're not, but it's okay. I will ramble a bit more to pass the time. Ransom will be right back, he needs to talk things through with Calix, my Old Man. So, you're Ransom's Old Lady, huh? I never would have guessed that nomad would be settling down, let alone here in Ohio. But between you and me...AF MC Ohio is lucky to have him. He's fierce, loyal, will be one hell of an enforcer, even with his arm screwed up."

"It's not screwed up," I mutter annoyed. "It only needs time to heal properly, and I'm going to make sure he'll gain more strength soon enough."

"Ah, nice. You almost made me think you're a little gray mouse. Glad to hear you're not, though." She gives me a wink. "Okay, just so you know, I used to be the VP here. That's right, me, a woman, the VP of an MC. It didn't have anything to do with the fact my dad was the Prez, because I totally earned the VP patch by making a business plan and getting the club out of money problems." She shoots me a proud smile. "My solution to everything was a car wash. It sounds simple, but imagine a pole dancer but trade the pole with a car. Nice visual, huh? Yeah, it's a huge success and business has been booming. Anyway, what I meant to say was, I can handle anything. If anyone is giving you trouble, let me know and I'll kick their ass. I'm the only Old Lady, well...next to you. We don't have many bitches hanging around the clubhouse anymore. There are only a few who come here from time to time to entertain the bikers who are single. But the chicks won't touch our guys. If they do...I'll make sure to throw them out, not before I rip all their hair out though...gotta make a point to show other bitches not to mess with us, right? But again, no worries about catfights, the only screw up one needs to worry about involves bikers' overbearing rude mouths or insane demands and misunderstandings because of their cavemen, alpha ways allowing their brain cells to evaporate for fragments of time. So, remember, I've got your back. Even if Ransom screws up, 'cause we all know men can be stupid from time to time, huh?" She smirks.

I have to blink a few times to process her waterfall of words. "Ummm, thanks?"

"Just holler if you get confused or have questions." Tenley takes my hand and leads me to the mattress. "Get off your feet, from what Calix told me it's been quite a day. Ransom claiming you on the spot, the shit with your ex, rushed out of your house and now here. Shit, I'd be off my rocker too. You need something sweet? Ice cream? Chocolate? Coffee? Something stronger?"

I pat Tenley on her knee. Even if she's a bit overwhelming, she seems nice and caring. "Thank you, but no. Though I would love something stronger, I can't." I unzip my hoodie and show off my little baby bump and point at it. "I'm pregnant. Also, something to add onto the eventful day...telling the father of my unborn child he's going to be a daddy."

"You're pregnant? Ransom's? Oh, wow. No wonder he claimed you on the spot. That's so…" Her grin slides right off her face. "Wait, that's one cute baby bump…more than 'I just peed on a stick and found out.' Did that asshole knock you up and bail?"

"No, no." Is she taking my side over Ransom's? While she's a part of his club? "We're neighbors. Well, you could say he gave me one heck of a housewarming party the first time we met. Which was at Christmas time, then he had to leave the next day and got back months later…today actually. He explained how there was some danger he needed to handle, he said it was club business, and how he didn't want to put me at risk and then he got injured right after. And when he left the day after Christmas, he didn't give me his number so I couldn't contact him. It's all a bit screwed up and we didn't even have a lot of time to really talk and you keep saying Old Lady and claimed and it's confusing…like I said, Ransom and I didn't exactly talk everything through yet. He does seem to want me and the baby but we finally kissed and then my ex showed up, which I hadn't even seen or heard from in seven months. Ugh."

"Shit. It's true, you know. I heard about the mess of things what went on over at the MC where Zack's the Prez, and how Ransom got hurt. Calix was with Zack's MC before he came here and later took over as the Prez. Shit…it sure blows we can't have a strong drink to take some of the edge off with all the crazy shaking up your life. But on the other hand, let me tell you to stop worrying. Even if you two haven't had the time to talk things through, I know for a fact you're not getting rid of Ransom. He's a good man, your baby daddy is here to stay. When a biker claims an Old Lady, it's like getting married. You're hooked, protected, cherished. Him being a nomad and requesting a meeting like he did? He's settling down here for you and his unborn child. Can't get any clearer than that, sweetie. As for your ex? From what I've heard from my Old Man, they are handling it. You need to let those worries go for now, all of it. This built up stress isn't good for you or your baby. You know what? You need to relax. Take a hot bath while I go and raid the kitchen to get you something to munch on."

"Thank you. Ugh, I keep saying it, but I really mean it. Normally I'd have my friend, Wendy who always has my back. My parents are sweet but always busy. Shit, I haven't even told them about the pregnancy yet. I'm sure if I did, they'd rush right in and my mom would drag me to their house and simply take over everything." My eyes widen. "Oh, shit. My father would drag Ransom into his office and give him a three-hour lecture for sure." I groan and take my head in my hands.

Tenley snickers. "Have you seen your Old Man? Does he look like the type to let himself be dragged off and lectured?"

I lift my head. "Ransom is too sweet, he'd,"

"Too sweet?" Her eyes bulge. "Again, have you seen your Old Man? He's inked from head to fucking toe, muscles bulging. I did mention he's an enforcer, right? You know what that means? Shit… don't tell me love is that blind. Ransom is anything but sweet and fluffy, Hedwig. Double shit. I don't want to freak you out, though there's no way out with the little bun in the oven…what I meant to say is…stop worrying. Ransom can handle everything and everyone. Alone, he's a force to reckon with, but this man has many MC charters at his back. There's very little this man can't handle. Well, maybe the frustration of not being able to ride his bike with his arm or becoming a daddy, but that's where you come in, am I right?"

"Right," I tell her with more determination in my voice than I have running through my body.

"Well, let's get you relaxed then," Tenley beams and strolls to the door. "I'll be back in about twenty minutes, okay?"

I give her a nod and stalk toward the bathroom. She's right, time to take a bath and let everything go, even if it's only for a moment. And it turns out to be just what I needed. Dressed in comfy PJs, I slide underneath crispy clean sheets and grab the file Wendy gave me as I dive into work. That's how Tenley finds me and hands me a bottle of water along with some comfort food.

Even if I want her to stay and talk some more, she excuses herself and tells me to get some rest. Something about having plenty of time for girl time since I'm part of their family now. And it makes me realize how this morning I was facing everything alone with only one friend having my back and now…now it seems I've been accepted into Ransom's world and although it's overwhelming, they also make me feel welcome and well looked after. I feel the bed shift and look up. I'm so absorbed in work, I didn't even notice Ransom coming into the room.

"Hey," he croaks, and gently rubs his knuckles along my cheek.

"Hey," I breathe, my cheeks heating from his touch. Shit. This man has such an impact on me it's unrealistic.

Ransom plants his ass on the mattress next to me. "You didn't even hear me come in, huh? What's sucked all of your attention?"

"Work," I tell him and show him two pictures, his eyes widening instantly.

"A senator and a rock star, what the fuck…oh, wait…they drop by for a massage or some shit?" His forehead crinkles. "Don't tell me your business offers a happy ending, and that's how those fuckers discreetly handle the media from finding out." Ransom winces at his own words.

Or maybe it's because I smack him on the head with the papers I'm holding. "No, you idiot. I told you my parents have a chain of wellness centers and one of those is mine. We don't do the happy ending thing, it's high class luxury with a reputation which precedes itself. We have a list of VIP members who come and go a few times a month. It just so happens I have two coming over on the same day and it's a bit of a hassle with security," I sigh. "Normally I hire extra security but now I also have to somehow divide personnel and the freaking building between two VIPs. Did I mention extra, extra, extra security?"

"I'm sure you're on top of things 'cause you make it sound like this shit happens on a regular basis." Ransom raises his eyebrow.

"Well, yes, but it's annoying because these appointments were made months ago…by Sandy. And it's not just the fact she screwed me over—which is an understatement with her having sex with my boyfriend at the time, in my own freaking office with me walking in on them, I might add. But it's also about how incompetent she was because I've told her over and over never to book two VIPS on the same day in our facility. Though the building is huge, it's a big risk with extra security and other clients and so on. Did I mention how it sucks I'm still dealing with her screw-ups and how my ex came over today of all days to ask me to hire her back?" I cringe at the way my voice squeaks during my rant. "Sorry, I promise I'm not a raging queen bitch with a crown tainted with overdramatic tendencies."

The man chuckles, making the whole mattress shake. "You could never be a raging queen bitch, Hedwig. Not one with overdramatic tendencies anyway."

I smack him in the chest. "How would you know? I could be. You don't even know me! We spent what? One freaking day together and we used our mouths for things other than talking. Most definitely not for talking to get to know each other."

"Hmmm, best memories, and best way to get to know each other."

Talking or no talking, I got to know you intimately and from watching you on my feed I know how kind hearted you are. Taking care of the neighbors' kids, searching for the old woman's cat who lives down the street, not to mention the dog that got hit by a car."

My eyes widen. "You saw all that?"

"I've been bed bound for fucking weeks at a time, with nothing to fucking do except watch my security feed. I hated the days it rained and you stayed inside so I couldn't get a fuckin' glimpse of you. Thank fuck you're a nature person and love outdoors shit when you have time off," my number one creepy video-stalker tells me.

I can only gape at the man. Okay, maybe my weirdness and his weirdness somehow fit.

CHAPTER 07

RANSOM

We keep staring at each other and it's as if time is standing still while we're daring our souls to disagree to the fact we fit so fucking well together. It's a gut thing. The way comfort surrounds you when you walk into your home.

I don't care we haven't spent months or years getting to know each other. We have all the fucking time ahead of us to do just that. We're tied to one another and not just through our DNA melding together into new life growing inside her belly. Fuck no.

Her becoming my neighbor, the condom ripping, me getting injured and needing to come home. I know for sure we were thrown together time after time for the sole reason we were destined to be together. I'm a firm believer shit always happens for a reason.

My eyes wander to the papers scattered in her lap. Fuck. Shit happens for a reason. Her ex popping up after months, Sandy doubling VIP appointments and wanting her old job back, power being cut and her ex being a damn electrician.

"Hedwig, why did Sandy double up those appointments? Any reason those two are needed in one place? Any special requests or shit happening?" I question, my mind running overtime trying to figure out what the fuck Sandy and her ex are up to.

"A yearly charity event is the reason these two VIPs are here at the same time. It's also the reason why the appointments were made months in advance. They also booked the special rooms we have for guests who will stay two days max. They will bring their own security too. I'm sure it's only my mind overreacting because Theodore showed up; it's nothing I can't handle. I just need a fresh set of eyes to focus and get everything set in time. Here, I'll stop working and look at it tomorrow, okay?" she tells me and starts to pile up all the papers.

My eye catches a list with headshots. I grab it before she can stash it away. "What's this?"

"Oh, it's the list of security guys Wendy gave me." Hedwig gives me a shy smile. "Wendy always gives me a list from the security company she knows so I can pick guys who are capable and available for the days I would need them. This company always handle things fluently when I hire them."

I let my eyes slide over the names and headshots while my anger rises. "What. The. Actual. Fuck?" I growl and jump off the bed. "How well do you know Wendy?" I question, wondering if I've been looking in the wrong direction to explain the shit happening.

Hedwig narrows her eyes at me. "Years. She's my best friend. Why?"

"These fuckers?" I shove the paper in front of her. "Thorns 'n' Bones MC, Hedwig. Every. Single. One. They deal in cunts and guns."

Her eyes widen. Fuck. "You didn't know?"

"Are you serious?" she fucking gasps.

I rub a hand over my inked-up skull. "Yeah, sunshine. I've dealt with these fuckers on more than one occasion. We're on neutral ground, no disputes, but we also don't get cozy because unlike us, they walk the balance of good and evil with a fucking blindfold on."

"I don't…I don't understand. Why would Wendy be involved in these things? Are you sure? These guys always do a good job, they all dress up pristine too and are very polite and nice…seriously. Shit. The security wasn't something I was worried about, Ransom. But now it is. Dammit, why is everything that can go wrong going wrong today? Turn off the lights, I need to sleep and get this screwed up day over with. I'll deal with everything tomorrow because I simply can't with the pile of insanity rising by the freaking second."

"No," I snap, and fucking flinch at the harshness of my tone. I bite the inside of my cheek while I try like hell to calm my shit. "Hedwig, you're my Old Lady now, and I'm the father of the kid growing inside you, yeah?"

She narrows her eyes and nods slowly, trying to figure out where I'm going with this shit.

I lick my bottom lip and throw my words, "AF MC Ohio will be handling security. I can't have another MC working for my Old Lady, that shit ain't right."

Great. We're at a standoff, each standing on opposite sides of the bed. She stomps her foot and strides to her bag.

"What the fuck are you doing?" I growl.

"Leaving!" she snaps and turns on her heels to stalk right out the fucking door.

I rush after her, passing Calix, Tenley, and two of my other brothers—Feargal and Quillon—who are drinking their beers.

"Stop for one fucking minute and let me explain," I growl, making her turn to face me.

She punches me in the shoulder. "No. There is no explanation for you to lay down your law about my business. And I'm not saying I don't like the whole alpha caveman act where you swoop in and save the day, hell...I'm thankful for it, but this is my work we're talking about. One that might carry my parents' name on the outside of the building but I've built it up for years. You don't get to swoop in and tell me I can't hire men I've hired countless times."

"They are not Willy from the fuckin' corner or some shit, we're talking about Thorns 'n' Bones MC," I growl.

She steps even closer but when I'm about to lean into her personal space, I'm being shoved back and suddenly my Prez's back is blocking my vision.

"Thorns 'n' Bones MC? Explain yourself and do it fast," I hear Calix snap.

I'm about to lose my shit. I'm furious about Hedwig working with another MC, even more because she didn't even realize she hires bikers as security. But mainly because Calix is stepping into my discussion and is snapping at my Old Lady. Normally I would punch the fucker but he's going to be my fucking Prez and I need to show respect.

Before I can act, though? A flash of blonde hair is in between Calix and Hedwig. "Calm down, that's no way to talk to her and you know it.

Even if this is about another MC, you respect my girl here to explain under normal circumstances, understood? Shit, she's here one bleeping moment and you guys get in her face, what the hell is wrong with you idiots?" Tenley reprimands.

She doesn't wait for an answer but snatches Hedwig's hand and guides her away from us and to the couch. "Fucking hell, you don't need this. Sorry about those overbearing idiots, they need to learn how to communicate less asshole-ishly."

"Tell me about it," Hedwig sighs. "They don't even ask but demand and take over. It's the exact thing my mom always does when she swings by my practice, as if I'm less competent to handle something than she is," she grumbles and now Tenley's words hit me even harder.

I should apologize but I'm not sorry for interfering. I lean my forearms on the back of the couch. "Hedwig hires extra security when she needs it. Her friend Wendy gave her a list of people working at a security company, I happened to glance over it and recognize all those fuckers as Thorns 'n' Bones MC. I might not have handled it well."

Hedwig turns and glances my way. "Might not have handled it well? Is this your way of letting me know you're sorry, because if so, it's a lame-ass apology."

"I'm not apologizing," I state. "Like I said, I might not have handled it well but I'm not changing my mind, you can't hire them anymore."

"He's right," Tenley says in a warm and gentle voice while touching my woman's knee. "I don't know why you need those guys but hiring them as security isn't something you'd want if something goes wrong."

"Nothing went wrong before but with Ransom popping into my life things seem to go from bad to worse, so you might be right." Hedwig flinches at her own words and I can't manage to hide the hurt spreading my face 'cause she's right.

I rub my temples. "I earned that," I sigh.

"No, you didn't," Hedwig states in a tiny voice filled with regret.

Tenley pats Hedwig's knee once more. "Tempers, you both got 'em, and it seems to me the two of you aren't shy on using them. Why don't you guys leave it be for now and get some sleep, huh? It's late and these things can wait till morning."

"Come on, baby," I whisper and hold out my hand. "She's right, let's get some sleep."

Instead of taking my hand, she stands and hugs Tenley, grabs her bag and stalks toward our room.

Tenley glares at me. "You're welcome," she grumbles. "Now go on after your girl and don't screw up again, she doesn't need the added stress."

I mutter an "I know," and head for our room.

Needless to say, she's already under the covers, lying on her side with her eyes closed. Fucking hell, what a day. I decide to thumb off a text to Casey. One requesting information I know Hedwig would hate me for if she knew, but it's something I can't ignore.

Shrugging out of my clothes I take a quick shower before I slide in bed next to Hedwig. I don't fucking care her body is rigid and stays that way even when I get close enough to spoon her. I wrap my arm around her and lace my fingers with hers.

"Sleep," I murmur next to her ear and place a kiss on her hair.

It takes a breath or two before I feel her start to relax against me. A few breaths more and she's sound asleep. Frustration overwhelms me. My hand slides over her belly, swollen with our child, yet I can't even grip her hip enough to pull her closer. Fucked up arm with no real strength.

I need to work my damn ass off to at least regain some strength back. Or fuck, find a damn way to make up for the shit my body lacks. Starting with keeping myself in check so we can avoid bumping heads like we did earlier. Everything consumes my mind as I finally drift off to sleep.

I wake up to the sound of my phone buzzing on the bedside table. Reaching out, I grab it to see Casey texted me. He's coming over to the clubhouse in half an hour. With the feel of Hedwig's body draped over me, it's the first time I'm not looking forward to meeting Casey any time soon. All I want to do is revel in the fact I have the warmth of this woman cocooning me, filling up the void I never knew could be filled.

Hedwig groans and rubs her cheek against my chest. Her lips feather over my skin and now I'm the one groaning. Fuck. The two of us ended up in bed together the same day we came face to face after months. Funny how it was exactly the same the first time we met.

I want to go slow this time. Slow as in take the time to get to know her, make her aware I'm here to stay and not just because she got knocked up. But if she keeps rubbing against my cock I'm going to be inside her very damn soon. Soon as in with my next damn breath.

She groans again and this time it sounds as if there's something wrong. Shit. Some women have morning sickness. Does she? Did she? Fucking hell, this shows I already missed so fucking much.

I place a finger underneath her chin and connect our gaze. "Are you okay? Feel the need to puke?"

Her eyebrows scrunch up adorably. "Why would I feel the need to puke?"

"I dunno, I just thought I'd make sure because I thought there was something wrong," I tell her and watch as her cheeks flush. "Ah, so there is something wrong. Tell me, sunshine."

"No," she mutters against my chest where she buries her head as she goes on. "There's nothing wrong and yet there is with me waking up like this and I'm still mad at you, and you're you and I don't even know you but I remember how good you felt and I feel like everything else is failing and all I want is to feel good again and I can't flat-out tell you I'm horny, because I am, and it's all your fault," she gasps as if she seems to be surprised at her own flow of words, and buries her head against my chest.

It takes a few heartbeats for me to process her words. For fuck's sake, ramble much? But then her words echo through me; I'm horny.

Rolling over, I hover above her, careful not to put any weight on her. "Let me make you feel better," I croak, hoping she gives me the chance, and add, "least I can do since it's my fault and all."

Her sharp inhale makes her breath hitch, and the way her eyes dilate shows eagerness and desire. I don't need any spoken words from her to know exactly what she needs. Besides, it's been way too fucking long since I've tasted her and my mouth fucking waters at the memory of the last time I had my mouth on her.

Rising slowly, I let my fingers find her pajama pants and slide them off. I take a moment to admire her pussy getting slicker under my appreciating gaze. My mind switched from cunt to pussy when it comes to her. The fact she's mine gives it the respect her pussy deserves. I inch closer and make a trail of kisses on her inner thigh, pacing myself instead of heading straight to my prize.

I nip her perfect skin and feel her fingers sliding over my head. I'm sure if I had hair on my inked-up skull, she would dig her fingers in there and pull me straight for her pussy. Good thing I shaved it all off;

she's not in control, I am.

"Patience, little firecracker, you're my woman now and I'll determine what you need and when you'll get it," I tell her and the huff I get in return makes the corner of my mouth twitch.

CHAPTER 08

HEDWIG

Oh, crap. It's been months and months since I last had sex. Well, ever since I got pregnant that is. But for real, the dragging seconds of this man between my legs, skimming kisses up my legs are even worse than all those months without having sex. Seriously. He's lighting sparks of fire with each touch of his lips but none are on the place where I crave him the most.

Infuriating. That's probably the best word to describe this man. Other than hot, sexy, over the top alpha, but…holy heaven that tongue. "Finally," I groan, making the vibrations of his chuckle tingle through my pussy.

This is what I need; to not think and be overwhelmed with pleasure. It's been too long since I've thrown my brain overboard and let myself go. Every single day since I found out I was pregnant has been somewhat stressful. Now, with all the added stuff from my ex, work, Ransom returning, and not to mention Wendy and those security guys. All thoughts disappear when he grazes my clit with his teeth.

"So. Damn. Good," Ransom groans and shakes his head against my pussy, giving me some extra pleasure from his scruff.

My nails dig into the back of his head, and I'm not sorry. Not one damn bit. I need him closer, I need him to work that mouth of sin of his harder. Faster. "I need to come. Please," I beg.

"Not yet, baby, not yet."

Asshole. I should clamp down on his head with my legs and give him an unholy death by pussy. But I need him, dammit. Not only for the pleasure he can give me—the sweet memories of him setting my body on fire all night long are still vivid in my mind—but for our kid, and to lighten the load together.

But most of all? This man intrigues me. I want to know more about him, share what lies ahead for us and grab hold. But for now, I'm going to settle with grabbing hold of his head to keep him in place. He might tell me 'not yet' and think he's in control, but I can feel tingles already building up. I'm so close, so close, I'm gonna...

"Ransommmmmmmm," I moan and revel in the sweet bliss that overtakes me.

My eyes close while I feel my energy draining. I slump back onto the mattress and shiver from the lazy licks Ransom gives my pussy. I almost push him off because I'm too sensitive but he's already crawling up my body.

He stares into my eyes, lust boiling over and so many other emotions all openly shared with me. My gaze slides down to his glistening lips. I don't have time to think when he slams his mouth down over mine.

His tongue slides between my lips, forcing me to taste myself and his dominance. I can feel how hard he is with his thick length caged in between our bodies. His boxers are preventing easy access to slide inside me. I'm not holding back as I start to claw at the fabric, wanting it gone.

"I need you inside me," I murmur between our kiss.

Ransom pulls back and places his forehead against mine. "I'm pacing myself here, Hedwig. For the both of us. We're not doing the full speed ahead thing with the raw fucking from day one like we did the last time."

"It's day two," I mutter in frustration.

The annoying man—who just gave me sweet pleasure but is withholding so much my mind and body is craving right now—chuckles. "We have loads of time ahead of us, sunshine. We're going slow this time around, build shit up the right way."

"So, we're only going to do oral from now on? Or am I the only one on the receiving end? And why are you making these decisions? Dammit, I don't know what's worse, finally getting some action or having limitations to said actions," I grumble, and mutter to myself, "Cock-blocking will only lead to frustrations, and mine are already sky-high."

Ransom tips his head back and laughs as he rolls off the bed and heads for the bathroom. Great. I went from bliss to shock and annoyed at warp speed. I don't think anyone manages to yank my emotions more than this man is capable of.

I hear the water running and I guess it's payback time. Because this man is naked underneath the shower and if he thinks he can decide what pace we take this thing between us, he's got another thing coming. He might show self-restraint but what if I'm going to poke the bear at every turn, and make sure to remind him of the limitations he set for us. Right. Payback.

Though I'm doubting my own strength when I stalk naked into the bathroom. This man is muscled and inked all over. It's been so freaking long since I've seen him like this and... Oh. My. Gosh.

"What's that?" I squeak and point at his dick.

Ransom's eyes find mine, mischief dancing all over before he checks for himself and shrugs. "My cock. The baby inside your belly isn't enough evidence you're very acquainted with it already?"

"I know that," I snap, as if the man thinks I'm an idiot. "But it wasn't...that...decorated the last time." Shit. "Is this the reason why you want to wait to be inside me? Afraid I can't handle...that." I wave at the monstrosity. As if his dick wasn't thick and big enough, the man had to go and get it pierced.

He slowly shakes his head with the biggest grin on his face. "Nah, I already know you can handle my cock, your pussy is made for me, we found out the first time I slid inside your body. Like I said, we're going slow this time. More talking, less fucking. But we'll hustle it up to the less talking and more fucking soon enough if you don't stop looking at my cock. I did it for you, you know...give you some extra pleasure."

"For me?" I squeak.

This time it's a slow nod. "For you. When I knew I couldn't return to you for a while, I had it pierced so I could let it heal during the time we weren't together."

"Let it...let it heal, no sex for weeks, for the sake of better sex." I cover my face with my hands.

Ouch. I can't even imagine the pain. Getting the piercing. To have a needle shoved right through it and then letting it heal. But shit...is it twisted this makes butterflies' heads bang in my belly because he couldn't have sex when he was letting it heal?

"No sex. At all like I told you already. I haven't had any since I've been inside you, and with the piercing, I'm dying to find out how it feels. Another reason why I'm pacing my-fucking-self because I might not ever want to leave the damn bed once I'm inside you again," the man growls with such intensity it makes me take a step back.

I swallow hard and realize he's right. The kind of connection we have is fierce and I have to admit, I do think it's sweet how he wants us to pace ourselves and get to know each other better.

Ignoring his hard, pierced length, I step closer and tell him, "Wash my back while we talk things over?"

"Make it harder, why don't ya?" Ransom mutters, making me snicker.

I give him my back and I instantly feel his hands roam over my body. He keeps his word, though. Even if his touch is making every inch of me aware of this man, we manage to talk about everything that worries me; work, my ex, Sandy, we share all the pesky things troubling our thoughts.

Ransom asks things about Wendy, making me uncomfortable because she's been my best friend for so long. But I do understand his worries, though. Not to mention I have concerns of my own as to why she would give me a list of men who are bikers and not tell me honestly about her connection with them or if there is one.

All too soon we leave the bathroom and it's time to get ready to start the day. I'm dressed for comfort with yoga pants and a sweatshirt as I watch Ransom pull on his jeans, no underwear.

"No underwear?" I keep staring as he tucks his pierced dick away and mutter, "Uncomfortable much?"

"It's only uncomfortable when you're near. Hence the reason I was wearing boxers to bed. I've got a constant hard on when you're around me, but the boxers ain't helping either so I'm ditching those." He eyes me from head to toe. "Since we're on the clothing topic, you could wear something to show off your body instead of hiding it."

My eyes widen. "Or not," I gasp.

"Why? And don't fucking tell me you don't like your figure," he growls.

Shit. There goes half of the excuses I had. "I don't know, okay?"

"Try better," he throws back with clenched teeth.

"Fine," I snap. "Because I am getting fat and nobody knew about me being pregnant until yesterday. I like to keep my stuff private."

Ransom rubs a hand over the back of his neck. "Oh, for fuck's sake. You're not fat. Your body is fucking perfect and growing a baby inside you means change, changes I happen to fucking love so don't hide that shit. I've told Casey and my brothers, you can be yourself and feel comfortable wearing whatever you like, but Hedwig…never do shit to hide something this good."

I point a finger at him and my mouth opens to say something back but his words seem to flow on repeat in my head. My hand drops as I mutter to myself, "I was getting used to being comfy in sweats, but now you're back and I have to dress up to look nice to keep you."

"Fucking hell, woman," Ransom groans and closes the distance between us. "I'm not sure I'm liking these hormones riding your body with your insecurities. And I can honestly say I'm not going anywhere. Fuck. We have a kid growing in your belly and even if you didn't, I would have come back to you. Hell, I did come back to you when I was finally able to. Now we're going to get some breakfast and,"

"Sure, motivate my ass to grow bigger why don't you," I grumble, making his head fall back while laughter rips out. I punch him in the gut. "Shut up," I mutter with a smile on my face.

AF MC OHIO

CHAPTER 09

RANSOM

"I thought women weren't allowed in church," Casey grumbles and though I want to punch him in the face because he's talking about my Old Lady, I do know his reasons for stating this.

He's got a pile of files in front of him with information I requested. Pretty sure Hedwig isn't going to like the pile of shit he's about to throw out in the open.

"Yeah, well, not your call, FBI agent, because your ass doesn't belong in here either," Calix snaps but tilts his head. "Unless you finally want to put on a cut. Pretty sure it will be a unanimous vote to make you a full-fledged member, Casey. We'd be fucking honored to have you."

Grunts of agreement ring out around the table from all the other brothers. I see the indecision and longing in his eyes before he shakes his head. "Thanks, man, but no. Pretty sure this club ain't ready for two retired lawmen."

Calix—who used to be a detective before he met his Old Lady—shrugs. "Invitation stands, brother."

Casey gives a thankful smile before his face morphs back to his hard business look. "You sure she needs to sit in on this?"

Calix doesn't even glance our way. "Ransom was officially voted in this morning. We discussed it and even my Old Lady made me fucking swear to let Hedwig sit in during this meeting. And Tenley made me ask Hedwig instead of demanding her presence. Pretty sure Tenley turning in her VP patch and cut was all show because she knows she got me by the balls anyway."

His words make everyone chuckle. He's right. Tenley, his Old Lady was the former VP of the Ohio charter. She turned in her cut when her dad resigned as the Prez and Calix took over. She put this club back on the road and I have to admit, she's the reason this club is back to the loyal brotherhood it should always be, and it's now stronger than ever with Calix as Prez and C.Rash as the VP. But like Calix said, Tenley still has a hard voice within this MC. As it fucking should be because she's earned that right, and the respect, of all brothers.

I don't glance at Hedwig because I know she's going to offer to leave with the discussion played out in front of her, but I won't fucking allow it. This involves her and she should sit in on it, and hear every single detail, because we can also use her train of thought and the extra info she might have.

I reach out and take her hand in mine, giving it a little squeeze to boost her confidence as I say, "Out with it, Casey. Let's hear what you have for us." I know the headlines since we already talked when he got here.

"It's not the ex who cut the power," Casey directs his words at Hedwig. "But we do need to keep an eye on Sandy and this Theodore fucker. I've checked out the both of them. Theodore is close to bankruptcy and Sandy's got a record for prostitution."

"What?" Hedwig gasps.

"Oh, yeah, not shitting you, doll." Casey takes a deep breath and warms his voice. "And I'm pretty sure they knew each other before she started working for you. Did she work as a masseuse? Because she did the whole happy ending thing at prior employers and I have all the intel I need to assume Theodore's her pimp. I might even bet Sandy was offering blow and hand jobs while she was working for you."

"I'm so glad she's no longer in my employment." Hedwig shakes her head in disbelief and I can only imagine her feelings about the intel Casey shared when it comes to Theodore since she doesn't mention shit about that fucker; blocking it out to stay focused.

"About that." Casey places a piece of paper in front of her, one I gave him from the files she had. "You have two VIPs coming to your facility. Ransom told me she had something to do with arranging the appointments on one day? Not to mention she had your ex contact you to get her old job back, correct?"

Hedwig slowly nods, understanding washing over her face as she snaps, "That bitch."

"Yeah," Casey chuckles. "I heard from Ransom she walked out, quitting instead of letting you fire her when you caught her and your ex together. Pretty sure she did it for a reason I can't figure out yet, but she couldn't use you firing her, that's for sure. But she needs to be checked out further. I'm going to take this on to expose whatever she had in mind but I'm pretty sure she wants to get one of those two VIPs in a compromising position to blackmail them or something. I'll find out and make sure to keep her far away from your facility so you don't have to worry about this. Your ex? I've paid him a visit and made sure he won't be bothering you either."

"What about the power cut at my house?" Hedwig asks warily. "Not to mention my old house going up in flames right after me and my ex ended things? Isn't it all a little too much of a coincidence?"

"I've read all the records. It might seem suspicious, but for now I think it might just be all a coincidence. Two separate cases, the recent one has my attention, but I'll keep a possible connection in the back of my mind, don't worry about it. Besides, we have bigger things to deal with." Casey's eyes harden and I squeeze my Old Lady's hand again because what comes next isn't something she's going to like hearing.

"I've asked Casey to look into Wendy," I say as Hedwig's head whips my way. "I had to, due to the fact she gave you a sheet filled with bikers to hire. I swear it's just a precaution, not just for your safety but also because it involves your business you work hard for."

"Hedwig," Casey says to drag Hedwig's attention away from me. "He was right to do so. Hear us out, okay?" He waits for her to nod before he continues. "Her apartment is cleared out and a record popped up about an electrical fire."

Hedwig gasps but nods warily. "I didn't know about an electrical fire, she just said her apartment was ruined. It happened about six weeks ago, she's either been staying with me or at,"

"At a hotel owned by Thorns 'n' Bones MC," Casey finishes for her and by the way her eyes widen she didn't know this little fact.

"How?" she whispers. "I've never heard her talking about bikers or Thorns 'n' Bones MC for that matter. I don't understand...I've known her for years, she's my best friend, how could I not know? And why didn't she mention anything about the electrical fire at her apartment? She was my roommate when the electrical fire happened at my old house...why wouldn't she mention it?"

The reason I stayed away from Hedwig is because I wanted to fucking protect her. And now I come to find out she's facing danger due to shit Wendy might have pulled her into? Fucking hell, what if I didn't come back?

I push the anger down; I need to focus. This 'what if' shit isn't doing me any good. We're all on top of this now, though the worry slices through me with Hedwig finding out about her friend, that shit cuts you deep on a personal level.

"My guess is she's keeping this side of her life hidden from everyone, though I'm curious as fuck why because now that we've put all of this together...she's the link connecting the dots," Casey growls before he mutters, "Well, other than she wants to protect her job, something I can understand."

"We need for her to come here," C.Rash, my VP, says. "Explain herself instead of us making assumptions."

Fuck. My VP. Sounds weird, and I never would have thought it would feel right to be here and a solid part of AF MC Ohio. Yet these guys didn't even blink to vote me in and face my Old Lady's problems with me. Though AF MC has always stood behind me, no matter what charter, but this to me is making me feel grounded.

They even voted me in unanimously, making me feel more than worthy to belong here with them. Though it's warming my fucking heart to know I have a solid family set in place for my woman and kid if something would happen to me.

"I understand," Hedwig swallows. "She's not going to like it. Not only is she too strongheaded, but she faces things head on and is not afraid to run her mouth to tell exactly how it is. There's a reason she's a coroner and doesn't deal with people on a regular basis. She punches through lies in a heartbeat and basically hates people with a double agenda. Dammit, she always says; the dead is the cold hard truth, can't hide behind it, it's equal and final to everyone. Why does it seem like she has a double agenda herself now? As far as I know she doesn't have any other friends besides me, she rarely opens up to anyone." Her voice drops to a whisper. "She must have her reasons for not telling me...I don't want to lose my friend."

Casey softens his voice for my woman. "Don't worry, I'll make sure to keep you out of it. She's already pissed at me so I'll take all the credit for this one too, okay?"

The thankful look in my woman's gaze says everything and is making Casey uncomfortable. He's always had my back and even with this he's embracing my woman as mine, shielding her from this as much as he can.

"You have to prepare yourself, Hedwig," Calix states. "You might be finding out shit she kept from you, even if she did it to protect you, it could turn nasty in the blink of an eye. You're under the protection of AF MC. If she's tied to Thorns 'n' Bones MC, and by the sounds of it keeps it locked up tight, she'll take sides with them. As I said...gotta prepare yourself..." He shakes his head and sighs. "Nasty in the blink of an eye I tell ya."

My woman's gaze goes to her lap and it doesn't sit right with me. "One step at a time, Hedwig, let's get Wendy here and talk to her, okay? If she is indeed linked to another MC, she knows how shit works, meaning she also knows how to handle it or work around it, yeah? You've said she's been there for you for years. The two of you have a solid friendship, right?" She just nods at my words.

"Can you send her a text asking to swing by?" C.Rash asks.

"No, you can't ask Hedwig to text her. Wendy will know she asked her here under false pretenses, it'll blow back on her. I'll go look her up myself," Casey states, stepping up to protect my woman again.

"Prez," Quillon snaps and points to the security feed. "Might not be necessary to make her come here."

"Fuck," Casey grumbles. "You guys stay here, I'll handle this. Calix, is it okay if I use your office?"

"Sure thing," Calix says. "Mind flipping the switch right next to the lights when you walk through the door? Then we have eyes and ears in there."

"Sure," Casey chuckles. "I might want to watch the rerun myself when I'm done with her."

Shit. I watched these two go head to head the last time, and with the stuff Casey wants to confront her with, it's bound to heat things up. Good thing Calix's office has secret cameras in place with the feed a straight line to church. It takes a few minutes before we see both Casey and Wendy enter Calix's office.

CHAPTER 10

HEDWIG

My hands clench into fists but I shouldn't get angry for Wendy's sake. I know she can handle herself very well. Not to mention I know all of us want answers. Yes, including me, though I'm torn about all of it. I know for sure she must have valid reasons to keep the connection between her and Thorns 'n' Bones MC from me, but it doesn't stop me from feeling hurt and for betrayal to sting through my heart.

Why wouldn't she share this part with me? She knows I would never judge and would keep her secret safe. Hell, she was the only one who knew that my biker neighbor knocked me up. Her words, not mine. And she was also the one telling me it would all work out, and how bikers protect and cherish their women.

Shit. Clearly, I'm the stupid one now because looking back, I realize she had some kind of inside knowledge about MCs. I lean forward to watch the TV screen that shows the security feed from Calix's office, cringing at the way Casey's harsh voice snaps at her.

"She's going to kick his ass," I mutter, making C.Rash, Calix, Ransom, and all those other bikers' eyes land on me.

Feargal chuckles and rubs his hands together. "Fuck, yeah, fifty bucks says she's gonna win."

"You're on, 'cause no one kicks Casey's ass. Even if I lose the fifty bucks it's gonna be worth having it on fuckin' tape," Hunter says, laughter tainting his words.

Casey locks the door behind her. Wendy is still standing near the door when Casey stalks past her but suddenly, he spins around, marches straight for her and backs Wendy up against the door.

"Oh, fuck. That's hot," Feargal groans when we all witness how Casey grabs Wendy's ass while his mouth is nipping at her neck.

Are they going to have sex right freaking now? Holy shit. Is all my mind can come up with when Wendy's hands reach for his head, holding him close while Casey's hand goes for the…

"No, don't, aw, dammit," Hunter grunts as the screen goes black. "Fucking hell, why did he kill the feed? He couldn't just let us watch, now could he? Selfish prick. Not to mention he'd have some good entertainment as a reminder he could watch over and fuckin' over again."

"Why doesn't this guy wear a cut? The fucker fits right in," Quillon chuckles.

"We've been trying for years, right, brother?" Calix says to Ransom.

I'm still trying to process the last few minutes. Hell, the last day with everything going explosive around me. Shit. Talk about explosive, Casey and Wendy really do have one hell of a connection. Don't think it's one for long term though, bumping heads, having sex the next minute. Crap. Talk about a lot of stuff happening at once.

Minutes pass when suddenly the screen turns on again and all of us watch as Casey zips up his pants while Wendy tugs down her dress as if nothing happened. Casually, they start to talk.

"Hedwig's here, right?" Wendy asks.

Casey leans against Calix's desk and crosses his arms. "She is. Depending on your answers, I'd let you see her."

"You'd let me." Wendy steps closer to Casey and snaps, "Asshole, you're going to let me see her right fucking now. I need to know if she's safe and unharmed. If not, I'm gonna…"

"You're gonna what, Wendy? Get your Thorns 'n' Bones MC biker buddies and rip her away from AF MC hands? Quite the mouth on you there, babe. I have to admit, I didn't take you for a biker bitch." Casey's ice-cold voice flows through Calix's office and we all watch as Wendy takes a few steps backwards as if Casey's words gave her a firm push.

While everyone sucks in a breath, the room goes quiet as we watch Wendy lunge at Casey. She surprises the hell out of him and takes the advantage to grip his jacket, twists, and throws him on the floor. She's straddling him the next instant, throwing punches at his face.

"Fucking hell," Calix snaps and jumps out of his chair, C.Rash right behind him as we all follow to see them rushing into the office to pull Wendy off Casey.

Casey who didn't do anything back but let her land punch after punch. He scrambles up and wipes his mouth with the back of his hand. Blood trickles out of his split lip as his tongue slides over the wound. The Prez and VP are standing in front of Wendy, like a human block to keep these two apart.

"See? The classy part of you is just an act, isn't it? Raging bitch is always there scratching at the surface. Why hide it, hey?" Casey snickers. "I think I like the raw one I had my dick inside a moment ago, nails scratching down my back…and just now fighting like a hellcat. Yeah, why hide behind the class? The hellcat's a better fit for damn sure."

"I'm not hiding anything," Wendy snaps. "Seems like you're the one who likes to hide…behind those bikers you're not even a part of. No cut on your body except for a stinking badge, so who are you to judge, Fed? 'Cause clearly they're not your family. So where do you belong? And who the fuck are you to judge?"

"A brotherhood—family—is stronger than wearing club colors, Wendy. It's about loyalty, honesty, havin' each other's back. You don't know fuck about me," Casey sneers and directs his attention at Ransom. "It's clear she's connected to Thorns 'n' Bones MC. I suggest you keep your Old Lady away from her 'cause the trouble with the electricity…I'm almost positive it's shit spilling from something she's involved in. No worries, brother. I'll dive right in and get all the details about this bitch's dirty life."

"Did your cock pump out the information you spilled just now?" Feargal quips while Wendy gasps.

Casey glares at the man. "I didn't need to talk or fuck her, I just wanted to see her reaction when she's pushed."

"Wow. Guess your cock did the pushing for you, huh?" Feargal chuckles but it's cut short when Casey punches him in the face.

Casey doesn't say another word but gathers his things and leaves the compound. Everyone is still eying one another when Wendy clears her throat. It seems like she's got some kind of magic field wrapped around her because she's got the brightest of smiles plastered on her face as if nothing happened and no one can hurt her. Such a contradiction to the sweet and kind friend I know.

"Wendy, what's going on?" I question.

Her eyes land on me and soften. She steps forward but Ransom pulls me behind him. "She's my Old Lady, Wendy. Hiding the fact you're clearly connected with Thorns 'n' Bones MC and not come forward with other shit? You risked her fucking life. I kept away from her all those months to protect her and not pull her into my shit. I lost fucking months with my Old Lady because of it. That's on me…but knowing you didn't have the fucking nerve to put her first and think of her safety? That's on you and your selfish ways. Needless to say, I have to protect my woman and our kid. Not to mention the fact I'm damn fucking sure you're aware you pulled her into your mess, don't you?"

Ransom's words are harsh and though I hated he was gone for all those months, the words he just said and with everything happening, understanding now settles. He put me first, even if we had one night together and wasn't there for me…in his way he was; I was his first priority.

Regret. There's regret in Wendy's eyes when she glances at me. "There was never a moment we weren't safe, I swear."

This makes me gasp and step away from Ransom to address Wendy. "You knew? They cut the power to my house because of you? What if they caused another electrical fire the night before? What if… shit, Wendy, what did you pull me into?"

"I don't know, okay? I have security set in place and…dammit, Heddy, I can't tell you because it's also tied to my work somehow," Wendy sighs in defeat. "It's complicated…so damn complicated."

"Connected to a case you're working on? Give me a name of the leading detective," Calix's voice rumbles through the room.

Wendy spins around and eyes Calix's President's patch before shaking her head.

"Fine, don't fucking say a word, I'll find out for myself. You keep my patch branded on your brain there, little girl," Calix growls. "I've been a detective for over a decade, though I'm retired but do you really think you can hide shit from us? I've got connections on the force so fucking deep, I could have you thrown out on your ass before you can so much as fucking blink. But first, though? First, I'm going to kick you out of my fucking clubhouse. Jeopardizing one of our Old Ladies by withholding information? Your own fucking best friend I might add. I don't even fucking care if you're a part of another MC, you know damn well you fucked up big, don't you?"

"Hey," a hard woman's voice snaps from behind me, making all of us turn to see Tenley standing there with her fists perched on her hips. "Why the fuck don't you guys let a girl explain the normal and easy way, huh? She's a part of an MC, ever occurred to you she has her hands tied herself? Not being able to give information to others outside of the club? Does it hurt to be nice for a freaking change? I had to rewind and see how Casey went all defensive the second they started to talk. Did you guys even notice the first thing she asked was to see her friend to know she was safe? Riiiiiiight. Ya'll's brain were probably clouded because of the raw fucking he gave her, or the lack of showing it since he cut the feed." Tenley clears her throat. "Now get out and let the girls talk, I'll even flip the switch again so you can all sit in church and watch from the freaking screen for all I care."

"I swear she traded her cut for Calix's balls 'cause she's using them at every fucking turn I tell ya. Either that or this club has another fucking VP besides me." C.Rash shakes his head as he leaves the room, all of the others trailing behind him.

Except for Ransom, he's still standing there looking unsure while Tenley gives him the stink eye until she finally sighs and shoos him with her hand. "Go on, Ransom. I'm right here and Wendy's been her friend for years from what I've heard. And did you not hear me mention a freaking second ago she asked to see Hedwig to know she was safe?" Ransom reluctantly nods and leaves the room, closing the door behind him.

"Are you okay?" Wendy asks while her eyes go from me to Tenley.

"I'm fine. Wendy, this is Tenley, the President's Old Lady," I say and they both nod at each other, deciding I need to cut the chitchat and head straight to the matters at hand, I start to ramble. "Can you please tell me why you would neglect to tell me you're in trouble? Oh, and while you're at it…why give me a list of security guys who all seem to be bikers? Do I need to mention they also own the place you're currently staying at when you're not spending the night at my place? What the hell, Wendy? So many secrets it's as if I don't even know who you are right now. Don't you trust me enough? Don't you know me at all? I would never judge anyone, you freaking know that!"

"You know me, Heddy," Wendy sighs. "Probably better than anyone around me. There are just things I can't share with you, but believe me when I say I only had to because I was protecting you. Am protecting you, and I still can't tell you anything about it, even if I wanted to. And the list I gave you? They have a security company, it's completely legit, I'm sure those new biker friends of yours told you. And I'm sure it's about the fact they don't like other bikers hanging around you. Hell, they might even want the job themselves, did they say they would handle the security themselves instead of you hiring outsiders?"

I have to blink a few times because of her words, remembering very well Ransom offering...no, telling me they will handle it. Is this about a job? Money?

"You really wanna go there, honey?" Tenley shakes her head with disapproval. "You know how bikers are, don't ya? Possessive, overreacting, taking lead without asking...you know damn well they would step up and handle a situation for their Old Lady they can take from her hands so she has one less thing to worry about. So, don't you dare try and get her on your side making her think her man is setting her up and just want the job for the cold hard cash, when you're the one with the skeletons in your pockets, missy."

Wendy's face falls. "Sorry," she mutters. "I just want my friend back. I want her back without having to strip bare. I really can't say anything or I would drag you into the stuff I'm tied up with and I really can't, and won't ever, do that. It's best if I go, just...just know I'm always here for you, Heddy." Wendy steps closer and throws her arms around me for a hug. Her mouth is right next to my ear when she whispers out words I need to focus on because they are so damn hard to hear, and I know she does it to prevent the security feed from picking it up.

And then she's gone and I feel like I just lost my best friend.

CHAPTER 11

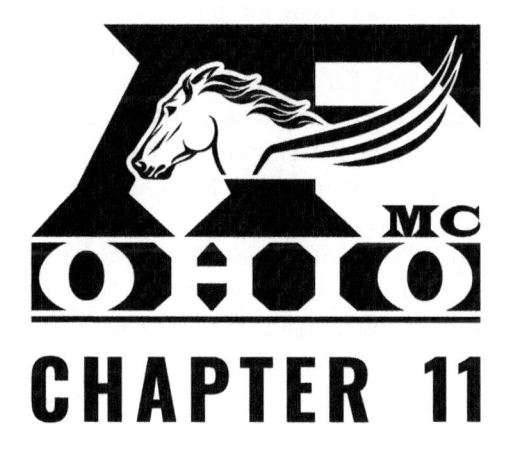

RANSOM

I'm bursting through the door to catch up with Wendy who's almost at her car. "Hey, wait up."

She spins around and pokes me in the pecs. "You keep an eye on her, Ransom. I don't know who has their eyes set on me, and they might not even care about your Old Lady but I'm asking you to keep her safe anyway. Oh, and chewy candy. Doesn't matter what kind as long as it's green. Stock up. And I mean really stock-the-fuck-up, 'cause it will make your life easier."

"Why don't you just tell me so we can help, Wendy? Or, fuck, why didn't you stay away to keep her safe, I fucking did," I ask, curious why she keeps her lips sealed but clearly cares so fucking much for her best friend.

Sadness hits her face. "You of all people should know, Ransom. I tried to stay away at first, but then she got knocked up by someone—who freaking left I might add—and I couldn't let her go through everything on her own," she sighs. "Shit, sorry. It wasn't your fault either. I knew it was a risk. Dammit, everything is fucked up. But I kept her safe, we kept her safe. And you damn well know club business is club business. I simply can't tell you, other than to let you know Thorns 'n' Bones MC is dealing with it."

I give her a tight nod, knowing there's nothing I can say or do to change her mind about giving me inside information. And to be honest? I damn well owe her for not leaving my woman alone to deal with the pregnancy. Even if she put her at risk by doing so. Fuck…she wouldn't have had anyone if Wendy would have left too.

I do want her to know one thing, though. "You keep in touch, ya hear? Call my Old Lady, text or you agree on a time and day for you guys to meet and I'll make it happen. I don't want you walking out of her life when she needs you the most, and I don't fucking care if you're tied to another MC or have shit happening, get me? You were there when she needed you, when I couldn't."

Fucking hell, how can I just step over the shit that put me on alert with everything I heard is tied to and around her? Oh, I know, because my gut is telling me there's more to the woman standing before me. I can see it in her eyes and the way she cares about my woman.

And shit, maybe because Casey fucked her within minutes of them being alone in a room. No one has ever gotten underneath his skin like Wendy seems to do. Hell, she punched him in the face a moment later. She's an enigma, but one who puts my woman first.

"Thank you," she fucking croaks, letting her emotions show how much this simple gesture affects her. "Take care of our girl, Ransom." Wendy gets in her car and when she's about to drive off she rolls down the window and yells, "Chewy candy, Ransom! Green ones. Don't forget 'cause your life might depend on it."

I catch her laughing as she drives away and it leaves me with a fucking smile on my face and shaking my head. Yeah, there's so much more to this woman none of us know about. And the little comment about the chewy candy shows thoughtfulness, that or she's fucking with me, but I'll find out soon enough.

When I stalk back inside, Calix and C.Rash both head for me. I don't want to fucking talk to them, I want to see my woman. Luckily, I see Tenley wrapping an arm around Hedwig while they're sitting on the couch talking. Seems like the Prez's Old Lady is stepping up again for my woman.

There was only one Old Lady in this club until now and this club couldn't have wished for a better one. A lot of things have changed since Calix became Prez of AF MC Ohio. Some of the older bikers moved away, leaving this MC with a fresh group who all have the same mindset.

"You need to ask your Old Lady what Wendy said when she left. We all saw her talk to her, fucking whispering, and we didn't hear shit. Might be crucial," C.Rash says.

C.Rash. I've known this fucker for years. Some think his name is Crash, but it fucking isn't. It's C.Rash, short for Carpet Rash, a nickname he got when he was still a prospect. Back then he was ordered to take care of three brothers who had passed out. They were bare assed and drunk with two whores in the hallway of a hotel. He put the girls in a cab, and dragged the guys by their hands into the room one at time. Let's just say we had three butts looking the same and with that, owning his new nickname.

C.Rash has changed a lot since then. Same as Calix. Also, a man I've known for years. He was one hell of a detective and used to own a BDSM club, all in the past, though. He sold it to one of his friends from what I've heard. He changed his whole life without one single regret.

Something I admire him for, turning his life around like he did, and I now realize isn't very hard to do because once you meet the right person, suddenly things are clear and fall into place.

"I'll talk to her, but I'm pretty sure our Prez's Old Lady got it covered. Besides, Casey is a pit bull when it comes to gathering intel, we don't need to hear Wendy's words," I state while Calix nods in agreement.

"I've worked with Casey in the past. Once he puts his teeth in a case, he won't stop till he's solved it. But he seems pretty driven and yet off his fuckin' rocker when it concerns Wendy." Calix keeps his gaze locked on mine.

"When I got home yesterday, Wendy left Hedwig's house and Casey saw her for the first time. He headed straight over to flirt with her. Then later they ran into each other again when Hedwig's power was cut and they immediately bumped heads," I tell him and C.Rash chuckles.

"We all know Casey can set women off within a few minutes." C.Rash smacks Calix's upper arm. "Remember when we went out to eat and the hot waitress got pissed at him in like three minutes flat? Fucking hilarious and not the first time either."

I shrug, knowing very well Casey is a guy with a personality not many women appreciate. Only this time, my guess is, there's more to it than that. "Casey has known about Hedwig and me since I told him the very next day after I met her. He's heard me bitch about it every other day since, how I couldn't go back to her 'cause it wasn't safe. He knows my issues, him and me go way back, we always keep shit real between us. I called him when her power was cut, he," I sigh and try to think of words to get my point across.

"Knows how much she means to you," Calix finishes and I can only nod 'cause he's right as fuck.

"Great." C.Rash rubs his hand across his face. "So we not only have the man ticked to bump heads with Wendy, he gets his cock involved to clear the air, and yet somehow flare up the heat a different way with the fight they had. But he also wants to get to the bottom of Wendy's problems to fight for his brother. Fucking great, can it get more complicated?"

My Prez's gaze hits C.Rash. "If Wendy doesn't have weird shit to hide, she won't have any problems. If she does however pose a threat, Casey will deal with it. Everyone knows Casey handles things flawlessly, always has. I don't see why it could cause any ramifications."

"That's because you ain't got sisters, asshole," C.Rash grumbles. "Okay, I'll enlighten you. When you have a chick, who has friends… you get issues with said friend…it causes a gap in between friends and leaves your dick to dry up. Still following me? Believe me, it's not pretty. The crying, the hurt, the blabbering, the 'oh, how I wish my bestie was here to see this,' and that's only the beginning. Then, in due time, they turn vicious."

Shit. Do I even wanna know? "You're full of shit, C.Rash," I mutter. "And I don't even care if my cock gets wet or not, look at my fucking woman. She's what's important; her wellbeing. I'll make sure she's cared for, and Wendy's got Hedwig as her first priority too and so does Casey. Might cause his dick to dry up 'cause for sure he won't get any more action from Wendy, and that shit ain't my problem either."

Calix snickers. "Something about hell freezing over causing his dick to shrivel up and die." His gaze goes to where the women are talking. "My Old Lady's already smitten with yours."

"Yeah," I croak, unable to keep my emotions in check, knowing everyone around us is fighting to make sure she's taken care of.

I rub my sternum with my knuckles. Fuck. Talk about a roller-coaster ride of feelings sliding though me, flaring that shit right back up from the first time I met her, and now back full force while I'm standing here. Knowing this woman is tied to me through life we created together.

"Go take her to your room, Ransom. The two of you need some space and time together." Calix slaps me on my back and I gladly take his advice.

I stroll over and hold out my hand. Hedwig takes it and I give Tenley a nod and a grateful smile.

Tenley touches my forearm as her eyes go to Hedwig. "If you need anything, come find me, okay?"

We both mutter our thanks and I drag her to our room, closing the door behind me. When my gaze hits her face, I can tell how much everything is draining her.

"When do you need to head in to work?" I question.

"I only have to swing by tomorrow at ten when I have a staff meeting. I had three days off, and the next couple of days too, it's the reason why Wendy picked up the files for me because she wanted me to take some time off. I've been so tired lately but I've been taking vitamins and cut back on some of my work. Oh, and the need of a nap in the afternoon. They said it would fade in a few weeks, every pregnancy is different," Hedwig sighs and sits down on the bed.

Gentling my voice, I tell her, "Why don't you lie down for a bit? I'll head into town and get us some food for later or did you want to go out to dinner?"

"A date?" she squeaks, eyes pinned on mine as if I just stated the room was on fire or some shit.

And to be honest? I'm questioning the same thing. Though the words flowed naturally, I didn't even think to look at it as a date, but come to think of it, "Yeah, I guess so. There's gonna be a lot of 'that's a first' when it comes to me and you. Fuck. I never even thought I'd have an Old Lady or a kid for that matter…so why not add dating to the pile? We both gotta eat, gotta get to know each other. And you don't need to worry about anything. I'll protect you and won't leave your side. Same goes for when you go back to work."

"Wait, what? You can't come to work with me," she fucking squeaks, again.

"And why the fuck not? Doing some shady 'happy ending' business yourself on the side you don't want me to know about?" Shit. That was out of my mouth before I could actually think what words to pick to handle this. "Sorry, I didn't mean to imply you would..." Her eyes widen before they narrow. "You're an asshole."

"I'm not thinking clear." I rub my hand over my inked-up skull. "Casey just rattled me with that comment about Sandy. I didn't even think...fuck. I'm sorry."

Shit. Way to put my foot in my fucking mouth, and without good reason—not that there ever is a good reason to put your foot in your mouth—what the hell was I thinking? Clearly, I wasn't.

Her shoulders sag. "You know how many times I've heard those very words from my ex? How I shouldn't keep it from him if I did... and how it probably was a good idea if I offered the happy ending stuff because my profit would skyrocket. Now it all makes sense with him being her pimp. God, I'm so stupid."

Double fuck. "No, you're not. He's the stupid one, and I'm an asshole," I growl at myself, rubbing my thumb and forefinger into my closed eyes.

"Yup, glad we both agree," Hedwig snickers. "If you only knew how many phone calls we get with this very question. Luckily I have someone who…" Her eyes go wide before curses leaves her mouth in rapid fire, leaving me to wonder why.

CHAPTER 12

HEDWIG

Ransom steps closer and tips my head back with his finger to connect our gaze. "Talk to me, sunshine, why the cursing?"

"One of her job descriptions was taking calls. Did I not just mention the many 'happy ending' jokes or freaking requests we get? With what Casey said I'm pretty damn sure she offered things on the side. What if Theodore and Sandy ran their shady happy ending business alongside of mine? Through. My. Business. Ransom!" Panic fills my veins. "Oh, shit. What if my parents find out?"

Can this get any worse? My friendship with Wendy is all screwed up and to become aware my business was tainted with stuff I had no idea about…underneath my own freaking nose. Gosh, how can I be so stupid?

"Calm down," Ransom mutters and takes me into his arms, his hand on the back of my head as he pulls me even tighter against him. "Not your fault and you acted accordingly. Your folks will see it that way too. Besides, you got rid of that bitch, it's in the past."

"I didn't." My throat clogs up at the emotions now running free. I'm a damn failure. "I walked in on my boyfriend having sex with my assistant...on her freaking desk. They didn't even stop while I just stood there, shocked. He came while looking at me, the asshole smirked, and they walked out of the office holding hands. Holding hands, Ransom. Then later I got the call my apartment burned down. I had nothing. Nothing."

"Fuck," the man says and only rocks us back and forth for a few breaths before he says, "It did get us together, though. Or you wouldn't have bought the house next to mine."

Great, screwed up way to see the good in the bad. "Glad to have had my normal life ripped apart...only to have it turned upside down all over again a few months later," I mutter into his chest, a smile tainting my words because he's right, and somehow I can't regret the outcome of my world going topsy-turvy when I have this strong man to lean on.

"Come on, baby, you need to lie down for a bit," Ransom says and places a kiss on the top of my head. "All this talk and the shit that happened only adds to your stress levels. It's not only yourself you need to look after, but the little cricket inside you as well."

"It's a baby, not an insect," I gasp, making him chuckle. Pulling back, I connect our gaze. "No, really, I'm not kidding. He or she has arms and legs and fingers and toes and...you'll see when they do the ultrasound."

His eyes soften and a goofy grin slides in place. "So, we're gonna find out if she's got your nose, huh?"

My heart skips a beat or two before it starts to race. "Or if he's got,"

"A cock like me? Then we're havin' a boy."

Oh. My. Gosh. "Weirdo," I exclaim.

"It just blows my mind we made something together. You know, something growing, turning into a tiny person the both of us are responsible for. And I'm going to make damn sure to be there for him or her, and if something happens to me...then our kid has a whole MC there, ready to jump in to make sure our kid will be cared for."

I reach out to cup his cheek. "Now I understand," I whisper.

He explained to me about his background, how he ended up in the system, what he's been through. Tenley mentioned it to me a few times, and how welcome she made me feel while I've only been here less than a day. This is his family and now, as his Old Lady, he's made sure it'll be mine too, as well as our child's.

He feathers his lips against mine. "Go on, get some shut eye. I need you fully rested because I'm going to take you out. We'll be staying here at the clubhouse tonight too but will swing by our houses tomorrow morning, okay?"

He's right. I crawl into bed and manage to get a few hours of sleep and when I wake up later that day, he takes me out to dinner. Well, the both of us wanted a burger so it wasn't fancy but the burger tasted amazing. Equally amazing as our casual conversation. Weird how this guy can pop in and out of my life and have such an impact.

When the day comes for me to finally get back to work, it's Ransom who drives me to work in his truck. I've been giving both his leg and arm enough attention and even gave him some homework to make sure he can do tiny things to stretch and strengthen the muscles. He doesn't say anything but I can see it in his eyes how he wants to ride his bike instead of dropping me off or picking me up in his truck.

He's so freaking attentive, surprising me at every turn. Like how he made Wendy text me the day she walked out of the clubhouse. She apologized about how things went and said how I was lucky to have Ransom as the father of my baby, and how it was Ransom who made sure she kept in touch with me. I smile at the reminder. She does have good instincts when it comes to character, though. But I already knew for myself Ransom's a good man.

I glance at the zipper bag of chewy candy, all green ones. I called Wendy and told her all about how Ransom spent time searching out the green ones for me. I heard the smile in her voice when she told me he was a keeper. I'm also glad she's not angry at me for not using the security company I always use.

There's a knock on the door and my assistant lets my next appointment inside. It's Beckett, the boss of the security company. I decided to explain myself face to face why I wouldn't be needing them this time. I'm kind of shocked to see the tall, muscled businessman with blond hair strolling inside in jeans, biker boots, a black tight shirt, and a leather cut with the patches of Thorns 'n' Bones MC stitched on it.

On his pecs it states he's the Vice President. Well, that's weird. The few times we had meetings this man was wearing a three-piece suit, and now...I guess with me knowing the security company is owned by the MC there's no point hiding it. I had no clue he was the VP of Thorns 'n' Bones MC.

He offers me his hand. "Thought I'd ditch the suit seeing Wendy told me you know the company is owned by us."

I give him a smile and meet his firm handshake. "I guess so. It's actually why I requested the meeting."

"Again, Wendy explained how the security will be handled by your Old Man. No worries, we can respect that," he says and is sporting dimples.

Oh, gosh, I bet this man can evaporate panties with just a flash of his cheeky dimples. He knows it, though. The confidence this guy radiates is extreme. And yet it does nothing to my panties. Doesn't have anything to do with the cotton granny panties I'm wearing. Nope. Doesn't matter this guy is standing here trying to impress me. I'm not interested in any man other than Ransom.

The door to my office bursts open and before I can see who it is, I'm looking at the Thorns 'n' Bones MC patch from up close. Beckett is blocking me from whomever burst inside my office. Though I'd recognize the growl flowing through the air any time of day.

"Ransom?" I gasp and step around Beckett. "What on earth are you doing here?"

He keeps his eyes pinned on Beckett but holds out his hand to me. Without a single thought I stalk over. Ransom wraps his arms around me and pulls me flush against his body.

The vibrations of his words flow through his chest. "What the fuck are you doin' in my Old Lady's office, Thorn?"

Thorn? Turning my head, I catch Beckett smirking at me. "Your Old Lady requested the meeting, Ransom. I was just explaining to her how we have no issue with you guys taking over security detail."

My mind seems to be catching up when anger starts to rise. How did Ransom even know Beckett was here? And what the heck is Ransom doing here for that matter? This is my business, my office, my stuff to handle and it's as if I'm standing on the sidelines while cavemen are discussing. My. Freaking. Business.

I push myself away from Ransom. "Get. Out," I snap and turn toward Beckett. "You too. Out, the both of you."

Beckett, Thorn—whatever the hell his name is—strolls forward. "No problem, ma'am. I think we exchanged all the words we needed to before your Old Man stormed in here." Thorn points at my belly. "Congratulations are in order, gonna be a daddy, Ransom? You ready for that?"

"None of your fucking business," Ransom snaps. "You heard my

Old Lady, get the fuck out of here. And a little warning…stay the fuck away from her, all of you."

I rub my temples while groaning. "This is sooooo not happening. Crazy. Totally out of place, stick your nose in my business, overbearing, asshole alpha cavemen."

Thorn is holding out his hand to me, ignoring Ransom's growl of disapproval. "Ma'am. Thank you for your trust in working with us in the past. If there's any need in the future, please feel free to contact us." He lowers his voice to a bare whisper to direct words that are clearly only meant for my ears. "You're Wendy's best friend, therefore you're still under our protection." He clears his throat and glances back at Ransom before he strolls out of the room. "Always a pleasure, Ransom."

"Fuck off," is all Ransom snaps, his hands fisting at his sides.

I'm sure he's not aware but I can clearly see the white in his knuckles and it makes me wonder how tight his grip is to see if he already made some progression in this short time. I shake my head because it's not the time and place to check on his injured arm because I'm freaking pissed.

"The same goes for you." I glare while perching my fists on my hips.

Ransom narrows his eyes. "Why?"

"Why?" I squeak. "You come barging in here while I'm having a meeting. You can't do that!"

"Thorns 'n' Bones MC needs to fuck off, they don't have any reason to come here. You're my Old Lady, AF MC, Thorn needs to know,"

"Oh, he knows very well I'm your Old Lady," I sneer at the alpha caveman who's acting like someone wanted to snatch up his favorite toy. "And I would have told you when you picked me up later today that he came by to tell me Wendy already explained to them how the security will be handled by my Old Man. He was very respectful and nice before you came barging in and ruined my workday. So, get the hell out because I'm pretty mad at you right now."

"Fine," Ransom growls. "But I'm picking you up after work." I'm about to snap how he doesn't have to bother but he points a finger at me. "Don't fight me on this. I'll leave but I will never fuck with your safety, okay?"

"Fine," I snap back and watch his ass stalk out the door.

Good thing he closes it softly behind him because if he'd left it open, I'm pretty sure I would slam it shut. My anger is still speeding its way through my body. Without thinking, I grab my phone and call Wendy.

I don't even mention who's calling but the words shoot out like rapid fire, "He's such an asshole!"

"Well, hello to you too. Bad day? Who's the asshole? Oh, don't tell me, it's your Old Man." I swear if she laughs, I'm going to hang up. Instead she sighs and asks, "Tell me what happened."

"I had an appointment with Beckett this morning. And why didn't you mention his name is Thorn? And how he's the VP of the MC. Could have come in handy, you know? Anyway, he shows up and then…minutes after? Boom! Ransom bursts inside my office, going all crazy eyes. All while Thorn was being nice and respectful, and telling me how you cleared everything up. Then Ransom goes and ruins it all, taking over my freaking meeting and leaving me no choice in anything…I'm so furious!"

"Oh, shit," Wendy gasps.

'Yes. Oh, shit is right," I mutter and sag into my office chair.

"What happened? Did they fight?"

"No," I sigh. "I kicked the both of them out of my office, that's what."

Full. Blown. Laughter. "I knew you could handle it. Look at you, nailing the Old Lady status already."

I growl into the phone and smack it twice against my forehead before I tell her, "You're insane, you know that? And how the heck did he get here so fast? Or knew Thorn was in my office?"

"Look out the window, Heddy. I'm sure there's a prospect somewhere near the entrance. Ransom won't leave you unprotected, not when you're carrying his baby and with the shit going on."

I block out the rest of her words while I stride to the window and glance out. She's right…there's a guy…well, he looks young enough. "A prospect?"

"Yeah, someone who's not a…you know, not a full member yet," Wendy chuckles.

"You've gotta teach me the lingo here, Wendy," I groan.

"All in good time, Heddy…all in good time. Now calm down. Your Old Man is just protecting you, as is his right, Thorn will respect that. Go pop some chewy candy in your mouth and relax," Wendy tells me.

"Fine," I grumble and hang up, grabbing the bag of green chewy candy for some sweet tooth comfort.

CHAPTER 13

RANSOM

She's been ignoring me. Ever since I picked her up from work yesterday afternoon. I hate it. The minimum reply if I ask her a direct question, the pretending she's sleeping while I can hear her breathing isn't the slow and steady as it would be if she's asleep. And then this morning, she was dressed before I woke the fuck up.

"Sit," I snap, when she's about to leave the room in a rush with her jacket on and purse thrown over her shoulder.

"I'm coming with, and you know it," I growl.

She huffs. "I was going to wait in the car."

I rub a hand over my face. "I'm fucking sorry, okay?"

"Yeah, it helps if you growl it out all frustrated. Really shows how sorry you are," she says and rolls her eyes.

I'm chewing on the inside of my cheek while I think whatever the fuck it is I need to tell her but there's no other way around it when I start to share my point of view. "A fucking VP, from another MC, walked into your office. The shit went down a few days ago. You're carrying my fucking kid, and you're you…I just got back to you. Fuck. What if,"

I can't even fucking say it, let alone think of what could go wrong if someone kicked her stomach or hurt her in any damn way. I close my eyes and let my head fall back, trying to get my bearings. Until she starts to talk, making me meet her gaze. "I have my own business to run, Ransom. Have been doing it for years before you came barging in. You can't expect me to just hand over everything for you to handle. It doesn't work that way. I don't work that way. This is me. My business. I make the decisions. Hell, I already made the decision to let you guys handle security, and Beckett…shit, Thorn, was supportive and understanding about it before you came storming in because Wendy already discussed it with them and he totally respects the decision to let my Old Man's MC handle it."

My shoulders sag as I realize I fucked up. I knew I did, but this shit is complicated. "You're…fuck. I know you're fucking good at your job and all, but this is you…our kid. I've never had this. Someone who makes my heart freeze at the very thought of losing you. It would shatter into a million fucking pieces and that's a fucking good thing too because now that I've felt how it is to have something that puts fucking sunshine on a dark and tormented road, there's no turning back for me. These things don't grow on trees. It's fucking precious and one of a fucking kind. I ain't prepared to lose it. But I now do realize I could very well lose it the same way too when I stormed into your office. You've made your point, I get it now. But fuck…no one was there for you if something did go down. I just couldn't. You're…" I swallow at the dryness in my throat and mutter, "…everything."

Her purse hits the floor when she crosses the space between us and wraps her arms around me. We stand there, holding each other in silence for minutes, soaking in the comfort of our closeness.

"My mother used to take over. She would just barge into my office, grab my files and make me step out of my chair and handle things herself. Even though I'm very capable of running my business—my life—she doesn't care, it's never enough." She snuggles closer against my chest. "It's also the reason why I haven't told her about the pregnancy."

Fuck. "I didn't mean to take over," I tell her, and place a kiss on her hair. "I know how it might have looked, and felt, especially with what you just mentioned about your mother. But,"

She doesn't allow me to say anything else because her lips crash against mine, robbing me from explaining myself some more. When she nibbles on my bottom lip, I can't hold back any longer and take over. My hand digs into her hair to angle her head so I can deepen our kiss. Her fucking taste is so sweet, it's a damn sugar rush flowing through my body. Addictive. One taste won't ever be enough.

Regretfully I slow the kiss down and brush my nose against hers before connecting our foreheads. "You make me want to ravish you for hours on end. But we have an appointment. One involving our kid."

The groan slipping over her lips makes my cock even harder, remembering all too well what sounds she made when I was thrusting deep inside her. Fuck. It's been too long. Why did I make the decision to wait with getting my cock inside her body? I fucking need it. Hell, we both need it.

"Then we'd better go," she says but doesn't move a damn muscle.

"Yeah," I agree but keep staring in her lust filled eyes.

She clears her throat and steps away, retrieving her purse from the floor where she dropped it. "Comin'," she croaks.

"Not any time soon apparently," I grumble, making her laugh as I lock the door behind us.

The ride over is uneventful but once we're there? My hands clench and unclench when we're in the room where gel has been spread on Hedwig's stomach while a woman is inspecting our kid on a screen while we're watching…inside Hedwig's fucking belly. I'm fucking nervous as shit. Why? I have no clue.

"Let's see if the little one will give us a good view if it's a…come on, little one," the woman says, searching between our kid's legs.

Holy shit. Yeah, there's my reason to be nervous. Boy or girl? Doesn't matter either way. In good health as far as the woman could see, and that's the important part, right? Then why the hell am I starting to freak out? A girl? Gorgeous as her mother. A boy? Reckless as they come. Fuck. Both will be torture to raise, I'm fucking sure.

I feel Hedwig's fingers sliding over my fist. "Your knuckles are white, did you see?"

My knuckles are white? What the fuck is that about? I glance down and understand what she means. I don't have the full strength in my arm, but it seems the little assignments she makes me do a few times a day already start to pay off when I can clench them enough to make my knuckles white. Yeah, boy or girl doesn't matter when I have Hedwig right there with me.

"The two of you will be parents of a…boy!" the woman gushes.

Fuck. A boy. Reckless it is. A fucking boy. My gaze hits Hedwig but her eyes are fixed on the screen. The woman has frozen the screen and hands Hedwig a picture of our baby. She tells Hedwig she can clean herself up but all Hedwig can do is stare at the black blob on the piece of paper she's holding.

I remove the gel on her belly and guide her up. Hedwig seems in a daze and when we're finally back on the road she mutters, "A boy."

"Yeah, sunshine," I tell her, now realizing we are indeed having a boy and shit is as real as it comes with the picture she's got a death grip on.

"What's your name?" Hedwig mutters while her finger slides over the picture.

A smile tugs my lips. "I guess we can ditch half the names now that we know it's gonna be a boy, huh? We need a strong name. Gotta live up to the name, our boy needs a strong name."

Her head whips up. "I asked what your name was, I wasn't referring to our boy. Besides Ransom, or is Ransom your given name?"

I glance over, making our gaze connect. Fuck. I haven't heard my own fucking name in years, let alone thought about it. I swallow hard and rumble, "Zander."

A fucking smile spreads her face so damn bright, it warms my heart. "Zander," she whispers and slides her gaze to the picture while she repeats my name.

Hearing my name slide over her lips does funny shit to my body. It tightens my throat and tugs my heart. I left my given name in the past when the bad memories would take me ransom. It's actually why I changed it to Ransom when I yet again was placed at a different foster family. Yet now? Hearing her whisper it to the picture of our baby boy? Fuck.

"I like it," she tells me and understanding dawns.

"You wanna?" If my throat would tighten any more, I won't be able to fucking breathe. She wants to give our kid my name? My given name?

"Well, it's not like you're using it," she mutters and sighs. "Sorry. It's a crazy idea. It's just...I love the name. It clicks." She releases a frustrated sound. "Never mind. It's just that you said he needed a strong name and then there's you and...ugh. It's a stupid thought."

I reach out and take her hand. I link our fingers and place our joined hands on my thigh. I keep my eyes on the road when I tell her,

"You're right. So...Zander, huh?"

One fucking glance at her face and the bright smile is back in place, boosting my body to a higher level. She's right. Giving our boy my name also gives me the opportunity to raise a kid who will experience none of the tragedy his namesake faced. I'll make fucking sure of it.

CHAPTER 14

HEDWIG

It's been four weeks since we found out we're having a boy. Only three more months to go before we get to meet the little one. I rub my hand across my belly and feel him press his tiny foot against me. There's no way to describe how it feels to have new life moving inside you. A smile tugs my lips when I think how thankful I am within this moment.

The visit with the two VIPs to my business went flawlessly. AF MC handled the security and I must say, I was very impressed to see Ransom wearing black slacks, a white dress shirt, and freaking loafers.

I didn't have to worry about Sandy since Casey had her arrested. He set a trap she walked right into and she was charged with prostitution, locked up so she couldn't cause any problems.

I glance out the window and see a prospect standing outside. About twenty more minutes before Ransom will be here to pick me up. I haven't heard anything about what's going on with Wendy or if they know who cut the power to my house. We've been back and forth from the clubhouse to either of our homes, but Ransom doesn't tell me anything other than "Casey's handling it."

And I trust him, all of them to be honest. I've spent time with most of the guys he calls brothers, and also Tenley is becoming a good friend of mine. And then there's Wendy. I'm worried about her. We've met just a handful of times but it's not the carefree moments we used to share.

For one there are people watching us from both sides. Well, not us but our surroundings to make sure nothing happens. It all adds to the tension when you have not one, but two MCs having guys set up at a safe distance. And I have no clue if it's because the threat became more serious or if it's just a precaution…but as I mentioned…no one tells me anything.

So, I rub my belly again and release a deep breath. It's not like I can do anything about it anyway. What I can do is get everything ready for when I take a few weeks off for myself. And I've been working up to it. The only thing left is to inform my parents seeing I need to hire a replacement.

Though I'm not becoming a stay at home mom, or a full-time working one, I'd like to find a balance in all of it and this will start by hiring a replacement who will be working full-time the first few weeks and later on part-time.

I'm still reminiscing when the door to my office opens and the voice of my mother flows into my office. I curse underneath my breath because today of all days I decided to wear one of the pregnancy bands Tenley gave me as a present.

She had a few specially made for me since she thought it was hilarious. This one says "Touch the belly and die." Funny, because Ransom keeps saying it when people come near me. Now I'm regretting wearing it because it's freaking red. And my belly is huge. Meaning it's a big beacon that shows I'm…

"You're pregnant?" my mother shrieks, making the hairs on the back of my neck stand on end.

Shit. Oh, how I wish Ransom would come barging in here to help me face my mother. Screw someone cutting my power or whoever is after Wendy. This. My own freaking mother is my biggest threat right now.

My father steps inside my office and glances between me and mom. "Does the statement apply to me too, since I've seemed to have missed the big announcement?" My dad points at my belly and chuckles.

He steps forward and open his arms. My eyes burn—stupid pregnancy hormones—and I run into his arms.

"Give her some room, Christian," my mother says. "She needs to explain how this could have happened."

"Pretty sure we all know how someone gets pregnant, Camila," my father says as he steps away and brushes his knuckles along my cheek. My mother is visibly fuming while my father rolls his eyes. "Oh, come on, Camila. Like you said, give our girl a chance to explain."

Great. Now I'm really put on the spot. I can hardly tell them I got knocked up at Christmas and the guy left the next day, only to return months later. Oh, and he's my neighbor. And a biker. And an outlaw. Yeah, where to start...

"Babe, I've got something you're gonna love to put your hands on and slide into your mouth," Ransom's laughter laced voice rumbles through my office before his massive body appears.

"Kill me now," I mutter while my mother chokes and my dad snickers.

Ransom doesn't even blink when he notices two people are inside my office. He strolls toward me and holds up a large bag of chewy candy—all green ones—for me to take.

My mother's eyes narrow and she strides to the door. "Security, get in here and remove this man from the premises." She glances over her shoulder to Ransom. "You might want to leave now, Sir. This is a respectable place and we do not have any 'ladies of the night' here to give you the kind of entertainment you're searching for."

The bag of chewy candy drops to the floor as I cover my face with my hands. Embarrassment engulfs me as I mutter again, "Kill me now."

I feel an arm go around my waist and I'm being pulled against Ransom's hard chest. My arms locked in between us, I hear his chest rumble. "Pretty sure you two are her folks, and though I respect the shit out of my woman—with it her parents too—and with her business being a part of your chain, it all needs to be handled with grace. And I don't even care you seem to judge me or put me in a box you like to shove people in who aren't wearing classy business shit, but with all-fucking-due respect. Get the hell out of my Old Lady's office because she doesn't need this stress from you. You're itching to swoop in and take over now that you're here and know she's pregnant. Well...no chance in hell I'll allow that shit to happen. She's fuckin' smart, capable, and very driven. But I'm sure you know all this since she runs this place flawlessly. She's gonna hire a replacement for the time she will be absent to give birth to our kid, to keep it the thriving business she made it to be. Hear that? She's got everything handled and under control. Now...Run. The. Fuck. Along."

When I try to peek at my mother, I'm cringing while warmth spreads through my veins. Oh, how I would have loved those words to be mine instead of Ransom saying them. I could never talk to my parents that way. But with my mother always stepping in without asking, belittling me, and making sure I get no words in between her lecture while she turns everything her way.

Now? She's gaping like a goldfish, eyes bouncing all over until they land on my father. "Don't just stand there, do something!" she seethes.

My dad steps forward, raises his hand to offer it to Ransom. "Christian Clark, and I'm guessing you're involved with our daughter? I must say, the way you stepped up for her gives me a good impression of your character."

I manage to step away from Ransom when he takes my father's hand to shake it firmly before letting go.

"Zander Zigmund, folks call me Ransom. And I wouldn't put it as lightly as being involved with your daughter. More like she's the reason I'm able to inhale fresh air into my lungs with every breath I take, making the world more bearable. Even if I've been breathing my whole damn life, it doesn't compare to what happened when I first breathed her in," Ransom says and pulls me back against him to put a kiss on the top of my head as he murmurs, "She's the fuckin' sunshine in my life."

A good thing too because I'm swaying on my feet with the gush of words the man so easily supplied, it knocks the wind right out of me. That is until my mother ruins it.

She snorts. "A little over the top coming from a man who has turned his skin into canvas and with it makes a statement to the outside world. A deeper meaning? More than meets the eye? You're not fooling me. You're,"

"Enough," my father barks. "Excuse us for a moment." He grabs my mother by her upper arm and turns in an effort to steer her out of my office and says, "We will be right back."

I dismiss them and give Ransom my full attention. "Sorry," I grumble, unable to keep my damn emotions in check and absolutely embarrassed by the way my mother is acting.

"Hey," Ransom says as he cups my face, brushing his thumbs along my cheeks. "Don't ever fuckin' apologize for other people, even if they're your parents. You don't have any control over anyone's actions. And those words I said were over the fuckin' top but that's what you do to me. You've pulled me out of darkness, spots on my soul still intact, and yet they don't seem to matter when I'm around you. Everything in life I've seen, blood dripping down my body…my own, my mother's, and many others after that…it burns holes straight through your soul until there's nothing left but one huge void. I fucking' thought I was unrepairable, nothing could ever take root…until you. It's like putting on glasses. The world was once a blur of colors turned dull, suddenly becomes clear and bright as fuck. Planting a seed that burst its roots and doesn't settle until its rooted deep enough to fucking bloom. That's us, we're solid and growing together, like it's meant to be."

"All right, Ransom. Have you been inhaling romance 101?" I shake my head but deep down this man is touching my heart.

His head tips back and laughter booms through the room. When he connects our gaze, there's so much emotion swirling in there, it takes my breath away. Even when he said all those words just now, it doesn't hold any value without this look. And this look he gives me? It's mine. No one else's. All mine.

"You don't know how fuckin' much I lo…" Ransom gets interrupted when a throat is cleared loudly.

Dammit, I wanted to hear what he had to say. Even if it was radiating from his eyes. Even if his words were enough to know, I wanted to freaking hear it. Pissed off from being robbed from our moment, I turn my attention to the door and see my parents still in the same spot. Shit. They didn't leave? They heard the words Ransom said—almost said—and interrupted?

Anger rises and takes over. "I'd like for the two of you to leave. The business is under control, my life is under control, and right now the only thing that isn't, is my freaking temper."

"We're not leaving!" my mother snaps. "Look at you, you're pregnant. I will handle the practice from now on and you can come and live with us so I can make sure you will take care of yourself and our grandchild."

"Camila," my father snaps. "That's enough. Our daughter is strong enough to handle everything on her own. I've held back every time you stepped in, and while you think you are helping her by shoving her to the side and running the business for her every time we visit, there comes a time when you need to step back and let go. The both of us know she's very capable and has shown to be so for years."

"But she's pregnant," my mother squeaks.

"And? So were you when we were building up our business, it didn't stop you from being successful." My father stares my mother down and this is actually the first time I've heard them argue over me.

My mother hangs her head in defeat, her soft voice cutting through my emotions when she says, "That's the very reason I know how hard it is and how much I want to help her and show her ways to make it easy for her."

The overbearing actions I've experienced in the past are now put into perspective and when I look at it from her point of view, it might seem like she was helping me, and yet she was suffocating me. Damn pregnancy hormones. I'm getting all teary eyed at her admission.

Ransom gives my hip a little squeeze, giving me the strength to gather the right words. "It might seem like you tried to help me but it felt like you were always robbing me from doing what I needed to do myself. And I've proven time and time again how competent I am while doing so. You guys raised me well, but it's time to let go, mom."

"I can see that now." My mother's eyes fill with tears and she quickly wipes them away before she rushes to me and grabs me in a hug. Her voice is still loaded with emotion when she says, "So I'm going to be a grandma?"

Laughing, I pull away to connect our gaze. "Yes."

"We're havin' a baby boy," Ransom says with pride.

My father smacks Ransom's shoulder. "You and I should have a talk."

Ransom raises one eyebrow. "A little late for a talk, don't you think? The only thing I have to talk to you about is getting your blessing to ask for your daughter's hand in marriage."

All the air rushes out of my lungs, making me lightheaded as I squeak, "What?"

CHAPTER 15

RANSOM

Weeks pass where Hedwig and I grow even closer together and form a routine where the both of us relax into. Thankfully her parents backed off a little after Hedwig had a long talk with her mother and showed her the file of the replacement she has now hired. Meanwhile her dad and I had the talk. Not just the one where he tried to threaten me if I hurt his daughter, but also the one where I asked for her hand in marriage to make the picture complete for all of us.

Me. As if I'm not the massive, inked up biker with a whole fucking MC behind my back. Gotta respect a man for stepping up for his kid like that though. I for damn sure will be the same way when the time comes. Every time I look at her belly, I swear I can see it grow. My eyes are fixed there right now when she grabs my head to guide it up to meet her eyes.

"As I was saying but clearly your mind is somewhere else...Do. It. Again," she snaps.

Fucking snaps. In these moments I don't fucking like her all that much. Not that I'd say it out loud, but yeah. She pushes my limits when it comes to my arm and leg, have me stretching and shit. Some sessions are so damn hard I'm useless for hours after it. But I have to admit, the progress I made is fucking worth it.

I'm not saying I'm back full force, but I have all the confidence I'm ready to ride my damn bike to-fucking-day. Well, if she doesn't wear me out too much, because then I wouldn't be able to so much as lift my damn arm to wipe the sweat off my fucking face.

"You should have become a drill sergeant," I mutter while following her orders.

Her laughter does funny shit to my head while my cock springs to life. Not what I need when I'm wearing sweatpants. Not to mention I haven't been inside her since the day she got pregnant. It's not the lack of lust or the fact she's pregnant, I just want to do right by her; to build a strong connection, one that's not driven by lust. Hard as fuck with her eyes set on my crotch, licking her bottom lip.

"Stop looking at me like that," I growl.

Her eyes slide up slowly to connect our gaze. "Like what?" All fucking innocent. Killing me.

I reach out and surprise her when I manage to swoop her up and carefully place her underneath me. As I hover over her, all thoughts of going slow evaporate. We have spent weeks together forging a strong bond, one where the both of us has shoved down the boiling lust we have for each other.

Yet now, with our connection solidified and set in place? Like I mentioned, it's been too fucking long since I've been inside her and every damn day the stolen kisses we have, the easy banter and chit-chat, snuggled close each night to watch TV and sleep tangled in each other's embrace.

"Lookin' like you're ready to be thoroughly fucked," I rasp.

Her eyes dilate and my lips crash down over hers. Thrusting my tongue in between, I make sure to thoroughly acknowledge every inch of her sweet mouth. Her belly doesn't stop her from grinding against me. Fucking humping my thigh as she seeks relief between her legs.

I know damn well I've been neglecting her body with the needs she's got running through it, but for fuck's sake…taking it slow means no sex because the lust can interfere and take over. She needs to know I love her mind, her sweet and perky character…fuck…I love every inch that's her and it's time she damn well knows it too.

It's got nothing to do with the fact I asked her father for his blessing for her hand in marriage or the baby growing in her belly or the months I've spent showing her I'll never leave her a-fucking-gain. I'm right here because she's worth everything to me.

Her nails rake over my skull and I'm so lost in her, I don't even care if the door to the room we're in is locked or not. And I'm damn thankful the weather is nice enough to have my woman wearing a sundress, granting me easy access. With my healing arm I reach out, grip her panties and with one hand I rip them away. Fuck, yeah, how's that for fuckin' progress.

I yank my sweatpants down, fist my cock and tease her opening with my tip, my piercing giving pleasure to the both of us. She's fucking drenched, allowing me to slide through the lips of her pussy with ease.

"Ready for me, love?" I fucking am, my pierced cock touching a pussy for the first time. I've never been inside a woman since I've gotten the piercing and my restraint is about to shatter.

"Stop stalling, get inside me already," she groans, making my cock even harder if possible.

Inch by slow fucking inch I slide inside her, holding myself back because I don't want to hurt her. I guess she's not on the same wavelength when she tilts her hips and with it, I slide in to the hilt, my piercing hitting the right spot for the both of us.

"Fuuuuuck," I groan and let my forehead connect with hers while I catch my damn breath.

I totally forgot how good she felt wrapped around me. Hot. Tight. Like the warm home I never had but always craved. Our connection when I first met her wasn't the cock twitching lust. It was the 'one look in her eyes and our souls connected' shit only romance books write about. Even if our paths were disconnected for those few months, re-fucking-route and we're back for good now.

For the first time in my damn life I make love to a woman. Not fucking; making love. There's a huge difference I now understand. Our gazes are as intimately connected as my cock sliding in and out of her pussy. Heat. Sizzling electricity powering up our bond and connecting us on a deeper level with each thrust.

Our eyes talk while our bodies finish the conversation. No matter how badly I want this to last, it's been too long since I've gotten my cock inside her, it's begging for release. When her walls start to grip me in a vise, demanding surrender, I make sure to rub my pelvis tighter against her to give her clit some more pressure, making her fall apart underneath me while she takes me along with her.

My cum shooting out deep inside her causes me to grunt her name in utter surrender while my body takes wave after intense wave of ultimate pleasure. Fucking hell, this woman is everything life is created for...and more.

Both breathing hard, I lean down to give her a sloppy kiss. I don't even have the energy to fucking focus but she doesn't seem to mind.

Her phone starts to ring and buzz at the same time with the ringtone she has in place for Wendy, instantly knowing who's calling.

Regretfully, I pull out and drag her along with me to our feet. She reaches over and taps her phone that's lying on the cabinet in the corner. She's trying to pull her sundress down so she hits the speaker button and the room fills with rustling sounds and rough pants. Her gaze connects with mine, eyes going wide. I'm right next to her when the both of us yell out "Wendy!" at the same time.

I grab my phone and hit Casey's number, he picks up but I don't have time to talk because Casey's voice rattles through the connection. "Can't fucking talk, three guys are after Wendy, I'm trying to keep up. Fuck." I hear gunshots, making ice slide through my veins. "They're getting...fuuuuuck!" Another round of rapid gunfire.

"What the fuck is going on? Talk to me!" I press because I can hear his breathing but he doesn't say shit while seconds are ticking away. Not to mention Wendy's phone disconnected too.

"They got her. Pulled her into an unmarked fucking van, Ransom. I was so fucking close but they pulled their guns on me. I managed to take one out...fuck. Fuck! Ransom, they got her. Fuck!" Casey's curses continue but we don't have time for this shit.

"Get to the fucking clubhouse, Casey. Now, goddamned, now," I growl and disconnect.

I keep my eye on Hedwig while I speed dial Calix. "Shit went down, I need backup for my brother and Hedwig's friend, they fucking took her. Casey was there and saw how the whole thing went down."

"I'll have everyone in church by the time you get here, so we can discuss options," Calix states and hangs up.

"What just happened?" Hedwig asks me in a small voice.

I don't ever want to fucking lie to her but in this moment, I wish I could...but I can't. "Pretty sure Casey saw a few men kidnap Wendy. We gotta go to the clubhouse, right fucking now. Casey will meet us there and I need you safe so you're coming with."

She doesn't say a word but nods warily. We head for her office where Hedwig gives the woman she hired to replace her some instructions before we hightail it out of there. When we drive up to the compound, we see Casey stalking to the entrance of the clubhouse, dragging a body behind him by a leg. The head of the body bounces on the stairs as he kicks the door open and stalks inside.

I take Hedwig's hand and we follow Casey into the clubhouse. I'm cringing inside and don't dare look at my woman right now with how Casey drags a dead guy behind him. Not something a woman needs to see.

But her voice is steady when she says, "What the hell happened, Casey?"

"They fucking took her right before my eyes," he roars.

"Calm the fuck down," Calix snaps.

The roaring of bikes fills the air. I'm guessing it's a few of my brothers when I hear footsteps coming closer, but when I turn around, I'm faced with different club colors. Thorns 'n' Bones MC.

"What the fuck are you doing here?" I growl and hear Casey roar the same thing along with me.

"I called them," Calix states. "Wendy is connected with them somehow and if shit was turned around, I would respect the fucking courtesy if they would inform me. Hence the reason I called them here, maybe they can either help out or have intel that could help."

"Fuckin' Lee, that fuckin' rat," the guy next to Thorn spits as he kicks the dead guy who's sprawled out on the floor where Casey dumped him.

"Save it, Ryke," Thorn grunts while his eyes meet Calix. "I'm thankful you called, though we were in the middle of some serious fucked up shit and could use your help."

"What the fuck is going on? What did you drag Wendy into and for fuck's sake, why?" Casey's chest is rapidly rising and falling as he drags a hand through his messy hair. I don't think I've ever seen him this disheveled.

"Ryke's sister is missing and when you called we were about to check her house. On the ride over here we needed to take a detour since our Prez was just assassinated by our own fuckin' guys," Thorn states, making the whole room fall silent.

CHAPTER 16

HEDWIG

No, no, no, no. This is a bad action movie, turning into a nightmare by the freaking second. This can't be happening. Glancing down at the dead man lying on the floor while all different bikers are staring at each other is really starting to freak me out. This is my friend who's missing. My friend who has always been there for me. And they are just standing around, looking at each other. Doing freaking nothing.

"Well, don't just stand there and do nothing," I snap, shaking everyone out of their staring match.

Thorn takes a step toward Casey. "For your fucking information... Wendy wasn't dragged into this shit; she was fucking born into it. She's my sister. The President's daughter; a fucking Princess. They killed our father and took her for leverage."

"Fuuuuuuuck," Ransom whispers beside me.

"What? What's wrong? What's going to happen?" I press.

Ransom's eyes land on mine, his face filled with sadness and regret...why? "It complicates shit, Hedwig. She's a Princess, the President's daughter...their Prez just got assassinated by their own guys. Wendy isn't tied to AF MC. The only link is your friendship with her.

Clearly, it's Thorns 'n' Bones MC club business, we can't interfere."

Oh, shit. No. I feel my whole world tilt. Nausea takes over as I rush away to the bathroom, Tenley and Ransom close behind me. How I wish I could freaking puke right now, I can't. I dry heave and clutch my stomach while Ransom holds my hair out of my face and tenderly draws circles over my back.

"Deep breaths, baby. Please, calm down, you're freaking me the fuck out." Ransom's voice is filled with worry.

"Don't tell her to calm down," Tenley snaps. "Hedwig, you're fucking strong, sweetheart. Don't you want to know what they're discussing in there right now? I would fucking like to know. Come on, it's your friend they're talking about. Get your shit together and get your butt inside the main room. No one wants premature labor in a time like this. Shut the feelings off, you're strong, babe. Come on, focus, and let's fight for your friend."

Shit. She's right. I take a deep breath and push away to stalk to the sink and splash some cold water on my face. A few deep breaths later and I've managed to somewhat push the nausea away. I need to be strong, need to know what they're discussing.

Tenley gives me an appreciative smile and follows me back into the main room of the club where everyone is talking at the same time.

"This shit ain't helping," Ransom grumbles behind me and I watch how he puts two fingers into his mouth, silencing the room with a loud whistle.

Calix glances around until his eyes land on mine. Regret and sympathy shine through. I don't know everything about the MC, though Ransom has told me a lot in the last few months, Wendy too for that matter, explaining the lingo. One MC can't interfere with another, I know…but it sounds so wrong. I mean, a woman was kidnapped, can't they just put their laws aside and help?

"Please," I croak.

Casey's eyes find mine, his anger clearly showing on his face and I take a step back by the mere force of it. Casey's gaze slides up, locking with Ransom's before his head swings toward Calix.

"Prez, I need a word," Casey demands.

"Can't you see I'm a little busy here, Casey?" Calix says without breaking eye contact with the VP of Thorns 'n' Bones MC, clearly annoyed by the interruption.

"Just wanted to let you know it's time. Give me my fucking cut. The one you promised would be there for me if I wanted it," Casey snaps.

This draws Calix's attention. Meeting Casey's gaze he nods. "You know it's yours, brother. We'd be fucking honored to have you, we'll settle this later."

"Not later, right fucking now because I also need to state a claim... Wendy is my Old Lady," Casey says, surprising all of us.

"Fuck," Calix mutters. "Then I guess we'd better brace ourselves and get ready to go hunt down—and fucking kill—those who fucking dared to touch one of AF MC's Old Ladies."

AF MC ⬥ OHIO
──── BOOK TWO ────

As a Federal Agent, doing what is right has always coursed through Casey's veins. The one thing he didn't expect was to give up everything he worked hard for in an effort to save the one woman who managed to crawl underneath his skin.

Wendy has succeeded for years to keep her MC ties separate from her personal life. Yet, in the end, there's nothing she can do to prevent it from getting tangled and mixed together.

Will the collision of two MCs become a slaughter party for every single one in their family? Or will brotherhood prevail and unite to save what's left of the ones who will fight for a better future?

*** When you've been living a shiny life, one might think you have it all. But when you're ready to trade everything you've worked for to save the life of a woman, you become aware life has been nothing but mediocre. Jump into the lives of Casey and Wendy, the final book in the AF MC Ohio duet. ***

CHAPTER 01

CASEY

Fucking hell, this is so not the way I thought how this day would go. Dammit. The replay of what took place earlier is still branded on my brain when I saw two guys grab Gwendolyn and drag her into an unmarked van. I had no choice but to take cover when another fucker opened fire. I did take the guy out though, but there's no satisfaction running through my veins as I'm standing here in the clubhouse of AF MC.

She's gone. They fucking took her. If I would have called it in—how I normally would do as a federal agent—it would take forever to gather a team and head out after them. I did the only thing I knew that would result in 'right the fuck now' action. Hence the reason I called Ransom and headed for the AF MC clubhouse to talk this through with Calix, the Prez of this MC.

All my damn life I wanted nothing more than to be a federal agent, making shit right in the world one case at a time. With my brother Ransom—blood or not, the man is my brother—being part of an MC it has been risky at times with them balancing the thin line of the law.

One woman. One damn woman makes me want to throw my

badge to the ground and grab hold of a leather cut that's been offered to me so many times in the past. Now it holds more meaning than ever because I need it for a chance to get her home safe. That's fucking right; a chance. I don't even know if I can get her home safe or if she's even still alive or not. One thing I do know is that the law can't do shit in this situation. Yet, I feel it in my gut, this MC damn well can.

Calix, the Prez of this MC? We go way back. Not as bikers but as law men. Calix used to be a detective. A damn great one before he retired because he took over as President of the Ohio charter. I've always envied his decision. The one he not only made for himself but also for Tenley, his Old Lady. The man changed so much, and not for the worst. Hell, no. If you ask the man, he'd tell you it was the best decision he ever made.

I can't say a woman has ever spiked my blood. Not one worthy enough to put my career at stake for, that's for damn sure. Until I laid eyes on Gwendolyn, Wendy as everyone else calls her, but I happen to love the sound of her full name. Long, red curly hair along with the face of an angel. High cheekbones, full damn kissable lips and those bright eyes you want to drown in. It's because of her hair I gave her the nickname Curls.

She's the best friend of Hedwig, Ransom's Old Lady. That's how I met her the first time, and also the second time, when we bumped heads straight away. She's feisty and clearly doesn't let anyone tell her what to do.

Now, I sure as hell respect an independent woman, but in that moment, she needed to follow my lead. Someone cut the power to Hedwig's house and I needed to check it out and keep everyone safe.

Curls baldly ran her mouth and seeing she had just arrived in her car, and with me having easy access to information…I had her license plate checked out and had all the basic info about her within a few minutes.

I never would have pictured the high-class woman as a damn coroner. A forensic pathologist trained in death investigation to be exact. Yes, I admit, it only made my dick throb even harder for her.

Those two times we met face to face were enough to get me hooked and I'm not even going to mention the third time we collided, because that's a whole different story. She's a surprise at every turn and the mischief in her eyes? Fucking phenomenal. And now she's gone. Taken by two guys and I have no damn clue why.

In anger my gaze lands on the fucker I killed and who is now lying on the floor in the middle of the clubhouse where I dumped him. The roaring of bikes fills the air. More bikers? I damn well hope so. But I watch as bikers with a different patch come strolling in. One of them is Thorn, the VP of Thorns 'n' Bones MC.

"What the fuck are you doing here?" I roar, and hear Ransom growl the exact same question along with me.

"I called them," Calix states. "Wendy is connected with them somehow and if shit was turned around, I would respect the fucking curtesy if they would inform me. Hence the reason I called them here, maybe they can either help out or have intel that could help."

"Fuckin' Lee, that fuckin' rat," the guy next to Thorn spits as he kicks the dead guy who's sprawled out on the floor where I dumped him.

"Save it, Ryke," Thorn grunts while his eyes meet Calix. "I'm thankful you called, though we were in the middle of some serious fucked up shit and could use your help."

"What the fuck is going on? What did you drag Wendy into and for fuck's sake, why?" I bark.

My anger is skyrocketing while fear is taking root inside my veins with the mere thought of not being able to know where Gwendolyn is. Minutes are ticking away while we're standing here and it could be minutes I need to save her damn life. All of it makes my chest heave rapidly as I drag a hand through my hair and tune back into the conversation.

"...Ryke's sister is missing and when you called we were about to check her house. On the ride over here we needed to take a detour since our Prez was just assassinated by our own fuckin' guys," Thorn states, making the whole room fall silent.

"Well, don't just stand there and do nothing," Hedwig snaps, shaking everyone out of their staring match.

Thorn takes a step toward me. "For your fucking information… Wendy wasn't dragged into this shit; she was fucking born into it. She's my sister. The President's daughter; a fucking Princess. They killed our father and took her for leverage."

"Fuuuuuuuck," Ransom whispers.

"What? What's wrong? What's going to happen?" Hedwig urges.

Ransom connects his gaze with Hedwig, his face filling with sadness and regret. "It complicates shit, Hedwig. She's a Princess, the

President's daughter…their Prez just got assassinated by their own guys. Wendy isn't tied to AF MC. The only link is your friendship with her. Clearly, it's Thorns 'n' Bones MC club business, we can't interfere."

Hedwig goes white as a sheet and rushes of to the bathroom, Tenley and Ransom rush after her. Fucking hell. I damn well know how shit in MCs work. Ransom's right, my Curls isn't tied to anyone in this MC so she's Thorns 'n' Bones MCs problem to handle. Except their fucking Prez was just fucking murdered and I'm sure it's tied to Curls' kidnapping. It's plain logic.

Everyone is mixed in discussions, throwing words around and no one is offering a solution; they're just arguing about boundaries. Fuck. My mind is reeling and I'm about to palm my gun and shoot a round to gather everyone's attention when I hear a loud whistle coming from Ransom, which silences the room instantly.

Calix glances around until his eyes land on Hedwig. Regret and sympathy shining through.

"Please," Hedwig croaks and it's fucking killing me how she pleads the Prez of AF MC to help save her friend.

My eyes find Hedwig's, and I'm sure she sees the anger showing on my face because she takes a step back. My gaze slides up, locking with Ransom's before I let my head swing toward Calix.

I've had enough. If no one steps up for Curls, I will. Daughter of an MC President or not—a fucking princess or not—I will risk everything to have her home safe. Not just because she spikes my blood and hardens my dick, while being the headstrong and independent woman she is and drawing my utter attention along with it. But also because she's Hedwig's best friend.

Hedwig, Ransom's Old Lady, is pregnant and will have his kid within the next two months. I'll be an uncle to the little one so Hedwig is already part of my family. Besides, Ransom deserves happiness, I fucking owe him. His whole youth was one fucked up tragic mess, where his father killed his mother, which resulted in him being thrown into the system until finally the two of us ended up in the house he's living in now.

The house he inherited from the people who took the both of us in. Blood or not, Ransom is my brother, we have a connection more solid than any DNA test can point out. He was a nomad for years, never staying in one place except to come home to that house for a few days every now and then to fucking breathe.

Until Hedwig bought the house next door and he knocked her up the same day they met. He only became aware she was pregnant when he was finally able to return home after being hurt by a gang related incident. He immediately asked Calix for a vote, he's no longer a nomad but a member of AF MC Ohio where he will stay in one spot.

The way he talks about Hedwig? I've never seen the man's face light up or be so damn positive about his future. It's Hedwig. She's the reason he's settling down and is planning a future neither of us thought was even slightly possible. I owe it to them, to the baby inside her who doesn't need the damn stress, and I owe it to my fucking self to step up for once and not think about my badge or what happens next. They fucking took her right before my eyes.

"Prez, I need a word," I demand.

"Can't you see I'm a little busy here, Casey?" Calix says without breaking eye contact with the VP of Thorns 'n' Bones MC, clearly annoyed by the interruption.

"Just wanted to let you know it's time. Give me my fucking cut. The one you promised would be there for me if I wanted it," I snap.

This draws Calix's attention and the man nods, "You know it's yours, brother. We'd be fucking honored to have you, we'll settle this later."

Thought so. We've worked together many times, but this can't wait. "Not later, right fucking now because I also need to state a claim…Wendy is my Old Lady," I say, surprising everyone in the room.

"Fuck," Calix mutters. "Then I guess we'd better brace ourselves and get ready to go hunt down—and fucking kill—those who fucking dared to touch one of AF MC's Old Ladies."

Shit, yeah. Their hands were tied before, but the second I claimed Curls she became my property and with it she's under the protection of AF MC Ohio. Since she's already tied to Thorns 'n' Bones MC, she now has two MCs at her back.

"Could we focus on how to go from here, we're wasting time," I growl, annoyed we're all still standing around doing nothing.

"We didn't know Wendy was missing until now. We had Lee here," Thorn kicks the dead guy I shot. "standing watch. There's something only a few folks know, and it comes in damn fucking handy right now."

Thorn pulls his phone from his jeans and taps a few times and eyes me. "You and I will have a chat later. Though I appreciate you claiming her and with it granting us the help we need to clean out the rats within our MC, I'm not fucking happy you claimed my sister, get me? Since I don't even know who you are and haven't heard shit about you from my sister." I give him a nod and the fucker turns the screen toward me. "The first time they took her, barely six years old, our father put a tracking chip inside her to be able to locate her at all times in case we needed to."

I couldn't care less what he says or thinks, but fucking hell...kidnapped at the age of six? Though I'm thankful she's got a tracking chip inside her, but the reasons are fucked up.

"The red dot is her? They're holding her at...fuck. Warehouses, empty ones are the only things around this location." My chest tightens at the way they took her and how easily things can escalate. "We're leaving. Now," I snap and head for the door.

"Now hang on one damn second," Calix grumbles and grabs my shoulder. "We need to think things through."

I spin around and face my Prez. Fuck. My Prez. Who knew I'd ever have one? I for sure didn't, but there it is. I demanded the cut he offered me many times, and now I have to show respect and damn well listen. Though the support and respect works both ways and for damn sure it's the kind that runs deep.

It's also the reason I know my words will lay heavy on his shoulders when I tell him, "What if it was your Old Lady? What if they took Tenley? Would you wait one damn second when you knew the exact location?"

The man can school his features like a pro but he can't mask the wince brought out from my words.

"Everyone weapon up," Calix bellows. "Tenley, keep an eye on Ransom's Old Lady. Ransom, you stayin' here or comin' with?"

Ransom meets my eyes and I can tell he's torn. To be honest? I understand him even more the second I laid eyes on Curls, and with the spoken claim, she's mine. Whether she likes it or not, but I'd rather fight over this shit than not have her breathing at all.

"Stay here, brother," I tell him. "Your Old Lady is pregnant and doesn't need the added stress." I direct my attention toward Hedwig. "You can bet your ass I'm going to do everything within my power to get her back. Even if it'll cost me my last damn breath." I vow to Curls' friend before I stalk to my car to—as my Prez called it—weapon up.

I've got two weapons strapped to my upper body, one more on my thigh, and a set of tiny knives strapped to my other thigh. Not to mention my backup piece is around my ankle.

"What. The. Fuck?" Thorn snaps as he stalks toward me in anger. Oh, yeah. I'm also wearing my FBI bulletproof vest.

"No worries, Thorn. Didn't you hear me in there? My loyalty belongs with AF MC now, and to my Old Lady. My wrath isn't focused on you, nor is the watchful eye of the law. Within this moment only my Old Lady matters."

"Fuck," Thorn grumbles and rubs a hand over his face. "A fucking Fed claimed my damn sister? What the fuck, man?"

Ryke is standing next to Thorn with a similar look of shock painting his face. I don't have time for this shit.

"Shove your issues up your ass and straddle your bike. His Old Lady is the only priority right now. He might have a badge but I'm pretty damn sure he's not bringing it with him. He's out for blood and justice in a whole different way, and so are we. Let's ride!" Calix slaps Thorn's back and I take this as my cue to get behind the wheel and drive off.

I don't even care if they follow me with their bikes. I have my destination and one damn goal in mind; My Curls. Hang on baby, I'm on my fucking way.

AF MC OHIO

CHAPTER 02

WENDY

Keep breathing. Deep one in...hold it...release. I have to get through this, one way or another they will come for me. Even if my last breath leaves my body, I'm damn sure revenge will rob these fuckers of their lives.

How do I know? Because this is not my first rodeo. Sad but true. I'm the princess or so they call the daughter of the President of an MC. I was born into this life with a huge arrow pointing at my head to show others I'm the prize possession when it comes to leverage for the Prez and the MC.

I've been successfully kidnapped—and saved—twice before. And to add to this count...three attempts that the MC has managed to end before they could take me. And now this happened.

And I consider this the worst one out of all of it. Though being kidnapped at the age of six does give a girl thoughts one doesn't need at that age. Want to know why I think this one's the worst? Because I know these fuckers.

What they don't know is the fact I have a tracking chip inside me. Only my father and brother know about this little fact, but it doesn't help me one bit if they don't know I've been taken. It may complicate things a little more though I hope Casey finds out I have a brother. Thorn needs to know I was taken so he can track me.

"Why use this instead of rope? You're nuts," Bandito says as he's tying me up.

Bandito. I never liked him, too slick and no respect when it comes to women. He wasn't one of the three who were responsible for taking me. Well, two were left since I saw Casey take one out.

Casey. I hope he doesn't go all vigilante and comes after me himself or get the law involved. Please let him contact my brother instead. Shit. How would he even know who my brother is because I've always kept the MC connection well-hidden when it comes to my family ties.

Ugh, dammit, and if Casey did get the MC involved? I wouldn't trust them. It's all screwed up because the one who should be watching over me? He was the very one who took me. Yes, betrayal within the brotherhood instead of loyalty and trust.

What for? I have no clue yet. They haven't said anything. They brought me to this empty warehouse with nothing but an old mattress on a metal bed frame where my wrists are now being tied to the iron bars.

"The electrical wire cuts into the skin beautifully," a dark voice states from behind me.

Ice fills my veins. For dang sure do I recognize this man's voice, but who is he? Pretty sure he's a biker, though not one staying at the compound...a nomad maybe? Shit. Think! Dammit, did he say electrical wire?

My brain overloads with all the information from the cases I've worked on, and all the incidences happening in the last few months. Like how my house had an electrical fire and my friend Hedwig's power was cut while I was supposed to be staying there, but most importantly?

I've had a few bodies end up on my table with injuries caused by electrical wire wrapped tightly around their wrists and ankles. Holy shit, this is bad. This is too much of a coincidence and I'm pretty damn sure this man is the killer who made all the bodies pile up on my table these past months. I don't have time to think when my pants are ripped off.

"Fuck, man. She's on the rag," Silas says with revulsion. "I ain't dipping my shit into a sea of red."

On the rag...blood. Oh, no. The beating I took...my stomach...I couldn't shield from them. It's not my period like this asshole claims it is. Pain slices through me and it has nothing to do with the injuries to my body or being kidnapped and lying on this bed. When they kidnapped me, I was on my way to see my best friend Hedwig. Mere minutes before that? I took a pregnancy test.

My period was a few days late and I was nervous because I had unprotected sex. One dang time—first sex ever—and the man manages to knock me up. Well, not anymore. More hurt slashes through me. I wish I never took the pregnancy test, then I wouldn't have known. Then my period would just have been late instead of knowing I'm having a miscarriage right now.

The dark voice rasps an eerie chuckle. "A bitch has more tight, warm holes to fill than their cunt."

Gael Murray. That's this bastard's name. I've heard him voice the same words once before, and back then I knew it was in reference to me. It was months ago during a barbeque where he said it in front of my father—the Prez of Thorns 'n' Bones MC. The man even had the nerve to ask my dad why no one had claimed my tight cunt or ass for that matter.

Needless to say, both my father and my brother kicked his ass and threw him out of the clubhouse. Dammit, why is everything falling into place now? He must be the one behind the killings and stalking me. Creepy fucker.

But why in the hell are Bandito, Lee, and Silas working with this idiot? Do they all have a death wish? No one turns on their own brothers; it's like signing your own death warrant.

"Move and let me prepare this pretty ass," Gael says as I hear him step closer to the bed.

Close enough for me to do something. I've stopped fighting when I knew I had no shot of getting myself free. I mean...the way they beaten my face, and almost every inch of my body, enough to miscarry and have the left side of my face swell, add the major headache, and not to mention my hands are bound...yeah, the only thing I can do is keep breathing and wait until I can get my revenge.

Because retaliation will be sweeter than...wait, I can't think of anything that would be sweeter. I'm in such a bad place, I better think about the best moments of my life. You know...the shit that flashes before your eyes right before you die? Not that I'm planning on dying.

Hell, no. I won't give up that easy. I just need something...a distraction from this hell I'm living in right now. Something to hold on to and what can pull me through.

But I won't draw myself inwards yet. Not before I try to lash out one more time. I put enough force into the kick to make Gael grunt but not enough to take him out. Dammit, I was going for his junk but only managed kicked his inner thigh.

"Watch and learn, Silas," Gael says as he binds my ankles and pulls the electrical cord toward my knees.

He wraps it so tight around my knees, I just know he's cutting off circulation. Pain is flaring up and running through my body from all directions. I need to focus, I need to keep it together...I just need to.

"See? This way you keep their cunt nice and tight without the risk of the bitch kicking out." With a crushing grip he easily positions me with my knees underneath me as he wraps the cord around my back, and then around my throat to make sure I can't move or I'll cut off my own oxygen.

Fear fills my veins. Helpless. I've never been driven to a point where I know there's no way out for me. I know I won't come out breathing with a beating heart, and if for some magical reason I do... it won't be with a sane and serene mind.

Burning pain bursts through me. "Like my fingers up your ass, Princess?" Gael rumbles. "Or would you rather I whip out my cock and pump this tight little hole? You'll have it soon enough."

His dark chuckle makes me gag as I try to keep my breathing steady. I have to keep focus, I can't freak out. Not now. If I do, I will panic and will turn into a teary mess. I won't ever give him the satisfaction. Never show weakness. Never. I've branded it into my soul at an early age.

You can say a lot from being raised into the hard life of an MC, even for a girl. But there's one thing you learn and you learn real freaking fast. Never, ever, show the enemy they've gotten to you. You show them strength and smile up until your last breath leaves your body. And you fucking fight for it.

"Tough one, ain't ya? I knew you'd be a prize to break. I fuckin' knew. All those women I killed before I could have you weren't even close to being a substitute for you, Princess. Fuck, no. I've been watching you for months. You're unbreakable while they were glass shattering with a single fucking touch. And you feel so good around my fingers."

I have to clench my teeth and I close my eyes in an effort to drown out everything around me. Casey's face flashes before me, his smirk, scruffy jaw and wild spiky hair on top with the sides cut short. Oh, and let's not forget his eyes; breathtaking.

There's a reason my mind drifts to this man. He's the one guy who has managed to light up my body in all the right and wrong ways. We bump heads as hard as we fuck. The kind of connection where the air starts to crackle around you and it's either going to explode or light up beautifully.

Shit. I've only had sex once—Casey being my first in every way—and managed to get knocked up from it too. It happened the third time we met and seriously it all took place within a few minutes of being in each other's presence. No small talk, no sweet words, only body language. And when the sex was over, we were back to bumping heads.

But being in Casey's arms—even those mere minutes—were the best dang minutes of my life. So, yes, I damn well going to put it on a loop. Anything to let my mind escape and not to be here—tied up in this filthy bed—with Gael's fingers up my virginal ass.

Gael leans forward and grabs my hair with his other hand to turn my head and let his mouth near my ear. His tongue licks along my earlobe. "I wanted you to myself, Princess. But I have to settle with these assholes being here when you take my cock down your throat. And don't fucking think of biting me, bitch,"

He hooks his fingers deep inside my ass and yanks them up, making it unable to keep the whimper inside. Fuck, that hurts.

"Because I will knock your teeth out and jam a knife underneath your chin." Gael releases a dark laughter and adds, "Exactly the same way I killed your daddy. A Prez no more, a Princess no more…quite fitting, don't you think?"

No…no…he's lying. I'm sure he is. My father can't be dead.

"Incoming!" Silas bellows and Gael's fingers are being ripped from my ass as he flashes up.

"Fuck. How could they have found us so damn fast? I'll go around and take a look," Gael snaps. "You guys take her and then bring her to the other location we discussed earlier."

"My brother will kill all of you!" I growl and I'm dang happy it comes out fierce and with determination because it's absolutely not how I feel.

"It's not your brother, Princess. Just an idiot who's at the wrong place at the wrong time. But a fucking interference we don't need. I'm going to make him and his car disappear before we travel to another safe location where I will have the chance to have my fingers up your ass and my cock shoved deep into your throat," Gael's laughter follows him as his footsteps fade, barking out one more time, "Take her, boys."

"Should we take turns fucking her ass? It's what he meant with take her, right?" Bandito asks Silas, clearly not one of the brightest but I already knew this little fact or they wouldn't have taken me in the first place.

In the distance I hear the rumbling of bikes. My brother or my father, they must have used the tracking chip to pinpoint my location. Gael was lying, he must have been, because the most logical reason for them to know I was kidnapped is Casey told them. And for real, the rumbling of bikes is music to my ears but dammit...they should be smarter than that. Talk about ruining the element of surprise.

"Fuck," Silan curses. "I'm out of here; they can't see we're a part of this shit, come on. Kill the bitch and let's split."

"We should take her with, man, and go to the other location like Gael said," I hear Bandito say. "Leverage and a warm hole to fuck in the meantime."

"The both of you will do nothing other than die," a harsh voice bellows and right after two gunshots ring out.

I close my eyes and brace myself. The voice I heard wasn't my brother's nor my father's. Deep breath in, deep breath out. Brace for what's to come.

"Hey, Curls...it's me, baby," Casey's voice slides through my brain and a sob rips from my throat.

Dammit, I'm supposed to keep my strength and now my mind is playing tricks on me. I wanted him, needed his memory to distract me from the hell I'm in. "You're not real," I whisper to myself.

"I'm right here and I'm as real as it gets, Curls. And you're about to become really pissed at me when I tell you how real." His chuckle is a warm caress right next to my ear, making my eyes flash open to see his smirk. And why the hell is he calling me Curls?

Oh, that smirk. It's what helped me push through this, and dammit, "Cut me the fuck loose instead of smirking at me, Fed."

Holy shit. Why does it have to be him finding me in this position?

Naked. Bound.

"They fucking raped you?" His roar makes me cringe. "Fuck, sorry. Careful, sweetheart...I'm going to cut you lose with a knife, stay still."

"What freaking choice do I have?" I mutter to myself. "It's not like I can move with the way that idiot tied me up. Please tell me you killed him." Finally, I'm free and the way the blood rushes back to my legs makes me rub all over my sore limbs.

Casey removes his bulletproof vest and grabs the hem of his black T-shirt, pulling it over my head and surrounding me with his scent.

"A little late to the party, aren't you, asshole?" Casey growls and I look over my shoulder to see my brother Thorn, Ryke, and a few bikers of AF MC standing there.

I'm thankful Casey cut me loose and covered me with his shirt and he also threw the bulletproof vest on me as if bullets can fly through the room any damn second. And who knows, maybe it could happen. But mostly I'm thankful because I can't imagine those guys finding me the way I was bound and exposed. Reminding myself of this fact makes me aware I have to be strong.

"I really hope you killed that fucker," I repeat, glancing around and eyeing every pair of eyes set on me.

Thorn points at the two dead guys, "There were more than these two?"

"Well, duh." I roll my eyes. "Otherwise I'd be rather stupid asking that damn question."

"Name," my brother snaps.

"Watch your fucking mouth," Casey snaps back, making my eyes widen. Did he really snap at my brother? A VP with other bikers standing around him?

Suddenly Gael's words hit me again. "Is dad okay?"

Pain, grief, pity. So many emotions are washing over my brother's face. I take a step back while fear takes root inside my veins.

"No," I gasp.

"For fuck's sake, blood is dripping down her damn legs, I'm taking her out of here, this shit can wait," Casey says and I'm not even able to process how fast he scoops me into his arms and strides out the door.

In the back of my head I'm aware my brother isn't stopping him but it's all a blur when Casey puts me inside a car and buckles me in.

Even the ride to the AF MC clubhouse doesn't make me wonder why the hell he takes me here instead of the MC I belong to. I should care, should worry, but I'm simply too numb. I can't process anymore. My brain is on overload with everything that happened and even more about the fact my father isn't alive anymore.

"What happened, is she okay? Are you okay, Wendy? Please, say something." Hedwig's voice is pleading and filled with concern.

"She needs a shower and some rest. Do I have a room here, Tenley?" Casey asks and I hear a woman's voice give him directions.

"Later, Hedwig," Casey sighs. "She's first priority right now. I'll come get you when she's caught her breath."

Casey carries me into a room and I hear the door close before he places me on my feet. I don't want to look at him. I don't want to open my eyes or do or say anything...I just...don't.

CHAPTER 03

CASEY

I can't get the image of finding her out of my head. Knees bound tight against her upper body and strapped to the damn bed like a dog. Fucking blood running down her legs. I feel like my whole world is about to cave in and yet I've seen so much worse in my line of work. But this? My damn woman...finding her like that? My heart was wrenched out of my chest and ripped to shreds in front of my eyes.

Seeing her standing here alive, and yet the life ripped out of her because of what she went through...and let's not forget her becoming aware they've killed her father on top of all of it?

"Fuck!" I roar and march into the bathroom.

I want to punch the fucking walls and smash everything within my sight but nothing will help me shake this feeling. This moment in time will slip by and will be a fragment of everyone's memory and yet it's burned into her goddamned soul forever, and I can't seem to grasp my bearings. I want...no, I fucking need to be strong for her but I'm losing my fucking shit here.

I take a few deep breaths and turn my head to see Curls still standing in the same position I've left her in. Blood still trailing down her fucking legs. I step over to the bathtub and start to run her a bath. I open the cabinet in search of some painkillers, and luckily find them, and flip on the faucet to fill a cup with water.

Stalking back to her, I hold out the pills for her to take and she throws them into her mouth without question and takes a few sips of water after them. I take the cup from her hand and place it on the bedside table. Closing the distance between us, she lets me take off the bulletproof vest I put on her earlier.

"I'm running you a bath, but I have to ask, Curls…do you want me to take you to the hospital? Are we going to need a rape kit? Do you want me to call the club doc to check you over…your face, those bruises?" My damn voice breaks and I'm glad I got all the words out, even if it was on a fucking whisper.

"Their dicks didn't come near me," she whispers. "I only got the hell beaten out of me…no doctors."

Thank fuck their dicks didn't come near her. "But, the blood…how…what?" I croak, unable to ask if they assaulted her in any other way.

Her head whips up, pain evident in her eyes but she blinks it away. "My period. Shocking, I know. It's the reason they didn't want to touch my pussy. Lucky me, right? Besides, if you killed Gael Murray along with those other two you shot before you cut me loose…then you've got it all covered. Well, maybe add the other one I saw you shoot when they pulled me into the van."

There's something more she's not telling, I can see it in her eyes. But it could also easily be the whole situation she was in just now. I leave it be for the moment because there are more crucial things at hand.

"The one I shot before you got pulled into the van is dead," I mutter as I let her words flow through my head, coming to the fucked-up realization that we missed one. "Who the fuck is Gael Murray? Was he in the room when I got to you? I didn't see anyone when I entered the warehouse. Just the two I shot who were there with you."

Her eyes go wide, panic filling her gaze, "Oh, no," she fucking gasps.

I dig my hand into my pocket and pull out my phone. "What's your brother's number?" She rattles it off and I wait for him to pick up. "You need to double check for one we missed," I bark into my phone.

"Name," Thorn snaps back. "And why the hell did you take my

sister? Get her here with me where she belongs."
Now this little fact makes my blood boil even more. "No. Fucking. Way. Bring her to an MC who killed their own damn Prez? Who fucking kidnapped their own Princess? I called to make sure we killed a fucker named Gael Murray 'cause your sister says he was there too. Now deal with it because my priority is my woman." I don't give him a chance to reply but end the call and throw my phone on the bed.

When my gaze hits Curls, I notice she's still staring at me with her eyes wide. Yeah, I might have unintentionally given her a large flow of information just now. Though I need for her to know I've claimed her as my Old Lady, it's not the thing for her to worry about. She's been through enough.

"Come on, let's get you into this bath and make sure you can relax. You must be hurting all over. We'll get you settled and then we'll talk, okay?" I tell her and she still doesn't move a damn muscle. "I'll tell you everything I know and what happened after I saw them pull you into the van. Club business or not, I will tell you everything I know, understood?"

There, I give her something a woman raised into an MC will understand and appreciate since—Old Lady or not—it's not allowed to share club business. I'm happy to say she gives me a slight nod and stumbles toward the bathroom. Fuck. I want to give her privacy and yet I need to keep my eyes on her to make sure she's okay.

Fucking whirlwind of things running through my mind when suddenly I remember her saying the blood was from her period. She'd need female stuff to handle it when she's finished with her bath. Dammit, and some fresh clothes for sure. Fucking hell, shampoo or that kind of stuff too. My brain clearly isn't functioning.

I turn on my heels and open the door, yelling Tenley's name. Damn. My Prez's Old Lady I now realize. Never in a million years did I ever made a spur of the moment decision that could have such an impact on my life, and yet with every realization it settles more and feels right, as if it was always destined to be this way.

Though I don't have a damn clue how things will continue from here on out. Me, a Fed, now an AF MC Ohio, full-patch status. An Old Lady to add to it and I also just killed two men in cold blood without filling out fucking paperwork to justify shit.

Tenley comes rushing down the hallway, Hedwig following behind her.

"What do you need?" Hedwig clips.

"Female shit," I clear my throat and add, "Shampoo and bath stuff, clean clothes, and the stuff you need when you have your period."

Tenley is about to turn to get the stuff but Hedwig is already rushing away so the Prez's Old Lady turns her attention back to me. "I'll make sure to bring you guys some food in an hour or two, okay?"

I nod warily, my mind already back with the woman currently dealing with personal stuff in the bathroom while I wait for the things she's going to need.

"I won't keep you any longer but I do want to mention I respect the hell out of you. Not only because I think you'll be a great addition for our MC but dude…the way you stood up for Wendy? For Hedwig? For your brother? You were crafted from the word loyalty. Thanks is just a word, but know if there's anything you'd ever need…ask, and I'll make it happen, yeah?" Tenley grabs my shoulder and gives it a squeeze.

Hedwig comes rushing back with two bags and hands them to me. "Here, I gathered a few things. Ransom put a change of clothes in there for you too. If there's anything else…or if she wants to see me, let me know okay? And…thank you, Casey. Really, I can't thank you enough for stepping up and bringing her back safe."

I take the bags and nod awkwardly. They each grace me with a smile before I close the door and head for the bathroom. The door isn't locked and I stop dead in my tracks when I see her standing like a statue in front of the bathtub—exactly how I left her—and still wearing my shirt.

I place the bags in the corner and step closer, "Hey, Curls. Let's get you cleaned up, okay?" I tell her in a gentle voice so she doesn't freak out on me.

She nods warily and I let my fingers grab the hem of the shirt and gently slide it off over her head. I should have let the women take care of her but my fucked-up mind can't handle anyone taking over. I need to be the one who takes care of her. Even though she's naked, there's nothing sexual about this. The only thing what she needs is to feel taken care of; to be cherished.

I gently scoop her into my arms and set her into the tub. She pulls her knees up to her chest and rests her head on them. I shut the water off and stalk back to the bags to grab the stuff I need before I get on my knees next to the tub and start to wash her back with a sponge.

"Is he really dead?" Her voice is barely a whisper and I need to think of how to reply, because she could be talking about the fuckers who took her or the one we missed, but I'm pretty sure she's talking about the only one who matters the most to her.

One thing I never do is lie to her. The first time my brother and I were thrown together in foster care, we made a pact. We would never lie to each other or to the ones we cared about. Even if the truth is cold and hard to face, it's always better to keep it real. Less chance for shit to blow back into your face.

"If your father was the Prez of Thorns 'n' Bones MC, then yeah, Curls. Thorn mentioned he was killed by one of his own." I keep stroking her back and add, "So sorry for your loss."

She doesn't say anything for the longest of times but then suddenly asks, "Why did you bring me here and not to my brother's compound? Seeing you know exactly who I am, or better yet, why didn't you let my brother take me home?"

Talk about fucked-up timing. She wants to do this right now? Screw it. "I couldn't do shit when they took you. I killed one and the others threw you in a van and drove off…I had nothing. I acted on instinct and instead of calling it in, I reached out to Ransom and he told me to get to the clubhouse. Calix called your brother since he knew you somehow belonged to them. When they showed up, they identified the fucker I shot and told us it was all an inside job. They didn't even know you were missing until we told them. None of us could do shit since Thorns 'n' Bones MC is divided and fucking compromised and AF MC's hands were tied because you're only connected through Hedwig." I clear my throat and brace myself to add the crucial part. "I asked for a full-patch status, since Calix had offered it to me many times before in the past, and I knew he'd give it to me no questions asked. Then I claimed you on the spot, and by doing so you were immediately tied to both MC's. Your brother wasn't too happy but shared the fact you have a tracking chip implanted and showed us your exact location. I headed out to get you straight away instead of waiting around and doing nothing. That shit was eating me up, I had to get to you…they fucking took you right from underneath my fucking nose," I growl out, raising my anger in full fury all over again as I relive the moment of seeing her being dragged into that van and fuck knows what happened until I was able to rescue her.

"And before you think of ways to justify my reasons to claim you…you might think I did it for your friend, the one who gave me my brother back. My brother who was ready to lock himself out of this world until she stepped in and pulled him right back into the center of it with a fucking child on the way and finally claim the woman he's been raving about for months. Fuck yeah, it had something to do with that, and the fact everyone was standing on the sidelines with their fucking hands tied because you belonged to an MC that's been corrupted from the inside out. But all this shit aside? You think I'd shove my cock inside any pussy? When I filled you up, it fucking meant something. Even if you took a swing at me right after and left, that moment right there? That's when I marked you as mine. So, let your mind run over all those things but in the end it doesn't matter. I claimed you. You're mine; my Old Lady."

"For a fed who's been a biker for a mere few hours you seem as if the MC has been the only life you've had," she mutters and tightens the hold on her legs. "How can this bath be warm while I'm so damn cold?"

"Come on, Curls." I reach out to take one of her flaming red curls between my fingers, letting it slide through before giving it a little tug. "Let's get you out of this tub and some warm food inside you. What's your favorite food?"

"Great. That's going to be my name from now on? Curls? Stupid bikers and their cheeky nicknames. I deserve a tough one, but no…dang curls," she grumbles.

Instead of getting in my face about me claiming her or the way shit went down or even with what she's been through…she starts to fuss about the nickname I give her. This strong woman in front of me grew up in the lifestyle and knows the ins and outs. Though it never defies a person from where they came from, and yet she's a person I've come to respect so damn much over the weeks I've gotten to know her.

Fucking hell, it's not like I've gotten to know her by talking to her. Fuck, no. I've been investigating, and surveilling, finding out what makes her tick and how she spends her days by laying low in the shadows. At first, I dove into her personal shit because of a threat to Ransom's Old Lady and it all lead me to her.

Her apartment was ruined by an electrical fire months ago. And before that, she was staying with Hedwig, and Hedwig's apartment was ruined the same way, that's where it all started. As if someone wanted to drive Curls out of her own home. Why? I have no clue but she's a coroner, a forensic pathologist no less, and the last few months females have been landing on her table with injuries caused by electrical cords. Fucking hell, electrical cords. I cut those loose from her body.

I hold out a large fluffy towel for her as she steps out of the bath. I don't want to address what she just went through and I try to soften the blow by using her full name. "Gwendolyn,"

"Crap," she gasps. "Don't call me that, it's Wendy. Or use the stupid nickname you picked."

"I'll call you whatever the hell I like," I snap, but I try to soften my tone once again when I explain the reason behind her nickname, "Your fiery red curls bounce with your attitude. When you pull, it straightens but it'll snap right back to their own way. Fierce with the kind of captured beauty one needs to appreciate it from afar without any interference. Fuck, yes, I call you Curls or the deluxe version of your name the way it was given to you." I clear my throat and have to look away from her piercing gaze and steer clear of this discussion so I dive right into the issue at hand, "You were bound with electrical cords. All those cases you've been working on,"

"Yes, pretty sure Gael Murray is the perp. Did you not hear me ask if you killed Gael Murray? If you had everything covered?" she sighs. "Right. Brilliant, just brilliant. Seeing you're a Fed, I suggest you put out a warrant or at least fill the detectives in who are on the case, maybe they can link it all together now that we know who we're dealing with."

"Dry off and get into bed, I'll get us some food and make a few calls. This fucker needs to die and I need to see it with my own damn eyes. I have to talk to Thorn, this shit's been going on for months. I need to know why you're being targeted by this fucker. Goddamned why did he slip through our fucking fingers?" I growl and stalk off. There's no way I'm going through legal actions and issue a warrant and sit on my ass to let detectives do the work they have been doing for months without any results.

"Tuna sandwich! Get me two," Curls yells out after me as I leave the room and head for my Prez.

AF MC OHIO

CHAPTER 04

WENDY

I glance at the clean clothes in the bag on the floor where I pulled out clean panties and a sanitary pad. I should put on some of those clothes and yet my gaze slides to Casey's shirt he left on the bed after he took it off me. The shirt he threw on me after he rescued me. I let the towel I was using to dry my hair some more drop to the floor and pick up his shirt. I can't help but take a deep breath to inhale his scent before I put it on and snuggle underneath the sheets.

My body hurts, my heart hurts, everything hurts while every single thing what happened runs through my mind. I try to block out the bad parts but I fail terribly; it's all too painful and overwhelming. My eyes burn and I hate myself for not being able to hold myself together. I don't want to cry. I never cry. Crying I consider a weakness leaking out of my body, I don't have any weaknesses. As always, I survived.

Words slide through my train of thoughts. Words Casey threw out how Thorns 'n' Bones MC has been ripped apart. My father…killed by one of his own men. One? There were at least three bikers of my dad's MC involved with my kidnapping and also Gael, a nomad. How many more are a part of it? Who can we trust? It's so messed up.

Hell, my feelings are even more messed up with the miscarriage. The painkillers aren't helping and neither did the warm bath. Nothing helps and even if he saved me and the way he treats me…Casey adds to it all.

These last few weeks we've met a total of three times, and though every time it's as if we have this pull to collide. Right or wrong; we just collide with force. And to find out it was him who stepped up for me, at a time where the MC I grew up in was at its worst, he found a way to have two MCs work together…he came for me.

No, he claimed me. I don't think he fully understands; it's not something he can switch on and off. It's something he can regret instantly if he gives up his badge for trading it with a cut or worse… when they take his badge away from him.

There's a reason I always kept the club and my life separate, I didn't want it to interfere with my career. It was easy enough to stick with my mother's maiden name seeing it wasn't connected—on paper or for the outside world—with the MC.

My father always wanted to shield me and yet enemies always found a way around it since I didn't completely stay away from the club. Family is a weakness and yet they can be the strongest connection you'll ever have, even if it has nothing to do with DNA. Every biker in the MC has my back. Had. Until now. Betrayal cuts deep but with this? In a brotherhood where loyalty is thicker than blood? I don't know how things will go from here on out.

It makes me even more aware what Casey did, stepping up by claiming me to have another MC step up to have his…have my back. Tears yet again sting my eyes however it's for a complete different reason now. Dammit, talk about having a bad day.

I'm never emotional, never. Not when it comes to my job, not when I saw people murdered when I was barely eight years old and a rival MC came shooting its way inside the clubhouse, making me hide underneath the pool table. See how I've learned to be strong and know how to control my emotions from a young age? Because one peep back then would have meant a bullet to my head.

Though it's a huge difference now. Alone in this bed I could let myself go for just a handful of seconds and no one would know. Well, except me, I would know. And if I would let it all out now? I'm pretty sure I won't be able to keep myself together and turn into a shaking, blabbering mess. Kidnapped, assaulted, miscarriage, the death of my father...everything.

I close my eyes and relay the mantra I always replay when I need it. "Keep breathing. Deep one in...hold it...release. I have to get through this," I keep whispering to myself repeatedly until it's too much. "I can't breathe, why can't I breathe," I croak and tighten my fists in the sheets.

The mattress dips, scaring the shit out of me, and I scramble back only to fall off the bed and hit the floor. Hard.

"Fuck, sorry. You're okay, sweetheart, it's me. Come on, you're safe," Casey says as he hovers over me.

"Up yours, asshole. I'm not okay, and as long as that fucker is still breathing, you know damn well I'm not safe until he's found and killed," I grumble.

"Everyone is on it. I told Calix and he's in church discussing it with Thorn as we speak. I've spoken with the detective on the case and he's also looking into things. I had to because I want all eyes open to find this fucker so he has nowhere to run. We'll get him and for once I fucking hope the law won't be the one who gets to bring him in. I want this fucker ripped into pieces for touching what's mine," his voice is deadly with enough strength a chill runs down my spine.

What Gael did to me? What I went through? What lives were lost because of it? Even if Casey only saw the way I was tied up he found me...I will never tell him how Gael touched, violated...No. Not going there. I shove the memory down deep and get to my feet.

I realize I have to tell Casey about the miscarriage. Somehow it doesn't feel right to keep it from him although I could because I only knew I was pregnant for less than an hour. But still, it hurts my heart not to share the loss with anyone, it's too hurtful to keep it inside.

"And why...never mind," Casey grumbles.

"Why what?" I ask and slide back underneath the sheets.

He shakes his head, "I can't believe you chose my shirt instead of the clean ones."

I refuse to answer and instead I fire back, "Did you bring food?"

"I ordered some, Tenley will bring it when it's delivered. Did you want me to get Hedwig for you? Or do you want some more time for yourself first?"

"Not yet, I'll...shit. My phone and purse. What happened to my stuff?" I gasp, only now realizing I lost everything when they pulled me into the van.

"I got your purse in my car," Casey says as he rubs his neck. "I snatched it up when I grabbed the asshole I killed while the other two dragged you into the van. Do you need it? I can go get it."

"Thank you," I sigh in relief. "Saves me from cancelling everything. No need to get it now, later maybe. I just thought I'd text Hedwig later to let her know we'll talk tomorrow. Right now, I need…" I can't even finish my sentence because I have no dang idea what I need.

"Okay, why don't I go grab it anyway? Then hopefully the food will be here and you can send her a text later. Would you rather be alone or can I crash here?" His gaze connects with mine and I can tell by the look on his face he doesn't want to give me a choice, but I'm thankful he did.

I look away from his piercing gaze while I answer his question. "The bed is big enough for two people." I shrug as if it's fine either way, but to be honest? I don't want to be alone.

"Good. Be right back," he mumbles and leaves.

I hate being needy. I hate the fact I want him. I've always been strong and by myself. Growing up surrounded by bikers I always told myself I won't end up with one. Seeing the handsome young guys… hell, even my brother…dating freely. Yeah, dating isn't the correct word for those guys and their 'activities'. Anyway, you get the idea why a biker wasn't my first choice.

I snort at my own train of thought. Even if Casey wasn't a biker mere hours ago, he is one now, while I'm supposed to be his Old Lady. Shit. Old Lady. What a screwed-up day where I feel as if I lost so much and yet Casey managed to touch my heart the way he stepped up for me…claimed me.

Let's also not forget the way he explained his reasons for picking my nickname. It's overwhelming to say the least. I snuggle into the pillow and let my nose trail along Casey's shirt, inhaling his scent, allowing myself some comfort only he manages to give me.

My best friend is having his brother's baby and only a few weeks ago I thought I'd lost her when they found out I was somehow secretly connected with Thorns 'n' Bones MC. Though I was under the protection of Thorns 'n' Bones MC, I never once thought we were in any danger.

Even if both of our homes had electrical fires. How could I've been so stupid and naïve? Dammit, I never would have thought the danger would come from within Thorns 'n' Bones MC.

The door opens and Casey steps inside. "Hey, I know you wanna rest up but someone is very anxious to see for herself if her friend is okay."

I sit up and give Casey a tiny smile and he steps inside the room to let Hedwig dash by him as she heads straight for the bed to sit down next to me.

Casey hands me my purse. "I'll be right back."

I don't get to reply because Hedwig is in my face. "I was so freaking worried! I can't believe everything that happened. Ransom is still in church, they're all working together. I have no clue what's going on or have all the details but the way Ransom reacted to Thorn mere weeks ago? As if he could go for his throat while now? Now he slapped his back and they walked into church together as if they've been friends for years. Not a good thing, right? Shit. I don't know. Sorry, I'm rambling. I just…shit. I'm so sorry about your dad."

And this is the exact reason I didn't want to see anyone. My throat gets cut off by emotions and I barely manage to swallow and give her a nod. I can't say anything. What do you even say to something like that? What are the correct words? I don't care if someone—anyone—is sorry. Sorry is just a word while my father is gone forever.

Swallowing hard, I try to find the strength to tell her, "Can you… can you get Casey for me? Sorry, I don't…we'll talk tomorrow, okay? I'm tired, I just…"

Dang, why can't I even form one coherent sentence?

"Oh, sweetie," Hedwig says before she gives me a quick hug, "Sure thing. If you need anything, let me know. I'm right down the hall, okay?"

My head slowly slides up and down as I watch her slip out of the room. Dammit. Does this mean I'm in shock? I mean, she's my best friend and I can't even muster the strength to tolerate anyone around me right now. Well, except for Casey, which is weird since I punched his face the last time me met, mere minutes after we had sex I might add.

Ugh, we have this twisted connection. Maybe I feel like I need him because he saved me? Some kind of screwed-up hero complex I've got going on. Shit, this is getting me nowhere. I don't want to do anything, let alone think.

I feel the mattress dip again and my heart stutters while I jump back, catching myself before I fall off the bed again. Dammit, why the hell am I so dang jumpy? I'm safe here, of this fact I'm very sure. Angry at myself, I huff and turn to see who entered the room.

"You're safe here, Curls," Casey's voice is soothing as he reaches out to cup my face, letting his thumb feather over my cheek. "I won't let anything happen to you."

I lean into his touch, "I know." Strange how I fully trust this man. Everything involving him suddenly seems so right in a world so wrong. I'm going with my gut. It's not like I can go home because Gael Murray is still out there.

Or to the Thorns 'n' Bones MC compound or the hotel they own because my father's murder was an inside job. Holy hell, why do I keep repeating these things? See? I don't want to think and just take a breath and...not think about anything.

"I've got the grilled pastrami sandwich, hands off, okay? I'm gonna take a shower, be right back," Casey states as he places the bag of food on the bed and heads for the bathroom.

First thing what comes to mind is eating his pastrami sandwich. What the hell with the hands-off threat? I grab the bag and check inside; the intoxicating smell assaults my nose and suddenly I do have the urge to eat his sandwich; it smells dang divine.

It takes me a few minutes to devour it completely and just as I lick my fingers with my eyes closed, I hear Casey's voice rumble, "You ate it, didn't you?"

My eyes flash open—hell, yes, I was savoring the taste. "What if I did?" I challenge.

"Then I fucking hope you only ate one so I still have the other one left," he gives me his trademark smirk and it makes my heart gallop in a whole new pattern.

"Yeah, well, no one showers that quick, I thought I had enough time to devour both," I mutter.

His head tips back and laughter slips out. It's the first time I witness this man laugh carelessly. It's almost magically the way his muscled body relaxes and tightens in all the right spots. Damn, this man has a six-pack, a delicious V pointing down, the works. And ink. Ink I need to lick and didn't even knew he had since it's in places it only shows when he's bare-dang-chested...a towel is riding low around his waist. Wow. Get a grip, Wendy.

I just went through a lot and yet it's this man who makes me feel normal with his attitude, appearance...hell, everything about him draws me in and makes me feel comfortable.

CHAPTER 05

CASEY

If she keeps staring at me like that my dick will push the towel off no matter how fucking tight I've wrapped it around my waist.

Three loud knocks rattle the door as Thorn's annoying voice rumbles along with it, "Open the fuck up, I want to see my sister."

Anger and annoyance rise and though it solves my boner problem, I seriously hate dealing with her brother. Especially at a time she doesn't need anything other than to have some peace and quiet time instead of everyone butting in. No matter if they mean well and want to let her know they care. The deep sigh—that by the sound of it seems to be ripped from her very soul—hurts my heart.

Unlocking the door, I open it in one swing, "Can't you manage enough respect to give her some fucking time to shake off the shit she just went through?"

"That'll be a first," Thorn snickers, "Princess doesn't need time to shake anything off, she's got balls of steel, enough to handle anything thrown her way. Hell, she's a fucking forensic coroner and can slice up a dead guy as easily as slice up a living, breathing one. Don't underestimate my sister or tell me she needs to shake off what she went through. A normal woman might shake, vomit, and huddle in a fucking corner, but not my damn sister. Now fucking move, asshole."

And just like that I want to kill this idiot with my bare hands. He's right how my Old Lady isn't like a normal woman but it doesn't mean she needs to put on a mask, grab her balls of steel and swing them around like nothing happened. She's allowed to take a breath and be normal to get her bearings.

This makes my gut tighten with a harsh realization. Was she never allowed to get her bearings? Fury consumes me when I feel soft fingers wrap around my forearm.

"Let him in, Casey. It's okay," she tells me with a strong voice and it only spikes my anger even more.

I take a step back to let Thorn in but at the same time I wrap my arm around Curls' waist and pull her close. "Make it fast because we were in the middle of some business we needed to deal with."

I don't mind throwing out a lie to protect her. Anything to get the asshole to get his ass out of this room faster.

"Gael is in the wind," Thorn grumbles. "I can't believe he's behind this shit but then again I could kick my own fucking ass for not realizing it was him sooner." Thorn's eyes land on mine. "Do you mind? I'd like to have a word with my sister without having you here."

"Not happening," I snap. Curls sighs again but I'm done with this shit. "You want to talk to her alone? Wait a few days and you can. Right now? She's attached to my hip. My Old Lady and you'll fucking deal with the limitations I set because I will always put her first no matter what the issue at hand is."

His eyes widen for a fragment before his jaw starts to tick, clearly annoyed with me.

"Look, we all didn't see this coming but we need to deal with it," Curls says as if I didn't just say shit. "Did you check the camera feed?"

"This fucker," Thorn points at me. "is standing here with his ears flappin', Princess, watch your tongue."

Another deep sigh rips from her soul, though this one sounds more frustrated. "He's a Fed, Thorn…"

"My point!" Thorn snaps.

"Let me finish," Curls bellows making even my head rear back from the mere force of those three words. "He's a Fed, which means he has valuable input we could use and is loyal to this MC and to his brother. And let's not forget the fact he's my Old Man. I trust him."

Fucked up connection or not, I could roar at the top of my lungs just to let the whole fucking world know my woman just openly stated for the first time to someone else that I'm her Old Man.

She could have picked the side of her brother, like how the guy barged over her wellbeing but instead of standing up for herself she chose to stand up for me. We haven't even had a chance to talk shit through properly and yet here she states she trusts me.

I keep my mouth shut and only give a gentle squeeze with my hand on her waist to let her know how much I value her strength. I don't need to voice words, nothing gives more meaning than me standing behind my woman.

Thorn eyes me for a few breaths more before he focusses back on Curls. "I haven't had a chance yet. And to be honest? I'm not sure I'm ready for it. I only know what others told me and what I've seen with my own eyes."

Now I do feel the need to butt in. "What camera feed?"

Without looking at me Thorn grumbles, "The one our father installed in the clubhouse. The one only me, Princess, and him knew about. The one I'm fucking sure his murder is recorded on."

"If you want me to check them first, let me know," I state in understanding. "And if you need help with anything else, I'm right here."

Thorn grabs his phone and taps a few times before he shoves it at me. I let go of Curls and take a step back so she can't glance at the screen. A few options present on this app where I can choose from a few different cameras.

I decide to check around the time Curls was taken because with this big shit going down in a club it makes the most sense that they would do everything simultaneously. I'm not at all surprised to see a guy stalking inside as two bikers from the main clubhouse come up to him. They exchange a few words, but I can't hear shit, then they head for church. I switch to another camera where I see an older guy sitting in church along with two men, papers scattered on the table in front of them.

The three bikers barge inside and immediately take out the two bikers sitting at the table. I glance around the room for my pants and grab the earbuds to plug them into Thorn's phone. Upping the volume, I hear one of the three bikers talk to Curls father, "Your time has come, old man. It's a shame I can't take you along to let you witness the things I'm going to do with your daughter. Hear what I said, asshole?

I've got her and I'm going to rip her cunt and ass apart while she screams to stretch her mouth wide enough to take my cock in there too. When I'm finished with the little cunt, she'll sign everything I place in front of her. I'm not just taking the princess but I'm taking this whole MC. Property and all, I've got enough bad blood on my side to bleed out the good. Thorns 'n' Bones will have a new President and a new VP. It's your own damn fault, old man. Shouldn't have tried to lean this club right. Dirty bikers won't settle for running a security business and fucking the maids every now and then at the hotel the club owns. Legal shit ties your fucking hands while the illegal shit makes you wash your hands before you eat. And you eat better when you have enough money and cunts to feast with, fucker. Isn't it what life's always about? They want money in their pockets and whores to bounce on their dicks and I'm going to give it to them. But not before I've killed you, your kids, and the hand full of idiots who'd dare to cross me." Gael's arm shoots out and he jams a knife underneath the Prez's chin. Gael's attention goes to one of the bikers, "Call Ryke, it's time."

I watch as all the three guys stalk out of the clubhouse. I click away the app and hand Thorn his phone back.

"How well do you know Ryke?" I question and while I'm at it, I ask, "Where was he when Curls here was taken?"

Curls groans, "Oh, come on, really, Fed? You wanna throw the nickname out in front of my brother?"

"I'm for sure as shit ain't calling you Princess. Now I need to know about Ryke because right after Gael killed your father, he asked one of the guys who worked with him to call Ryke and tell him 'it's time.' I need to know where the fucker was and what's it about because the fucker is here with us in this fucking clubhouse and if he's working with Gael, he's a dead man. Thorns 'n' Bones or not, he'll pay for setting shit up to capture my Old Lady."

"We were at our security company's office when he got a call. He said he needed to swing by his sister's house. I told him I'd tag along and when we did there was no one there. She didn't open the door and when I glanced through the window, I saw her living room was a mess. We couldn't check shit out further because we got the call from Calix, demanding we'd swing by the clubhouse. Since he mentioned it involved my sister, I didn't think twice and headed here. Come to think about it...Ryke wanted us to check inside his sister's house. Obviously,

I told him I understood but that I had to check on mine. I told him to stay and got on my bike, but he got on his bike too and we headed here." Thorn shakes his head as if he's trying to wrap his mind around the fact Gael mentioned Ryke, and he might somehow be involved.

"We need to have a chat with Ryke," I state. "And Thorn? Gael's got a personal vendetta somehow for my Old Lady. She comes first at all times, no matter if she's got balls of steel or not, yeah?"

He gives me a tight nod, "Anything else I should know about what you saw on that tape?"

"With hearing Gael's rambling thoughts on tape it's clear he's got the other guys to work with him because shit ain't going how they want it to go. And with this I'm talking about club business, the one-eighty you guys pulled, going from illegal to making a turn to walk a straight path. That shit won't ever go well with some of the more hardened criminals. The money flow is less and when they're used to the good life they've known since forever...yeah, Gael didn't have a problem finding partners in crime, so to speak."

"Fuck!" Thorn roars. "Everyone was in on this...we agreed...it was a club vote and we all knew we didn't have a damn option. It was either this or all end up behind bars."

Curls turns to me. "About a year ago, the club went through a rough spot. Two members went to jail and we had so many legal eyes on us, dad suggested the change. We already had the security company and the hotel in place as a legal way to obtain money but with a deal going south, the members arrested...in the end no one had a choice and it was voted in."

I try to wrap my brain around this shit but it's not so much the stuff she told me just now, it's the fact she told me and seems to know every detail.

Which raises the question. "No offense, darlin' but why the fuck are you telling me club business?"

Thorn smirks, "Because she's not only the Princess, but she's the one who vouched for us. She created some kind of business or silent partner shit with her lawyer so we could start back up again since we had a huge debt."

"Fuck," I growl and run my hand through my hair. "That explains the reason Gael said he'd hurt her so bad she'd sign anything he'd put in front of her. Listen, like I said, she comes first and not just the normal lockdown, and keep her here either. I'm going be in the same room as her at all times, and if I'm not, I want two brothers with her at all times. Brothers I know who can be trusted. And no offence, but they won't be wearing a Thorns 'n' Bones MC cut."

"Done," Thorn snaps. "Fuck, I never would have forgiven myself if..."

Curls sighs, "Casey got there just in time, I swear."

The hurt in Thorn's eyes gives him away and before he can say something, I shut him down. "What's done is done, in the past. Leave it there, fucker. We have bigger things on our hands right now."

"But if it wasn't for you," Thorn releases a string of curses.

"What?" Curls grabs Thorn's biceps, "What's this about?"

"Don't do it," I growl, but it's against deaf man's ears when Thorn starts to wallow in self-pity.

"We all wanted to talk things through first, if it wasn't for Casey claiming you, walking out of the clubhouse and dragging everyone along with him...I don't...fuck," Thorn sighs and takes his head in his hands.

"I hate wasting time. Like now, can we skip the self-pity 'cause we have bigger fish to fry here. Starting with that Ryke fucker." I grab the door handle and look back. "Calix gave him a room here? Because if he is in on this, we have a fucking rat among us compromising the safe setting I created for Curls."

"Dammit, it can't be Ryke. I've known the fucker his whole damn life," Thorn sighs.

"You know we have to look at every single one to be sure we have everyone who even had the slightest thought of going against dad. And all of this lands on you, I can't be involved," Curls tells him in a soft voice.

Her words process but it's confusing the hell out of me. "What do you mean with I can't be involved? Are you normally in this shit? Women aren't allowed in church or club business, what the fuck is going on?"

"Everything is tied to me. When the club was drowning in debt I stepped up but I made the contract they signed. I made it so I had to veto every huge decision to protect my investment," the woman casually says.

"What. The. Fuck," I growl underneath my breath and lock eyes with Thorn. "Don't tell me you're brainless to think brothers won't go nuts over a damn woman having the club by the fucking balls."

I shake my head and release a deep sigh before locking eyes with Curls, "And you…really? You grew up in that biker world. Hell, even within the normal business world people go cuckoo over a woman sitting in a high position because success raises envy and in particular when it's about cavemen who see a cunt shaking her tits in front of them and they can't fucking touch," I roar. "You fuckers shouldn't have put her in the middle of all this. Even if she offered her fucking self you should have never taken her up on it. This was bound to fail from the start."

CHAPTER 06

WENDY

The grunt that leaves Casey's throat gives me only a hint of satisfaction. Asshole. I know he's right, but it just sets me off. Hence the reason I punched him in the stomach.

"I saved the club when I stepped in. They always had my back and when I offered them this deal, they were all fully aware I wanted to keep them straight so the club would grow to be healthy and strong again. They didn't want to have more members thrown in jail with their Old Ladies left behind and kids only seeing their fathers behind bars. They knew. And it wasn't like it would be a forever deal, there was an option they could buy me out, and they would be able to sooner or later with profits growing slowly but steady." I seethe.

Casey's eyes pierce mine and I know he wants to say so much more but all he grunts is, "It only takes one rotten apple to taint others, Curls. Now this shit's all behind us and we'll deal with it, but I want you out after this. You'll transfer everything over to your brother who my guess is going to be Prez, right?" He swings his gaze to Thorn who gives him a tight nod. "I'm sure you can settle and keep the payment plan or whatever. Respect and trust your brother to lead his MC the way your father set the course and pull your hands off. I want you safe and I want you out."

I am beyond pissed. I open my mouth to spit out my words but I get robbed from doing so because it's my brother who speaks first. "Curls,"

What. The. Fuck? He's switching from Princess to Curls? Oh, no. They're backing each other up. Surprise, dang surprise. Assholes, all of them. I wave my finger in front of Thorn's face. "No, just…no. I'd like for you to leave and handle shit with Ryke. I'm too pissed right now to even talk to you so be glad I even manage to find words to tell you this."

"It's 'cause you know your Old Man is right," Thorn tells me in a soothing voice. And I might just hate him, embracing the fact I'm now claimed and my Old Man makes it possible to be of influence on me.

"Oh, you're a piece of work, you know that? Not agreeing to the fact Casey claimed me, but then looking back on how it went you're suddenly happy because he did save me in time for Gael to take his fingers out of my ass? That he prevented Gael from knocking out my teeth to fuck my mouth 'cause my pussy was leaking blood and it wasn't clean enough for a cock to pump? But because it's a convenience for you to have your sister shoved away and claimed as an Old Lady; to be just a bitch who's standing on the sideline. Right? Just a cunt who's…"

"Enough," Casey snaps and pushes Thorn against his shoulder to bring him out of the daze I put him in.

Shit. Why in the hell did I spill what Gael did to me before Casey saved me?

"Go find Calix and explain so you can take a few AF brothers to stand behind you when you confront Ryke. Make sure you do it in Calix's office, he's got a camera installed in there so you have it on tape in case you need it. We'll talk tomorrow morning or if you have crucial info you come find me but for now? Leave her the fuck alone." Casey holds open the door while Thorn gives him a warily nod and walks away as Casey locks the door behind him.

Fury still burns its way through my veins but Casey points a finger at me, "No. You do not get to fight me on this. Can't you fucking see what this shit has brought you? I learned you were taken the first time at the age of six and have a tracking chip in your fucking body so they can find you whenever that shit happens again. Happens again, Curls!

What you went through today? What you just…fuck, no. I just fucking claimed you. I never even once cared enough to step up for a woman, let alone give up my whole career for one. Now you think about how many lives you touched in this fucking world and what you think you're worth before you fight to hold on to something you can easily hand back to family you trust to continue to guide shit in the direction you all agreed upon."

Shit. My anger deflates when his words hit me hard. He takes a step toward me but all of this is too much, making me take a step back.

Casey stalks over to the bed instead and plunks down to lean his forearms on his knees. "You know this MC has an Old Lady who was once the VP?"

His words shock me enough to sit down next to him, hoping he will continue because I had no clue. I gathered a lot of info when I became aware Hedwig was living right next to a biker of AF MC and became pregnant. But this? No. Though my curiosity is spiked.

"Calix, my Prez and I go way back. We've worked together when he was a detective but he's also a guy you can have a drink and a good discussion with from time to time. He told me how Tenley saved the club like you did. And not just because she was the Prez's daughter, but because she fought for it, she always works hard to put the club first. It was like a contest of sorts, the one who could come up with a plan to pull the club out of debt. She made a business plan, one that was voted in and she earned it fair and square. The club now has a carwash with hot chicks washing the car you can pick out of a menu. Like a strip bar but change the pole with a car. As you can imagine, it's a huge success."

"Why isn't she the VP anymore, what happened?" I question because why would she?

"Calix happened," he simply states and gives me one of his panty-wetting smirks. "Her father's terminally ill and stepped back as the Prez. Calix was voted in and Tenley chose the club. She stepped aside to become the Prez's Old Lady instead of his VP along with it so he could have C.Rash as his VP, By doing so she made the club not only stronger but gave back the unity the club needed. But don't think twice about the fact she's just an Old Lady. Fuck no. Even the brothers openly state she's got the Prez by the balls and maybe she knew when she traded her cut that she would still have her voice heard no matter if there was a patch on her tit or not. They respect her, they listen to her input; she doesn't need the cut and title. Though I'm not saying you two are alike or even this whole situation...I'm just saying...I dunno, you probably should chat with Tenley, she's a woman who would understand this shit."

"Thank you," I sigh, defeated and oh so tired.

He leans toward me and bumps my shoulder, "Let all this stuff sink in. Talk it through and make the right decision; it's all I ask. Now go on and lie down or eat my sandwich for that matter."

His last statement makes me snort. "It's all yours but next time you better order me two of those too."

"Deal," he says and places a soft kiss on my temple, making my stomach flip with a current singing through my body I wasn't expecting.

How can he bring up such a strong emotion inside me? Not only lust but every single emotion intensifies when he's around. And safe. He makes me feel safe and with all the things he said flowing through my head, I see how everything this man does revolves around protecting me and doing what's right...for me. Even if it's overbearing.

He stands and snatches the sandwich out of the bag while I admire his strong body, imagining what's hidden underneath the towel. Dammit, the first time I have sex and I didn't even see what entered my body.

And why am I thinking this with what I just went through? What I'm going through with the miscarriage. This man, he does things to me I tell you...it shouldn't feel so right and yet it does. Even if my body is hurting, I still want him.

"Not happening, Curls," Casey states and gives me his trademark smirk right after.

His words make me huff, "You and I need to have a talk about how things are going to work between us. You can't be the one who makes up all the rules and lays down the law."

Yikes, even his laughter spiked a flow of tingles between my legs. Ugh. I really hate him, equally as much as like him...or not, the verdict isn't out yet.

"Now, darlin' with all the stuff we just discussed in this room you don't bring this up, but when I mention you're not getting my dick you go tell me we need to have a talk about laying down the law? Good to know you've got your priorities in check." One day I'm going to punch that smirk right off his face.

"Never mind, I've made it through life using my fingers and toys before you popped it in there, I could continue a lifetime with just battery driven substitutes," I shrug and crawl onto the bed, only to be spun around as Casey's hovering over me, his sandwich long forgotten.

"What did you just say?" he croaks.

Shit. What's with my mouth, blabbering out stuff I should keep inside? "It's nothing." I try.

"Bullshit and you fucking know it, try again."

"Wake up, Casey. Weren't you in this room with me when everything about the club was discussed? I'm the princess, daughter of the dang president, the one no one is allowed to touch. Not to mention I threw all my attention on becoming a forensic coroner so I didn't have time or any interest in dating. What else is there to say? Even if you had no clue you were my first because I popped the damn hymen myself with a vibrator, but you were, okay? Is that what you wanted to hear? You popped but didn't officially pop my cherry" I keep my gaze locked with his because I'm not ashamed nor a prude.

Ugh, and I should have expected the self-assured alpha pride his features wash over with.

"My dick only touched what's mine," he croaks, his voice dripping with lust.

I have to swallow at the dryness of my voice when I tell him, "The one and only."

"For fucking sure it will be the one and only," he growls fiercely and slams his mouth over mine.

For the first time. My first time having sex was with this man and we didn't even kiss. So, this is also a first. And if I thought his smirk, his words, or even his body would get my body pumping…it's his kiss that pulls me closer and makes me want to merge with his body to seek more heat than he's already tainting me with.

All of my pain and hurtful emotions are long forgotten when I let my hand travel over his muscled back until I reach his waist. My fingers dig into the towel and with one firm tug it falls free, allowing my hand to grip his bare ass. Hot damn. Sculpted so dang powerful, making me dig my nails in to pull him closer.

He groans into my mouth while his tongue swirls around mine. His length is hard between our bodies and I hate the fact my period—yes, I'm going to stick with the fact my period was just late because I can't deal otherwise—is stopping us from having sex. And it reminds me of the way my kidnappers were revolted by it. Hate swirls up but I manage to push it down when I feel Casey's hand slide down my body.

My body that's hurting from all the blows I took. The blows that turned life inside me to a pulp, preventing me from becoming a mother. Pain slashes through me and it has nothing to do with the physical injuries but everything to do with my mental state.

It's as if Casey knows what I need when his hand starts to slide up and down my belly while his lips go to the crook of my neck. He's trailing kisses and setting my skin on fire while he's whispering such sweet words. The attention he gives my body is making me feel wanted. The exact opposite of how the kidnappers were.

I shove the memories deep into a part of my brain I don't ever want to visit again and just relish in the way Casey makes me feel. As if I'm the only thing he needs to feel grounded. Maybe it's just me but the way this man connects with me is different than any other person I've met in my life.

I wish I could have sex right now, to take him inside my body again like the first time. Yet the thought only brings out the fact I got pregnant in that moment in time and how I lost it today. Tears fill my eyes and sobs rip from my throat.

Casey's arms wrap tight around me and his comfort is making me calm down. Kisses. The gentle tone of his voice while his words not only give me strength but also warmth. It now makes my tears fall for a completely different reason.

I'm treasured by this man who not only wants me, but who saved me, who comforts me here in this bed and is not repulsed by me when he discovered about my period. The way my body is reacting from the things I went through and being in this man's arms...my tear stained face is a mess and I'm shaking while my body is hurting badly. Even if his touch is tender, I can't prevent to hiss from the pain when I try to shift.

Casey pulls back and glances at my face. "Come on, we're getting a shower. Even if you already had a bath, you're hurting and need the warmth of the water to relieve your muscles."

Oh, yikes. After effects of my meltdown. Though Casey doesn't seem to be fazed by any of it. He just drags me up and guides me toward the bathroom. Turning on the water, he slides underneath while I make fast work to ditch the shirt, panties, and throw the pad in the bin before I accompany him.

He reaches out and pulls me flush against him. "Are you okay?" I tilt my head back and let his warm gaze settle upon me. Doesn't this man realize what he does to me? "More than okay. I didn't even realize how badly I needed the meltdown I just had."

Shit. Good thing the shower is hot and my skin is already flushed because I can't believe I just admitted to this. His gaze slides down to my lips. Slowly closing the distance, he captures my bottom lip between his teeth and gives a gentle tug, brushing his lips against mine in a feather light kiss right after.

"You're perfect, you know that?" He takes a few steps forward and it makes me gasp when my back hits the cold tiled wall. "I fucked you bare the first chance I had when we were in a room alone together and I have to admit it takes everything within me to keep myself in check not to jump inside you right now. Fucked up, I know. Even if you're on your period, condom or not, I don't fucking care. I've never buried myself bare inside anyone; only you. I'm clean…a little late to mention, but, yeah."

"Clean…but," I whisper out the rest of the words on a rush so I know I said them but obviously not loud enough.

"But?" He presses.

"I'm not using birth control," I sigh.

"Don't need it either," Casey simply states.

"Didn't you just hear me?" I squeak, words fail me and I need to tell him what happened today, even if I only knew myself for an hour. One freaking hour of a new found and lost life.

"I'm fine with whatever life throws at us. Even when we decide to fuck bare in the future, and we damn well will." The man shrugs. Shrugs!

I roll my eyes at the way he casually waves this off. "Well if you keep throwing cum inside my pussy, I'm bound to end up pregnant…" Emotions rip through me when I add on a whisper, "again."

"Maybe that's my plan, to bind you to me in all ways possible." His husky voice makes my lips open with a slight gasp, even the ones between my legs.

That is until his head rears back, "Did you say again? As if…did… what?"

I close my eyes, unable to look at him while my whole body grows tight with the burning hurt I now put into words. "When they took me, I was on my way to see Hedwig. I was late with my period and took a pregnancy test...I only knew for less than an hour before I lost...maybe it was a false positive."

"The hell it was," Casey roars, making my eyes snap open.

His anger makes me cringe and my head drops. Again, with the hurt and devastation slicing through me. My body is still sore from the blows I took, I can barely open one of my eyes and yet only minutes ago I was lying in a bed being treasured and taken away by extreme kindness but it's all gone now.

I can't deal with any of it and it makes me feel weak. I'm never weak. Never. Yet now? I feel as if life itself is draining away from me. Just like the blood that's running down my legs because of the miscarriage.

And I know I shouldn't lie to myself like I just told him but if I let my mind travel over the fact that they kicked life right out of my body? A sob rips straight from my soul at the same time I hear Casey curse as he wraps his arms around me, preventing me from crashing to the floor as I grab hold just as tightly.

"Shhhh, sweetheart. I'm sorry. So. Fucking. Sorry. I shouldn't have lost it like that, but fuck...shhh, darlin', I've got you. We'll make it right, somehow...we'll get through this. Fuck, Curls." The roughness in his voice cracks with emotion as we stand there holding on to each other. "I swear to avenge what was taken from us. I'll kill them with my own fucking hands...but all in good time, you hear me? All in good time, 'cause you're what's important now, you gotta heal. Come on, we're gonna clean you up and I'm gonna talk to Calix to get the doc here to check you out. You should have mentioned it sooner... maybe we need to swing by the hospital."

"No," I croak. "No hospital, I just need to rest. I have a medical background, you know...but I've also double-checked information on my phone...it says exactly how it is. It doesn't look any different than my normal heavy menstrual bleeding. I should have never taken the test, then I wouldn't even have known..."

"Searched for information on your damn phone," he grumbles and shakes his head. "Woman, you have to realize right fucking now I will be beside you every step of the damn way from now on. I'm done with everyone expecting you to deal with things on your own. And don't start with saying you're strong enough to handle everything, because

I know you're more than capable. But…you shouldn't have to… not at times where it matters anyway. And you will let me, hear what I'm saying?"

"I hear you," I mutter, a little dazed by how well he knows me. "I'm used to doing things myself so I can't promise anything."

His soft chuckle relaxes me, "I know, darlin'. But I'll even kick Thorn's ass if I have to. Hell, I'll face the fucking devil himself if need be; you're mine and I will make sure everyone knows to treat my Old Lady with respect and those who don't will feel my wrath. As Gael will soon enough," he adds on a growl.

Crap. What in the hell have I gotten myself into with this man who doesn't seem afraid of anything and makes me think he can make everything right. And yet realizing this makes him the perfect man for me, making me feel safe enough to know with him at my side I can truly face everything life throws at us. Even if it's Gael…I'm sure Casey will kill him with his last breath if need be.

CHAPTER 07

CASEY

"It's been fucking weeks! He can't have crawled underneath a damn rock and stayed there," I growl in frustration since this meeting is almost over.

It's as if the fucker went underground with his scum buddies. We were able to narrow it down to four other dirtbags who teamed up with Gael, and those fuckers are also missing.

"Believe me when I tell you we're all frustrated, angry, and want to nail this fucker. We're working on it," Calix sighs.

"As are we," Thorn adds.

"And it's brought us jackshit," I mutter to myself, knowing these past few weeks we had a funeral to deal with and also dove into the fact Ryke's sister, Claudia, is still missing.

Thorn swears Ryke's clean and never was on Gael's side but I can't help but stay suspicious, even more because of his sister. I did some digging and with the club going through a rough patch and switching from illegal shit to legal? They closed down a whore house and Gael's sister, Kate, was running it together with Claudia.

From the two bikers I talked to who were there when they shut down the whore house for good, they mentioned Kate flipped. I know it's connected. Gael's hatred for Curls' family and the way they handle the MC runs deep and in many ways.

Again, Ryke's sister missing? Leverage if you ask me. But it seems my hands are tied and I'm sick of this shit. Though having my hands tied by the law is one thing...my Prez doesn't hold me back but he does have limitations too. All of this make me even more sure about starting my own company.

I haven't told anyone—besides Curls—about my plans, but I turned in my resignation the day after Curls was kidnapped. I've been talking to a former associate turned friend who I once worked a few cases with. He has his own company where he takes on cold cases. Picks his own jobs and, from what he's told me, is quite successful. I'm not talking about a solid income but also the personal gratification. To be able to make a change, it's basically the whole reason I started working in law enforcement.

"Prez?" I get his attention while the wheels in my head start turning and for fuck's sake why didn't I think of this sooner? "Can I have a word with just you, Ransom, and C.Rash?"

He gives a tight nod and closes the meeting that's already come to an end since the flow of information has been less to nothing anyway.

"I want to dive into Ryke's missing sister's case," I state.

Calix nods thoughtfully and a grin slides over his face. Figures. We were in the same line of work, he knows very well I want to dig into the connection while searching for the woman. It's a new angle while we're waiting to find Gael, and who knows I'll stumble on something to either soothe my suspicion about Ryke working with Gael or clear him from any involvement.

"Let me know if you need me or anyone else to help out," Calix grunts.

"Will do." I tell him, and realize, "I would probably need some extra brothers available when I need to head out while my Old Lady is either here or at work. She has to be protected until Gael is found."

"Done. Ransom, C.Rash, Quillon, and Hunter will be available when you need them. C.Rash, make sure the other two brothers know."

C.Rash and Ransom both nod at Prez's words as he turns to me, "And I'm here too if you need me."

I'm glad Calix dismisses us right after, my hands are itching to work. I checked into Claudia's missing person's case the day after

Curls was taken but didn't find anything relevant to be linked with Gael or the fact she's missing.

But knowing about the whore house and Gael's sister and Claudia working together? Add the fact Curls is Thorn's sister? I get a feeling this is all about sisters and fucking payback. Three sisters of guys within one MC involved is too much of a coincidence not to be connected somehow.

I'd like nothing more than to stay with Curls. She seems to have bounced back pretty quickly the last few weeks. Even with the huge emotional load, she's damn strong. But I have to head out and check into things.

I'm glad Calix assigned the VP and even himself along with a few other brothers and not prospects. Even if the few prospects we have around here are solid, I need my mind at ease when I head out and leave Curls' side.

My mind couldn't handle her being taken when she wasn't even mine. Then afterwards hearing she was pregnant at the time? I shove the thought deep down because I still can't handle it.

Even if I've always lived for my job, I never realized how fast my life would switch when I found the right woman. And now that I've found her…I ain't ever letting go. Nor do I want the risk of having her taken from me. I need to make sure she's safe, and she isn't as long as Gael is still out there.

"Ransom, you're with me. C.Rash, can you check in on the girls a few times until we're back?" I ask and he gives me a nod as he takes a spot at a table in the main room, giving him a clear few of the hallway where Curls and Hedwig are spending time together in Ransom's room.

We've been on semi lockdown ever since Curls was taken. We're not risking any of the other Old Ladies either. So, it's semi lockdown until we've found and killed Gael. Not to mention there are four others who chose his side and they need to be taken care of too. Since Hedwig has a few more weeks to go in her pregnancy, Ransom and Hedwig have created two nurseries. One in Hedwig's house and one here at the club.

Anyway, it's a good thing the girls have something to focus on and being this far in the pregnancy Hedwig doesn't have the energy to be very active so lounging around with Curls is just what they both need.

Though Curls is strong, I can see how the miscarriage pains her.

It's in the little things flashing through her eyes only I seem to notice. Even with her body healed it's something what's left a scar on both our souls. The only thing we can do is move forward together.

Every night we end up wrapped in each other. Even with life fucked-up as it is, the exquisiteness of having her in my arms—consuming and comforting each other—is what makes it all worth it.

"Bike or cage?" Ransom's question rips me out of my thoughts.

"Bike," I tell him. "Thought you never wanted to sit in a cage again, unless you need to go somewhere with your Old Lady."

It's true, the fucker worked his ass off to regain all the strength back in his arm that was injured months ago. Once he was finally able to get on his bike, he swore he would never crawl into a cage when he could ride.

"Yeah, but I gotta escort your pansy ass," my brother chuckles.

Fucker. "I was riding a fucking bike before you could so much as point at one, asswipe. Hell, if it wasn't for me you wouldn't even be wearing a patch in the first place."

"Oh, do tell," Quillon quips from behind me.

"No, he fucking won't," Ransom growls, grabs my cut, and drags me out front where our bikes are parked.

"You gotta admit, it's a nice damn story," I snicker and straddle my bike.

"No one needs to know how I fell over every damn time and how you laughed your fucking ass off not even trying to pull the heavy bike off me," Ransom grumbles, making me laugh harder at the mere reminder.

Damn. The both of us have been through bad times growing up but there are also a lot of highlights and even more when we were both placed at the home Ransom lives in now, the one we inherited but we both decided it was his to live in.

With both Hedwig and him owning a house next to each other, our Old Ladies being best friends, a thought hits me and I turn off the bike to relay my thoughts to Ransom. He sees the look on my face and turns off his bike too.

"What's up, brother?" he questions.

"When all this shit is cleared, I'm thinking me and Curls should move in next door to you guys," I tell him and watch as his eyes go wide in surprise. "Well, if you don't mind having us as neighbors."

"You sure, man? It's...fuck. It's perfect. Need to check with Hedwig but I'm sure she'd be okay with me moving in with her and you guys take the other house, with Curls being her best friend and all. Hell, they've been roommates before and living next door will give us babysitters within reach," Ransom chuckles.

"What makes you so sure me and Curls won't be needing fucking babysitters," I growl back, suddenly annoyed.

Ransom just shakes his head and chuckles as if it's the most insane shit I've ever told him. We didn't mention the miscarriage to anyone. Curls didn't want to talk about it and knew with Hedwig being pregnant it would be hard for everyone but in this moment, I need for Ransom to understand—to know—how strong my woman is and what we already overcame together. But most of all? To know fucking well I want my woman pregnant again.

I glance around me to double check but we're completely alone in the parking lot in front of the clubhouse. "She miscarried the day they took her. They fucking beat her so she fucking miscarried, okay? My baby. My kid was in her belly and they ripped it from her. Even though she only knew she was pregnant for one hour before they kidnapped her. They killed our fucking kid before it had any chance to grow. She was on her fucking way to tell Hedwig about it."

Ransom pales and leans his forearms on his bike while one hand covers his mouth to mute the "Fuck," slipping from between his lips.

"Yeah," I sigh. "We all carry heavy burdens and sometimes it feels like stacking shit is waiting for everything to crumble down and drown you in it. I have no clue why I fought the biker life for so long, Ransom. For fuck's sake this woman had my heart the first time I laid eyes on her when I saw her through your kitchen window. Then we go head to head, the second time we met. Hell…fucked our brains out the third time we met and made a fucking kid right then and there, only to have it ripped from our lives. It's…fuck. Knowing they took her that day and the mere thought of losing her had me going insane and yet those fuckers took something from us we won't ever get back. The kind of hatred my body is filled with, Ransom? It's damn good I turned in my badge the day after Curls told me about the miscarriage, because I can't live with handing this shit over to the law."

"Hey," Ransom's face morphs into a fierce look. "One thing you'll never have to do is justify your actions to me. I have your back no matter what, and you know it. Though I know you're gonna miss catching bad fuckers, even if you're not gonna be squeaky clean yourself after we've handled this shit."

"I've been thinking," I quip.

Ransom shakes his head muttering, "Well, fuck, here it comes. You sayin' 'I've been thinking' always transfers into 'I'm doing something and I'm now telling you how shit's going to be.' Just like you just dropped on me how you turned in your badge weeks ago."

A smile tugs my face, this guy knows me too well. "I'm gonna start up my own business. Gonna handle cold cases. I'm treating Ryke's missing sister as my first case. Hell, you and I both know I have enough cash saved up I don't even need to work and could even take on some pro bono shit to soothe my mind every now and then. But I need to do this...I need..."

"You need to do good, Casey. Like you've always done. Handle your own piece of doing right in this world. And with what you just mentioned? Fucking perfect. Even makes me think Calix would like to help out every now and then. The man has an itch like you to dive into something that needs to be handled. You should mention it to him or even bring it to the table so all the brothers can handle cases from time to time if need be."

I nod as I take in his words. He's right. "I could use some help from time to time," I mutter.

"Then with this case, you'll have me. Future shit? Think it through and run it by Calix. Even if you don't want the club involved...an ex lawman can give you his input from his side of things."

I lift my chin and fire up my bike, "Thanks."

"Don't mention it," Ransom barks over the roar of the bikes.

The ride over takes about fifteen minutes. Thorn and Ryke have been here to check on his sister the day Curls was taken. They saw the living room was a mess as if there had been a struggle. A few days later I swung by the place to check it out but everything still looked the same and still there was no trace of her.

We leave the bikes in the driveway and decide to stalk around back first but fresh footprints in the dirt make me hug the house and swing my arm back to have Ransom press his back to the house too.

I take out my phone and call Thorn while I point at the footprints to show Ransom. "Thorn, Casey. Hey," I tell him at a low whisper. "Ryke near you? Do you know if he went by his sister's house in the last few days? 'Cause I'm there now and I'm seeing fresh fucking footprints and they seem to be from a woman by the size of it."

"Nah, man. Ryke has been with me for the last few days. We've been checking all over this town to follow up some leads we had on the four guys working with Gael but we didn't find shit. Hang on," I hear him question Ryke. There are muffled voices until Thorn's voice comes through loud and clear. "No, he hasn't been there like I mentioned and we still have no word about or trace on his sister. What are you doing there anyway? I didn't hear Calix mentioning something to me when we were in church this morning."

"I asked our Prez if I could take on the case of Ryke's missing sister. We're all doing something but getting nowhere. I need to focus on something else in the meantime and maybe Claudia missing is connected so who knows? I'm still working on getting Gael."

I don't hear his reply because gun shots ring out, making me end the call and shove the phone away to free my hands. Ransom curses next to me and I can hear him growling into his phone, demanding back up. We both palm our guns and I risk a glance around the corner of the house.

"Pool house," I grunt, "I think two, maybe three by the sounds of it."

A bullet lodges into the house right above my fucking head and my body pumps with adrenaline. I need to get through this, need to come back home to my woman. More gunshots ring out and one grazes my knee. I push myself closer against the house but I damn well know I need to confront these fuckers instead of hiding out. We're sitting ducks if we don't do something.

"Stay here and glued to the wall, I'm going around," I grunt to Ransom and don't wait for a reply but run off and around to the other side of the house.

Checking around the corner I see it's safe enough. Bullets are still being fired from the backyard in the other direction and I hear Ransom returning fire. Staying low, I risk a quick glance and instantly my blood boils. Gael, his sister, and at least two other guys are standing near a pool house.

I take aim and suck in a deep breath. I need the first shot to count because it will give away my location. Kate is standing in front of her brother, blocking a clear shot to take Gael out. Fuck. Gael says something to the others and I see him starting to retreat. Dammit, no time to think.

I fire three rapid shots, one hitting Gael's sister, one hitting Gael, and the other misses a target. Dashing behind the house, I hear Ransom taking over while there's only a few shots being fired my way. Then everything goes silent.

There's a chance I can get my damn head blown off if I check to see if they're still standing, but not doing anything gives them a chance to slip away, and I can't let that happen either. Fuck it. Crouching down, I take a quick peek and curse under my breath. Three bodies are down and from the look of it, Gael isn't one of them.

I hear the rumble of bikes roaring through the air. Backup. Fucking sweet but a little too damn late. Rushing forward with my gun raised I shout, "Better come out fuckers, you're dead either way." Just so Ransom knows I'll be in his line of fire.

"Well, that's new," Ransom chuckles. "Pretty sure your line used to be 'Freeze, FBI.'"

"Very fucking funny, asshole," I grunt but there's a smile tugging my lips and a righteousness in my heart how I stopped being a fed without a single hint of regret.

Ransom keeps an eye on our surroundings, allowing me to check on the three bodies sprawled out on the ground. Gael's sister was shot in the chest, the other two have multiple gunshot wounds. One's still alive though. Knowing it's one who helped Gael take my woman and kill her father, it only takes one squeeze for me to end his life.

I hear Calix voice coming from near the house and I bark out my words, "We're out here."

Around twenty guys—all AF MC brothers—come rushing toward us. Calix assesses the situation and connects his gaze with me. "You left one alive, nice."

"Yeah, not my intention but there you have it. She was standing in front of her fucking brother and I couldn't get a clear shot. The fucker got away," I growl.

"And you'll never catch him. He will kill all of you," his sister pants.

I press cold steel against her temple, "You won't get the chance to see me skin him alive for you'll be burning in hell yourself, bitch."

"Now, now, Casey. Let's take her for a ride and show how we can create hell on earth for her before we send her to hell itself, huh?" Calix's words make me smile and I give him a nod, allowing him to address the others. "Quick work guys! Get this cunt to a safe location and these two others need to be disposed of."

"Aw, fuck, what's that smell?" Feargal asks, stalking away from the back of the pool house. Stepping closer, the smell assaults my nose and I instantly recognize it, "Dead body." I grunt and follow my nose. It leads to a garden tool storage shed. I'm not surprised to see a body sagged in a dark corner. I grab my phone and hit the flashlight button revealing the fact this body is clearly a woman. Shit, it's Claudia. I guess my first case is solved. Though it does raise a question or two. One being 'how the hell did she end up back here when we searched the place a time or two since she went missing?'

AF MC OHIO

CHAPTER 08

WENDY

Something's going on. When Hedwig and I were in the nursery we heard shouting and when we went down the hall, we saw all the bikers leave. Well, everyone besides C.Rash, Hunter, and Quillon. And the prospects, they stayed behind too. Not to mention Hunter and Quillon are both pacing, both palming their guns.

"What's going on?" Hedwig asks Tenley who comes rushing into the clubhouse.

She nods and waves the both of us to the couch. "Sit you two. Our job is to sit and let our boys handle it."

"Handle what?" I snap, annoyed Tenley seems to know more than we do.

She rolls her eyes at my attitude. "Whatever it is they're dealing with, Curls."

Over the last few weeks I've become used to the nickname Casey gave me and everyone around here has picked it up. I never once thought I'd have one besides everyone from Thorns 'n' Bones MC calling me Princess. At first, I wasn't all too happy with being called Curls, but the way Casey explained the strength behind it…yes, it suits.

"Is it always like this?" Hedwig grumbles while rubbing her huge belly.

Tenley shrugs. "Depends, normally it's kinda boring. It's not like they have a shooting every other day."

"What?" I squeak, "There's a shooting?"

Tenley rubs her fingers across her forehead, "Fucking hell. Come on, Curls. Casey is a Fed, he's used to things spiraling out of control, he's done it for years, have a little faith in your man."

"Yeah, well…we weren't together when he was doing the whole shooting, risking his life, thing. And we've been together like a blink of an eye and he's already got me in all kinds of knots," I sigh.

"Shame our girl here's got a bumper on the front, otherwise we could do shots to calm down," Tenley quips.

Though I'm all about supporting my friend, my nerves are shot. "The hell with the bumper, she can watch, I need some and I need it now."

I dash to the bar and grab two glasses, filling up both with a few fingers of whiskey before I hold one out for Tenley to take but her lips part and it's as if she wants to say something and yet she doesn't.

Suddenly it clicks, "Oh, shit, don't tell me you might have a bun in the oven too."

"I might," she whispers.

"Great," I smack both glasses back on the bar, "I don't know if I should guzzle the whole bottle down or decline 'cause with ya'll being pregnant, it might be infectious. Though I haven't had sex in weeks."

"What is it with these bikers and not using condoms when it comes to Old Ladies? As if they can't knock us up fast enough to tie us to them for life," Tenley sighs but a smile tugs her face.

"Ransom hit bullseye at first strike," Hedwig chuckles.

"So did Casey," I sigh and two heads spin my way. Shit. That slipped out without realizing it. I'm so stupid. "Only kidding." I squeak, stalking back to the bar to grab the whiskey, guzzling down the whole bottle it is.

"Put that shit down and get your ass here on this couch and spill," Hedwig snaps. "because I can tell you're not kidding. Pregnant and not tell me about it. How far along are you?"

I take a sip of the whiskey, earning a glare from the both of them but I need it before I tell them, "I miscarried when I was kidnapped… they kicked the pregnancy right out of me."

I sink into the couch and let both girls hug me.

"Why didn't you tell me," Hedwig scolds, hurt equivalent in her voice.

"When I took the test and saw I was pregnant I was on my way to tell you. Then they kidnapped me...kicked me around...they pulled down my pants and Bandito said I was on the rag...I knew...I knew then and there I miscarried. I wish I'd never taken the test, then I wouldn't have known and would only have been a few days late," I sigh in defeat.

The both of them give me the comfort without any words. And really, what's there to say?

Until Hedwig squeezes my hand. "Does Casey know?"

I nod and swipe away the stray tear gliding down my cheek, "I told him the same day he rescued me."

"Good, good," she mutters, rubbing her belly and wincing.

My gaze connects with Tenley and I manage to point out how Hedwig is rubbing and wincing.

Tenley's eyes widen. "Hedwig, is your belly giving you trouble?"

"It's nothing," she shrugs. "It comes and goes."

"It fucking comes and goes?" Tenley snaps.

"What Tenley is trying to say is that you might be having contractions," I smile as Hedwig's face flashes toward me, eyes wide enough to fall out. "Come on, let's get you checked out," I state and pull her up.

"Holy shit, is this happening for real?" Tenley gasps.

"Go get her bag," I tell Tenley and she dashes off to Hedwig and Ransom's room.

Hedwig is digging her nails in my arms and keeps staring at me while her face fills with panic. "It's too early."

"Stop stressing, Hedwig. You got this. You're only a few weeks away from your due date. Everything was fine with your last appointment, breathe, sweetie," I tell her.

"Do I need to puff? Is that what you're telling me to do? I'm not doing the whole labor puffing thing, Wendy," Hedwig screeches.

Everyone calls me Curls but Hedwig, guess my best friend is either stuck to the normality of using my name or she's refusing to use it. Or, and this might be it...she's consumed by other things, mainly keeping her legs closed so no baby can pop out.

"I said breathe, Heddy. Not huff and puff, now relax because stressing isn't helping," I calmly tell her and start walking toward the front of the clubhouse but C.Rash stops us.

"We need to go through the back," he says.

Is he kidding? "She's in pain, can't you drive the car around?"

C.Rash doesn't reply but simply scoops Hedwig up in his arms and leaves me to follow. Tenley is behind the wheel, C.Rash puts Hedwig in the back and I scoot in beside her while C.Rash jumps in the front. Hunter and Quillon follow on their bikes while we make our way to the hospital.

Everybody's on edge though the guys seem to have different reasons. The hours that follow gives us some reassurance when it comes to Hedwig. She's fine and so is the baby. They were false contractions, but she was also dehydrated and was given fluids. Rest. It's what the doctors described and it will take a whole lot to make her follow up on this, but she needs to think about the baby.

Good thing she realizes it too and Tenley and I are there to make sure she takes good care of herself. Not to mention I made sure to text Ransom to let him know we went to the hospital to run a few checks for Hedwig. He didn't even text back but remembering the way C.Rash and the others acted I'm sure Ransom had his reasons for not replying.

When we get back to the clubhouse it's filled with bikers from both MCs. C.Rash is walking in front of us along with Tenley as Hunter and Quillon have our back. C.Rash barks out Ransom's name and the door of church flies open. Ransom stalks forward and takes Hedwig's face in his hands.

"You need to lie down," the man says and plants a hard kiss on her mouth.

Pretty sure C.Rash kept either him or Calix up to date because Ransom starts to relay the exact same words the doctor told us. Hedwig huffs and I'm actually glad C.Rash made a big deal out of being in the room when the doctor gave the results.

Something about being there for his brother and even if it's something I've been brought up with, it's heartwarming to see someone—a whole MC—standing up for my best friend.

Well, besides me, but she won't listen much when it comes to me but with Ransom now knowing? The fierce look on his face? Yeah, I'm seeing a lot of naps in my best friend's future.

Strong arms surround me and I instantly recognize Casey's scent.

"Missed you," he says on a whisper right beside my ear, making me shiver.

Turning around in his arms, I need a breath or two before I manage to say something. Shit, the worry carved on his face is something that makes my chest constrict.

"Missed you too. Do you need to head back into church or can we talk for a few minutes?" I question because I'm worried about why he looks so disheveled.

His gaze goes over my head and he barks, "Calix, be back in five." He laces his fingers with mine and drags me off to our room.

When he closes and locks the door behind us, I have no time to say anything because his mouth covers mine while his tongue demands entrance. When I moan from the way he dominates my mouth, it seems as if all limitations fall away.

He grabs my ass and hoists me up. The dark green summer dress I'm wearing is shoved out of his way and while I'm being consumed by this man, he manages to somehow slide my panties to the side while releasing his dick as he slides deep inside me with one stroke.

"Caseeeeeeey!" I gasp while digging my nails into his shoulders.

A roar of triumph rips from deep inside him while skimming kisses along the line of my neck. "I fucking love the way my name spills from your lips when I bury myself inside you. No better place on this earth I'd rather be than inside you. Gripping me like a vice, cocooning me with your warmth. Fuck, darlin', you're the one who makes my heart beat to the tune called living."

If I could only focus on his words but I'm absorbed by the way pleasure is building, getting closer and closer already to the orgasm that's bound to take over; ready to consume my body. And then it hits. My whole body lights up as I scream his name while Casey keeps pounding inside me until he too finds his release.

"Fuck, you don't have any idea how badly I needed you. Hell, I didn't even realize it myself until I saw you." His head is buried into the crook of my neck and it seems he isn't in a hurry at all. In fact, even if he's softening inside, he keeps me caged between the wall and his body.

I let my fingers lazily slide through his thick dirty blond hair, keeping his head buried against me. Comfort. It's as if we're sucking up energy from each other with every breath. The stress from the last few hours of being worried for Hedwig and not to mention not knowing what was happening with the club.

I can only imagine what was going on with Casey and it's something that causes more worry to run through my veins. I think I might come to hate the term 'club business' when it comes to the safety of my Old Man. Yet I do respect it, don't get me wrong, but the not knowing is killing me.

"Everything okay?" I question.

"No," he mumbles and releases a sigh so deep I think it's been ripped from his very soul.

"What happened?" I whisper, afraid of hearing those two words that prevent me from helping him with the load of emotion this club business carries with it.

Another deep sigh before he steps back as he lets me slide to my feet, feeling his cum slide out along my leg. Shit. I seriously need a shower.

Casey rubs a hand over his face and when I don't expect an answer from him, his voice cracks with the words, "We found Ryke's sister. Dead."

"What?" I gasp.

CHAPTER 09

CASEY

Curls has been in this life from the day she was born. Even if women are kept out of it…fuck, what the hell am I talking about? My damn woman is a forensic coroner, she cuts into dead bodies for a living. Anyone who can do that can handle a lot of shit if you ask me. So, if she wants to know, club business or not, I will damn well tell her the truth.

Though she has to know, "What I tell you has to stay between us. I don't have to tell you what club business entails, right? 'Cause I want to be able to come home to you and…"

She steps forward and places her fingertips on my lips. "I want to be there for whatever you need. But mostly I want you to be able to lean on me, no holds barred. I'm here. I can deal with anything you throw at me and I won't ever repeat any of it and you know it. Everything, Casey. Let me be everything for you because you're everything to me."

Fuck. She's has now idea how turned on I am because of how perfect she is.

"Stop looking at me like that," she rolls her eyes. "We just had sex and we are having a discussion right now. Besides, you need to get back to Calix. You said you'd be back in five and I'm sure we already used up double the time."

"Worth it though," I smirk and watch how her eyes flare. I damn well know how every move I make affects her, my smirk being one of her favorites.

But there's enough time to be consumed by one another later, I hope. Right now, I need for her to know a few details so she won't be in the dark. I've also told her my goals for the future—job wise—and she's aware I've turned in my badge without any regret. She was the first and only one I told before actually doing it. Even if they're my actions and decisions, I made sure she's a part of it since I consider her a part of my future.

"I asked Calix if I could look into Claudia's missing person case. We checked out her house, neighbors, and friends, a few weeks ago but we're kinda stuck with Gael being off grid. Besides, I wanted to bite into something like I intend to do when I start up my own company." When the words leave my mouth, I look at my Old Lady who has the proudest of smiles painting her gorgeous face.

"Perfect." She beams.

"Yeah," I sigh. "But it was a little less perfect when Ransom and I showed up at her house and found her dead body in a garden tool storage shed."

She nods warily. "Do you know how she died, how long ago or why for that matter?"

"That's more your line of work, huh?" I give her a wink and continue. "When Ransom and I arrived at Claudia's house, we went around back and walked into a shit storm. Bullets flying. Turns out Gael, his guys, and his sister were staying in the pool house. They probably thought it was safe enough since the last time we went there was a few weeks ago. I do know the why and how...because we were able to capture Kate. Gael, that fucker, got away probably with one or two others who helped him. We managed to kill two others, though. As for Kate? It didn't even take any effort to make her talk. The raving bitch told us all about how she was supposed to keep her locked up, her brother's orders, but things didn't go as planned. Fucked up part was that Gael wanted Ryke's sister as leverage, just like you. But his fucked-up sister killed her by accident. Well, if you'd call plunging a knife into a person more than a few times an accident...I did mention raving bitch and fucked up, right? Yeah," I sigh and shake my head. Curls eyebrows scrunch up, "Did you guys find out why Gael would want to have leverage over Ryke by using Claudia?" Her eyes go wide, "Never mind, I don't mean to pry into club business." But she's forgetting one thing, "We agreed, Curls. Between us, no secrets, and anything delicate stays between us. And no, we just checked if Ryke was clean, there's no obvious link between Gael and Ryke. What are you thinking?"

Fuck. The smile she's sporting is making my chest fill with warmth. "My mind is just always popping up questions at every angle and in this I see no reason. I mean...Ryke isn't the VP, he's just one of the brothers. Other than Thorn's best friend...oh, shit."

"Oh, shit is about right. Damn. Are you thinking what I'm thinking?" I knew letting her in was what we both needed. She's too fucking smart to keep on a low information level. "About how they wanted him under their control so he could take out Thorn?"

"Yes!" she exclaims. "And now I'm worried. Because...shit."

"What? Come on, woman, didn't I just point out you need to spill out your thoughts. Even if they don't make sense or sound crazy, I need to know." Because it fucking helps my own thought process.

"Now I really would like to know when Ryke's sister died because you asked Thorn in this room, the day I was kidnapped, how well he knew Ryke. For one? I don't trust Ryke at all anymore. Even if his sister died, I'm finding it all too damn weird with them hiding out at Claudia's house, don't you think? And it also raises the question if Ryke put any effort in finding his own sister. And for real...has Ryke left Thorn's side? That fucker is here, Casey. In this clubhouse where he's trusted. Makes sense you couldn't find Gael if someone is giving him inside information, right?" Her eyes are a clear window to her worries.

She's not alone in this though. With the things she just mentioned? Fuck. "We're going to have a hard time getting to the bottom of this."

"I need to get my hands on Claudia's body. Because Ryke's sister carries the first bits of information, I just know it," Curls muses.

"And you, me, Calix, C.Rash, and Thorn need to have a little talk about this," I state. "This is too much of a risk to leave them out. Dammit...everyone is here, how do we fucking manage a meeting with just us? If that fucker is in with Gael he would get suspicious."

"Maybe through Ransom? Send him a text asking to have Ryke check his bike or something? Ryke is a mechanic, it wouldn't raise any suspicions, and then we could meet after Ransom and Ryke go outside so he wouldn't notice," Curls brilliantly suggests.

I lean in and brush my lips against hers, "Smart. Maybe it's also a good idea to get the others in our room instead of church so others don't see us go in there."

Grabbing my phone, I shoot off a couple of messages to make it happen and also let them know not to rise suspicion and get them here one by one instead of all coming over at the same time. Within a few minutes there's a knock on the door. C.Rash stalks inside first and slowly the others start to come in as well.

"Okay, you got us here, Casey, what's up?" Calix asks.

"Curls and I were talking about the case I was working on," I start but Calix cuts me off.

"You're not on any fucking case, Casey. You're dealing with club business," he growls.

"Be that as it may, you'll thank me later so let me get it all out first." I wait for his reluctant nod before I continue. "With us finding Ryke's sister, Curls was wondering when she died because she's suspicious."

All eyes land on Curls and it makes her hands fist as she places them on her hips. "It's just weird, you know…why would Gael target Ryke's sister? What would he gain by controlling Ryke?"

"Fuck," Thorn curses. "Me, this is about me, right? But we've cleared him, his fucking sister is dead, there is no way my brother would deceive me."

Curls throws her shoulders back and stands a little taller. "Let the facts speak. Let me investigate the body to determine the time of death."

"And that shit will tell us what exactly? We all know Kate killed her. Claudia's house was a mess the day our father was murdered. If she was killed before that, during or whatever it doesn't prove shit. Dead is dead and what's done is done," Thorn growls at his sister and I'm seconds away from punching the fucker.

"I think Ryke is in on it. Those two women were never on good footing and both Kate and Claudia worked in the whore house until it was shut down. Claudia was the manager, those two weren't seeing eye to eye, and you know it." Curls states and it's the first time I'm hearing this and I now even more stand behind the reasoning of my woman. Thorn steps closer to his sister and leans down into her face, "That's club. Fucking. Business. And none of your fucking concern." In one smooth move I've got her behind my back as I'm about to face off with Thorn but Calix's growl rings through the room. "This true? About Claudia and Kate? If so, Ryke is going on the shit list whether you like it or not. And I now realize why Casey has full disclosure with his Old Lady and I'm fucking glad he didn't request it first, though I might be pissed about it, he made the right choice."

"Agreed," C.Rash says. "You're too close to see it through reasonable eyes, Thorn. Fucking think. You're the Prez now, they're about to take a vote who the VP will be. Are you really going to vouch for someone you're not a hundred percent sure of? Because I can fucking see it in your eyes you too are thinking of possibilities. This fucker is the only one who hasn't left your side and is in on all fucking details. No wonder we can't find Gael and if it wasn't for Casey asking me and Prez to dive into Claudia's missing person case without anyone overhearing...I damn well know they wouldn't have a confrontation like they had with Gael, Kate, and those others. They would be long gone since Ryke would have tipped them off. Just fucking think."

"I can't fucking think, okay?" Thorn bellows. "They killed my fucking father. The Prez! Including a few of my other brothers who were sitting at the table with him. They took my sister and we can't even find the one responsible and now you guys...another fucking MC...is telling me what I need to fucking do? I've blindly trusted Ryke with my life more times than I can count. I've always thought he'd take a bullet for me. It's always been like that between us, and now he wants said bullet between my fucking eyes? I might need more than a damn minute to think it through, for fuck's sake."

"As long as you spend those damn minutes well enough to realize you have other brothers ready to step in front of a bullet for you. Ones you can fucking trust and are ready to fight this shit with you head on," Calix tells him with a stern yet understanding tone.

Thorn closes his eyes and lets his head fall back. Minutes tick by until he releases a deep sigh and connects his eyes with Calix. "When you called, I was back on my bike, making my own sister my priority instead of checking Claudia's house. Ryke was there with me and he tried like hell to persuade me to get off my bike and check the house.

At the moment I thought his concern was his sister. Now? Knowing Casey saw the tape where Gael ordered to call Ryke, it makes even more sense. I think he wanted me inside his sister's house to kill me. He took a call and then was frustrated because I refused to go inside and stayed out in the open with people around us. Knowing Casey saw the tape where Gael ordered to call Ryke, could very well be the call for him to kill me. I asked what was up but he didn't say shit. I had to drop the discussion 'cause I got the call shit went down at the clubhouse. Fuck. I just can't..."

"Yeah, you can," Calix states. "You're already taking the first step. You're sucking up information and throwing it around in your head to let it fall into place. It's fucking hard but it has to be done. First things first, we need to keep this between us."

Sounds of agreements rip from all of us.

"Sis, you gonna put Claudia on your table?" Thorn asks, quite the turnaround from when we started this discussion.

"I will, if you guys let me or need me to. And...can we maybe tap into Ryke's phone? Or would he use a burner if he's on their side?" Curls questions.

Smart, and I have the right equipment to do it too. "I can handle it if I have his phone, but how are we gonna get it?"

"You guys have a bitch you can trust? Ryke likes to give his cock enough action, seeing he was always at the whore house before we closed it. The fucker has a revolving door when it comes to club pussy. Offer him something new and I'm sure he'll bite. Might give us enough time to get a bug in," Thorn suggests.

"Dixey, for sure. As far as I've heard she's been around for over two years, and from the time I've been here I've seen with my own eyes this chick follows orders like a pro. She can be trusted to do the job and when she's finished, we can send her away for a few weeks' vacation to make sure nothing blows back...just to be safe," C.Rash says. "Normally I would trust her to stick around but this isn't normal shit."

"Agreed," Calix rumbles.

A plan of action. Might not lead to anything but it's damn better than how the day started out. Where we're all hoping we're wrong and Ryke is a good guy, but it sure as hell doesn't seem this way. I'm damn proud of my woman's involvement. But it ends here, there's no way I will risk getting her pulled into shit that will put her life at risk again.

CHAPTER 10

WENDY

How on earth can I be nervous about something I'm not even a part of? But my nerves are shot, I can't help it. It took a day to get everything set but C.Rash arranged a woman, Dixey, who will...I have no clue if Dixey will handle Ryke's phone or if she will give it to Casey so he can handle it and then give it back. Yes, maybe I'm nervous because I don't know how and what but I know enough to put me on edge.

There are only three Thorns 'n' Bones MC bikers here along with Thorn and Ryke. Calix made a big deal out of double checking every single biker Thorns 'n' Bones MC had left. Even if Thorn hated it, he appreciated it with the same ferocity. The music is booming while Tenley, Hedwig, and I are sitting in a booth in the far corner of the clubhouse just watching all the bikers relax with some booze and some girls who are hanging out. It's all part of the scene Calix organized to set Ryke up with the woman.

And it doesn't take long for Ryke to take the bait. Dixey has been throwing 'fuck me eyes' at him for the last hour or so and has been rubbing her tits on his arm long enough it actually makes me wonder why his arm hasn't caught fire yet.

"Go on, take the last one or I'm going to shove it in my mouth and I feel like I ate the whole stash already," Hedwig sighs.

She's sitting across from me and has her feet up and a pillow behind her. I scrunch up my nose and snatch away the red velvet cupcake before she can grab it. I start to nibble on it when my eye catches movement from where Ryke was sitting. Excitement courses through me when I see him drag off the woman in the direction of a room that's available for those who need it.

The nerves I had start to drain away. I guess I was afraid Ryke wouldn't take Dixey up on her offer, but it's good to see he's still the old Ryke I knew when it comes to women; take whatever is offered and freely bounce them off his dick.

"Oh, this is delicious," I groan and direct my attention to Hedwig. "Why did you eat all of them and leave me just this one?" I question, appalled she didn't even share.

"Don't look at me, Tenley brought them. She's got more and won't give 'em to me." Hedwig pouts while Tenley laughs.

"First of all, you told me to keep an eye on your food intake. Second, you damn well gave your last one to Curls because you would need to pop out the kid to create more space if you want to eat more," Tenley tells her and I can see she's having a hard time not to laugh out loud.

Hedwig starts to sputter but loses any retort and falls into full blown laughter as we all do.

Hours pass and the party slows down. Calix and Casey joined us when Ransom dragged Hedwig to their room. Ransom said they needed an early night and both could use the rest. Well, make that Ransom demanded Hedwig take an early night and it seems having her feet up and tucked in with a pillow at her back here in the clubhouse wasn't rest enough.

But it's okay, though. My heart actually overflows with warmth when I see how those two are together and how Ransom treasures her. Hedwig deserves it and so does Ransom. Those two are a perfect match, that's for sure.

"He hasn't left the room," Casey grumbles. "We should have gotten some camera's in there so we could see what's going on. Now we don't even know if she got the job done or not and it's obvious the fucker is going to be in there the whole damn night."

Ah, so the woman was the one who would make sure his phone could be bugged.

One thing's weird, though. "All the times I've been at the clubhouse Ryke has fucked and dropped. Hell, I did mention he used to be a one of the brothers who frequently visited the whore house they owned, right? Not only to keep an eye out for security reasons, but also to test the merchandise. Or so I've heard."

Casey and Calix stare at each other and it takes a moment or two before Calix tells Casey, "Check with Thorn if he doesn't fuck a bitch all night. If this is true, we're checking the room. Now."

Casey pats my thigh and stalks off to find Thorn. The nervousness creeps right back in and my gut is telling me something bad is about to happen. Casey comes back into view with Thorn at his side, a concerned look on both their faces.

"Curls is right, Ryke won't ever share a bed with a bitch, he throws them out or he walks out," Thorn tells Calix who stands up.

"You two stay here," Calix grumbles and leaves in the direction of the room Ryke and Dixey went, followed by both Thorn and Casey.

Tenley mutters, "I don't like the sounds of this."

"Tell me about it…my gut is firing up alarm bells, but I guess we're about to find out, right?" I keep my eyes pinned on the hallway and a few breaths later, Casey comes rushing toward us.

"Curls, you need to come with me…I…we need your expertise." His head goes to Tenley, he leans in closer and I have to strain to hear the whisper of words. "Ryke is missing, Dixey's dead. Stay here and keep an eye on the damn room if anyone acts suspiciously."

Tenley's eyes dismiss Casey and scan the room immediately while Casey takes my hand and drags me off. When we get in front of the door of the room he leans in and whispers, "I know you see a lot in your line of work…so have I, but fuck…take a deep breath and brace yourself, darlin', 'cause this shit is as fucked up as it can be."

I do as he says and when we step inside and the door falls shut behind me, it's then I understand the meaning of his words. Holy. Dang. Shit. This is as fucked up as it can be. The room is painted red. The directions of the blood stains on the walls indicate arterial spray. It's everywhere. The pattern though? Severed carotid.

Careful where I put my feet, I walk around the room and see an arm on the floor behind the bed. Stalking closer, I see Dixey's slaughtered body. She's sprawled out naked and at an odd angle, clearly thrown there by someone. She didn't just have a severed carotid… she was butchered; knife wounds all over her body.

Inching closer, I lean in and glance at the wounds. "Someone give me some gloves." I mutter and it seems they were prepared for my question because gloves appear over my left shoulder.

I put them on and my hands start to linger around the wounds on Dixey's body. Clean cut wounds, both ends pointed, some are gaping…twisting cuts, irregular. Dammit, why don't I have her on my table so I can measure the length of the wounds.

I asses her face, hands, and her feet. "Her face muscles are starting to change, rigor mortis is starting to setting in. She's still warm but not stiff…she was still alive around three hours ago."

I'm still glancing over the body when I hear Casey say, "That's a huge fucking window for someone to disappear, but Calix, see what I'm seeing?"

"Two…fuck, three sets of footprints?" Calix grunts. "The blood near and on the window with the bloody handprints might be hers or hell, Ryke's or someone else's. Two other people thrown in the mix?"

"Do you have any security set on the outside of the building?" Thorn asks.

Standing up, I glance at the both of them while Calix answers, "Not really. I only put in new security in my office. Big fucking mistake not doing every other fucking room in the clubhouse inside and fucking out too. There's one or two outside of the building but the system is old. Didn't think it was needed and I put priority on other things that needed to be replaced. Fuck."

"What about the one I saw locked on the garage? Might give us enough of an angle to see who came and went through this window. It's worth a try, don't you think?" Casey suggests.

"Nothing much I can do here unless I have her on the table along with my instruments," I tell them, making them aware I'm still in the room.

"Get back to my Old Lady, spill what happened without anyone hearing shit, and stay put," Calix says and directs his attention at Casey, "I'm gonna text C.Rash to get his ass in here so I can tell him what went down and have him lock down the clubhouse and get everyone in the main room. Have Ransom stay with the Old Ladies. We're gonna check the outside perimeter and the security feed. Then we'll reevaluate."

I'm about to step out of the room and look down at my shoes. Shit. There's bound to be blood underneath and...

"Just wipe your feet on the carpet, we ain't gonna get the cops here for a damn crime scene investigation, we're gonna handle it," Calix grunts behind me and I internally cringe, knowing Dixey won't end up on my table and they just wanted my opinion to hear how long Ryke would have had to get away judging from how long Dixey was dead.

I do as Calix says and head for Tenley. Her eyes land on mine when she sees me but they quickly slide back to observing the room. Instead of sitting across from her, I chose to slide in next to her and lean in.

"The room turned red, she was stabbed so many times...as you know Ryke's missing but they saw multiple different footprints...two, maybe three people? They're going to check the outside and the feed from the garage security camera," I tell her and she reaches over to take my hand and give it a gentle squeeze.

"No one acted suspiciously. No one. And to be honest? The last few hours didn't raise anything out of the ordinary. Hell, I didn't even hear anything coming from the direction of the room and it's not like the music is blaring too fucking loud. It's a party, yes, but not the kind where we need to shout to hear what you're saying when you're standing right next to me. It's fucking weird," Tenley muses.

Calix, along with Thorn and Casey stalk through the room and head out the front door. Ransom strolls over to us but doesn't sit down, instead he observes.

C. Rash comes into the room and kills the music. "Brothers. Church. Now. Stray pussy, sit your ass down and you only move to be able to breathe. You don't even lift your damn ass to take a piss, you stay in your fucking seat," he bellows.

C.Rash doesn't turn the music back on but heads into church along with every other biker in this room.

Tenley looks at me, "Guess I only have to keep watch over eight women."

A bike roars outside along with gunshots. I'm out of my seat before I think things through and rush out the door. I watch how a bike comes racing from the left side of the building. Casey runs toward it and he jumps through the air, grabbing hold of the biker as they crash to the ground on the other side.

My heart is in my throat but I'm being pulled back into the

clubhouse by a strong arm while another arm is shutting the door. Turning around I see Ransom glaring at me and pointing toward the table where Tenley is stalking toward, pretty sure she was right behind me when I flew outside.

"I don't even know what the fuck is going on but I do know you should know to stay put when shit goes down," Ransom growls into my face. "My brother would spank your ass red if he knew you'd put your life at risk running straight for the sound of fucking gunshots. Not to mention he'd kick my ass for not protecting you enough, even from your damn self. What the hell are you thinking, Curls?"

I don't even care about his warning, I dang well know he's right but my mind is still processing what I just saw and I shove him hard against his pecs. "Get out there, Ransom! I just saw Casey take down a biker and I need to know he's safe."

Ransom doesn't even wait or questions me but rushes around me to head out. I have to swallow a few times at the lump in my throat. I hope Casey is all right. I don't want him hurt. The things I just saw in the room…all the blood…the people who did this…were they waiting outside? The shots I heard. Dammit, I can't lose him.

CHAPTER 11

CASEY

My body is pumping with adrenaline, even if I just got the wind knocked out of me when I collided with the fucker I pushed off his damn bike. I can't believe this fucker was standing watch. He must have seen us through the window. Fuck, he could have easily killed Curls or hell, maybe even all of us.

I pull my arm back and hit him in the face. I go blind with rage and keep hitting him until I feel someone grabbing hold of me and start to drag me off the guy. It only makes me more enraged until I hear my brother's voice.

"You got him, Casey, come on, leave some damn life in the fucker so we can drain some info out of him," Ransom grunts while I let him drag me to my feet.

"Fuck, bro, that could have turned bad in a nanosecond. How the fuck did the both of us handle this shit with our damn heads up our asses," Calix growls.

"Sweep the area, I doubt there are more hiding out. This one was already on his bike, he was just watching. Doesn't make it any less fucked up," I say, and step away from Ransom in an effort to get my bearings.

"Leo," Thorn sneers the name of the biker who's lying bloody on the ground. "You're gonna die tonight, fucking rat."

My hands go to my head as my fingers dig through my hair. Fucking hell. I close my eyes and tip my head back in an effort to get my bearings. When I open them, my gaze is locked on the roof and I have to blink a few times to process the shit I'm seeing.

Pointing up I tell the guys, "I found Ryke."

All eyes follow the direction I'm pointing in and turn to shock when the scene registers. Ryke's body is on the roof, slightly tipping over with his head and arm as if he's thrown up there like a ragdoll.

"Looks like they climbed onto the dumpster to throw him on there, but for fuck's sake, why?" Ransom questions. "Why not throw him in the dumpster, leave him in the damn room or throw him in the bushes? This is fucked up."

"Not going to discuss it right now, but it's going be the first damn question this fucker here is going to answer," Calix growls and grabs Leo off the ground to drag him with him into the clubhouse.

We all follow them into the office. Calix points at me. "Tell C.Rash it's gonna be a while and make a list to make sure we know who was here when this shit went down. Then make sure to empty the clubhouse and get the stray pussy out of the damn club. And make damn sure no one goes around back. Then return here."

I give him a nod and leave the room. Curls' eyes land on mine and she narrows them, "I know you're doing your job—club business and all—but I don't appreciate you risking your life by throwing yourself at moving motorcycles."

The corner of my mouth twitches, "Understood." I tell her and the only reaction in return I get is to see her shoulders relax as she turns her attention back to Tenley.

Fuck. I know for damn sure the reason she's as relaxed in this fucked up situation is because she was born into the MC life. Even if I've been on the outside of one—my brother in one—I know the ins and outs and how Old Ladies handle themselves. Yet Curls? She's stronger than any women I've ever met.

I realize it even more as I escort the stray pussy out of the clubhouse. Every single one is wide eyed while scurrying out as if the club's on fire. They know very well to keep their mouths shut. Seeing Calix drag a guy inside who's face is beaten up is enough for them to internally freak out.

Pride courses through me as I glance back to see the strength Curls radiates. But then a thought hits me…how the hell would she have known I launched myself at a moving motorcycle? She would have to have left the clubhouse to see me do it since no one told her. Fuck.

I take a detour to stride to my woman, catching her by surprise when I place my hand at the back of her neck to grip those flaming curls and pull her head back gently to crash my mouth against hers.

Though the kiss is quick and rough, leaving her lips swollen and well used, I tell her, "You just earned yourself a spanking by stating what you just did…'cause it lets me know you ignored a direct order to stay put or you wouldn't have known what I fucking did."

Her eyes go wide before they dilate, "Okay," she fucking breathes.

"You two, break it off. My Old Man just dragged a bloody Thorns 'n' Bones MC member into his office, get your ass back to work, Casey," Tenley snaps.

The corner of my mouth twitches and I see the mischief in Curls' eyes and when they slide to Tenley and back to me, I can clearly see the understanding going through her mind of what I've told her. How Tenley might have given her cut and VP status back to the club and yet there's no doubt of the authority she still holds.

I brush my lips against hers one last time before I pull back and give Tenley a tight nod. I rush over to church to find C.Rash to get things moving. It was already a night filled with tension but the way it spiraled out of control is something completely different.

Hours tick by while my brothers handle two dead bodies and we interrogate Leo. When we're sure he hasn't got any other info to share it's the end of the line for him and his body is disposed of too.

It's early morning before we decide to get some shut eye. We have a meeting later today to discuss everything we discovered and we need the rest and a fresh brain to process this twisted shit.

I follow Ransom to his room where Tenley, Curls, and Hedwig decided to stay in together. It's a room without a window, and with Dixey and Ryke both dead with perps going in and out of a window, I'm damn glad these three decided this was the best place for them. Even more when we are met with a gun pointed at us by Tenley. She lowers it as soon as she sees us.

"Your Old Man is waiting for you," I tell her and she turns to the other girls to say goodbye before rushing out of the room.

"Come on, let's get some shut eye," I tell Curls and hold my hand out for her to take.

She takes it without questioning and follows me to our room. Even if I'm drained, I still need to feel her underneath me. With just a few weeks having her as my Old Lady I know the life ahead of us will be spend together. A connection as strong as ours simply can't be ignored.

Lust turning to love and entwined with my soul where we're set on a path to explore everything as we go. Hell, even if it was only for a fragment of time this woman was the mother of my unborn child. This is something no one can change, it's a straight up fact.

For me it also made the thought settle to have her belly swell with our child someday soon. I was just inside her bare two days ago, my cum yet again sliding out of her pussy. She might already be pregnant this very second.

With Ransom and Hedwig becoming parents any damn time now it would hold even more value to have our kids growing up together. Exactly how me and Ransom found support in one another.

Hedwig and Curls being tight friends…me and Ransom with the paths of our backgrounds crossing, it makes all our connections more solid. I'm now more focused than ever to find and kill Gael to prevent anything from hurting the family we've build together.

"Get naked," I growl, unable to keep my emotions in check.

Her eyes find mine and she slowly obeys, making me watch every single fucking move until she's standing naked in front of me. Perfect tits with nipples all pink and begging for my mouth.

They're inching closer and all rational thoughts leave my head when she drops to her knees in front of me. Her hands going for my belt, rushing to open the zipper to free my hard as fuck cock that's bursting out of its confinement to bob in front of her face.

I shrug out of my cut and let it slide to the floor, my shirt follows as I shove my jeans down. I want her mouth on me right this fucking second but I don't want the feel of fabric on my skin. It's the complete bare feeling of her warmth radiating on every inch of my fucking body I crave.

Once I'm standing in front of her with every inch of me bare, I feel like I have my sins and soul in hand. I'm more than worthy of her love because in return I damn well love her more than all the love a universe can hold.

I reach out and cup her face while I wrap the fingers of my other hand around my cock, giving it a tight squeeze. "At the end of a fucked-up day, you in front of me ready to give me anything I will ever be able to handle means more than the breaths I take. I love you so damn much already, baby, and it will only grow stronger." Her eyes fill with tears and spill over her cheeks, but I'm not done telling her the shit pouring from my soul. "See through your tears, Curls. See the man who's standing in front of you for I'm the father of our child that never was, and I damn well will be the father of our future children."

A sob rips from her throat and if it's because of the raw intensity or the overflowing love we have for one another, I can hardly shove my cock inside her mouth now. Though, I seriously want to feel her mouth on me.

The way things spiral into fulfillment for the both of us, might be too much of a speeding train ready to crash at any second, for some people. It doesn't matter, because they don't understand our connection and it will only be proven every day that follows.

We will hold strong and stay together. A love so fierce, so damn hot, so fucking strong…others will only understand when they will either see the result or experience it for themselves. I don't fucking care, though. In my heart, in my mind, in my fucking soul, there's only room for one thing…and that's her; my Old Lady.

My hand falls away from my cock and I cup her face with both hands to guide her up to her feet so I can kiss her. Our mouths connect and the way things shifted between us can be tasted in the way our kiss deepens and raw emotions turn to delicate lingering.

The love we both pour into it is equal and it fires up the craving between us. I want to bury myself inside her so damn bad but she rears back and with our gaze connected she yet again drops to her knees.

Between realizing what's coming and her taking me in her tiny hand and sliding her tongue over the tip of my cock, all common sense evaporates. My hands dig into her hair and even if I let her set the pace of sliding her mouth on and off my cock, I can't help but hold her head.

Euphoria. Utter pleasure is running through me with the vision before me and it has me close to blowing my load. But I can't; I want to be inside her when that happens. And it will happen very fucking fast if she keeps sucking like that. Hell, her other hand starts to fondle my balls and I know I'm seconds away from blowing my load down her throat.

I step back and with it my cock falls from her mouth. My thumb traces her bottom lip, "So. Fucking. Good. But my cum needs to hit another place inside you. One where I know it belongs so we can work on our future; plan a family," I croak, my voice loaded with the emotion of this moment between us.

"Sooner rather than later, that's your motto?" she fucking chuckles as she gets to her feet.

"When it comes to you? Damn sure it is," I tell her.

"Since you already came inside me once, I could be pregnant right now," she muses.

I groan, "Don't fucking tease, but let's fucking hope so. Not only is having you in my life worth everything I ever worked for...but to plan a future together, having the same mind set? All of it makes it complete, darlin'. Emotions burn and grow deeper and I can't wait to see months pass to know we will stand even more solid and connected to our dreams than we already are."

"You can stop talking now, I'm convinced, get inside me already," she moans.

Who am I to delay pleasure for the both of us? I swoop her off her feet and let her bounce on the bed, immediately grabbing her ankle to open her legs. I can smell her arousal and I need her taste on my tongue when she orgasms again around my cock.

I settle between her legs and I take a deep breath to consume her sweet scent. Turning my head to make a trail of kisses, I turn again to do the same on the other leg until I kiss her mound. I let my tongue slide down to her clit, flicking it a time or two before I cover it completely with my mouth and start to suck.

She gasps my name as she digs her nails into my hair to pull me close. I leave her clit and start to lap her pussy, penetrating it with lazy strokes to drive her crazy. I relish in the way curses fall from her mouth and even more the way her hips move to grind her pussy against my face to seek the release she needs.

Ultimately, I give in and take the bundle of nerves between my teeth and nibble and suck and...screams of pleasure rip through the air while her taste hits my tongue. Pleasure. Hers and mine, the whole damn room is crackling with it.

It's exactly how it always is between us. Everything heightens when we're near each other and even if it's the third time I'm burying myself deep inside her, it feels like the first time all over. Tight. Unbelievable. Hot. The way she grips me like a vice is taking my damn breath away.

I need to focus and when our gaze connects, I know it's useless to delay the inevitable. Hovering over her, I start to piston inside her. I crash my mouth over hers and I don't even have the focus to kiss her correctly because every cell in my body is chasing the orgasm we both crave.

And then it hits. It's as if it's shooting from my damn soul and straight into hers when she comes at the exact same time. Completely drained I let myself fall on top of her. Barely managing to turn, the both of us crash and slowly drift off to sleep. And even in my dreams the thoughts of my cum still in her pussy fills a void inside me enough to know what the future might bring for us.

Nothing in life is a sure thing...yet the thought of her being comfortable enough to fall asleep with me still dripping out of her makes me even more aware of the fact we belong together. Fucked up, I know. But it's a primal instinct that needs to settle. Maybe because we were robbed from what might have been and it's making me eager to obtain what we lost.

CHAPTER 12

WENDY

"But it doesn't make any fucking sense," Thorn sighs.

He knocked on our door early this morning and has been talking to Casey while I'm sitting on the bed looking at the both of them as they try to understand why Ryke was found dead too.

I don't mind Thorn waking us up early and discussing things with Casey in front of me. Absolutely not. In fact, I'm being quiet and haven't said one single thing since my brother entered the room. Mainly because I want all the details too. I know, it's twisted and it only makes me worry even more but it also settles a part of me that needs to know.

"The only thing I can think of is that Gael didn't trust him in the end either. And to be honest? We might never get to know whose side he was on because he's dead and dead men don't talk. See? Another reason why Gael could have had him killed or the fucker came here to do it himself since he had a few guys to spare. Well, not anymore…it's only him and one other guy we got to link back to him, right? We're getting close with finishing this fucker for good. Calix mentioned he wanted to see if we can get some more intel from Gael's sister. We'll see," Casey says and my brain perks up enough to break my silence.

"What if Ryke was seeing Kate? What if Gael was staking out the clubhouse and saw Ryke cheating on his sister?" With me stating this I now have two pair of eyes glaring at me as if I've lost my dang mind. I roll my eyes, "Oh, come on. It makes some twisted sense, right? Ryke's twisted loyalties, him hanging out at the whore house before it was shut down…and if I remember correctly Ryke was one of the three who were against closing down the whore house when it was first suggested but since there was no choice and the majority ruled, it went through and the whore house was shut down. When you go over to squeeze Kate for information, casually mention Ryke's dead and be sure to have a close eye on her reactions. I'm sure if there was something between those two, she won't be able to hide her emotions."

I'm biting the inside of my cheek. The two idiots are still staring at one another as if I've managed to pull a frog out of my ass.

Thorn clears his throat and completely ignores me. "Right, church in half an hour, see you there," he tells Casey and stalks out of the room.

I'm still pissed they didn't even consider my suggestion. It's as if Casey feels my tension and he strolls over to cup my face but I manage to dodge and rush to the other side of the bed.

Jumping off, I point at him, "Don't try and sweet talk, I know you think my suggestion was way out there to even consider. But with Claudia and Kate not getting along, Kate killing Claudia while she was supposed to be leverage? What if Claudia threatened to get between Ryke and her? Or even mention she would go to Thorn and rat them all out if she was in on it. You have to consider all the angles even more when everyone ends up dead. Stabbings are personal. The rage I saw of those knife wounds? The details you told me about Claudia's body? For some reason, I think everything in this messed up situation is personal. Even more because Gael came after me because he was put into place due to his comment…the whore house closing, it all falls together and they've waited for months while planning all of this. Throw in personal issues and you have mad men filled with blind rage who do stupid stuff and spiral. But maybe it's because I'm suggesting these reasons it doesn't come across as an option but it's ignored instead. Yeah, when an opinion comes from a woman it's hard to,"

"Do not fucking finish that sentence," Casey growls angrily. "You damn well know I value your input and have followed your thoughts before. We're all on edge here and we all need to take a deep breath and look at it from all angles. And we will. Like Thorn said, we have church in half an hour. The things you just mentioned are also in his head and he's throwing things around as we speak. I swear I will also mention all of this while we talk things through in half an hour but don't ever fucking think your voice isn't heard because I damn well live for your voice. And while we're in this discussion I would also love for you to put your nose in my business once I start my own company. That's how fucking much I value your input, okay?"

"Well, okay!" I snap back, but inside I'm smiling.

He wants my help in the future, and to be honest? I like the thought of changing careers or adding to it. I've always loved my job but I've always wanted more. Not just writing a report after my findings but diving into the why and how. And when Casey started talking about how he wanted to start his own company with solving cold cases it starts to itch even more to change things up.

I stalk around the bed until I'm in front of Casey and stand on my tip toes to give him a kiss on the lips. "Thank you," I tell him.

Stunned, he asks, "Why?"

"For everything," I simply tell him. "And for what's to come. Maybe I'll quit my job or work part time instead to come work for you. I'm good at writing reports and I could also handle the phone."

"What?" he sputters. "You can't quit your job and do something completely different."

"Judgy much, Mister Kettle? Because I remember not too long ago you turned your badge in for a leather cut," I state and glare at the annoying man. "Besides, I did mention working part time."

Crap. Why can he yank my emotions like no other? Oh, I know; because I've fallen hard for this man and love does crazy things when your heart is involved.

"You got a point, I just don't want you to have any regrets. You've worked too hard to get to where you are," he sighs.

"You also have a point, don't get me wrong," I give him an understanding smile. "but I've always felt there was something missing, you know?"

"Me," the man states and it makes me roll my eyes but on the inside my heart is skipping because he's right; he was the one thing my life was missing.

Now I do let him cup my face and it makes me feel extremely special when he keeps our gazes locked. As if he needs to brand every inch of my face into his mind.

His voice is raw when he says, "Life truly started when I met you, then I was finally able to dream and chase them into reality."

"Life is mediocre unless you dream," I tell him breathlessly.

"You're my dream turned reality," he whispers right before his mouth covers mine in a hard kiss.

I could let myself drown in this man. The way he takes me in his arms, wraps me with comfort and consumes me with lust and love in an equal dose. Yet, he slows down our kiss and steps back.

"I need to get ready, are you going to keep Tenley and Hedwig company?" he questions.

I'm still in a daze when I simply nod, but I snap out of it when I think what Casey will be doing.

"Make sure someone checks Kate's reaction," I mutter and start to get dressed while I let my thoughts flow. "Claudia always had a secret crush on Thorn, it wouldn't surprise me if it got her killed."

"What did you just say?" Casey steps closer and narrows his eyes. "Why didn't you mention this sooner?"

I stare at him for a few breaths because, "I thought Thorn knew. She never acted on it but for me it was obvious."

Casey sighs and rubs a hand over his face. "What might have been obvious for you might not have been for Thorn. He's a dude, he might have needed action or words."

"Well, dang," I mutter. "Maybe he would have believed me if I told him before all of this happened, but now? Everything is a touchy subject. And it's not that I blame him, a lot happened and it all practically lands on his shoulders…I just…I want my brother back."

Casey cups the side of my face and lets his thumb slide over my cheek, "This will all be over soon. It's escalating quickly and Gael doesn't have anyone else to fall back on. His plan failed before it started but it's caused a ripple effect we all are dealing with. Thorn not only has to deal with this but also has to push forward to get his MC up and running again. Today they're voting for a new VP and since your brother is now the Prez, it's also a lot of pressure to fill the shoes that were once your father's."

"I can't help him," I now realize. "I've been a part of Thorns 'n' Bones for so long but I now realize I can't do anything, it's all him."

"It is," Casey simply states. "The whole MC and the club business that goes with it is all him. But the support, the family outside of the

MC, that's you, darlin'. And since he's stepped up and showed us the change Thorns 'n' Bones MC went through Calix has told him we also have his back. It might seem a lot in this moment but your brother has shown he's got the backbone for this shit. He too was born into this and will lead his brothers to a better future."

I take a few deep breaths and give Casey a soft smile, "Thank you," I breathe with all my heart. "Even if I thought you were an overbearing asshole the second time we met, I have grown very fond of you."

Casey snorts, "Just very fond, huh? Well, shit. I think I need to up my game here to get a high score from my Old Lady since I won't settle for anything less than over the top, hot burning love."

"Give me a few orgasms and I might be dazed enough to admit to the fact I have indeed fallen for your pretty face," I reply through easy banter and yet this moment is as serious as it gets.

"I wish we had more time. Later," he growls and kisses me with such ferociousness I need to grab his shoulders to steady myself.

Both panting hard, Casey places his forehead against mine and softly rubs our noses together.

"I adore you," he murmurs softly.

"Right back at ya," I croak, overcome with emotions.

Even if we've been through a lot these last few weeks and our connection is solid, this moment right here is where the both of us acknowledge our feelings have settled and from here on out there's most definitely no going back. Nor would I want to.

Casey clears his throat, "I need to go."

"Yeah," I sigh. "So, you mentioned…the reason I won't be getting orgasms any time soon."

"For fuck's sake," Casey chuckles and shakes his head while he grabs his cut and throws it on. But his face turns serious all too soon. "Do you have a gun? They came into this clubhouse to kill Ryke and Dixey, we took precautions not to let it happen again, but I need to know you have a gun on you at all times. Even if a brother will be in the same room with you as well because no one will be left alone until Gael is caught and dead."

"I have a gun, it's in my purse," I tell him and stalk over to get my purse.

Casey groans, "In your purse, what good will that do. On. You. You put it on you where you can grab it with your next breath and not tell the fucker, who's ready to kill you, to hold on because you have to go through the shit in your purse to find the damn....what the fuck is that?"

"My gun," I shrug. Not at all ashamed I have a Wonder Woman Glock, I'm all about the pretty visual, and it's small and fits right into my hand.

"Does it even work?" The overbearing man asks, clearly annoyed by my choice of weapon.

I roll my eyes, "Duh, it's a Wonder Woman, of course it works."

All he does is shake his head and waits for me to place the holster on my belt. I'm wearing jeans shorts along with sneakers and a yellow stripped tank. I have no plans for today since they decided I can't go to work until Gael is dead.

Another day with Tenley and Hedwig and this is me not complaining because spending time with these two women is a treat. Though Hedwig is getting grumpy. She's tired of the huge belly and not being able to do anything other than rest. She's ready to be done with it, and it could happen any day now. I follow Casey out the door as I head for the main room and Casey stalks off to church.

CHAPTER 13

WENDY

"Do you remember when I had those false contractions?" Hedwig muses while she's dissecting her sandwich.

I watch Hunter put on his large black beanie and with the hoodie, along with his cut over it, he's looking more dressed for winter time instead of the warm and sunny day it is. I shake my head at the man's weird wardrobe.

"I'm going out to get some more stuff for the new security cams I'm installing," Hunter says to Feargal who got the assignment to keep an eye on us, even if we're in the main room of the clubhouse.

"Bike or cage?" Feargal questions.

"Cage," Hunter grumbles. "I need the space for the equipment I'm buying."

"Later," Feargal nods as Hunter stalks off and out the door.

Focusing back on Hedwig, I see her rub her stomach and remember she said something about the false contractions she was having a few weeks ago.

"What was that, Hedwig?" I ask while I watch her face pinch with pain. What the hell? "You're having contractions? Now?"

Tenley's head whips up, the book she's holding in her hand long forgotten. "What?" she squeaks.

"I might," Hedwig grunts and it seems like she's holding her breath.

"Breathe, woman!" I snap and stand up, my gaze connecting with Feargal whose eyes are about to fall out. "Feargal, get Ransom here, now."

"Right, right," he muses, stands up, and suddenly his eyes are focused on the window. He curses loud and rushes to the door.

I turn to look over my shoulder and see through the window how Hunter is slumped over his steering wheel. What the hell?

"Casey! Ransom!" I bellow as loud as I can, hoping they can hear me through the thick door and walls of church.

But I can't focus on them because Hedwig stands and water is dripping down her legs.

"Holy shit," Tenley gasps, "her water broke. She's gonna pop out the baby. We need to do something."

"Well, we need to not panic, that's for sure." I glare at Tenley and she seems to jump into action.

"I have to go grab her bag, right?" she asks but doesn't even wait for my answer and rushes off down the hall to get Hedwig's bag she packed for her and for the baby.

One breath I'm staring at Hedwig, the next I'm looking at the back of a leather cut with the AF MC patch stitched on it.

"Are you okay, what's going on?" Ransom's voice is filled with worry.

Hedwig is puffing away another contraction so I tell him, "Her water broke, she's having contractions, and we're going to the hospital."

Ransom's head whips back and he looks at me with horror. "Fuck."

"No, you did that part nine months ago, now it's time to reap what you've sowed," I tell the silly man and roll my eyes.

"You guys take the car. Tenley will drive, when she gets here with the bag, while I'm gonna follow behind you guys in my car," Casey says but get interrupted when the door of the clubhouse swings open.

Feargal is carrying Hunter into the clubhouse. Or more like half dragging him since he's got Hunter's arm hooked around his neck to keep Hunter somewhat upright. Hunter's face is covered with blood and his beanie is pulled down. He seems unconscious though his feet move and his other arm is going around his back.

Time slows down when I see Hunter ripping the beanie off over his face to clean off some blood or at least it seems that way. He throws the beanie to the floor and is palming a gun the next instant. Oh, God! He shoots Feargal in the chest who crashes to the floor, freeing up his other arm to palm another gun. Hunter starts to…Fuck. It's Geal pretending to be an injured Hunter, and he's now shooting up the clubhouse.

I palm my gun and only get one single shot fired before I'm being pulled down by Casey who's cursing and my eyes meet with a panicked Hedwig. She's in pain; it's written all over her face. My first thought is the baby but when my eyes scan her body, I see blood staining her dress. It seems to be coming from her thigh. I reach out and she takes my hand in hers while Ransom is hovering over her.

"I'm going to get out of my tank top and try to stop the bleeding, okay?" I tell her and regretfully let go of her hand and the gun I was still holding.

But she starts to scream and grab my upper arm. I have no other choice but to use my hand without the protection of a glove and instead of my tank, I use her own dress to put pressure on her wound. There's nothing I can do right now with the bullets flying everywhere. I have to stop the bleeding as much as possible. Casey grunts above me.

Calix's voice booms through the room, "Die, fucker."

As if thunder crackles, making the room fill with such loud noise, I have to close my eyes, then…nothing. Hedwig whimpers and my eyes fly open to connect with hers. I wish I could sooth the pain but I only have two hands who I both need to put pressure on her wound. Dammit, she's shot and going into labor, how fucked up is that?

"Motherfucker," Thorn bellows and I manage to raise my head some to see him stalk through the clubhouse in the direction of where Gael was standing.

The heavy weight on my body is preventing me from standing and when I glance back, my heart stops. Casey is slumped over me and he's not moving. I can't do anything because it would mean I have to remove my hands from Hedwig's wound and she could bleed out. While she's having contractions, shit, this is so screwed up.

"Ransom, help! Calix! Thorn!" I start to bellow all the names of every biker I know in here, anything to get help.

It's Ransom who turns and tucks away his gun. My chest squeezes with the same pain ripping through his eyes when he glances at both

Hedwig and Casey.

"Call an ambulance, Ransom. She needs to get to the hospital. Now!" I scream. "Tenley," I sigh in relief when I see her head coming from behind Ransom. "Check Casey, he's not moving."

"Ambulances are coming," Ransom grunts and is kneeling next to Hedwig but his gaze is set on Casey.

"Ransom," I snap, while Calix is at Tenley's side as they are turning Casey to lift him off me. "Focus on Hedwig right now, let your Prez take care of Casey. Hedwig, Ransom," I press. "and your baby."

His face is torn from pain and indecision but he seems to shake it off and is cupping Hedwig's face, giving her gentle words in an effort to calm her down. The way she's losing blood from the wound in her leg and being in labor? The ambulance needs to get her as soon as possible for her to survive this.

I want to look behind me to check on Casey so damn bad, but I'm afraid to. What if he's dead? What if I shift my hands and lose pressure on the wound so Hedwig bleeds out? Dammit, I need to keep myself together. Sirens, I'm hearing them in the distance and they're getting closer. Help is on the way.

I take a deep breath and close my eyes. Prioritize. Like I just told Ransom, I need to trust other people. My eyes flash open when I hear Thorn start to curse and rush toward Calix and Tenley…Casey. I can't look. I'll fall apart. I can't look. I can't…

EMT's are rushing into the clubhouse. Two crouch down next to me while others rush past me to help Casey.

"Gunshot wound to her upper thigh. She's in labor. Her water broke and contractions started," I blurt out but it seems they are already starting to help Hedwig and only nod at my rush of words.

"Ma'am, I'm going to take over, I need for you to remove your hands," he tells me but I can't seem to process. Tugging at my arms makes me nod warily and for the first time I'm able to turn around to focus on Casey, and the second I do, my whole world stops.

My heart plummets when I see Calix perform CPR while the EMT's are now slowly taking over. My ass hits the floor as I watch them connect wires and give him oxygen. There's beeping…his heart is beating, right? Blood. So much blood. I look down at my hands and there's more blood. I can't…I can't breathe…I…I can't…

"Look me in the eye, Curls." Thorn's angry face appears in front of me. "I need for you to be fucking strong now, sis. He's gonna need for you to be his strength, you hear?"

Thorn hoists me up by my arms and he guides me out of the clubhouse to see how they load both Casey and Hedwig into the waiting ambulances.

"We'll follow," Thorn grunts and pushes me toward his bike.

It's when he starts to fuss with his helmet on my head when I snap into the now. "Stop it, I can damn well handle it myself," I growl.

"Good," Thorn bites back and straddles his bike.

The ride to the hospital is a blur and the only thing what keeps me upright is the fact I have my arms wrapped around my brother, and it gives me the strength I need right now.

Thorn pats my knee, indicating I need to get off and the both of us rush inside to get an update on both Hedwig and Casey. We don't get any information, though. All they mention is how someone will be with us shortly to update us. We're guided into a waiting room and it does nothing to calm my nerves because Ransom is sitting there holding his head.

His head whips up and his gaze connects with mine but it returns to the floor when he sees it's just me and Thorn. I don't have to ask him about Hedwig. With him sitting here, and not with her, I'm sure there isn't any information about her status.

Instead of sitting down, both Thorn and I are pacing through the room until the door opens. I expect a doctor or a nurse but Calix stalks inside along with a few other brothers, all with grim expressions. Tenley enters the room and she rushes forward and hugs me tight.

"Any news on Casey or Hedwig?" She asks.

I shake my head. "Nothing."

"Feagal is hanging on, they don't know if he's going to pull through," Tenley says. "They found Hunter's body underneath his truck. There was another dead guy underneath it too, the one who was working with Gael. We assume he was killed when they attacked Hunter. We have three of our own brothers with gunshot wounds but not life threatening."

"I'm glad you weren't in the room when the bullets started to fly," I croak and my chest tightens at the thought of all the others who got hurt.

"They're gonna pull through," Tenley whispers next to my ear as she hugs me tight. "They just have to…all of them including the little one."

I damn well hope she's right.

AF MC OHIO

CHAPTER 14

CASEY

I'm gasping for my next breath as I raise my arms to pull the trigger. Fuck. Where's my gun? Where the hell am I? I'm being pushed down by Calix and Curls. My whole fucking body hurts and my head is pounding.

"Calm down," Calix growls. "Go get a nurse or a damn doctor in here, Curls."

"No," I croak, my voice raw. "Stay."

I don't care about anything other than having her near me. Even if my stomach rolls and it takes everything in me not to throw up. Fuck. I try to breathe through the nausea.

"I'm here, right here," she whispers and slides her fingers along my cheek.

"Fine, I'll go get someone. Just don't do anything idiotic like surging up again. You'll rip the damn IV out," Calix grunts while he spins around and leaves the room.

Hospital room I now realize. "What happened?"

The only thing going through my head is that I was firing my gun before everything went black.

Curls searches my eyes. "What do you remember?"

I try to wreck my brain but I come up empty, I start to think about the shit I do remember, "We were sitting in church...gunshots. Fuck." The beeping in the room spikes and my head whips that way to see my heartrate is accelerating.

"Calm down," Curls urges.

"Gael?" I question, needing to know if the fucker is still alive.

"Dead, and so is Hunter. They found his body underneath his truck. Geal killed him to pretend he was him. Feargal thought Hunter was hurt when we saw him slumped over the steering wheel. Instead it was Gael who covered his face with Hunter's blood and put on his beanie, hoodie, and cut. Feargal is still fighting for his life. He made it through surgery so that's a good thing but his body went through hell and the doctors have no clue if he's going to pull through or not."

"Ransom...Hedwig? The baby?" I'm afraid to ask with everything she just told me.

A bright smile paints her plump lips. "You're an uncle, Casey. Ransom is fine and Hedwig had an emergency C-section because she took a bullet to the leg and needed surgery. Their baby boy, Zander, is healthy as a horse."

"Zander," I croak.

Fuck. They named their son after his father. I haven't heard Ransom's given name for a long damn time. Mainly because my brother started to use Ransom to step away from his dark past, one he connected with his name. It seems to me he's grabbing this chance to give the name he lived through to his son.

And I damn well know my brother will be a great father and will move heaven and earth to give what he needs. Knowing this new family is safe and complete soothes me. I don't even care my body is hurting because I'm staring at the very person who makes life worth living.

And yet the loss of my AF MC brothers hits me hard and it's also something we all have to live with. They gave their life to make ours safe.

Calix rushes back in and a nurse is close behind him. "Sir, you need to rest," the nurse says and Calix smirks behind her.

"Your Old Lady okay?" I question, totally ignoring the nurse because I will fucking rest when I'm dead because I'm fucking thrilled to be alive right now.

"Yeah," Calix rubs his sternum. "Thanks to your Old Lady she wasn't even in the room when shit went down. I can't fucking thank your Old Lady enough."

"We needed to go to the hospital since Hedwig was having contractions and her water broke. Tenley was grabbing the bag Hedwig prepared. It's not like I sent her out of the room because I knew things were going to...shit. I just...never mind," Curls mutters and keeps her eyes on the nurse checking all the machines.

The nurse turns her attention to me. "The doctor will be right with you."

Curls glares when the nurse starts to fuss with my IV, probably checking to see if it's still okay after I tried to get up when Calix held me down, he must have mentioned something. I reach up with my other hand and let my finger trail down Curls' bare arms.

"Hey, gorgeous," I croak, my voice loaded with emotion.

Without looking she reaches out and holds my hand between both of hers, eyes still pinned on the nurse.

Frustration, along with annoyance, makes me snap at the nurse, "Stop touching me." Resulting in a full-on glare from the nurse.

I know I shouldn't snap at the woman, and I'm thankful she's looking after me, but in this moment all I need is my Old Lady and some quiet time to appreciate what I have right in front of me. Now Curls' eyes do land on me and she gives me a bright as fuck smile.

"Feeling better, huh?" she beams and leans in to whisper, "I dang well love how you can agitate females within mere minutes of being in their presence."

"I only care about one and even if I manage to agitate her, she stays and gives me hell just as fierce in return," I tell her and shoot her a wink.

"I'm not going anywhere, and neither are you." She swallows hard. "You took two bullets and lost a lot of blood. For a moment you passed out and...I almost lost you...your heart...you were..." Curls sucks in a shaky breath as if she needs other words and to skip what she intended to say. "But you're here and the doctor mentioned full recovery. But you need to rest."

"Yes," the nurse chimes in. "You need to rest."

Now it's my turn to glare at the nurse and she spins around and leaves the room. The hours that pass is filled with visits from the doctor and finally also a few of my brothers. They each take turns so it isn't crowded or too stressful for me. The annoying nurse's words, not mine. But she's right. I feel drained with every minute that passes. The next day Ransom is in my room along with his son. They managed to put Hedwig in the room next to me for the next few days seeing Hedwig will be able to leave the hospital sooner than me. I still need to be bedbound and let my body heal before I can start PT.

A few weeks later, when the day finally comes for me to leave the hospital, it's Ransom who's in my room while we're waiting for Curls to come back with the nurse to go over my discharge papers. All while I keep staring at the papers Ransom put in front of me.

"Are you sure?" I croak, unable to process what he just shoved in front of me.

"Fuck, yeah, I'm sure. We talked about this so it shouldn't come as a surprise, but you know what this means, right?" He challenges. All I can do is stare at Ransom and wait for him to expand. "When shit hits the fan at home, we need to build a man cave in the backyard. A huge one. One with a barbeque out front and two couches inside along with a huge flat screen where we can watch football. Not to mention a stacked fridge, microwave, bathroom…gotta have everything we need, right?"

The smile I feel spreading my face is hurting my damn cheeks. "Like how we used to camp outside together and watch the dark sky while spilling the shit we wanted in life when we were teenagers. Only we'll have the deluxe version surrounding us instead of a damn tent."

Ransom points a finger at me. "That exact fucking spot, fucker! You and me, our Old Ladies, and our kids growing up together. Neighbors, brothers, friends, for life."

The way we grew up, the way we each had our dreams and ended up with two women who were fast friends before we met…his woman living right next door to him and making it possible for us to become neighbors. Because that's what the papers state in front of me. Ransom has signed the house over to me.

He moved in with Hedwig because she had the nursery ready and he explained how he's just as happy in her house with me living next door than the other way around. Because there wasn't another option since we decided a long fucking time ago, we were gonna be brothers for life.

I can't even muster words right now so I only nod. Ransom shakes his head. "Didn't you hear me say our kids growing up together?"

"I did, and they will," I croak, my voice loaded with emotion when I add, "hopefully sometime in the near future if life grants us another chance."

"I said our kids because your Old Lady is pregnant, fucker," Ransom tells me with the biggest of smiles and I'm absolutely stunned.

"Great," Curls sighs and stalks further into the room. "I leave you alone for a few minutes and you manage to spill the news I'm supposed to share myself with my Old Man. It's dang personal, Ransom." She smacks his chest with the discharge papers she's holding.

I'm glad I've made huge progress and can stand, walk around, and function normal if I don't do any weird shit or lift heavy stuff because I only have to raise my arm to cup her face and let my thumb travel over her bottom lip.

"You're pregnant?" I ask and her cheeks flush while she gives me a slight nod, confirming the best news ever. "How long have you known?"

"She peed on one of those things before we came over. Hedwig and her were in the bathroom watching the two lines appear. Apparently, I wasn't allowed in there," Ransom grumbles.

"Oversharing personal stuff again," Curls sighs.

Ransom shakes his head. "You're the one who put a stick in your own pee with my woman standing right next to you…who's the one who's oversharing, huh? Not me."

"Okay, you guys, enough. I really like to go home now," I state and the both of them rush into action.

Ransom grabs my bag with clothes while I grab the papers of the house. The house. The one where I grew up and now it seems I'll be raising my own family in while my brother is living right next door, living his live while we still share our dreams and turn them into reality.

Curls' fingers lace with mine and I follow Ransom down the hall with my Old Lady right next to me while she carries our unborn child inside her belly. Even if my body isn't back to full health, I've never felt better in all my damn life.

CHAPTER 15

WENDY *One Year Later*

"I can stare at them for hours," Hedwig says from beside me.

We made fresh lemonade and instead of bringing it over to the others, the two of us just stand on the deck, watching our husbands and our kids. They built the man cave they've talked about ever since we moved into the house. It actually looks like a tiny house all on its own, with a bathroom and a living room complete with a bar, flat screen TV, two large couches and a sound system.

It's where they go to watch any sports game or have a talk with other brothers for some club business they need to discuss or hell… they sometimes open up the sliding door and have a barbeque. Just the two of them while Hedwig and I have our own girl time. All while our kids are sleeping safely in their bed while we enjoy a movie or just talk.

Not in a million years did I think we would end up with two guys who grew up as brothers and good friends. We're all a tight and solid family that's grown stronger and bigger over time.

Ransom and Hedwig's son, Zander, is standing against his father's leg while his hands are up, his tiny fists clenching and unclenching reaching for Luna. Just a few months into our lives, Luna, our daughter, has stolen the hearts of all of us.

"Same here," I croak.

"I can't believe we're going to add to it, are you ready to tell our men?" Hedwig smiles and it immediately triggers a smile on my face too.

"Ready," I state and a flutter of excitement fills my veins.

Before we headed into the kitchen to make lemonade, we took turns going to the bathroom to pee on a stick and then switched so we could tell one another if we were pregnant or not. Turns out, the both of us are and it makes it even more special to share this with my best friend. And the scene we're staring at? Two brothers who grew up here and are clearly enjoying themselves along with their kids is extremely special to watch.

Strolling into the backyard, we place the lemonade and glasses on the table and join our husbands. Yes, not only is Casey my Old Man, he's also my husband. He managed to persuade me into wearing a wedding dress while I had a baby bump.

All worth it though because we did the whole double wedding thing and a huge wedding reception at the club. Some might say we spend way too much time together but the truth is, our lives are hectic as it is and we could go days without even seeing each other even if we live right next door.

Casey has his own company and has Calix as a partner so he can count on his brothers to assist if he needs help hunting down a perp or for a stakeout or whatever is needed for the cases he works on. I chose to work part time and assist him where I can too.

Hedwig also works part time and this gives us the freedom we need to spend time with our kids but it also has days like I mentioned where our schedule doesn't allow for us to sip coffee in the kitchen or have playdates for our kids. So, living next door to each other and having these moments in life we get to share together? Hell, yes, we're taking them and enjoy life to the fullest.

Even my brother spends time with us every now and then. Though Thorn is very busy with the club and running the legal businesses he's set up with his brothers. Gael's suicide mission with the attack on the club where Hedwig and others were injured and Hunter was killed is still branded on my brain and I think about it all the time. But then I see the warmth and peaceful moments we have now and I treasure them even more; thankful to have them.

"Hey, darlin'," Casey leans in, brushing a kiss on my lips. Luna is in his arms and she takes her chance when her tiny fists grab hold of my hair. Casey chuckles and helps get my hair loose.

"If she keeps this up you might have to go with another nickname because I'm gonna shave my head," I grumble, making Casey laugh even harder.

When my hair is freed, I take the hair tie from my wrist and twist my hair up into a messy bun to take our daughter into my arms. I connect my gaze with Hedwig and she's also holding her son as she stalks over to me.

Ransom elbows Casey. "I'm having a gut feeling our Old Ladies are up to something."

Casey narrows his eyes, "We just took three more cases, can't have the little getaway you girls asked for last week, it'll have to wait till next month."

Hedwig snorts, "What we have in mind can't wait and will last a lifetime."

Both Ransom and Casey's eyes widen and bulge when Hedwig and I say in sync, "We're pregnant."

Clearly, we both expect our husbands to come to us but instead they turn to face each other and high five one another, causing me to roll my eyes at their brotherly weirdness. But then they do turn to us and Casey wraps his arms around both me and Luna, inching his face close to the both of us.

"Best news ever. This makes me so fucking happy," he croaks and it makes my chest tighten with love. My eyes sting and if he doesn't let go soon, I'm sure I'll be a blubbering mess.

"Ouch," Casey gasps and when I check to see what's going on, I can't help but laugh instead of help him. Luna has buried her tiny fist in Casey's short hair and is pulling at it with all her strength.

We untangle and Ransom appears next to Casey, shoving his son in Casey's arms.

"Be right back," Ransom says and grabs Hedwig's hand and starts to drag her off toward their house.

"Hey," Casey snaps, "Not fair!"

"Be a good neighbor, brother, and watch the kid," Ransom chuckles while Hedwig's giggles drift through the air as they disappear into their house.

"Fine but you're watching ours next, so hurry up," Casey bellows, making me smack his arm.

"Hush," I tell him, my cheeks burning from embarrassment.

Casey steps closer and murmurs, "I love watching your face flush, exactly why I told them to hurry."

My body heats with desire. I quickly step away and put some distance between us. It's always like this with us, the strong connection of our fire, flaming with lust, tangled with love and desire. Never once does it fade or grow dull, it only expands and evolves into something deeper and more valuable.

Casey takes a seat in one of the garden chairs and bounces Zander softly on his knee. His eyes are connected with mine when he says, "I love you so fucking much."

My body tingles from his words and the anticipation grows of what's to come when Ransom and Hedwig come back to watch Luna for us so we can have our own time together.

"Love you right back, but Casey? Watch your mouth in front of the kids," I scold, making the corner of his mouth twitch.

"So, I can't start talking about all the ways I'm going to worship the place between your…"

"Casey, stop," I gasp, making his booming laughter fill the air.

This man. Not a dull moment and most definitely not a boring life. He challenges me, worships me at every turn, and the way he completes me and makes sure my whole life is filled with people to fall back on—with the family and friends we all need to build a life with—is more than I could ever wish for. Our life. One we will make sure to enjoy to the fullest.

EPILOGUE

CASEY
Twenty-one years later

"No, you cannot go out on a damn date," Zander growls in Luna's face.

Luna puts both her hands on his chest and he lets her push him away, "It's none of your business. If I want to go out, I'm going out."

"I'm not talking about going out, you're meeting the dude who asked you out this afternoon. While. I. Was. Standing. There. Next. To. You," he snaps.

Luna gives the brightest of smiles and she looks so much like her mother with the bouncing red curls and the feisty attitude as she crosses her arms in front of her chest and shrugs. "He asked, I had nothing planned, we're going out."

"He wants in, Luna," Zander shakes his head, anger painting his face.

Ransom is standing next to me. We're both leaning against the wall of the clubhouse while we're watching this play out. It's been a long time coming. Hedwig and Curls aren't moving a muscle either. They're leaning their heads on their hands while staring at them from across the room.

Zander was given full-patch status over an hour ago after being a prospect for a long time. Hence the reason this is playing out here in the main room of the clubhouse. Mainly because I think he feels more confident to have his brothers standing around. He's underestimating my daughter, though. She could care less whose ass she needs to kick to get her point across.

Both of them work for me in their spare time, and both of them take every case on together. These two have been inseparable but this head to head thing has only grown stronger over the last few years. Hormones. They both have them screaming through their bodies and either one...hell, both of them, need to step up or cut loose because this is getting worse.

"So what? Can't stay a virgin forever," Luna purrs and I put my hands over my own damn ears but just as easily let them fall away since it didn't help shit to protect my damn hearing.

"Didn't need to hear that," I mutter, making Ransom snicker beside me. "Oh, shut up, what if your daughter was the one stating it?" I throw at the man who now cringes. Yeah, thought so.

Ransom and I both have a daughter and a son—in fact, me and Curls have two sons—but our oldest kids are the ones who go head to head, and if they would just see what everyone else sees when it comes to them...then they'd realize they belong together. But no, denial or plainly dodging the subject. Hell, they might just like fighting for the hell of it, but this tension is sparking fire to combust at any second.

"Agreed," Zander hisses through clenched teeth.

Luna snorts, "Glad we finally agree to something."

When she's about to stalk past him, he grabs her hand, "Where do you think you're going?"

"Out, we just agreed, I thought that was very clear." Luna tells him with a 'duh' tone of voice.

"Motherfucker," Zander hisses and he spins her around and backs her into the wall behind her, caging her in.

Both Ransom and I curse and are ready to close the distance but Zander's words make us stop dead in our tracks. "You're mine, Lulu. Mine. Am I being clear now?" Zander's head turns and faces the room, "Lulu is my Old Lady, clear?"

"Finally," I hear Calix sigh from our left while cheers erupt all over.

Luna seems to snap out of the daze Zander's words put her in when she gasps, "You can't...you don't...you don't even want me...I...no,"

"Fuck, yes," Zander faces her again and leans close. "I've wanted you for as long as I can remember. Hell, from the time I could barely walk, I've wanted to pull you close and hold you."

"I can vouch for that," Ransom chuckles and it makes me snort, remembering all too well how Zander and Luna grew up closely together and from the time Zander could speak he called her Lulu and never used Luna, she has always been 'his Lulu'. I guess it only took this long for him to voice the words so she too understands how it was and how it always will be.

I glance over at my Old Lady and watch how a dreamy look washes over her face. Hedwig's got the same look and it makes me glance back at Zander and Luna who are now kissing. Also, not something I need to see.

"Get a fucking room," I growl, and freeze when the words I just stated enters my own ears. "Fuck. No. No, no."

Ransom chuckles and slaps my back, "You'd better get a room yourself since they're not moving."

Best advice ever. I speed walk toward my woman, snatch her up to throw her over my shoulder, and hightail out of the room at full speed.

"Oh, come on." Curls complaints against my back until she gasps as I slide her down my body.

We're standing in the backyard of the clubhouse. A couple of fire pits is giving us some cozy lighting but there's no one else here.

Curls grabs my cut and pulls me close. "Why did you do that?" She questions and leans in to bite my bottom lip.

It makes a growl rumble through my chest and I make sure to connect our lower bodies. "There comes a point in our kids' life I have to pull back and don't want to know. I've reached that point. Hell, call it me giving her private time...or me wanting my own private time."

I don't leave room for reply when I crash my mouth over hers. My tongue demands entry which she happily gives. I damn well love summertime with the soft breeze and the late warm evenings. Not to mention the easy access due to the summer dress she's wearing.

My hands go to her ass and easily lift her up, allowing her to wrap her legs around me. Leaning her back against the wall, I fumble between our bodies and though I love to fuck her against the wall, my balls start to tingle with the thought of smacking her fine ass and I can't if I'm holding her up.

She always pushes back harder and lets me fuck deeper when I take her from behind and for that reason alone, I let her slide down my body again. She starts to sputter but when I put my hands on her hips, twist her around to face the couch that's only a few feet away, she simply stalks over and lets me place a hand between her shoulder blades to push her slightly down...she hums and knows exactly what's coming.

I grab the hem of her dress and slide it up. Black. Lace. Thong. If my cock wasn't hard, it would be steel right fucking now. I wrap my fingers around the lace and with one rough yank it gives way and I've got the most gorgeous ass and pussy to my disposal.

Even if the lighting is dim from only the fire pits, it's clearly glistening for me as her arousal draws me in. Ultimate pleasure. One surge up when I've freed my cock and it's pure bliss for the both of us. Even after all these years. Even at our age. Even with kids who are just exploring the first steps of feelings and relationships. It's indescribable how a connection hits right from the start without an end date in sight.

Her moans spur me on to pound into her more fiercely. My hand gripping her hip leaves for only a moment to smack her ass cheek, making her moan loudly as she pushes back on my cock at full force. I know I won't be able to last long but it doesn't matter because my woman is grabbing my cock in rapid waves while my name is screamed through the backyard.

Cum shoots out my cock at full force and I hold her steady as I let the orgasm overtake me. I slump forward and huff and puff as an old man needing to catch his breath. Fuck. I'm getting old.

"Aw, gross," our daughter's voice gasps out from behind us.

"You can say that again," Zander mutters. "I don't need to have your dad's naked ass burned into my corneas."

I'm about to curse them out over my shoulder but the door already slams shut behind them as they've made their escape back into the clubhouse.

"Fucking kids," I growl. "We're never getting rid of them, no matter how old they get. Cock block at any age."

Curls giggles underneath me and it makes me slide out of her. Pushing up, I grab the hem of her dress and cover her ass before I smack it.

I'm tucking my cock back into my pants when I say, "Wanna head over to the clubhouse of Thorns 'n' Bones MC?"

"Lars and Axel?" Curls asks while rubbing her ass cheek, making me smirk as I pull her close.

"They're on a run, won't be back until tomorrow," I tell her.

Both our sons are members of Thorns 'n' Bones MC, making their uncle—and the both of us—proud as fuck. Because in the end, Thorn lived up to be one damn fine Prez who faced hell with his MC but made sure nothing will ever come between him and his brothers. All of them have the same mindset, loyalty, and respect.

"Or..." Curls purrs, "We could head home and lock ourselves in the bedroom."

"Smart woman," I counter and lean in to whisper, "Since the cum is still leaking out of your pussy I might as well take your ass."

How I hate the dimmed lights because I know for damn sure her whole face flushes. Still, after all these years I'm able to make her flush as she can make my chest tighten with the love I hold for her and the sweet anticipation of having her underneath me again.

Even if I just had her a few breaths ago, I won't ever get enough of her. One life time doesn't seem enough but it's worth to take every second and make it count. I lace my fingers with hers and take her with me to continue to enjoy our lives to the fullest.

AF MC OHIO

AF MC · OHIO
──── BOOK THREE ────

One nameless encounter six years ago leaves both C.Rash and Magnolia with scorching memories. After all these years they both would like to find the one they shared a one-night stand with, though both for different reasons.

Memories can either haunt you or give you the strength to hold on and pull yourself through dark moments. Magnolia experienced both. The ones who gave her strength involve the rugged biker who comes back into her life to face the danger returning to torment her.

Christmas is a time to come together, to love, to share heartwarming gifts, and to make new memories. Yet everything is at risk when danger from the past threatens to take away everything.

AF MC Ohio (Book Three) is a complete standalone, second chance romance novella with an HEA, no cheating, and no cliffhanger.

AF MC OHIO

CHAPTER 01

C.RASH

Those who have sisters know how much of a pain in the ass they can be. I love them, don't get me wrong, but sometimes they just ramble and nag until I give in. And yes, I always give in, since, you know…they're my sisters.

Yesterday my younger sister Darby called me out of the blue and when I picked up she squeaked my name and told me not to freak out. Yeah, say something like that and I'm as calm as a fucking tornado. Right after there was a rustling, as if she held the phone to her chest because someone else dragged her into a discussion she needed to deal with first. Then she came back on the phone a few breaths later.

It was weird to say the least and I was heading for my bike the next instant. But her tone suddenly changed and she said not to worry, that it was all a misunderstanding and she would call me later to explain everything.

She did and strangely enough the phone call wasn't about her, it was about Magnolia, one of her friends, who needed help. Darby hadn't seen her friend in years but ran into her, and Darby demanded I should be the one to help Magnolia.

Fact is, I had nothing to do anyway. It's a week before Christmas and everyone is either off shopping, decorating, making dinner plans, or doing fuck-knows-jolly-what with their kids. I'm the VP of AF MC Ohio and even the clubhouse looks like Santa himself shit all over the damn place. So, yeah, I'm all for helping one of Darby's friends to drag me away from Christmas freaking-jolly-ness.

I've met a few of Darby's friends. Hell, I'm not ashamed to say that over the years, I picked up one or two. Don't judge, it's hard enough growing up with sisters I need to protect, so I earn some benefits in return. At least that's how I see it.

There was this one girl…yeah, not going down that road…let's just say I had a magnificent one-night-stand—I might have fucked-up a tiny bit—but she left my bed before I could get her number.

And I needed a way to contact her because of my fuck-up but like I said, she was gone when I woke up. And still, until this day I still regret the fact I never heard from her again. I always considered her "The one that got away." I've told all my brothers the story countless times.

But I sure as fuck didn't mention it to Darby. I'd rather not face her wrath and I figured the hint of running from my bed was enough of a statement not to pursue the girl. Not to mention the fact I didn't even knew her name because we might have just thrown ourselves at each other for carnal reasons.

Oh, and I wasn't even sure if she was one of my sister's friends in the first place, because it was during a neighborhood holiday party thing Darby organized. Imagine that awkwardness of me describing the girl to my sister and why I need her number. Yeah, no. I repeat, she's the one that got away.

Anyway, my sister's friend, Magnolia—the one she called me about—needs help. Unless it's club business, I wouldn't normally mess with other people's problems. But, needless to say, my sister asking me something for a friend of hers isn't club related.

Though, this friend? Years back Darby told me what happened to her. Hell, back then I didn't even know who this friend was, nothing. Just the shit that happened to her since Darby asked me to keep my ear to the ground because the cops had no lead on who did this to her.

Magnolia was kidnapped, held hostage for three damn weeks. She was beaten and left for dead alongside of the road. Darby lost touch with her a few years ago since Magnolia moved and she just ran into her again at the grocery store.

Magnolia mentioned they never caught the guy who did it and how he's still been tormenting her over the years and still the cops can't do shit. Plus, the woman seems to have a kid and is living alone, scared out of her mind about this fucked-up situation she's still in. Reason enough for me to help out.

I glance at my phone, looking up Darby's text to double check Magnolia's address. Yeah, this is the place all right. The street doesn't look high-class but it seems nice and friendly. Most of the houses have their Christmas lights up and number nine, the one my sisters told me to go to, has a large deer silhouette wrapped with multicolored lights.

I park my bike and grab my backpack from my saddle bags. It holds a few changes of clothes and some other stuff I need to stay here for the next couple of days. I have another bag with my laptop and some other technical stuff since I'm installing cameras around Magnolia's house tomorrow morning to keep an eye on things.

It's been six years since she was left for dead alongside of the road. She's scared of what the fucker is going to do this time since he comes back around the same time every year and leaves twisted messages. I'm not sure about every single detail, only the birds my sister mentioned. Along with something else I thought was weird. Something about me not being allowed to become angry and to let Magnolia explain. Whatever that means.

Maybe it has something to do with the fact this fucker seems to come back each time around Christmas. No matter where she lives or where she hides, he finds her. The asshole leaves dead birds with their heads ripped off as some kind of message for her. I try to ring the bell but there's no sound. I'm about to knock but the door swings open and a tiny as shit woman is standing there. A tiny as shit woman I instantly recognize.

"Sorry," she whispers. "Joshua is sleeping."

I swallow hard and blurt, "You left my bed without a word."

Her eyes widen and she nods warily. "I didn't think you remembered that night. Can you come inside, please? I don't want to be standing in the doorway when I explain everything."

She steps away and I go inside, locking the door behind me. I follow her into the living room and I have to place my two bags on the floor because she's holding up a picture for me to take.

I take it but don't give it a glance, because for real, "Back then…I wanted you to stay, but you left and I didn't even know your name. Hell, I didn't even know if you were a friend of my sister's so I couldn't ask Darby."

Her eyes hit the floor. "I had to leave early that day because my parents were going on a trip and I needed to house sit. I was supposed to swing by that holiday party for only a few minutes...but then you happened, and...well, obviously I didn't plan for any of it to happen the way it did. And I had the same problem, I didn't know you were Darby's brother. Not until today when Joshua and I ran into her at the grocery store. We hadn't talked in years, which was my fault because I moved and cut everyone out of my life after what happened six years ago. But, if I had known you were her brother, I would have contacted her to let you know sooner. I didn't mean—"

Somehow her words soothe me. Stupid, I know, but when a hot woman leaves your bed without a second glance it kinda bruises one's ego.

"Hey." I reach out and grab her upper arm to give it a soft squeeze. "I understand, it's no big deal."

"It is," she whispers. "Look at the picture. I'm sure you'll regret what you just said, but do remember I didn't plan any of it, and I would have told you if I knew who you were or how to contact you. I mean...I also went back to the motel but...yeah, let's just say that didn't help."

The corner of my mouth twitches. "I paid cash, and the motel we picked isn't very well known for keeping their administration up to date."

"I'm sorry," she says as she grabs my hand and guides it up, making my eyes land on the picture I'm holding. "When they eventually found me alongside of the road I was taken to the hospital. After all the tests and exams they told me I was pregnant. The timeline pinpoints back to our night. I couldn't...I didn't want...he's been the only good thing in my life. I wish I had a way to contact you sooner, I would have."

It's as if I'm holding a picture my mom took of me when I was about five years old. Except...it's not me. It is me. But it's not. Fuck. Reality comes crashing down as realization sets in. I stumble back and manage to place my ass on the armrest of the couch. My head starts to spin. I have a kid? A fucking kid?

"I'm so sorry," she croaks, making my head whip up.

"Stop saying that," I snap and rub my eyes. "Dammit, I don't mean to snap at you but it's not your fault. It's…fucked-up to say the least. Shit. Fucked-up. I did. If anything, this is all my fault. The second time we fucked I didn't put on a condom. I forgot. I should have said something, but the way we ravished each other that night? Yeah, I'd say there wasn't any time to put it on but I should have. So, I'm the one who's sorry."

She gasps and it makes my head swing her way. "You wiped away your stuff to hide the fact we didn't use protection?" A low growl rumbles through her chest and she starts to pace back and forth. "If you had said something, I would have asked for your number. Or left mine, whatever. I would have made sure I had some way to contact you. I can't believe I bought that shit you said about cleaning up the taste of rubber so you could eat my pussy."

A noise has both of us swinging around as both our eyes land on a little boy standing in the doorway. His eyes are wide and he points a finger at me. "Mom?" His voice is shaky and his eyes start to water. "Is this man going to eat Ketchup?"

Ketchup?

The little kid runs around me and I watch how he drags a black cat from its peaceful sleep as he quickly backs away from me.

"For fuck's sake," I grumble, making Magnolia glare at me, probably due to my cursing but for crying out loud, how is this insanity my reality? Talk about some fucked-up secret Santa shit.

CHAPTER 02

MAGNOLIA

Oh. Come on. How can this day go from bad to worse to insane? Damage control. I need to compartmentalize. Joshua first. I open my mouth to say something but I'm prevented from doing so because there's suddenly a broad back in front of me.

"Hey, kiddo. Everything is okay, all right? This is your cat? Did you give him the name Ketchup?" I stare at the man who's now crouched down in front of my son.

Shit. I swallow hard. Our son. There's not a single day that goes by where I don't think about leaving this man's bed that day. He absolutely gave me the night of my life and it's also safe to say I used his memory to pull me through some dark times in my life.

"You're not going to eat him?" Joshua says as he turns slightly but still holds Ketchup away from him.

Ketchup starts to squirm and jumps out of his hands and onto the floor as he runs into the hallway. Probably heading upstairs to find a nice quiet place to finish his nap.

"I don't eat kittens, pussies, cats, whatever. Seriously. I don't." He sounds desperate and suddenly blurts, "I'm a vegetarian. I don't eat meat." He looks back at me for help.

If this moment wasn't so messed up, I would laugh. I hold out my hand for Joshua to take. "Come on, sweetie, let's make you a cup of hot cocoa. Okay?"

Joshua takes my hand and we stroll toward the kitchen, almost there he digs his heels in and glances back.

He's eyeing Darby's brother and I'm still not sure what to call him. Other than the father of my child. Ugh. Darby said his name is Easton, but he doesn't use it because he's a biker and everyone calls him C.Rash. I have no clue why or if it's short for something.

Like I said, I have no clue what to call him or know anything else about this man. Other than he's a-freaking-amazing in bed and the night we met was mostly driven on both our animal instinct. When he mentioned there was no time to put a condom on the second time I did understand. We had sex four times and spent hours enjoying each other's bodies. I crashed into a deep sleep and woke up late and had to rush out to meet my parents in time.

"Would you mind joining us in the kitchen? I'm pretty sure Joshua is digging his heels in because he needs to keep an eye on you so you don't rush upstairs."

"I'm not eating the f—" He stands up and rubs his neck. "Fine. But, can I have some hot cocoa too?"

I glance down at Joshua and I raise my eyebrow. It's something I always ask Joshua myself, and he always gives me the same reply. I'm hoping he does the same thing now because I kinda need it to break the ice between them.

"I don't know," I say as I tap my chin and direct my question at Joshua. "Can he?"

Joshua crosses his arms in front of his chest. "I'm not sharing my cookie."

"Well," I say, and can't help to keep the laughter out of my voice when I connect my gaze with the father of my child. "I'm not letting him eat my cookie either."

A deep sigh rips from his chest and he shakes his head. I swear I thought I saw a smile tugging his lips. "Just some hot cocoa is fine." He stops heading our way and holds up his finger. "I'm just gonna make a quick call first, okay? I'll be right there."

Panic starts to flare up. What if he's calling a lawyer? Or his buddies from that motorcycle club he's in, so they all come here to help him take Joshua away from me. Would he do that? Oh, shit.

I glance down at Joshua. "Can you please head into the kitchen and grab the cookies for me? I'll be right there to fix us some hot cocoa, okay?"

He nods and heads into the kitchen without a word. I'm pretty sure he's going to stuff a cookie into his mouth, but right now I have other problems to deal with.

Stepping closer, I lower my voice to a mere whisper. "Are you going to take him away from me?"

His head rears back as if I slapped him. "What? No. Why would you...? Ah, me mentioning calling someone freaked you out. Listen," he says and releases another deep sigh. "To say I'm shocked, surprised...hell, I don't even know what to say, how I feel, or how to react. Before you told me about the kid, you and I agreed, we should have handled the morning after we met differently. Clearly, we need to stop looking back and look forward. I don't know what to do right now or how to handle anything. I just found out that little man—whose first impression of me is one where he thinks I'm gonna eat his damn cat—is my son. I'm his father. I—"

"That's my Daddy?" Joshua says with a mouthful of cookie.

"Motherfucker," Easton mutters underneath his breath as he glances at me. "The little dude has impeccable timing. I...what...I...a little help here," he croaks.

I glance at Joshua and realize I need to know something first. Stepping closer to Easton, I lean in and whisper, "You have two choices here, either you want him in your life or not. Right now, I need an answer."

A hard look slides over his face. "He's mine and I never turn my back on my responsibilities."

I give a tight nod and feel my heart start to beat again. Dammit, it's as if my whole life depended on this man's answer.

"Thank you," I tell him and I have to swallow at the emotions clogging my throat. I rush out my words on a mere whisper. "He knows he has a daddy who loves him. And this sounds weird, but I always mentioned to him how I lost his daddy and didn't know where he was and how his daddy didn't know where we were either. It might not have been one of my best choices or wrong of me but lying didn't feel good either. And I gave him presents from his daddy for each birthday and so on."

Easton nods. "Thank you. And I guess it sounds weird, though it was the truth."

Joshua is now standing next to me and is pulling my shirt. "Mommy? Did you finally find Daddy?" The hope in his voice is killing me and makes my eyes sting. "Santa helped, didn't he? Yes, he must have." His gaze hits Easton and uncertainty washes over his face, making him step closer to me and suddenly he's shy and wants to hide behind me.

Easton squats down. "Maybe Santa did have something to do with it, but it doesn't matter, because I found you, buddy. They say you don't miss something until you find it...but it sounds like you missed your daddy. If only I knew—" He chokes up and slams a hand over his face, covering his eyes as he starts to rub furiously.

"Mommy?" Joshua pulls my sweater. "Daddy needs hot cocoa. And you need to share your cookie, because I'm not sharing mine."

Easton snorts a laugh. I furiously blink my tears away and can only nod as I let my hand slide over Joshua's hair. He's staring at Easton and is now giving him a whole different look. As if he's taking him in and seeing him through different eyes.

"Can you play baseball?" Joshua blurts before he starts to rattle, "Danny's dad plays baseball with him when he gets home from work. Mommy can't throw a ball and catching one always goes wrong too. Can you?"

I clear my throat. "Okay, sweetie, there's enough time to talk about any of this tomorrow. Let's get into the kitchen and make some hot cocoa so we can all calm down while we eat a cookie. I'm sure he will answer some of your questions and then it's time to brush your teeth and get into bed to get some sleep."

He takes a step into the direction of the kitchen but turns to Easton. "You're going to stay, right? Or you might get lost again and Mommy couldn't find you for a very long time when she lost you the first time."

Oh, my damn heart. Tears are now freely falling down my face. Dammit. I should stay tough for Joshua and yet I don't have an answer to give him.

Easton steps in front of me and squats down to Joshua's level as he points at his bags. "See that, buddy? I'm going to be here when you wake up."

Joshua's eyes slide to the bags and happiness spreads his face. "Okay," he says and runs off into the kitchen.

Easton turns to me and my body fills with emotions, thoughts, everything is a blur and yet I do know one thing for sure. "You're welcome to stay as long as you like. But please, don't confuse him. I know you said you never turn your back on responsibilities, but Joshua is more than that. He's—"

He leans into my personal space and my breath catches as my lungs fill with his scent, making memories from the night we shared together many years ago rush back. Great. Add it to the many things I can't deal with right now.

"I know," he says in a low voice. "I might not have been a father, but many of my brothers have kids. I've seen and been around them to know what having a kid entails. Just give me a moment to breathe and to let my mind catch up. We need to talk and I am taking you up on the offer to stay. Even if I…wait. This thing Darby mentioned, about that fucker who did that to you years ago, how he's still tormenting you by coming back each year. Please tell me it was all a scam to get me here, 'cause if it's not, I have to take other precautions since my mind is all over the place now."

Fear slams through me. Dammit, I'm such a mess. I swallow hard. "I wish it was."

"Fuck," he snaps and it makes me flinch. "Shit. Sorry. Dammit. I guess I have to watch my language from now on. Listen. I need to make a phone call, okay? Like I said, I'm not going anywhere. Then I'll come into the kitchen and we'll drink some hot cocoa with the kid. Our kid. Holy fuck. Our kid. Yeah. This is gonna take some getting used to." He rubs a hand over his neck. "I also need to install some security cameras around the house, but that might have to wait till morning. I want eyes on this place. I would take you guys out of here, but my sister mentioned the fucker returns every year around the same time. I want to catch him; this needs to end and it will end now."

I nod warily. I've heard this a few times over the years, either from the cops, or from the private investigator my parents hired. No one seems to be able to end this ongoing nightmare. I lived through it, thought I was saved, and heard nothing until exactly a year later when the headless birds started to show up.

Easton snorts. "I can see you don't believe me. Doesn't matter, you're bound to find out what kind of man the father of your son is."

CHAPTER 03

C.RASH

I watch the woman—whose sinful memories popped into my head more than a few times over the years—disappear into the kitchen. I have to take a few deep breaths to let the fact sink in I'm now tied to her by blood. Have been for years, dammit. Neither of us knew how to contact one another and yet faith made it possible for us to reconnect.

Damn. If my sister hadn't run into her today, I still would be oblivious to the fact I have a son. I shoot a text Darby's way to thank her for getting my ass here or I wouldn't have known I had a son. My phone instantly dings with a reply.

DARBY:
I was shocked when I saw Joshua. He looks so much like you. Easton, I swear Magnolia didn't know who you were. I saw the relief on her face when I bluntly asked her if Joshua could be my brother's kid. I showed her a picture of you and she told me what happened that night you two met. I'm here if you need me. Call me!

I text her a quick reply in return to let her know I'm dealing with everything right now and promise to call soon. How fast can things take a damn turn? When I woke up this morning, I was having a hard time deciding what to do today and yet here I am, no longer alone but suddenly connected to a tiny person who is half of my DNA.

I wait for the panic and turmoil to flare inside my head and yet it all settles. Pretty sure it also has something to do with the fact his mother is Magnolia, the one chick who managed to burn sweet memories into my brain, even if it was one damn night we spent together. I can do this. I've seen my brothers and their old ladies grow tight and raise their kids.

I know for sure they all have my back, and from what Magnolia said and the impression she gives me…she's open to have me in her life to be there for her son. My son. Our son. Dammit. Seriously, this will take some getting used to. I reach for my phone and without thinking call one of my brothers who I know would understand.

"Hang on," Pokey barks into the phone and I hear rustling and then a few doors slam before his voice is back. "I can't tell you how glad I am you're calling, pulling me out of a discussion with my old lady and kid. Well, not so much of a discussion, mainly my old lady reprimanding our oldest. And for fucking real, man…don't ever have kids. Adopt grown-ass people if you get affectionate. Me for instance. Adopt my old ass, I could use an escape. Because teenagers? I think I'd rather swim in a tank filled with sharks while sticking myself with a fork, because take it from me, the adrenaline spike for survival is fairly the same."

The nonsense falling from this guy's mouth is something that always makes me snort and yet this is something that hits the nail on the head about my reason for calling.

"Too late, man. I just found out I'm the father of a five-year-old," I tell him and only silence greets me.

"Mind running that by me again? Because with what you just said, I'm fairly sure you got a head start in becoming a daddy and you kinda missed the boat for the first five years," Pokey states and his voice is tainted with a hint of shock before there's some anger sliding in when he says, "Or did some bitch come knocking on your door, demanding money or some shit? Then you need to take distance first and demand a DNA test, 'cause there are some women out there trying to grab you by the dick and squeeze for some easy money."

"Did I ever tell you about the one that got away?" I ask, knowing very well I did.

There have been a few times over the years where some drunk discussions turned into talks about "the hottest piece of ass" or "the one that got away." I would always bring up the nameless one, 'cause she was the perfect package. Well, she's not so nameless now.

"You're talking about the 'oops I forgot the condom but if I don't tell it didn't happen' one? Well," Pokey snorts. "I'd gather she won't be getting away now, right? With the kid you just mentioned. And fuck, man. Why didn't she say anything? Why now? Wait. You didn't know who she was…did that mean she didn't know who you were either? You're talking about the night you went to your sister's neighborhood holiday party and had the best pussy ever, right? I mean, you've told the story more than a handful of times. That's the only reason I remember."

"Yeah," I can only answer in reply before I add, "Neither of us knew anything about each other. So damn stupid but it wasn't like we exchanged more than a handful of words, it was more like instant lust and the both of us acting on pure instinct. My sister stumbled into her at the grocery store today. Joshua looks exactly like me, that's how Darby knew he had to be my kid. She bluntly threw the question at Magnolia and showed her my picture."

There's more silence before Pokey says, "What do you want, now that you know? Because all I can tell you is to listen to your heart and follow your gut instinct along with it. I did, and look where I am now. And fuck, forget what I said about the sharks and sticking a fork in me. As a parent you will know what it's like to love the shit out of your kids while voluntarily letting them pull out your fingernails, because that's what family is all about, man. The whole love hard, fight dirty, and reap sweet victory for the rest of your life. Completion shit, that's what I'm talking about. But I stumbled onto my kid when he was a mere baby, you're skipping the whole diaper phase. I probably shouldn't have reminded you. Damn. I'm talking too much. Like I said…what do you want, man?"

His words tumble over me and again I wait for the panic and turmoil to flare inside my head but still it doesn't hit. Being a father, and to have these added responsibilities, doesn't scare me.

"I want it all, Pokey," I tell him with determination. "I can't turn my back on either one now that I know she wanted to reach me. It's all so damn easy to explain and then add all the fucked-up circumstances

...talking about the fucked-up circumstances...exactly six years ago something happened to her, about three weeks after we met, and this fucker who hurt her seems to return every year around the same time. I need him found and handled because six years ago? He kidnapped the mother of my kid, held her hostage for three weeks, beat her and left her for dead alongside of the road."

"You need me, I'll get on my damn bike right now. I will always have your back, whatever you need," Pokey growls.

"I know, brother." I let the pride and thankfulness I feel shimmer through my voice. "I'm gonna put up a security system bright and early tomorrow morning, and I talked to Casey and Calix before I got here. Casey is going to have his contacts at the FBI look into her case."

"Good. If there's anything we can do, call." His tone is fierce and I know he will be there for me in a heartbeat.

I might have switched chapters years ago but we never cut ties. Calix and I were both a part of Areion Fury MC where Zack is the president. All before Calix and I switched to AF MC Ohio, and Calix became the president while I became his VP. Like Pokey just mentioned, we're still brothers; we're there for each other no matter what.

"Will do. And thanks, man," I tell him and hear him grunt before he hangs up.

I stare at my phone for a few heartbeats before I tuck it away. Things might still be all scrambled and up in the air, but I feel like my talk with Pokey made me realize everything can work out as long as you fight for what you want and are straightforward with it. And I sure as fuck want this. Even if I didn't plan any of it or never so much as thought of wanting kids in my future. He's here. He's mine, no doubt about it, so I am damn well going to live up to the things life throws in my path.

I stalk into the kitchen and watch how Magnolia places a steaming cup in front of her while there's already one in front of Joshua. The look she gives him is all love and devotion. To think this woman faced everything all those years on her own is unbelievable. Not to mention the shit she went through, and the fucker is still out there tormenting her.

And it's also hard to believe the things that fucker did to her when that boy just took root inside her belly. For fuck's sake...she could have lost the baby without even realizing she was pregnant. Then I wouldn't be standing here looking in on this intimate mother and son moment. Fuck. I rub my sternum and try to shove the feelings rising inside me down. I need to focus on the now and keep them safe. I clear my throat and both their gazes swing my way. "Did you make me a cup?"

Magnolia gives me a shy smile and turns to grab a steaming mug from the counter to place in front of me.

Joshua jumps off his chair and breaks his cookie in front of me, crumbles all over, as he holds out his hand. The corner of my mouth twitches and I try to cup my hands and catch all the crumbs but I'm sure some will end up on the floor anyway.

There's a huge smile on the kid's face when I take a bite of the chocolate chip cookie, and I have to say, "This is amazing. Where did you buy them?"

"I made it," Joshua says and I'm pretty sure his cheeks are hurting from grinning so damn big. "With a little help from Mom."

"Thanks for sharing with me, kid," I tell him and grab the mug, blowing over the hot cocoa as I watch Magnolia over the rim.

Her face is exactly how I remembered her all those years ago. Delicate, oval-shaped with piercing eyes and plump, strawberry lips. Except for the tiny faded scars I now notice as I let my gaze travel over her features. The longest one slides from her chin down to her throat and I quickly admire her hair because anger flares when I see those scars. It makes me feel as if I failed her. Nonsense, I know, but still.

Her hair was darker back then, and her eyebrows are still the same color and yet her hair is dyed different shiny shades of gray. It dances around her shoulders as she wipes the counter. I remember how good she felt in my arms but she was a bit slender back then. Still a magnificent ass, though. I've always been an ass man and it seems this woman tipped the balance of awesomeness on the curvy scale.

A cloth hits my chest and I glance down at it and back to Mags. Mags. I don't know why my mind came up with the short version of her name but I'm liking it. She raises an eyebrow and it's then I realize I was absolutely picturing her naked and remembering every minute of what my tongue, fingers, mouth, dick…dammit, I need to focus, there's a kid in the room. A kid we made the last time I was balls deep inside her.

Yeah, it seems this woman is still branded into my brain, even if it was years ago. Pokey's words come to mind again; what do you want? And I know for damn sure…I do want it all. I've wanted this woman when I first laid eyes on her, and I got her into my bed...regretting every second she walked out and not knowing who, or where she was. I'm not making the same mistake again. I'm grabbing hold and not going to give her an option to slip out of my life this time.

CHAPTER 04

MAGNOLIA

I clear my throat. "Okay, little man, time for bed."

I can see the panic in his eyes and I know the reason why. I'm about to say something but Easton beats me to it.

"I'm gonna be right here, little man. And now that you shared your cookie with me, and knowing you're the one who made them, I'm not going anywhere. You're gonna make me some new ones tomorrow, right?"

Again, Joshua's face lights up. He's not one to be very shy but he's also not a kid to open up to anyone instantly. Of course, it might have helped that I always told him his daddy was out there looking for us, just as I was looking for him.

I know it's insane and probably not one of my smartest ideas but I couldn't lie to my kid, I had to tell him something. In the end it was the truth. The both of us did want to reach the other. It might have been for different reasons, I'm sure, but still.

Joshua rushes up the stairs and as I pass Easton, I mutter, "Stop looking at me like that."

His head tilts. "Like what?" A smirk slides on his face and I don't have to say another word because he damn well knows what I'm talking about.

I shake my head and head up the stairs to make sure Joshua brushes his teeth before bed. After he's all snuggled in, I give him a goodnight kiss and reassure him yet again how Easton will still be here when he gets up. I do hope he will be and I'm a bit scared as I make my way downstairs.

We still have a lot to talk about and it seems he takes everything very well, but I also don't know what he has in mind for the future. How much he would like to be involved in Joshua's life. I don't even know if he has a girlfriend. A wife. Other kids. There's so much more to consider if there are others involved. My heart squeezes at the thought of someone else living with this man and yet I know it's none of my business. Joshua is who's important.

"All tucked in?" Easton says as I stroll back into the kitchen.

"Yes," I mutter and grab the mugs from the table to put them in the sink. I turn to face him and place my hand on the table. "Is it Easton, C.Rash, or something else? What do I call you?"

The corner of his mouth twitches. "We're doing the whole name thing? All while we have a five-year-old kid together? Kinda funny when you think about it, huh?"

"Believe me, when I walked out of that motel room and the door fell shut behind me, I did realize the very next second I should have left my number. But I couldn't leave it in front of the door or at the desk. I was in a hurry, I overslept…nothing about that evening was planned."

He reaches out and covers his hand with mine. "I don't regret one single moment. Well, maybe falling asleep, 'cause I should have prevented you from slipping out of my bed. Oh, and I should have—"

I slide my hand away from underneath his and lightly smack his forearm. "Believe me, the whole 'should have' thing? It's overused. And it doesn't change anything. We're here now and you telling me this means a lot. Now we need to move forward and you have to realize the boy sleeping upstairs is, and will always be, my first priority. And you looking at me the way you did before I put him to bed isn't really helping when we need to focus on Joshua."

"Why not? Do you have a boyfriend?" he suddenly snaps. "An ex-husband or someone on the side in your life?"

My eyebrows scrunch up. "What does that have to do with

anything? And it's not like I owe you anything, but really? Do you think after everything I went through I'd open up to a relationship of any kind? It took me weeks to comprehend everything that happened. I don't know where I would be in my life if it wasn't for Joshua. I had all those months to mentally heal from what that nutcase put me through. The outer scars are only a visible reminder, the ones on the inside still give me nightmares from time to time but Joshua gave me a purpose, love, something unconditional. It's also why I won't ever regret what happened between us. Well, obviously the part where I was stupid enough not to give you my name or ask yours."

"Easton," he roughly says. "C.Rash is what all my brothers call me, but I want this between us to be more…personal." He lets his fingers slide through his hair. "C.Rash is the nickname I earned when I was a prospect with Areion Fury MC. It's short for carpet rash. At the time I was ordered to take care of three brothers that had passed out in the hallway of a hotel. Found them bare ass and drunk with two girls who were still trying to get some action from them. I put the girls in a cab, dragged the guys by their hands into the room one by one. Let's just say those three brothers all had their butts looking the same; flaming red due to the carpet rash. But like I said, you, me and Joshua…I would like it if you used Easton when we're together. Use C.Rash if you're talking to my brothers, 'cause they know me by my nickname. But in the end…it's your choice. I answer to either one, though over the years not many call me Easton anymore."

I give him a smile, and realize we also need to know something else since it's not just us two. "And Joshua? What would you like him to call you?"

He places his forearms on the table and leans in. "I think that's up to the little man. You've told him he has a father; he is now aware it's me. Don't bring it up and let's see how he handles everything himself, okay? All of this is hard enough, let's not complicate matters."

"Okay," I croak. "I think I need some coffee. You?"

His smile is warm as he gives me a nod. There's a loud thump followed by another one and it sounds like something hit the window, twice.

"Stay here," Easton grunts and jogs out of the kitchen.

My eyes slide in the direction of the stairs and I fight the urge to check on Joshua. He's safely in bed. For the first time in years I'm not as scared as I used to be. For the first time I'm not alone with my son.

And hopefully, this will be the time when fear stops running my life completely.

I hear Easton's voice rumble from the living room. It takes a moment before he steps into the kitchen, his phone glued to his ear as his eyes are locked on mine. "I want a prospect keeping watch to be sure, though I don't think he'll show his face again tonight, but I want an extra pair of eyes and hands here if I need it. Okay. Good. Talk tomorrow."

He ends the call and slides his phone into the front pocket of his jeans.

"Two dead birds. Do you have something I can clean the window with? I don't want Joshua waking up tomorrow morning to see anything smudging the window. And I want those birds checked out as evidence too."

I nod warily. "I can do it, no worries."

He's in front of me cupping my face the next instant. "Hey. I didn't ask you to do it. I asked for cleaning stuff, and some Ziploc bags, because I'm handling it. I know you've been on your own for years. And Calix, my president, just gave me an update on the background I asked about your case. I know a private investigator has researched the case, and I know the kind of limitations the cops have. But you have to understand…we work differently. I'll explain the dynamics of our MC at a later point, but just know I'm the VP of AF MC Ohio and have a whole motorcycle club backing me up. Calix is a retired detective and one of my brothers used to be FBI. What I'm trying to tell you is…I am going to fix this, okay?"

"I know, but you have to understand how many times I've heard people voice they are going to fix it. How they are going to find him." I swallow hard and realize, "But I also know this time it's different."

He gives me a tight nod. "I was heading here tonight as a favor for my sister. I would have been there for you like I am now, though you're right when you say it's different. That little man sleeping up there is linked with me and tied to you. This?" His finger is going back and forth between us, indicating him and me. "Might not have been settled, and what I'm about to say to you might scare you and sound insane, but you're the mother of my kid. The both of you are mine to protect, and not because of some request or some shit. And I have more than one MC at my back. I swear to you this fucker tormenting you is going to be dealt with."

I don't trust my own voice and can only nod while my eyes spill over and a stray tear slides over my cheek.

"Fuck," he snaps and wraps his arms around my waist to drag me against him.

"I'm not alone anymore," I whisper out the words, mainly to myself.

AF MC OHIO

CHAPTER 05

C.RASH

I'm not alone anymore. The mere whisper of words slides through my damn heart and makes all different kinds of emotions pour out. The need to protect and comfort her is sky high. This woman has faced so much shit on her own and had to keep herself standing and raise a little boy along with it.

"Never again," I vow. "I'm right here, Mags. I swear you'll never have to face anything alone again."

Her arms tighten around me and this time satisfaction flows through me. She accepts my words. And I know trust takes time, but the way we connected when we first met shows we're compatible on many levels. I mean, we have a kid to prove our bodies bonded.

The reminder of Pokey's words and how he too managed to fix things with his old lady and have been together many years since… everything gives me the reassurance I can do this. I want this. I fucking need this. And I will make it right. Even if no one is to blame for missing out on both of their lives; I need to do this for all of us.

I place a kiss on the top of her head and pull her slightly away from my body. "Can you fix us some coffee while I deal with the mess outside?"

She nods and wipes her face with the back of her hand. "Yeah, sure. I can do that."

"And I'm gonna need one of those damn cookies if you have one left," I tell her and get the result I was going for when she snorts a laugh.

She points at a cabinet and says, "Cleaning stuff is in there. I'll have coffee and a cookie waiting for you."

"Thanks, Mags."

Her eyebrows scrunch up adorably and she grumbles, "That's twice you called me Mags. People never call me Mags. Mag…maybe my mother every now and then, never Mags."

I shrug and simply say, "I like it." I head for the door and throw over my shoulder, "Don't forget about the cookie, Mags."

The soft snort that fills the air makes the corner of my mouth twitch. Yeah, she's a fighter all right. Everything she went through screams she's a strong woman. I remember my mother being one, my sisters too. Not to mention all of the old ladies my brothers have. Though, I also remember very vividly how everyone has their breaking point. And for damn sure I won't allow for it to happen to her. I will have her back, whatever comes our way.

It takes some time to safely tuck away the dead birds and then clean the window. I try to search for some footprints with the help of a flashlight but I don't see anything. I wish I would have got here sooner; I would have installed the security system along with the cameras. I guess I'm going to wake up at the crack of dawn to get it done; I need eyes everywhere to nail this fucker.

My phone rings when I'm finishing up and I see it's Casey. "Hey, any news?"

"I'm at the door, want to let me in or are we discussing this on the porch?" Casey says and it surprises me to hear he's here.

I stalk over to the door and open up for him. "Come on in."

He holds up a file. "Are you sure?"

I give him a nod and he strolls in so I can lock the door behind him.

"I don't want her kept in the dark about this." I take a deep breath. "She has a son, he's mine."

Casey blinks slowly and says, "Come again, VP?"

The corner of my mouth twitches. "Remember the story I've told a few times; about the one time I forget to wrap up?"

"You're kidding me? You found the one who got away?"

"Great, I'm a story? Everyone knows about me, but...doesn't know me?" Mags says with a smile in her voice.

I automatically hold out my hand and to my surprise she takes it and she lets me pull her against my side.

"You are," I murmur. "The one who got away makes you somewhat of a legend in my book."

She groans and now an actual chuckle slips past my lips.

"The case you wanted me to dig into? Can we discuss a few things?" Casey holds the file up again, and I feel Mags go rigid against me.

I glance at my brother. "Mind waiting in the living room? I'll be there in a sec."

Casey nods at my words and takes off.

I turn toward Mags and make sure to watch her face when I ask, "Casey is the one who I mentioned earlier, he used to be FBI. He runs his own company where he picks his own cases to solve. I've asked him to look into yours when Darby asked me to help you today. Do you want to hear what he has to say?"

Determination washes over her face. "Yes. Though I hate going over details because the many times I've had to do it over the years it always resulted in nightmares. And with Joshua waking up early it takes a while for me to recover."

I hate hearing this but things will be different from now on. "Like we agreed, you're not alone anymore. I'm here and I'm not leaving. I'll be there to pull you out of those nightmares, watch over you sleeping, or take care of Joshua if you need a quick nap on the couch, whatever you need."

She gives me a tiny smile. "The one that got away won't be given another chance to slip through your fingers, huh?"

"We have a kid together, you're never getting rid of me ever again," I simply reply.

She gives me a curt nod. "Yes. Joshua. Right. I...we shouldn't keep your friend waiting."

I don't understand her reaction and it's as if she's putting distance between us. Probably because I mentioned Joshua. I grab her hand and she glances down before our eyes lock.

"Not just Joshua, Mags. I'm here for you too." I give her a little squeeze and I hope she sees the promise I just gave her.

But she gives me a tiny smile and says, "Yeah, sure."

A low growl rumbles through my chest. "I mean it, Mags. I wasn't done with you when you walked out that first time. And unless you're tied to someone else, I'd say we can see what this pull between us can give us while we focus on our kid. That's what I meant when I said I'm here for you too. The both of you are mine. I told you."

"You said something about protecting…mine to protect and being there for Joshua. What are you implying? You want me? As in a relationship? We don't even know each other. We jumped into bed for a nameless one-night stand the first time we met, and that was years ago. It's not as if we can be careless like we were back then, Easton. There's a little kid involved. If we throw the whole you, me, sex, relationship in the mix too it will complicate things. I have to think about him first."

I can feel my gut start to clench. She's not even open to the suggestion of a chance for us to be together. And believe me, I know very well Joshua comes first, but we were so good together.

"Shit," she mutters and reaches out to cup my face. "Can you maybe not be so freaking adorable when you pout? I think you did that the first time too when I mentioned I couldn't go with you because I had plans, and it's the very reason I ended up in bed with you."

A sly smile spreads my face because I remember our conversation very vividly. "You said you had plans. Then I said you needed to change them because—"

"Because your heart just took a ride with mine," she snorts. "I can't believe I fell for that line."

My head tips back and laughter rips out, and when our eyes slam into each other, it's as if everything around us falls away and we're back in that moment in time where nothing else matters except the longing to connect. I grab my chance and do what I did back then… lean in and taste her.

CHAPTER 06

MAGNOLIA

His firm lips cover mine and my heart beats faster as pure pleasure flares up inside my body. His tongue slides over my lips and I gladly give him access to let myself drown into this moment. The last time I felt someone spark anything similar was years back, and it was the same man who's heating up my soul this very instant.

A rumble flows through his chest and I can feel my nipples harden in return. My hands fist his leather cut and I'm ready to pull him closer or rip off his clothes—whatever I can manage first—but he suddenly pulls back.

He places his forehead against mine and whispers on a hot breath, "Joshua comes first, we come second. But the three of us will be together. Understood?"

"Okay," I answer breathlessly.

And I absolutely surprise myself with this answer because the second I knew I was pregnant I swore I wouldn't get involved with anyone because Joshua would always come first. Not to mention the turmoil I went through. A relationship was never going to happen. Yet Easton steps back into my life and suddenly I'm swooning from one mere kiss.

I'm about to tell him I need to think about it, but he places his finger on my lips. "No. No taking it back. I can tell in your eyes all the reasons are flooding your brain to backtrack, and I won't allow it. We're not jumping into bed together without thinking things through this time, okay? We'll set rules, boundaries, take it slow, whatever. First, we need to deal with the past and that fucker who still thinks he can torment you, and we will start by talking to Casey."

He slides his hand to my lower back and guides me into the living room. Casey is sitting at the dinner table and has spread out some documents. He's holding a pen and tapping it on an empty piece of paper.

"Would you mind if I ask you a couple of questions? I'm sure you've gone over it multiple times over the years, and I've read everything in your file but—"

I hold up my hand as I cut him off. "No reason to explain, I understand. If you want, I can tell you what happened from the start. You know, in my own words instead of answering questions. Then, when I'm finished...and if you still have questions...I will answer those too."

"Thank you, that would be a great help," Casey says with a warm smile and in a gentle tone.

I take a deep breath and start at the beginning. "I drove back from spending three weeks at my parents' house. They went on a cruise and since they own a cat, I offered to house sit for them. The only thing I remember was stepping out of my car, which I parked in the garage. Everything is fuzzy after that. The next thing I remember is waking up in a cage. Well, it was more like one of those large dog kennels. I couldn't stand or turn. I didn't have any clothes, only a blanket. The man who held me captive always wore black clothes, gloves, and a ski mask. He would enter the room which looked like a dark basement, grab a hose and hit me with cold water. I remember the cold...shivering so hard, my head would hurt from the way my teeth would chatter. I still hate cold showers or when the tap water is too hard of a stream and hits my hands. I hate it."

My chest is rapidly rising and falling and I have to close my eyes for a moment to take a deep breath and hold it in an effort to calm down. "Days blurred. I didn't know how long I was in there. The only thing he gave me was a dog bowl with oatmeal once a day, quickly followed by the cold water and then he'd throw a clean blanket into the kennel. The first few days I'd scream for help, yell and ask why he was doing this. He would just laugh, so I stopped asking and yelling. Then he started to poke a stick through the bars and just…torment me. Other days he would sit and stare and whistle. 'Come on pretty birdy, why don't you sing for me.' That's what he used to say. It didn't matter what he or I did, it's the only thing he kept repeating. In the end I think it was my screams he got off on. When the water hit, when he would poke me with a stick. Eventually I didn't care anymore and kept quiet. He dragged me out of the cage and—"

My hands tighten to fists. I can do this. I've worked very hard to put it behind me. I'm safe. I'm still me, and my body still functions. I lock eyes with Casey as I feel Easton place his hand on my shoulder, giving me a little squeeze.

My voice comes out steady as I continue. "He would punch my face, step on my hands if I moved and used a bull whip to draw out my screams. Until…until I stopped screaming. I stopped fighting. I stopped eating. I just…stopped. I remember how he dragged me out of the cage. I kept staring at him while he whipped me. My mouth stayed closed. I must have passed out and next thing I remembered was waking up in the hospital."

"Do you remember anything about your attacker?" Casey asks.

This is something I've been trying to remember but I can't. "He always wore a ski mask. His whole face was covered and he also wore gloves. His eyes were dark, that's the only thing I could clearly see. Not blue, not gray, dark." And something that still haunts me when I get nightmares. "He would always use voice distortion so I couldn't tell you what his voice sounds like."

Casey nods. "You were held captive for a little over three weeks, correct?"

"Yes. I always call my parents when I get home from the long drive and this time I didn't. They tried calling my roommate but he didn't pick up."

"You've mentioned in your statement you thought it was weird your roommate didn't pick up the phone, correct?" Casey checks as if he's going over the police report step by step.

"My roommate, Peter, was always home, he didn't have a job. I was always home too because I used my room as a workspace. No matter what time, Peter would always pick up the damn phone. Even if all the calls were always meant for me." I rub both hands over my face. "At first, I thought it was Peter who held me captive because the week before I left for my parents, I gave him my one month's notice since I bought this house. He was grumpy about the fact I was moving out while he knew I only needed a room for about six months. He was always lazy and annoying but those last few days when I gave him my notice he turned into a mean jerk."

"Didn't the police check his alibi?" Casey points at the file. "Because I couldn't find any record of it."

I stand from my chair and head for the tiny desk in the corner to find the file I have stashed away in the bottom drawer. Handing it over to Casey, I say, "This might explain why. The private investigator my father hired when the first birds showed up collected all of this, but he didn't make any progress in linking Peter or finding any evidence that could incriminate or show who did all of this to me."

Casey starts reading and I can see Easton staring and I know he wants the information too.

I turn to look at him as I explain, "Peter's father has money and connections. It's the reason why Peter doesn't work; because his father pays the bills. He needed a roommate because he wanted some extra spending money and this was the easiest way. Plus, I was fanatical about cleaning. He didn't do anything and I hated a messy kitchen so I kept cleaning up after him. I was happy I finally found the perfect house for myself so I could move out. I hated the way he was always there watching me, even if I cleaned the damn kitchen."

"Peter's uncle is a detective. Pretty sure that's a big help with credentials. He didn't have an alibi for the day you were taken. Other than being at home and getting some gas for his truck," Casey adds.

"His truck was in front of the house. I paid extra to use the garage. And Peter didn't mind because he always parked in front of the house anyway. He was lazy. Like seriously lazy. But the cops never found a link so, I guess it wasn't him." I release a deep sigh of frustration.

"We'll see about that," Casey grumbles. "Do you still have any injuries? Are there any new things you might remember? No matter how little or irrelevant you might think it might be."

"No. I've been wracking my brain for years on end, trying to remember anything that might help explain who did this. Even the days or weeks before it happened. The only thing out of the ordinary was the night I spent with—" I almost let the name Easton fall from my lips but suddenly remember he doesn't use that name around his biker friends. "C.Rash. That night wasn't planned while all my life I've planned every day to the next."

Casey chuckles. "Well, obviously we can rule out C.Rash. Not only because it's very easy to backtrack and show you evidence if you need it, but I—along with every brother of the two MCs he's always around—know for a fact he wouldn't have let you go if he knew who you were. Whenever he's drunk, he always mentions the one woman who got away."

I can't help but smile. "Well, if I go missing again, be sure to check C.Rash's bed first, okay?"

Casey barks out a laugh. Easton joins him but clears his throat and sits down next to me. "I want this guy found. This Peter guy sounds like a good start."

"Agreed. I'll start digging and keep my eyes open for any other perp that might pop up. I'll widen my search because he could have followed her from her parents' house. From everything I've read about her case, the cops have been keeping it localized to her house and the place she was found." Casey shoves all the papers back into the file and holds up the ones I gave him. "Mind if I take this with me?"

"No, sure, go ahead," I tell him.

Casey stands but Easton's voice stops him from turning. "Casey, be sure to tell Calix this is now about the VP's old lady."

A slow smile spreads his face as he gives him a nod in return. "You got it, VP. I'll call if I need anything or have something to share."

I offer him my hand and Easton walks him out and makes sure to lock up. When he walks back to me the first thing on the tip of my tongue to question is the very explanation falling from his lips.

"I just claimed you as mine, Mags. My old lady. The VP's old lady. With my claim you have my protection along with every single brother looking out for you along with it. I want you safe. I want Joshua safe. And like I mentioned to you before…the three of us are together now. I might as well make it official."

With the turn of events, along with the explanation he just gave me—not to mention how he's managed to put people into action to dive into my case—my mind can't think of any reason why I should fight this. And I might as well listen to my gut because this feels right.

"Fine," I fake grumble. "But if you think that will earn you another chocolate chip cookie, you're sadly mistaken."

His head tips back and a full belly laugh rips from his body. My throat turns dry as I take in this magnificent man. He's exactly how I remembered him all those years ago. Strong. Handsome. Dark scruff to accent his strong jaw. Muscles in all the right places and even if he's wearing clothes, I remember all too vividly some of those muscles are inked. And he knows very well how to use his ripped body.

Okay. Maybe it's more than fine to be his old lady. To finally have a man around the house—something Joshua has craved to do dude stuff with—and for me to do grownup stuff with. His laughter stops and our eyes lock, instant lust skyrockets and suddenly it's getting very hot in here.

I dash up and take a step back. "There's a spare bedroom upstairs. The door is open and I'll get some clean linens. I'm gonna…I'm tired. I'll be upstairs. Goodnight."

I rush out of the living room and head upstairs. I know I'm making an escape and it's silly because he basically said he's here to stay. Though right now I need space. And if he is here to stay, I'm sure he won't mind taking it slow because my heart is racing and my body is pulsating with the need to kiss him and the intensity scares me a little.

CHAPTER 07

C.RASH

I steal another heated glance at the woman who is putting away the groceries we picked up. It's been a handful of days since my life was turned upside-down by this woman. But I guess it takes something life-changing to make you realize your life before has been seriously lacking. Even if I repulsed sappy shit, it's not so sappy if it involves these two people.

And tossing ball with Joshua in the garden is very satisfying to say the least. To see that little dude smile because of something so damn simple as throwing a ball back and forth is making my heart tug.

I've even spent some time online ordering shit to make sure I have some presents for the both of them. Yeah, I'm up to my neck in jolly shit and I shamelessly admit I'm liking every damn second.

A prospect is coming by later tonight since I had everything shipped to the clubhouse. And even this little fact of me shopping for gifts says something about a change in things because most times I wing the whole Santa stuff. It's more like a necessity. Making sure I have some gift cards at the last second to give to my friends, but this is different.

This is my kid. Another thing I had to do; research stuff five-year-olds like and do. Because if I remember what I like to do compared to nowadays...let's just say times have changed. I climbed—and fell out of—trees, while now they have loads of technology to spice things up. And the fact I cringed about choosing educational stuff over fun shit makes me aware I'm already leaning to the whole sensible parenting thing. But I guess that's good, right? Because the one thing I'm very sure of is the fact I'm here to stay. And ideally staying here with them in this house. But that would be too soon, too fast.

Though it's necessary, I'm staying here twenty-four-seven until this asshole—who is still tormenting her after all these years—is caught. And believe it or not, I'm grateful to be this close to them while living here but I'd rather have that asshole locked up or dead.

This because I can see the stress and fear slicing through her multiple times a day. She hides it well and I'm pretty sure Joshua is oblivious to his mother's worries, but I can tell and it needs to end.

Me and my brothers—either AF MC Ohio or Areion Fury MC—have been working hard to track down every single detail and information about this case and those involved we could find. Casey has been focusing on her former roommate. Everything smells fishy about this guy, and it's safe to say we think this is our guy. What we need now is evidence or to catch him red-handed.

I've installed cameras all over the place but nothing has happened since the first day I came here. If I had to voice my suspicions, I'd say the fucker is smart, laying low and is staking out the place. And I would try to set him up and leave the house to wait at a safe distance to catch him, but I'm not risking my son or Mags.

"Did you want to watch a Christmas movie with us?" Mags says and grabs two mugs. "Joshua wants hot cocoa with marshmallows. You?"

"As long as it involves those Christmas cookies you two made this morning, I'm in," I tell her and rub my belly.

Damn. I've been doing extra sit-ups and push-ups with all those extra calories, but it's hard to pass up the goodness these two can create in the kitchen.

She rolls her eyes. "Men. All they think about is their stomach."

"Hey," I snap, faking anger. "That's not all we think about."

Her eyes automatically slide down to the front of my jeans. Yeah. It's been too damn long since I've had sex and the best pussy I can remember was hers, and it's been too damn long since I've tasted it.

The thought makes me groan. "Yeah, you need to rephrase it as 'Men are always hungry.' Because for sure as shit that's the damn truth." My voice is husky as I lazily slide my gaze over her body. She might be wearing yoga pants and a long, thick sweater covering up all her curves, but I've had my hands on her naked body. I remember very vividly how good she feels. It doesn't matter if it was years ago, both my body and mind crave her with fierce ferocity.

The doorbell rings, well not exactly rings since it's a Christmas tune that lasts until I'm actually at the door. I swing it open and see it's Casey and Calix instead of the prospect I was expecting.

"Guys?" I question while stepping back to let them inside.

Calix hands me a large box and my eyes connect with Mags. "Can you show them to the living room? I need to bring this up to my room, okay?" I turn and head for the stairs.

"It's that way, we'll be right there," Mags says as I hear her walking up the stairs behind me.

I place the box on the floor near my bed and turn to see Mags pointing at the box while she squeaks, "What's that?"

"Sex toys," I say without blinking.

"Wha…what?" she whispers and takes a step back.

I can't help but chuckle and grab the knife I have in a sheath on my belt. Opening up the box, I reach inside and grab one of the books I ordered for Joshua. "I bought a few Christmas presents. This is the same one my mother used to make me read and I vividly remember loving it."

"Oh," Mags says and she visibly relaxes and it makes me wonder. "What did you think was in there? You were freaking out before I joked about sex toys." There's a guilty look sliding over her face and it puts me on edge when it suddenly clicks. "You thought it was my stuff? That I was moving in without discussing shit, is that it?" I swallow hard in an effort to hide the rising anger and disappointment. "Why am I getting the impression you don't want—"

"I do want you here," she rushes out. "It's just…I'm…" She groans and takes her head in her hands while she mutters, "I'm screwing this up." Her hands fall away and guilt is written all over her face. "I'm so sorry."

She steps closer and grabs my cut with both hands. Fisting the leather she gives a little shake. "I freaked out. And yes, seeing those guys bring you a large box and you rushing it up to your room made me think you were moving in without discussing it with me first. I'm a bit of a control freak when it comes to the normality around me. I thought you were forcing…it's not you, it's not…dammit." Her forehead is now leaning against my chest as she's breathing heavily.

I wrap my arms around her and pull her closer. "Freedom of choice," I mutter and softly rub her back as I ramble out my thoughts, trying to make sense as to why she would freak out. "Once it's taken away it's hard to put your guard down. It's the same as trust and doubt. I might be a straightforward guy and also have to admit, I'm not letting you go. I won't be walking away when we catch the guy who gave you all the scars on the inside and outside. But I won't do anything without running it by you first. Well, obviously buying our kid presents and other minor things don't need to be discussed. But when I buy him his first dirt bike, I'll ask you what color, okay?"

"He's not getting a dirt bike," Mags gasps.

The corner of my mouth twitches. "I guess I have to think about something else to give him for his birthday then, huh?"

She places her forehead against my chest again as she shakes her head. "You and your jokes. The rush of adrenaline you give me at times makes me dizzy."

"I'd like to think it's the lust for my body that's making your head spin with the need to have me."

Her head tips back and I'm stunned to see the desire swirling in her gaze. I cup the side of her face and let my thumb trace her bottom lip. Her eyes flutter close for a breath or two as if she's relishing in my touch. Leaning in I feather a kiss on the side of her mouth. I repeat the action on the other side until I place a soft one full on her lips. Pulling back, I brush my nose against hers.

"Just so you can get used to the idea…I do intend to move in at some point. I do intend to be the best father on this fucked-up planet, and I do intend to become your lover. And eventually, I really hope we're both going to be voicing out the words I do, if you understand what I'm saying because I want it all. I knew you were damn magnificent the first time I laid eyes on you, and I don't care if there's been years in between or how our lives were split until our paths crossed again. I feel it. Deep down I know you're it for me. The way you make me feel when I'm around you or see Joshua and you interact with each other. This morning, the whole making cookies and letting him do everything and not even getting mad when there's flour everywhere... you have patience and so much damn love for that kid it absolutely takes my breath away."

The lust in her eyes shifts and I'm afraid I went too fast, too soon laying it all out until there's mischief flashing those pretty eyes when she says, "You're just addicted to the cookies and all the other stuff you've eaten over the days you've been here. It's the sugar rush."

"Woman," I growl.

She laughs and steps away from me as she pats my chest. "I'm gonna cut you off. No more sweetness for you, mister."

A low rumble flows through my chest and she glances over her shoulder and playfully squeaks as she dashes away. She doesn't even get a chance to leave the room because I've caught her and have her caged against the wall with my body.

"Take it back," I demand, our noses touching.

"Never," she answers breathlessly and her eyes are locked on my lips.

"If you won't give me any sweetness...then I'm going to have to take it from your body," I tell her and slam my mouth over hers.

CHAPTER 08

MAGNOLIA

Lust. Desire. Heat. Longing. My whole body lights up with pleasure that's building and has been building ever since this man stepped back into my life. I hate the way I jumped to conclusions because I should have known Easton wouldn't force his way. Only when it involves our safety but that's something that goes without saying.

It was my own insecurities. I should have given him my trust. It's just that the last few days I've been on edge. And if I'm completely honest with myself…I want him to move in because I've never felt this safe with him being near. And yet seeing him carry a big box upstairs made me think he would take away my decision on things.

Like I said, it was my own stupid brain jumping the gun on things. I should have known I could trust him because he's been caring, thoughtful, open, and honest ever since he walked back into my life.

The reason I'm on edge has everything to do with what happened six years ago and what has been happening each year around that date ever since. Until Easton arrived. Only the first day there were dead birds thrown at my window. Normally it's each day for the full three weeks I was taken and held captive.

The sonofabitch always torments me as a reminder, as if he still has me in his grip and then doesn't do anything for the remainder of the year. It's driving me insane and instead of acting the way I did to Easton, I should be begging him to move in. Though I want him to be with me not because of this asshole, not for me to feel safe, and not just as an obligation to our son.

Yet...the way he's kissing me as his hands roam my body makes everything fade to the background. It doesn't feel as if he's here out of obligation for his kid or because he needs to end the threat that endangers the mother of his child. No. He's kissing me as if he can't get enough of me. Me as a person. As the woman who has been missing a man's touch.

So. Freaking. Bad. And I've been dreaming about him specifically. Not just because he was the last man I had sex with, but because he was the one who gave me the most perfect night of my life. Even if weeks later I went through hell and back. It was his memory that gave me the reminder there were still good things in life; things that make life worth living. I wanted that back and it's kept me going, along with our son.

All of this makes me emotional and I don't want to be emotional right now. I want to feel desired. I want to give in to the craving of being pleasured by this man. I want to step outside of the 'mom person' I've been for years on end and actually feel like a woman who lights up for the touch of the right man.

His mouth slides from mine as he buries his head into the crook of my neck. He's nipping my skin and it shoots electric jolts through me as it starts to settle and build between my legs. He grabs my ass and lifts me up so I can wrap my legs around his waist.

This position allows me to rotate my hips in an effort to rub myself against him. I need the friction. I'm so close already. The way his hot breath spreads all over my skin and his rough groans tease my ears, all of it burns me even more while we're dry humping the shit out of each other.

"So close," I pant.

His lips leave my skin and settle right next to my ear. "Let me taste you," he rumbles and I seriously think about questioning his sanity because how in the hell could I deny him or myself?

"Yes," I groan. "Hurry."

My head spins—or it might be my body that's flying through the air as Easton throws me on the bed. He quickly strips away my yoga pants and my underwear along with it. He doesn't waste a single second as he pierces my pussy with his tongue.

My hand digs into his hair at the same time as I tip my head back and release a long moan. Shit. This feels so freaking good. I let my other hand find his head and shamelessly start to rub my pussy all over his face. His growl vibrates against my pussy as he laps away. Suddenly he captures my clit gently between his teeth and changes it up by grazing, sucking, flipping his tongue.

"Aaaaaaaahhhh," I gasp and moan his name in a soft prayer for him to never stop the flow of pleasure bursting through me.

Easton gently lets his tongue slide through until he softly places a kiss on my mound and then on each of my thighs. He moves up my body and glances down at me.

"Better than any cookie on this fucking planet." He shoots me a grin and tells me, "Speaking of cookies...we need to head downstairs before either Calix or Casey eats any of the Christmas cookies."

My eyes go wide. "I can't believe I left Joshua alone."

Easton places a hand on my shoulder to keep me in place. "Hey, we didn't leave him alone. Two of my brothers are downstairs. It's okay, we were only here a few minutes, now breathe."

I don't have time to reply because he gives me a fierce kiss right after. He pulls away all too soon and takes my hand to pull me from the bed. He's standing there, a huge bulge tenting his jeans.

I clear my throat. "You can't tell me to breathe and then steal my breath away with a scorching kiss," I scold, licking my lips at the sight of his bulge, remembering all too well how big and good he felt inside me.

"Stop looking at it or I'll explode inside my pants, and I don't have the time to shower because we're heading downstairs," Easton grumbles. "Remember. Joshua. Cookies. All the important stuff."

This man. He gives me pleasure but skips himself completely.

"You're important too." My thoughts slide right out my mouth.

His hand flashes up and cups my nape, giving it a firm squeeze as he connects our foreheads. "Not as important as you. You've been on my damn mind for years; I can wait a while longer to slide my dick inside your heavenly pussy. Because I remember taking your tight heat. I've dreamed about it, about everything. And...you taste even better than I remember. So, believe me when I say I will for damn sure even the score, but for now I'll settle with your taste on my tongue."

I swallow hard while my breathing picks up again.

"Fuck. Come on. We need people around us," Easton grumbles and takes my hand as he starts to lead us out of the room.

"Wait," I squeak and rip my hand away. Bending down I hear Easton curse and I risk a glance over my shoulder as I snatch my yoga pants off the floor along with my panties.

"I can't believe I almost dragged you down the stairs half naked." He swallows hard and slides his fingers through his disheveled hair.

"But you didn't." I smirk and this time I take his hand as we head downstairs.

Joshua is sitting in front of the TV and has a cup in his hand. It looks like someone made him some hot cocoa.

"He told me his mom was gonna make him some hot cocoa and with you two dashing upstairs and taking your time I thought you wouldn't mind if I made him some," Calix says as he shoots me a wink.

"Thank you," I tell him, and try like hell to keep the blush on my cheeks from spreading.

Geez, talk about awkward. I feel like there are big bold letters on my forehead stating, "Easton ate my pussy."

"Mind telling us why you guys are here? Other than bringing me the stuff I thought a prospect was gonna bring by," Easton rumbles and reaches out to slide his arm around my waist as he pulls me close.

Casey holds up a file. "Mind if we talk in the kitchen? I don't want to interrupt the little man's cartoon marathon."

We follow Calix and Casey into the kitchen. Casey slides the file over the table until it's in front of Easton but his eyes stay on me.

His voice is soft when he says, "The birds. They always start around the date you were taken and end around the date they found you alongside of the road, correct?" I slowly nod in agreement. "You haven't had any incidents in the last few days, correct?"

I almost nod again but instead I say, "Yes, why are you asking me this?"

Calix clears his throat. "Peter Milvisson was arrested for driving under the influence a few days ago. Three blocks from your house, the night birds were thrown at your window, the timeline...it all fits perfectly. His father managed to get him out of the charges and put him into a rehab facility. He walked right out and no one has seen him since."

"What?" I gasp.

My head starts to spin because I always had the nagging feeling it was Peter who held me hostage and did all those things, or at least he was involved in some way. But there was never any evidence.

"And that's not all," Casey adds. "When they arrested him, they found a large box inside his car with birds. The same kind he left for you."

My heart starts to beat out of control and my eyes start to sting as a tear slides over my cheek. I can't believe it.

"This is proof, right?" I croak. "Proof I was right all along. Proof that can tie him to what he did so he can be brought to justice."

Calix and Casey both share a concerned look, but it's Easton who speaks this time. "Not exactly, sweetheart. But—"

"No," I growl angrily. "Don't tell me it's not enough. Don't tell me you can't do anything."

I'm so sick of not being able to do anything. I was feeling damn good a moment ago and this asshole who tainted my life with darkness and kept me in fear for years is still out there, somewhere. And he just keeps getting away with it.

CHAPTER 09

C.RASH

"Calm down, Mags," I tell her and I know that's not the smartest thing to say, but there's more information and she needs to see it. "Look," I tell her and smack the file in front of her.

"Motherfucker," Casey growls underneath his breath. "She doesn't need to see that shit."

"Yes, she does," I growl back. "It's the only way to let her know this fucker isn't getting away with anything. She needs to see the truth. To know it's real and the visible evidence is right here. You need to tell her everything you know because she will want to hear every single detail."

I place a hand on her shoulder and she covers it with her own as she glances over the information and the pictures along with it.

"Those pictures were taken by the cops early this morning. Peter probably didn't realize his father would report him missing if he walked out of rehab. Daddy dearest demanded everyone jump into action which led to them searching the house. There was a K9 unit in the neighborhood who dropped by to talk to his brother who was a cop at the scene. He had a cadaver dog with him who alerted his handler, it's how they found the first body," Casey says and sits down across from me. "So, as C.Rash mentioned, the birds aren't exactly something we can tie him to your case with. Though we have someone on it to see if all the birds came from the same breeder. But for now, we're focusing on nailing this fucker for what he did to you six years ago and those other girls he killed over the years. They've found four buried underneath his house and one girl they found alive. She has been missing for four days and was locked up in a dog kennel in a hidden room in the basement."

I can tell everything Casey just said to her is hitting hard. I can only imagine how it is for her to hear that fucker killed all those girls while she lived to tell about it.

I squat down next to her chair to be close to her as I glance up at Casey. "I'm sure you're here to tell her the police would like to question her, right? I mean with all of this she's the one who got away together with the girl they found alive."

"Yes," Calix says as he sits down next to Casey. "But the girl they found alive isn't talking. They are keeping her sedated at the hospital. Seems like the fucker became more aggressive over the years."

"What's the plan, Pres?" I ask and grab a chair and slide it right next to Mags. She might look strong, but I know this is hitting her hard.

Calix's eyes turn hard and this is a look he always gives when he doesn't allow any disagreement. "The plan is to get you guys out of here and into the clubhouse until this fucker is found. I'm not trusting this Peter one damn bit; he's got nothing to lose and it makes him more dangerous. And let's not forget he's been coming back to Magnolia each year."

"It's almost Christmas, we have gifts, it's our first Christmas as a fucking family," I hiss.

"VP," Calix snaps as he throws a set of keys over the table in my direction. "Can you get my bag from the car, please? It's in the backseat. I should have known you didn't want to leave so we're staying the night, but I have to discuss something with Magnolia and it's not meant for your ears, understood?"

I grind my teeth. I know very well he's not asking; he's giving me an order as my president.

Mags places her hand on my thigh and gives it a squeeze. "I'm okay, go get his stuff. I'll be right here."

I reluctantly stand and stalk out of the kitchen. Throwing a quick glance in the direction of the living room, I see Joshua sitting on his knees in front of the TV, enjoying a Christmas cartoon. Not bothering with a coat, I open the door and head for Calix's car.

I notice his bag and have to smile because even if I hate the man for sending me out here to talk to Mags in private, I also know he only thinks about her safety. And the bag I'm holding only amplifies it because it's not filled with a change of clothes, it's filled with extra guns and ammo.

Locking up the car, I head back to the house but the shatter of glass makes me aware something is very fucking wrong. Horrified, I watch as someone is now standing in the living room, pulling up Joshua and holding a knife in one hand while he has Joshua by the throat and plastered against his body.

Calix, Casey, and Mags rush into the living room but freeze at the sight before them. I let Calix's bag hit the dirt and snatch my phone from my jeans. I know for damn sure my brother Ransom knows everything about this case because he always works closely with Casey.

He picks up on the first ring and I get straight to the point. "Perp broke into my old lady's house; he's holding my son hostage."

"On it, brother," Ransom grunts and the line disconnects.

Everything seems frozen before me, though the fucker is waving the knife in Calix's direction, who is holding his hands palms up in an effort to calm Peter down.

I glance at Calix's bag and squat down to open it. There are four guns in there but I take the Beretta I've used countless times. Inching closer to the house, Casey locks eyes with me for a second and I can tell he understands what I'm about to do. Not thinking twice, I take aim and wait for the perfect moment.

Joshua sees me and my heart skips a damn beat. I realize in this damn moment everything I hold dear can shatter beyond repair. I hope to fuck he keeps quiet and stays still. Peter holds the knife away from Joshua again and waves it at Calix with an outstretched arm.

I gently squeeze the trigger and the bullet smashes through the glass before it impacts Peter's head. His arms swing away from Joshua as Calix rushes forward and grabs my son before Peter's body hits the ground.

I burst inside and almost bump into Calix who is running into the kitchen with Joshua, Mags is right on his heels. I want to follow so damn bad, but I can't. I head into the living room and see Casey standing over Peter's body while his phone is glued to his ear, barking out orders. Stepping closer I see my aim was a perfect hit.

"Gimme that," Casey snaps and takes the Beretta from me. "Good job, man. He's not breathing anymore. Now get your ass to your old lady and kid, they need you. And I need for you to get our Pres in here, understood?"

"Yeah," I croak and swallow hard.

I head for the kitchen and see Mags sitting on the floor holding Joshua on her lap. Calix is leaning against the counter with his arms crossed in front of his chest as if he's standing watch to make sure they're okay.

"Casey needs you," I grunt and squat down next to Mags.

Joshua's head flashes up. "Daddy," he says and holds out his hands.

Without thinking I lift him into my arms and hold tight as I stand up. "I got you, little man. I got you."

Emotions are burning through me and I tighten my arms. Tears are stinging my eyes and I'm not holding back. I won't ever hold back because I'm holding my son, alive and well.

"You saved me, Daddy," Joshua says. "I wasn't scared. I saw you."

"My brave little man," I croak.

Mags steps closer and wraps her arms around the two of us. I don't even know how long we stand there but it doesn't matter. Nothing fucking matters except us. Right here, right now. Together without anything threatening to rip us apart.

CHAPTER 10

MAGNOLIA

"Are you sure he's okay?" Easton whispers to ask me for the second time and I see him scratch his forearm repeatedly.

We're standing in the bedroom of a large luxurious apartment Calix brought us to. Joshua is finally sleeping in a big bed and the reason he didn't want to sleep was because he wanted his Daddy to keep reading the book he gave him. Ketchup is curled up beside him and the cat is purring with his eyes closed.

I glance at Easton and wrap my fingers around his wrist to stop him from scratching and to pull him out of the room. I close the door but leave it slightly open. We move to the living room where a large couch sits in front of a big screen TV along with a fireplace and some comfy chairs along with it.

A Christmas tree stands in the corner. I'm touched how the bikers of AF MC Ohio and their old ladies all came by with Christmas stuff they wanted us to have to decorate the tree and this place with. Calix arranged the tree, but it was Easton who brought it in all by himself.

I'm pretty sure it's the reason he's been scratching his forearms, due to irritation from the tree. Maybe he's allergic but he didn't mention anything when the three of us took our time decorating everything. Calix owns the apartment and told us to stay as long as we wanted. I don't know how long that will be, but for now I'm glad we have a place that doesn't remind us of what happened so we can spend the next few days together without worry and just relish in the fact it's Christmas and we're together.

"I'm sure he's fine, Easton." I plant my ass on the couch and pull him down beside me. "I know it sounds crazy but all of us saw and experienced it differently. Joshua for sure. He saw us, he saw you. All his eyes caught was you firing a gun while the one holding him was waving a knife. When you shot the guy, Joshua didn't see anyone getting hurt or so much as a speck of blood. Calix was right there to grab him and he pulled him into his chest. He didn't see a body, any blood, nothing."

He nods warily and I know it's hard to accept for him, but I know my son. Okay, things can backfire, but from what I've seen in the last couple of hours was still the same cheerful boy he was before this happened.

His nails drag over the skin of his forearms again and I can see the redness spreading. "Stop scratching," I scold and head for the bag where I know I have a tube of ointment in there that will help with the rash spreading his skin. A giggle slips out when I sit down next to him and grab his forearm.

"What?" he grumbles as I start to apply the ointment.

"C.Rash," I snicker. "If I didn't know any better, I would think it stands for Christmas Rash."

Easton chuckles and shakes his head. My heart skips a beat when I look at him. The last few days he's been involved in every second of Joshua's life and the way he shows how important he is to him has made Joshua open up to him completely.

At first, I had my doubts and fears about how all of us would react to these new circumstances, but we easily fell into a routine and all enjoy every minute of our time together. I clean up and wash my hands and when I stroll back to the couch, Easton isn't scratching his forearms anymore but has his intense gaze locked on me.

I clear my throat as I sit down next to him. "He really liked the book you gave him. And I think it's even better you gave it to him, instead of putting it underneath the tree as if Santa put it there."

A slow smile spreads Easton's face. "You're right. I feel better already knowing I'm getting the credit for giving my little man that book. And now I can tell the reason I gave it to him and how I loved it as a kid too, instead of the old man with the beard and red suit stealing my thunder."

I can't help but snort. "First priority on Daddy's list...never let Santa steal your thunder."

He bumps his shoulder against mine. "Hey, I'm still new at this, okay?"

I release a deep breath and pull my legs up on the couch as I lean into him and snuggle close. "You're amazing, Easton. Don't worry so much. For the first time I feel completely safe. And with you sitting here, how you reacted and handled everything? Not just your quick reaction by handling Peter, I'm talking about what happened after you saved our kid. The way you were there for him, how gentle you were and how you listened to every word Joshua said and nothing else mattered but him. You made him feel strong and safe. You did that, and that's why he's sleeping peacefully. Hell, I'm pretty sure he's dreaming about becoming an astronaut because of the book you gave him. See? It's all about how you handle things and I'm thankful you're a part of our lives now."

His arm reaches around me and he pulls me closer, placing a kiss on the top of my head as if he's finally at ease. Though the tightness of his muscles tells me differently. He's still tense and filled with worry. This used to be me every second of the day.

I close my eyes and let my thoughts flow. "All these years, there has been a kind of restlessness dominating my life I couldn't take away no matter how hard I tried. It was always right there at the surface, as if I needed to be ready for anything at every second; always on edge. Tight as a string like the way you feel now. I don't feel it anymore, it's gone. It's as if the bullet you fired took that down with it too. It's over. I can finally put all of it behind me and this is why I know Joshua will be fine too. I'll be there for him if he needs me. You will be there too. There's no risk of Peter taking me again or tormenting me. One of my biggest fears has been the risk of being taken away from my son, or worse...having something happen to him because of me. No more. It all ended today. You made it possible and I can never be more thankful."

Easton's breath rushes out. "I have never been more scared in my life as I was today." His voice cracks and his arm tightens slightly around me. "I've been shot a few times in my life. Hanging on the balance of life and death, not knowing if I close my eyes it would be for good. But standing outside of that window while my son was in the arms of danger? Fuck."

I take his face in my hands and the torment edged on there is slicing through me. "You're here. He's here. I'm here. We're all safe. You saved us. Don't dwell in the past, let it go and look forward. I had to force myself to look forward countless times. Years ago, when it all happened...when I woke up at the hospital and knew the nightmare was real...I didn't know if I wanted to live. Then they told me I was pregnant and there was no doubt in my mind Joshua was the gift I needed to move forward and give my life meaning. The night we spent together all those years ago has given me strength over time. They were the kind of memories I needed to live through and spark my life with. A reminder that there are good things worth living for. The scars Peter inflicted, the pain, the torment, humiliation, the beatings...with what we know now, and those girls found dead. If I didn't escape, I wouldn't be here. Joshua wouldn't be here. And I still don't understand how I managed to escape and why I can't remember how or recollect what happened those last few days of captivity. Maybe I didn't escape, he let me go instead because he was sure I couldn't identify him or couldn't say anything to incriminate him. Maybe that's the reason he kept coming back, because it didn't matter if I was in a cage with him or free...all those years he still had me in an invisible cage built by fear. And you...you smashed that cage for me today. So, don't you dare create a new cage with thoughts, fear, or uncertainties. No more, you hear me? We're going to pull through this together and finally have no other worries than our little family where hard decisions are something like...like...what cookies we need to bake tomorrow."

A chuckle slips past his lips and the sound makes me sigh in relief. His lips gently feather over mine. "You're really something, you know that?"

I shrug. "Meh, I've been told once or twice."

Finally, his body relaxes and though silence wraps around us, I know both our minds are busy with working through everything that happened. But we're sitting here. Comfortable and soaking up each other's strength.

Time passes when Easton suddenly says, "We need to wrap all those presents I bought and place them under the tree before Joshua wakes up."

I dash up and with wide eyes I tell him, "I can't believe I forgot. He can wake up at any time. Everything I bought him is already wrapped. We need to do yours behind the couch, if he walks in one of us can distract him and he won't see anything. Oh, and you're not coming near the tree. Well, no touching the branches anyway."

He glances down at his forearms and lets his gaze slide back to me. "Sounds like a plan."

The smile spreading his face warms my chest. I dash off the couch and head for the large bag I placed in the bedroom. Stalking back, I take out the few gifts and place them carefully underneath the tree. I glance over my shoulder and see Easton on his knees behind the couch, taking out the stuff he bought along with the wrapping paper. He glances at it as if he's thinking up a plan to tackle it.

"Need some help?" I question and make my way toward him.

"If you could show me a few times how this whole wrapping thing works, that would be great. I want to do a few myself too. I can hardly let you wrap your own presents, right?" the man easily supplies.

And in this moment I realize, "I didn't get you anything."

He leans in close and brushes his nose against mine. "You gave me so damn much already. There's no better gift than to be here with you two, fussing over wrapping gifts while knowing the three of us are just starting out together. Don't you realize it's the best present ever? Just don't give the old man with the beard any credit, though. Cause you and I both know it was us who did all the hard work."

My head tips back and laughter flows out. Instant joy spreads my body and I hug the man who's crawled back underneath my skin. I tighten my hold because I don't ever want to let go of this moment.

His words flow on repeat through my head. The three of us are just starting out together. Yes, we are. And I can't wait to see what the future has in store for us.

EPILOGUE

C.RASH

One Year Later

I don't know who's more excited, me or the kid. Probably me. I glance to my right and see the reflection of the Christmas tree twinkling in his eyes. We're sitting on the last few steps of the stairs, staring at the tree with all the presents underneath. Sure, I know what's inside all of them, but Joshua doesn't. Well, he knows what's inside one of them because we just placed it underneath the tree together.

Maybe that's why I'm more excited or it's the nerves flaring up because the present we added contains a ring. The little man helped me pick it out. It's a white gold, diamond ring in the shape of a snowflake. According to Joshua it was the prettiest one in the store.

Sometimes I still can't believe how damn lucky I am to have these two in my life. I remember all too vividly when I was standing on their doorstep a year ago. No plans at all and ready to protect a friend of my sister I didn't even know at all. Yet now? I hope to make this woman my wife and around this time next year there will hopefully be two kids sitting right next to me on these steps.

That's right, Mags is pregnant. We found out three weeks ago. Best news ever. This because we've been trying for the last four months.

Still fast, though, but I guess with everything in life the things you want most can't get here soon enough.

I glance up the stairs and my eyes lock with the woman who holds my heart. She's leaning on the banister while staring at us. It's the same spot she was in when we first saw this house almost a year ago. She didn't want to live in the house where Peter burst into the living room and died. I completely understood and I have to say, building memories like buying a house together are the rays of the sun that warms your life. Like now, the way she's standing there with the smile on her face.

It's the same smile she had when she said, "This is it." And I didn't even have to ask if she was sure because of that very smile and besides, I instantly loved this house too. It's close to the clubhouse, closer to her parents, and even my sister lives two blocks away.

Not to mention it has an amazing garden. And that reminds me of the present we didn't wrap but is staying in our bedroom, sleeping in a box. Well, not any longer in our bedroom since I can see the box standing near her feet. A puppy. Yeah, the best presents aren't underneath the tree. They are alive and breathing and spread joy in my life every damn day. My old lady—and soon to be wife—along with my kid, and the peanut growing in my woman's belly.

"Mommy," Joshua squeaks and dashes up.

He heads straight for the Christmas tree as Mags descends the stairs.

"Look, there's a present for you. But it wasn't Santa who put it there. Go on, Mommy, open it," Joshua rambles and is bouncing on his feet.

This is not how we agreed to do this but the smile on my face is hurting my cheeks. It doesn't matter how this moment goes; the important thing is the answer falling from my woman's lips. She glances at me while fumbling with the tiny box. Her chest is rising and falling and I'm seriously getting turned on here.

Damn. It doesn't matter what this woman wears, even if she's all covered up by layers of clothing or like now in just a robe with pajamas underneath. I know her. Her body, her mind, every inch of this magnificent beauty standing in front of me while she's holding a box and staring at the ring we bought her with tears in her eyes.

"Daddy said I could ride the rings on the wedding day because I did good with picking out this ring. I did good, didn't I?" Joshua rambles some more.

"Ride the rings?" Mags asks, confused.

"On a dirt bike, Mom! Daddy said he'd get me a dirt bike."

Mags is now shooting a glare at me. Shit. I lean into Joshua's space and whisper, "Didn't we agree to wait with telling her until she said yes?"

Joshua's eyes grow big and his head swings to his mother. Her face softens at the pleading look he gives her. That's my boy. Not that I need any help winning her over because I know for a fact this woman loves me with the kind of ferocity that will last us a lifetime, because I feel the exact same way.

It's for this reason I sink to one knee and stare right at her. "Mags, you already hold my heart. I told you that the very day we met how your heart took a ride with mine. You and me? Us as a family? Best ride of my life, so you might as well take my ring and make it official."

Her eyebrow raises and I know the words I just gave her aren't the standard ones where a guy asks the woman to be his wife. But nothing is standard in our lives and you sometimes are thrown into situations where you don't have a choice, though you know deep down what road to take because you're strong enough to face anything. This because you find your strength holding on to good things. She is my good thing in life, along with our son and the family and friends we surround ourselves with.

Her gaze shifts slightly and out of the corner of my eye I see Joshua mimic my pose as he says fiercely, "Yeah, Mom. What Daddy said."

Mags is fighting a smile as she whispers, "How can I ever resist you two?" She reaches out and cups Joshua's face as she shoots a loving look my way. "Yes," she says and a jolt of utter pleasure shoots through my body.

I rise to my feet and say, "Joshua, go see what Santa brought you."

There's no need to check if he's heading for the tree with all the presents underneath because the squeals of happiness followed by the ripping of paper is enough. My eyes never leave Mags as I step closer and take her into my arms.

My mouth finds hers and I close my eyes to relish in her taste, in the way we connect and the righteousness of it all. The both of us finally come up for air and when she places her hand on my chest, the way the ring sparkles on her finger, it really hits me how truly blessed I am.

"I love you." The words she gives me are the subtitles of what's vividly displayed in her eyes.

My throat clogs up due to all the emotions ripping through me. "I love you so damn much. I...fuck, this is bad," I blurt.

Mags's eyes go wide and confusion hits her but I have to act quick. I move her to the side so I can rush up the stairs. Her laughter rings through the air as I barely manage to scoop up the moving present that's bound to tumble off the stairs. Dammit, that damn puppy is already a load of trouble.

When I'm at the final step both Joshua and Mags are standing next to each other. I place the box on the floor and Joshua sinks to his knees to open the top. A fluffy black head dashes up and the little fluff jumps out of the box and straight into Joshua's arms, licking his face all over. The little man's giggles bring a smile to my face and me and my future wife share a look.

Yeah. You can plan your life and the things you want to the T, but it's the unexpected turn of events that might lead to the best things life can give you. I'm always going to follow my instinct and give into the things that feel right. It has led me to this woman, the gift of our son, and everything else that we've welcomed into our lives.

"Thank you, Santa," Joshua squeals.

Mags and I share another look and I slowly shake my head while whispering underneath my breath, "Yep, there you have it...the old man with the beard and red suit stealing our thunder again."

"Not possible," Mags whispers back. "Wait till we get to the clubhouse where we can slip away for a few minutes so we can create some new thunder for ourselves."

"I knew there was a reason I loved you," I murmur and kiss the top of her head.

She laughs and steps away to pick up the remainders of the wrapping paper that's scattered all over the floor. "Just for the thunder, huh?"

"Among other things," I shoot back as I grab a garbage bag to stuff all the trash in.

I rip my gaze away from her heated one and focus on the task at hand and not the need to bend her over the couch and take her from behind. Shit. There are hours in between that prevent me from taking her. But I guess that's why they have the saying "all good things come to those who wait." And I know it will be good because it's Mags.

The woman who blew my mind many years ago; who I lost but

somehow spiraled her way back to me around Christmas time. Shit. Maybe the old guy with the beard and red suit did have something to do with it. The thought makes me snort. Yeah, no way am I going to let the old fart take credit for that. It was all us. We connected and it shows each day we're together, growing stronger as we enrich our lives as a family.

Thankfully the hours pass quickly and before I know it, I'm placing the puppy—which Joshua named Thunder—in the backyard of the clubhouse while Ransom and Casey are standing there along with one of their kids, Zander and Luna. All of them are fawning over the little fluff and I clear my throat to catch Casey's attention.

I shoot him a look, and the smile and shaking of his head lets me know he can see the question I'm not asking out loud. He lifts his chin and that's my cue to snatch my woman's hand and lead her back into the clubhouse.

My room here at the clubhouse nowadays is mainly used as an escape for me and Mags. Four walls where we can put life on hold for a few minutes, knowing my brothers are taking care of our son while we take care of each other. Wow. That sounds dirty and a necessity.

Though on some level it is, but the speed of which my old lady's clothes hit the floor is a vivid reminder how badly we burn for each other. Shrugging out of my cut, I throw it on a nearby chair and grab the hem of my shirt. I close my eyes to pull it over my head but groan when I feel Mags' fingers slide over my naked chest.

Damn. Her touch always manages to spark fire. I quickly toe off my boots and let my jeans and underwear hit the floor; no time to waste when there's a gorgeous woman in front of me that's all mine. I grab her around the waist and throw her on the bed, quickly following her to cover her body with mine.

Her beautiful tits are right there for the taking. With our eyes connected I cover one tight peak and let my tongue swirl around it. She groans and lets her head tip back as her hands flash up to my head to keep me in place. As if I would ever stop what I'm doing. No. Damn. Way.

My dick has been hard for what seems like forever. I will never stop craving this woman and thank fuck I never have to. I switch to the other breast and let my fingers slide to her pussy. Drenched. So damn wet for me already. I draw tiny circles over her bundle of nerves and she starts to lift her hips off the mattress in an effort to chase her orgasm that's clearly threatening to boil over any damn minute. My fingers leave her pussy and I reach down to fist my cock. I line up perfectly and slowly thrust inside the sweetest, tightest pussy that's all mine. When I'm rooted deep, I glance down to watch her face but her eyes are closed and the look of pleasure painting her face almost makes me blow my load.

I start to lazily slide in and out and watch how her lips slightly part as soft moans tumble out. Eventually she captures her bottom lip as her eyes flash open and both her hands capture my ass.

"Harder," she moans and my hips almost falter hearing the need in her voice.

I pull out completely and slide down her body before she can so much as utter a single word of complaint.

"Yessssss," she groans and rotates her hips when my tongue slides through her pussy.

I determine what I give her and even if she wants me to go harder, it's the soft way I lick her clit that drives her over the edge. Her body starts to shake the same time her taste intensifies and freely coats my tongue.

I wait for most of the waves of pleasure to fade before I flash up and grab her hips. I flip her over as I place her on her hands and knees. I cover her body with mine and lean in close to her ear. My dick slides home at the same time I sneak my arm around her to grip her shoulder and pin her in place.

"This hard enough for you?" I grunt and tunnel roughly in and out, the sound of skin slapping skin fills the air.

She doesn't have a spare breath to give me a reply because she needs it to scream through the orgasm that's blazing through her. The way her pussy is squeezing the life out of my dick gives me no other option but to follow her into the blinding pleasure we're wrapped in.

Utterly spent I crash down on top of her. She grunts and I could curse myself for putting my full weight on her. I let myself fall to the side and turn her, placing my head on her belly I murmur, "Sorry, little one."

Her body gently shakes underneath me and I know she's laughing at me, but I don't care. The way her fingers lazily slide into my hair makes me close my eyes and relish in our closeness. Fuck Santa and gifts underneath a tree, this right here is where we create our own magic. This woman is the biggest of gifts my life is ever graced with.

One who freely gives and accepts my heart while in return gracing me with hers.

"What time did Tenley say dinner starts?" Mags says and tries to get up.

"Shhhh," I shush and throw my leg over hers to keep her in place.

"We're going to tell everyone about the pregnancy, right?" Mags questions, and I know she's right because we talked about it but now, I'm having second thoughts.

"Maybe we should wait," I tell her and lift my head to look at her. I can tell she's about to ask why so I let her know. "The little ones will think the old dude with the beard had something to do with knocking you up and I won't have that fucker stealing any more of my thunder."

Her laughter is the sweetest of sounds and I can't help but smile with my whole heart. Though, I'm dead serious. But in the end? Who cares about the thunder, or the darkness life is clouded with at times? Deep down we know how bright a day filled with sunshine can be. One look into the eyes of the woman I adore is enough to see my future is just as bright and filled with all the love my heart can hold. Because she's in it, along with our kids.

THANK YOU

Thank you for reading
AF MC OHIO

Gaining exposure as an independent author relies mostly on word-of-mouth, so if you have the time and inclination, please consider leaving a short review wherever you can. Even a short message on social media would be greatly appreciated.

Click here for another Areion Fury MC chapter, and connecting, standalone books:
https://books2read.com/rl/AreionFuryMC

Check out all my other MC, Mafia, Paranormal MC, and Contemporary Romance series!
https://books2read.com/rl/EstherESchmidt

SPECIAL THANKS

My beta team;

Neringa, Tracy, Judy, Tammi,

my pimp team, and to you, as my reader…

Thanks so much!

You guys rock!

Contact:
I love hearing from my readers.

Email:
authoresthereschmidt@gmail.com

Or contact my PA **Christi Durbin** for any questions you might have.
facebook.com/CMDurbin

ESTHER E. SCHMIDT

Visit Esther E. Schmidt online:

Website:
www.esthereschmidt.nl

Facebook - AuthorEstherESchmidt
Twitter - @esthereschmidt
Instagram - @esthereschmidt
Pinterest - @esthereschmidt

Signup for Esther's newsletter:
esthereschmidt.nl/newsletter

Join Esther's fan group on Facebook:
www.facebook.com/groups/estherselite

MORE BOOKS

AREION FURY MC

R OHIO MC

BROKEN DEEDS MC

WICKED THROTTLE MC

DEATH BY REAPER MC

LOST VALKYRIES MC

THE DUDNIK CIRCLE

PEACOCK
THE FAULTS OF OUR SINS

MARLON
NEON MARKSMAN MC

THE FALLON BROTHERS

UNRULY DEFENDERS MC

FREDERICK

UNRULY PROTECTOR

Swampheads
SERIES

Printed in Great Britain
by Amazon